INFINITE

Also by Jodi Meadows

Incarnate

Asunder

INFINITE

JODI MEADOWS

KATHERINE TEGEN BOOKS
An Imprint of HarperCollins Publishers

Katherine Tegen Books is an imprint of HarperCollins Publishers.

Infinite

ISBN 978-0-06-206081-5

Typography by Joel Tippie
13 14 15 16 17   LP/RRDH   10 9 8 7 6 5 4 3 2 1

First Edition

For Jeff.
My husband. My best friend.
See title for how much I love you more.

INFINITE

1

ENDINGS

MY DEATH WOULD not be another beginning.

For millennia in Range, death meant another rebirth. Another life. Then someone died the night the temple went dark, and I was born in their place.

A nosoul. A newsoul. A soul asunder.

I was a mystery others sought to control, a frightening creature that made the world reconsider what it knew of life and death and what happened after. But I was only one. I could be desperately ignored as a mystery, a mistake that would never be repeated.

Then my father devised another Templedark, and for dozens of oldsouls, it was their final death. Violent. Terrifying. Inescapable.

Within the year, newsouls were born and the world mourned darksouls even more fiercely, never realizing the sinister truth about reincarnation. They had thought rebirth was natural, but the opposite was true: while oldsouls lived and died and lived again, millions of newsouls were consumed by the very entity that provided reincarnation.

Janan. The Devourer. The once-human who had reached too high and who would soon burn the world.

And then, there would be nothing left but endings.

Midnight struck.

The Year of Souls began with a thunderous crash and rumble from deep within the earth.

"What *is* that?" My voice sounded hollow in the parlor, the floor still littered with the remnants of destroyed instruments and tattered rose petals. Light from the kitchen bathed a square of the dusty hardwood floor, but otherwise, the room was dim with night. We'd awakened only a few minutes ago, having dozed on the sofa after friends left last evening.

Across the parlor, Sam tilted his head and listened. Black hair shadowed his eyes as he searched his memory for the strange crash and rumble.

The floor swayed under our feet. I yelped and braced myself against the wall. Janan's heartbeat thudded under my fingertips.

I dropped to my hands and knees, spreading out my

weight for balance. "What's happening?" Panic pitched my voice high and thin.

Sam staggered toward me, unsteady on the shifting floor. "It's an earthquake. Don't worry. It will pass."

Decorations rattled on the honeycomb shelves that divided the parlor and kitchen. Obsidian figurines danced and dove off the edges of their shelves. Wood and stone and glass thudded to the floor, crashed or rolled or shattered as they struck. Even the shredded rose petals swirled.

The shaking slowed, but it wasn't over. The world jerked again and hurled everything sideways. Furniture crashed upstairs. Trees snapped outside. The whole earth roared. I screamed as the hand-carved shelves cracked and splintered all around the room.

Sam stumbled and dropped, just out of my reach. Surprise and pain flared across his face as he clutched his hand to his chest, keeping his fist closed. His gray nightshirt darkened with seeping blood.

"Sam!" I crawled toward him, fighting the moving floor. "What happened to your hand?" Even as the question left my mouth, I spotted the glass near him, stained with crimson and glistening blood.

"Nothing. It's fine." The world steadied and he sat back on his heels, trapping his injured hand in his good one. "That wasn't so bad."

His idea of bad must have been the whole world rattling

apart. And now the earth's silence stretched through the house, heavy and alive. Waiting.

Not trusting the floor to stay put, I sat up and scooted toward Sam, giving the glass a wide berth.

A couple of weeks ago, Councilor Deborl and his friends had come through and smashed all the instruments in Sam's parlor. The piano, harpsichord, cello, and even the smaller instruments locked inside protective cases. Only the instruments upstairs had been spared, including my flute. It had been in the workroom, waiting on a small repair. Only chance had saved it.

I'd cleaned up most of that destruction right away. What remained on the floor had been pieces that might one day be useful again, as well as dried rose petals left over from a party with our friends.

But now, the parlor was more of a wreck than Deborl ever could have left it.

Shelves hung at odd angles, leaving books and boxes and bits of decorations scattered everywhere. The shelves looked like teeth, ready to bite down.

A lamp had fallen, leaving a glittering river of glass. We were lucky the light hadn't caught fire. Who knew what the kitchen looked like, or the upstairs, or the outbuildings. There'd been so much crashing and thumping; anything could have happened.

"Is your hand okay?" I crouched next to Sam and pried

his fist away from his chest.

"It's fine." A lie. His hand trembled in mine, and his skin was slick with blood. It was hard to see under the red smears, but it looked as if the glass had shredded his palm and fingers.

"We need to get this cleaned up. Hold still."

Sam nodded and braced himself while I picked out bit after bit of glass until my fingertips ached, but I couldn't find anything more. Cleaning the wound would help, but first I needed to stop the bleeding.

"This might hurt."

"It already hurts." Sam's voice was rough.

I wanted to say something reassuring, but I didn't know near enough about what had been damaged to make promises. If it looked bad after we rinsed the blood, I'd call Rin, the medic. For now, I grabbed a big shard of glass and sliced off a length of my nightgown to make a bandage, then wrapped the length of cloth around his hand as many times as it would go. "Hold on to it. Keep pressure."

"My hand will be fine." The words came out hard, like commands. Like he could will the cuts to heal.

"Let's go upstairs and get it properly bandaged. It didn't sound like any of the support beams broke, so the stairs should be safe." Hopefully the water lines were intact, too. The lights and everything else seemed all right. That was something.

I started to stand just as the earth jumped and an explosion sounded in the west. Not another earthquake. Something else.

Sam and I scrambled to our feet, careful of the glass as we hurried to the front door. I slipped into the night, icy air stinging my face. "Can you see anything?" I asked.

Sam shook his head. "No, but it sounded like an eruption."

"Not the caldera." The Range caldera was enormous, stretching in all directions with the city of Heart at its center. If the caldera erupted, there'd be nothing left of Heart.

"Not the caldera," Sam agreed. He put his arm around my shoulders, holding me close against the chill. "A hydrothermal eruption. Like a geyser, but bigger."

"How much bigger?" I peered into the night, but clouds obscured moonlight. Even if there'd been enough light to see by, the city wall blocked the horizon completely. The eruption had been outside the city, but it could have been just beyond the wall. There were geysers everywhere.

"Depends. Sometimes much bigger. They're a response to a pressure change underground."

Pattering sounds filled the trees and yard, tapping on the house in a strange rhythm. A pebble fell from the sky and hit my head.

With his good hand, Sam took my elbow and drew me toward the house. "Hydrothermal eruptions take rocks and trees with them sometimes, but they don't happen very often.

8

I've seen only two of them, and they were a long time ago."

As he spoke, a second eruption thundered in the north, and a third in the southwest. The world came alive with tapping, hissing, clattering. Animals grunted and darted through the evergreen trees. Birds squawked and took wing, but there was nowhere safe to fly. Earth rained from the sky as though the world had turned upside down.

"Inside." Sam's voice hardened as more bits of stone pattered against the walls of the house. "Inside now."

"How is this possible?" As we turned for the door, a flash of light caught my eye.

In the center of the city, Janan's temple shone incandescent.

2

INTRUSION

THE FRONT DOOR slammed behind me, muting the quiet cacophony of the world falling apart. I hugged myself as Sam moved into the shadows, away from the light of the kitchen. "Did you see the temple?" he asked. "I've never seen it so bright."

"I saw."

"Do you think it's Janan's doing?" He leaned on the wall, head dropped as he clutched his hand to his chest. "The earthquake? The eruptions?"

"It seems likely." I eased into the shadows with him, resting my cheek on his shoulder. His arms circled my waist. My chest and stomach pressed against his, only our nightclothes separating us. "I'm afraid," I whispered. It was easier to be honest when he was holding me, and when we stood in the dark.

He rested his cheek on top of my head. "Me too."

"If the caldera is going to do this a lot from now on, maybe the Council exiling me isn't such a bad thing. It's probably smart to get away from Range. I'm glad you're coming with me."

"I'll always go anywhere with you."

We stood together for a while, listening to each other's heartbeats and the patter of debris on the house. I touched only Sam, avoiding the white exterior wall even more now that Janan's pulse was stronger.

"Let's go upstairs and get this fixed." I straightened and cradled his hurt hand in both of mine. The strip of my night-gown was soaked with blood.

He nodded and allowed me to guide him upstairs. We took the steps slowly, testing the wood before trusting our weight to it. The exterior of the house would be fine after the earthquake—Janan would never allow the white stone to be damaged while he was awake—but the interiors of the houses were all of human construction.

But the stairs were well enough. None of the support beams had snapped.

His bedroom was cool and dark. Shapes hunched within the shadows: a warm bed, a wardrobe, and a large harp. We made our way into the washroom, and I flicked on the light.

Both of us squinted in the white glare. "Sit," I ordered.

He leaned and scooted onto the counter while I closed the door and turned the shower knobs, water as hot and strong as it would go. A sly smile tugged at the corners of Sam's mouth. "Ana, I'm not sure this is the best time, but if you'd like to—"

"Shut up." A relieved grin slipped out. If he could joke, he would be fine. "The steam will help loosen the glass, if there's any left."

"That's less fun." He pretended to pout as he unwrapped his hand and rinsed the blood away in the sink. I found bandages and ointment, and together we picked out the last slivers of glass while steam billowed from the shower. The mirror fogged, and the pounding water on the tub drowned out the sound of the world beyond the room.

"This doesn't look too bad," I said, spreading ointment over his fingers. Most of the cuts were superficial.

"Told you." He held still while I wrapped his hand in clean bandages. "And it's my left hand, which is a relief because I write with my right." The shower made his voice deeper and fuller. "I'll get along fine until my left recovers. And I don't need either hand to kiss you."

With a quiet gasp, I dropped the roll of bandage tape. "We should test that claim. I seem to remember you using your hands quite a bit when you kiss me."

"Hmm." He slid off the counter. "Perhaps this does deserve

some experimenting." He closed the short space between us and smoothed a strand of hair off my face. "Oh," he murmured, "you're right. There's one."

I stood on my toes and wrapped my arms around his shoulders. His lips were warm and soft from the steam filling the room.

"Two," he said, curling one arm around my waist to pull me close. Lips breezed over my cheek and neck. "Three." With his good hand, he nudged my nightgown off my shoulder and kissed bare skin, then trailed his fingertips down my arm. His touch ignited sparks that traveled all the way to my stomach. My breath fluttered. "You're very right." His lips grazed my collarbone. "I use my hands all the time when I kiss you."

I would have melted if he hadn't been holding me up. The steam, his touch, his kiss: they made me light-headed and giddy, in spite of everything that had happened not an hour ago. Safe in his arms, with only the sound of the shower running, I could forget about the outside world and the rest of our problems.

"Do you remember what we talked about last night?" I kissed his ear, his cheek.

Sam gave a low rumble of assent. "You said you love me."

"I did say that, didn't I?" Pleasure poured through me. After years of believing I wasn't deserving of love, Sam had shown me I was. But that was different from accepting I could love others. Wrestling those feelings had been diffi-cult, but last night, I'd said it, and it turned out that I'd loved him all along. "Guess what?"

He pulled away and met my eyes.

"I still love you today."

His smile grew wide and warm.

"I heard a rumor," I went on, "that the first day of the new year is your birthday."

"Did you?" He suddenly looked shy.

"When we first met, you told me we shared a birthday."

"Did I?" Panic flickered across his face, and his cheeks darkened. "I did. Oh."

I kept my face as serious as I could manage, though laugh-ter gathered in my chest and I had to bite my lip to keep from smiling. "So?" I lifted an eyebrow.

His whole face was dark with embarrassment. "Would you believe I forgot when my birthday is?"

I snorted and laughed. That was exactly what I thought he'd say, because when I looked back on that day, I remem-bered the hesitation and momentary confusion before he declared we had the same birthday. He *had* forgotten. "It's all right. I love you on your real birthday *and* on your fake birthday. And all the other days."

He grinned, relaxing. "There's nothing more we can do tonight. Would you—" He seemed to fumble for the right words. "Would you like to sleep here with me? In my room,

I mean. Not the washroom."

The mess would still be downstairs in the morning, and his bedroom had appeared relatively unharmed when we passed through. We could take care of everything else in the morning. Or not. Yesterday, the ruling Council had exiled me from Heart, and Sam was leaving with me. Soon, we'd be on our way east. We didn't *have* to clean the house.

We could put off real life until dawn.

"If you steal all the blankets, you'll be sorry." I reached inside the shower and turned off the spray. After dealing with the Council, visiting friends who'd come to express their outrage, and then the earthquake and eruptions, curling up with Sam was the most appealing thing I could think of.

The shower dripped for a moment longer, and then the house was silent. Maybe the debris had stopped falling outside. The whole world was still, and quiet, and waiting.

I felt behind me for the doorknob and pushed the washroom door open. Soon, everything would be perfect, if only for a few hours.

Sam's smile fell away. A question formed in my mouth, but he grabbed my wrist, yanked, and spun me so I stood behind him. "What are you doing here?" he growled. He reached behind him with his good hand, palm on my hip as though to keep me in place.

My heart raced at his sudden shift. I peeked around him.

A stranger stood in Sam's bedroom, clutching a long knife.

He wore a filthy coat that hung to his ankles, but even in the dim light and with the heavy layer of fabric, I couldn't miss the bulge of another weapon on his hip when he faced us.

"Dossam. Nosoul." His voice sounded familiar, but I couldn't place it. "We were hoping you'd been crushed to death."

We?

I twisted my hand in Sam's shirt, desperately wishing I were wearing something more serious than my nightgown as I stepped out from behind him. I didn't need a shield. "You're one of Deborl's friends."

"And you were in prison," Sam said. "With Deborl and Merton."

The stranger showed teeth when he smiled. "Janan used the earthquake to free us." He pulled back his coat, revealing a laser pistol tucked into his waistband. "We have a calling."

"Mat, no." Sam tried to step in front of me again, but I jabbed my elbow into his side. "Why would you do this?"

The stranger—Mat—leveled his gaze on Sam, apparently unworried about our escape. We were trapped in the washroom, after all. "She's an abomination. They all are. The plague of newsouls *must* be stopped."

We were trapped in the washroom.

I stepped back, letting Sam block the doorway. "Newsouls are the natural order of things," he began. "Other animals are born, live, and die forever. Haven't you considered that what we do is unnatural?"

"They're an offense to Janan. He created us. He gave us immortality. And soon he'll return to reward the faithful. He'll ascend. The faithful will ascend with him."

Meuric hadn't thought so. He'd been convinced he needed the temple key to survive Soul Night.

I tuned out Mat's arguments as I considered the items in Sam's washroom. Shampoo, soap, painkillers. I wished for my SED—then I could call for help—but both our SEDs were downstairs.

"Ana's done nothing to you," Sam said. "Nor have the other newsouls."

Gauze. Painkillers. Ointment for cuts and burns. If my nightgown had pockets, I would have grabbed those, because the plan budding in my head involved going outside.

"They were born," Mat said. "They replaced oldsouls. *Real* souls. They take what isn't theirs. Life. Keys."

Mat's identity snapped into place. He was the man who'd attacked me when I'd stumbled out of the temple. He'd stolen the temple key from me and given it to Deborl.

"This must come to an end. I'm sorry, Dossam. I have no quarrel with you, but Ana has to die."

Cleaning powder. I snatched the can and unscrewed the lid just as Mat pushed past Sam and aimed his laser pistol. The blue targeting light flashed—

With a shout, I hurled the powder at Mat's face. Sam

shoved Mat into the counter as the man screamed and his eyes watered. White particles floated in the air, glowing bright blue as the targeting light on the pistol shone. Air sizzled and a hole appeared in the ceiling; Mat was too busy clawing at his eyes to pay attention.

Sam grabbed Mat's collar and slammed the man's head on the stone counter. A wet crack sounded and the copper odor of blood filled the space, but I didn't have time to see if he would live. I grabbed the pistol and fled the washroom with Sam.

We raced downstairs, pausing only to get our SEDs and shoes before we ran outside in our bare feet, carrying our belongings into the dark.

"Stay quiet." Sam's voice was low, all warning. "There may be more."

Shivering with fear and shock, I let Sam guide me. He could navigate Heart blindfolded, but I needed a light, which we didn't have and couldn't use even if we did.

We slowed as the cold settled in and the sharp debris on the ground stabbed our feet. "Here." Sam turned us toward a patch of black on black. Trees. Pine needles pricked at my feet and shudders racked my body. I could hardly breathe around the cold and adrenaline. "Put your shoes on," he whispered. His hand fell from mine, and I realized I'd been squeezing it tightly from fear. It was his left hand, his hurt hand. He hadn't made a sound about it.

I crouched, shoving my feet into my shoes as quickly as I could, straining my senses to hear footfalls from more intruders. But all I could hear was my pulse in my ears. Was Mat dead? Were there others? Deborl had more friends than Mat, so where were they?

"Do you need help with your shoes?" I asked.

"I've got them." His voice was rough, from pain or cold or something else, I couldn't tell. "Get your things."

I scooped up my SED and the pistol I'd stolen and followed Sam through the darkness, keeping hold of his shoulder. How soon before someone found Mat in Sam's washroom?

Was he dead? Had Sam killed him?

My thoughts spun as we crept through the trees. Our shoes made more noise than bare feet, but the risk of stepping on something was too great. Already, my body ached with chill.

Light shone beyond the trees, a pale and fractured glow. We'd reached Stef's house.

"Wait," I hissed, and squeezed Sam's shoulder. His profile flashed against the light as he turned his head. "What if they sent someone to watch her?"

"Ah." He retreated into the trees and knelt, then fumbled with his SED. "I can't— It will take me too long to type a message with my hand like this."

"I'll do it." I sank to the ground, shivering in my thin nightgown, and sent a quick message to Stef.

19

Mat attacked us. Deborl and Merton have escaped prison.
We're outside your house, but afraid it's being watched.
Call Lidea and Geral. Warn them. Meet us in the library
with other trusted friends. Please bring us clothes.

Sam read the message over my shoulder. "The library?"

"Even if they look for us there, we'll be able to hide. Plus, I think there's something I need to say to all our friends."

"Will you tell me what it is now, or do I have to wait?"

I lifted my eyes as a light flickered on upstairs in Stef's house. "If Janan is responsible for the earthquake and eruptions, it will only get worse. They deserve to know, and a chance to get away while there's still time."

Sam caressed my shoulder, my spine. "Good. They deserve to know." He went rigid as a shadow moved across Stef's yard. "Stay here." He grabbed the laser pistol and crept away. A second later, blue light flashed and the shadow crumpled. Dead or not, the person didn't move as Sam darted across the yard and seized something—a second laser pistol.

I sent another message to Stef, updating her. She wrote back immediately.

Go to the library. I have a plan.

After a quick acknowledgment, I doused the light on my SED. Sam was back.

"Is he dead?" I asked. But maybe I didn't want to know.

He just handed me the second pistol.

"Let's go." I didn't have a waistband or pocket to hold my SED and the pistol, so they stayed in my hands.

"Okay." Sam looked up, not at Stef's house, but at the blaze toward the center of the city: the temple shone like a torch. "We can't go any of my normal ways. If Deborl has anyone on patrol, they'll be watching for us. Surely Mat was supposed to check in by now."

"I agree. So we creep through the trees in the dark?"

He frowned as he hefted his pistol. "We don't have much choice. Are you ready?"

I stood and linked my arm with his. "I'd go anywhere with you, Dossam."

3
WORLDS

WE REACHED THE market field an hour later. Sam hadn't wanted to go in a straight line from our house to the center of Heart, thinking that was a good way to get caught, so we sneaked around in the cold, doubling back on our path a couple of times before we finally reached the wide expanse of cobblestone at the middle of the city. Debris from the earthquake and eruptions littered the ground. Cobblestones had buckled and broken.

The four main avenues probably didn't look much better, but Sam hadn't been willing to use them—or even get near them until we had no choice. Hopefully the roads weren't completely destroyed; we had to leave Heart soon.

I still couldn't believe I'd been *exiled*. By all accounts, that was a death sentence. The world beyond Range was incredibly dangerous, filled with all kinds of creatures.

Though maybe Heart was just as dangerous now.

The temple flooded the market field with brilliant light. How many souls did it take to make the temple that bright? At least a hundred million.

Next to the temple, fused with it in some places, the Councilhouse stood immense and regal. Janan had built the Councilhouse before everyone arrived in Heart, as he had all the houses, but the columns and relief, which stood in shadow now, had been added later. I could just see the statues around the market field, all pockmarked from battles and age. The field was empty, but in the mornings and afternoons, it bustled with groups of friends, opportunistic sellers, and people simply wanting the sound of other voices. Once a month, colorful tents filled the space for the market; it was one of my favorite times, though newsoul-haters made it hard for me to do any shopping on my own.

"Too much open space," Sam muttered, shivering in the winter wind. "Make sure your pistol is on."

I checked the switch and nodded. "Give me your SED." I clutched both SEDs in my left hand, leaving us free to fire our pistols unhindered. Still, I hoped I didn't have to use mine. "That man back at Stef's house. Did you kill him?"

Sam's eyes were shadowed. "Would it make you think any differently of me?"

Reincarnation made it almost pointless to kill someone. They would just be reborn, and they would seek vengeance. No one *liked* dying, because it hurt, and whatever you were doing—romances, projects, or exploring—had to pause while you waited to be reborn, and then waited to grow up. But they always came back, at least until recently.

According to our friend Cris, when Janan ascended, he wouldn't bother reincarnating people. That meant with only three months until Janan's ascension, death would be death. No one who died now would be reincarnated; there was no time for them to be reborn. If Mat was dead in the washroom, he was dead forever.

As far as thinking differently of Sam, though? "No," I whispered. My whole body quaked with cold. "I know you're protecting me."

"I would do anything to protect you." He kissed my cheek. "Let's go."

Together, we crossed the market field, scanning all directions for movement. The temple burned so brightly, and the space was so wide and empty. Crossing here felt like *asking* for someone to shoot us.

But we made our way across the rubble-strewn field, and nothing happened. No attacks, no earthquakes. Our shoes crunched and wind hissed along the streets, but otherwise the world was silent.

At the library entrance, Sam tucked his pistol under his

left elbow, then hauled open the door. With one last look over my shoulder—the field remained empty—I ducked under Sam's arm and into the library. He followed, letting the door swing shut behind us, casting us into complete darkness.

"Careful." Sam's voice seemed loud in the stillness. "Things might have shifted during the earthquake. There could be books on the floor."

I tapped one of the SEDs to life. The white light extended only a short way, but it was enough to let me find a stained-glass lamp and switch it on.

The earthquake had indeed been hard on the library. Books were sprawled on the floor. Bookcases and chairs had toppled over. A lamp had crashed against the hardwood, leaving a rainbow of glass shards. Papers lay across everything, like a shroud. I couldn't see the upper levels clearly, but no doubt the eleven other floors were just as damaged.

Sam picked his way through the mess. "Will you send a message to Stef and let her know that we arrived safely? And maybe find out what her plan is?"

I set my pistol and Sam's SED on the table and sent the note from mine. The library was warm, especially coming in from the midwinter night, but my skin still ached with cold, and I couldn't stop shivering. "Next time we get chased out of our own house in the middle of the night," I said, "I'll be wearing more than a nightgown."

Sam grunted agreement as he dragged a table in front

of the door. It swung outward, so the table wouldn't keep the door from opening, but it would certainly slow anyone, should they rush in to attack us.

By the time we covered all the entrances, Stef had replied. *Lidea, Geral, and Orrin are on their way to you.*

I relayed the information to Sam and responded.

What about everyone else?

She didn't answer immediately. I sighed and dropped the SED back onto the table. "How's your hand?"

Sam shrugged. "It's going to hurt for a while, but I don't think it's bleeding anymore."

"We can walk to the hospital wing." I picked up a few books and put them on a table. "See about getting your hand stronger medicine."

Sam helped pick up a few more things from the floor, leaving a clear space around one of the cushiony chairs with a blanket draped over the back. I wanted nothing more than to sink into it, but . . .

"Let's just visit a washroom and get cleaned up," Sam said. "Then come back here. My hand will be fine."

A few minutes later, we returned from the washroom with clean faces and combed hair. Before I could suggest curling up in the big chair, though, a low rumble sounded outside. "What's that?"

"Sounds like a labor drone. A plow, maybe, to move the debris."

26

Now the market field and streets would be clear. Better late than never. "I suppose we're lucky they're still working after the earthquake. Will the drones clear the roads outside Heart, too?"

"They should."

That was good. Our trip out of Heart and Range would have been much more difficult without roads.

Banging sounded on the door. A second later, it pulled open, revealing darkness. I jumped to turn off the light, but Lidea said, "Watch out. The earthquake moved a table here." A small cluster of people waited at the door. Lidea and Geral held babies against them, while Orrin carried bags.

I sagged in relief. "Actually, that was Sam." I hurried over to drag the table out of their way, and when they were safe inside, we sat around the lamp to trade stories.

"Mat tried to kill you?" Orrin sounded incredulous.

"He was one of Deborl's followers." Maybe one of Meuric's followers before Deborl. "I think he attacked me once before."

Orrin glanced at Sam. "When did that happen?"

"Remember when Ana was missing a while ago?" Sam said, and everyone nodded. I hadn't actually been missing. I'd been inside the temple, but thanks to the memory magic Janan worked on oldsouls, Sam hadn't been able to remember where I'd gone. He'd told everyone I was sick, while he and his friends searched for me.

I wished I could tell my friends the truth about the temple, but they wouldn't be able to remember it without months of my reminding them, like I'd done for Sam. It was easier not to burden them with knowledge they couldn't hold on to.

"Well," Sam went on, "she appeared in the market field one morning. Shortly before I found her, someone shoved her and stole a key from her, but she was so exhausted and afraid, she wasn't able to identify him."

I nodded. "But it was Mat. I recognized him tonight." I didn't add that he was probably bleeding to death in Sam's washroom. "After he attacked, we contacted Stef and came here."

"What happened to you?" Sam asked.

Lidea and Geral glanced at each other, and Lidea started, "Well, there was the earthquake."

"Ariana wouldn't go back to sleep," Geral said, "so I was already awake when Stef sneaked into my house. Orrin was with me. We had to pack in the dark, in case anyone was watching the house."

Orrin took up the story. "We went to Lidea's house, and then Stef activated the labor drones and told us to ride to the library."

"Clever." That sounded like the kind of plan Stef would come up with.

"Are you worried they'll attack newsouls now?" Lidea asked. "I thought the Council promised to protect newsouls. I thought your demonstration worked."

I shook my head and repeated what Councilor Sine had told me once. "There's a law about killing me. Murder is frowned upon, of course, but with me, they didn't know whether I would be reincarnated, so they made it illegal to try to kill me. The law extends to the other newsouls, but Deborl, Merton, and their friends—they don't care. They think any punishment is worth it. They just want us dead."

"Why?" Lidea held Anid to her chest. "I just can't understand why."

I didn't want to explain Janan and their misguided devotion to him. Not right now. So I shrugged and leaned against Sam's shoulder. "The Council is working to protect newsouls, but this is the truth: they won't succeed. They can make rules, assign guards, and lock up everyone they think will cause trouble, but there will always be someone they miss, some hole in their security they overlook. Newsouls aren't safe in Heart. And neither is anyone else."

"What are you saying?" Orrin leaned forward, darkness in his eyes.

"I'm saying I'm not the only one who needs to leave Heart. We all need to get out."

After changing into the spare clothes Geral and Orrin had brought, Sam and I headed upstairs to where the maps were kept.

"I thought you knew where we're going." The dusty air

of the library smothered his words. "Back to Menehem's lab, right? For the sylph?"

"Yes, but then where? We can't stay there." We *could,* I supposed, but there had to be something better. "I don't know. I think the sylph will have answers. I'm sure they'll be there. They were before."

Sam nodded.

"I need a better idea of the world surrounding Range. There's so much of it. I need a plan." I slumped into a chair when we entered the map area. "Sam, I don't know what I'm doing. I don't know how to stop Janan."

He looked at me, all longing and sadness, and said nothing of my confession. "What maps do you want?"

I gazed around the space, filled with rolled sheets of paper and large books. There had to be a hundred maps. Maybe more. "I don't know."

"Perhaps let's start with Range." Sam drifted around the small, closed area until he found a rolled map. Together, we spread the thick paper across the table, smoothing the corners with our hands. I didn't know how to read it, not as far as figuring out distances or elevations, but I recognized familiar locations.

Rangedge Lake was in the south, near where I grew up in Purple Rose Cottage. Midrange Lake was a huge body of water right by Heart. Small *X*s marked geysers and fumaroles, while *O*s marked mud pools and hot springs.

Mountains were everywhere, continuing northwest in a line of jagged peaks. Forests covered the map, all across Range, and everywhere beyond the human haven.

I dragged my finger eastward, until I found the twin peaks visible from Menehem's laboratory. "The lab should be somewhere here, right?"

Sam nodded and pointed at what looked like a random spot. "There." He moved his finger. "See, here's the road."

Now that he pointed it out, I did. It had almost been lost in the other lines and splotches of ink. While I bent to study the land surrounding the lab, Sam fetched more maps and laid them on the table.

North of Range, the forest grew denser and the details less frequent, as though few people had bothered to explore and chart that area. A line of writing warned of dragons in the frozen north, though I wasn't sure how far out one had to go in order to see them. Would it take a week to get there? Probably more.

"Sam."

He paused next to me, arm around my waist.

"Remember when you told me about how you died in your last lifetime? You went north, saw a huge white wall, and there were dragons?"

He hesitated. "Yes."

"Where would that be on this map?"

"I . . ." His bandaged hand drifted over the map, but never

paused. "I'm not sure. You don't want to go there, do you?"

"Of course not." The last thing I wanted to do was put Sam in the path of dragons. He'd died by dragons thirty times. By some fluke, I'd managed to save him from dragons twice this lifetime. I didn't want to risk him a third time. "I'm just trying to get an idea of the rest of the world, since I won't be able to come back here."

Sam sighed a little, like relief. "I didn't mean to be suspicious. We've learned a lot about sylph in the last few months—enough to know they might not be as evil as we'd thought—but dragons still terrify me."

Thirty times. I couldn't imagine dying thirty times because of dragons. "I wouldn't put you in danger."

He gave a weak, exhausted smile, and we both dropped our attention back to the table. "Stef can put maps on your SED for you. It's not as good as seeing the whole land on paper, but it's better than nothing."

"Oh, good." I found warnings of trolls in the east, centaurs in the south, and rocs in the west. And these things were only the creatures that citizens of Heart might encounter on the edges of Range. There were more creatures beyond, though this map didn't show that far. "I think I need a bigger map."

Sam produced a globe, the whole world on a piece of polished stone. Continents were outlined in gold and silver, dressed in green and brown and beige and white, depending on the vegetation or lack thereof. Oceans and large lakes were brilliant, beautiful blue.

I caressed the globe, stone and metal smooth beneath my palm. "I had no idea there was so much beyond Range. Where are we?"

"Here." He pointed toward the middle of a northern continent. "Range is smaller than the space my fingertip takes up."

"Oh." I turned the globe. It was tilted—one of my teachers had told me the world was tilted, but on *what*, I wasn't sure— and gazed at continents that suddenly seemed so far away it was pointless even thinking about them. "Range feels so big."

"It *is* big." Sam smoothed hair off my face. "The rest of the world is even bigger."

"It makes me feel small. I don't like it."

"Me neither." Sam sat on the edge of the table and watched while I looked through more maps, dismissing some and moving others into a pile. He answered whenever I had questions, but for the most part, he kept his eyes closed and seemed lost in thought.

I yawned as I finished with the maps and rolled them up again. "Let's go to sleep, Sam."

"Right here?" He eyed the floor. "Right here looks good."

I helped him off the table and we headed downstairs, dousing lights as we went. As we reached the stairs, my SED buzzed with a message from Stef.

Get down here. Big news.

33

4

GATHERING

HEAD ACHING FROM lack of rest and too much mortal peril, I slumped down the stairs to find that Stef had arrived with several other friends.

"So much for sleep," Sam muttered.

"Rin is here." I nodded toward the crowd. "She can look at your hand." Rin was a small girl, about ten or eleven years old, but she was one of the best medics in Heart. For some reason, she liked me. She'd stuck up for me several times, even before I'd known who she was.

"Wow." Stef looked up as we descended the stairs. "You two look terrible."

"Ana!" Sarit jumped up and threw her arms around me. "You're okay."

I hugged her back, relieved she was here. Everyone knew Sarit and I were best friends; Deborl would target her if we left her behind. Stef could take care of herself, but Sarit was gentle. She wouldn't hurt anyone, even to protect herself.

"Are we safe here?" someone asked.

Stef nodded. "I've secured the library entrances. And when we leave, no one goes anywhere alone. Take groups of at least five."

People nodded.

"What's your news, Stef?" Sam glanced around the crowd, and found an unoccupied chair to collapse into. Everyone looked exhausted, their coats on over nightclothes and hastily packed bags by the door. Weapons had been piled onto one of the tables, and several people were hunched over SEDs, sending messages or checking some sort of function that involved a map.

Everyone was newsoul-friendly. Some had given me lessons on various subjects, while others were simply close friends of Sam. There was another handful I recognized from a list Sarit and I had made: they were pregnant women. They might be carrying oldsouls, but . . . they might be carrying newsouls, too.

"It's all bad news." As usual, in spite of the chaos, Stef looked like she'd spent an hour grooming herself. Not like she'd just been sneaking people out of their houses, and possibly killing others.

I glanced at Sam on his chair, but there wasn't room for both of us unless I sat on top of him, and no one else was sitting *on* their friends. Even the other newsouls were tucked away somewhere, sleeping. Grudgingly, I claimed my own chair on the other side of the crowd.

"Everyone knows that Sam and Ana were attacked tonight. They asked me to bring most of you here in case there were other attacks, but the truth is there's much more for us to worry about. I've sent a program to all of your SEDs. Whit and Orrin already had it, of course, but the rest of you should pay attention." Stef held up her SED. "This program is linked to the monitoring stations around Range. They read all seismological activity and translate it into information that's useful to us."

As she spoke, I found the new function on my SED and opened it. Several small red dots appeared over a map of Range. A large one was centered right under Heart.

"The dots are recent earthquakes," Stef went on. "The bigger the dot, the bigger the earthquake. If you tap the menu, you can switch between different types of events. There's another that shows where the hydrothermal eruptions took place. We won't know all the details on those until someone actually goes to look. I'm afraid some of the equipment was damaged or destroyed, but this should give you an idea of what's going on."

"And what *is* going on?" Rin pulled a blanket around her

shoulders and yawned. "Sorry, I'm just tired, not bored. Stef woke me up, even though no one was trying to kill me." She flashed Stef a dark look, suggesting she should probably not sleep anywhere close to Rin or risk waking up dead.

And that was curious. Why were all these people here? I'd been expecting the parents of newsouls and a few of our closest friends. Ten or twelve people. Not forty.

Whit spoke up. "The caldera is unstable. The ground has been rising measurably over the last few months, and Midrange Lake is draining, probably from a crack at the bottom. The geysers have been going off more frequently, and the number of earthquakes—even small ones you never feel—has more than tripled." He looked all around the group, meeting my eyes for a moment. "The caldera is going to erupt. I don't know when, but I know it will be soon."

"It will happen on Soul Night," I said.

Everyone looked at me.

The seconds stretched like minutes, and finally Sarit said, "Well, are you going to explain how you know that?"

"Meuric told me, the night of Templedark. He said something would happen on Soul Night, and that nothing would matter after it. I think he meant the eruption. And"—I glanced from Sam to Stef, who nodded encouragement—"that Janan will ascend."

Someone gasped.

"Janan isn't real," Aril said. I only vaguely knew her from

mathematics lessons; while she was always friendly, I'd never realized she'd cared about me that much.

"He is real. Menehem proved it the night of Templedark. He stopped reincarnation with a poison, remember?"

Everyone shuddered.

"Janan is real," I went on, "but he's not what you think he is. He's not what Meuric and Deborl have told you." That was probably safe to reveal, though the truth—that Janan had once been nothing more than a human—was no doubt something they would immediately forget. "He's going to return on Soul Night. Or rise. I don't know how. I don't know why. I don't know what will happen after. But it's pretty certain that his ascension will cause so much instability in the caldera that it will erupt. Not just hydrothermal eruptions like we had tonight, but a cataclysmic event."

Stef nodded. "I agree. Whit? Orrin? You've been studying Rahel's work."

People winced at Rahel's name—she was a darksoul, a soul lost during Templedark—but Whit and Orrin nodded. "That does seem to be what all this is pointing toward," Whit said with a sigh. "But what can we do? There's no way to stop it."

"No way to stop the caldera," I said, "but if we stop Janan from ascending, perhaps that will put everything else back in order."

"That sounds impossible." Sarit leaned back in her chair

and crossed her arms. "It sounds a little crazy, too. I believe what you've said about Janan, but it sounds crazy."

"I know."

Stef put her SED in her pocket. "I agree with Ana about stopping Janan." When she met my eyes, I knew she was thinking of Cris and his sacrifice, and everything else that had happened inside the temple. "But let's debate that later, because there are other things we need to discuss before everyone passes out from exhaustion."

I shot her a grateful look. I didn't want to discuss a plan for stopping Janan in front of all these people. Particularly since I didn't have a plan.

She looked at all of us. "Deborl and his friends want to harm newsouls. We know this. The laws the Council has been working to pass won't do anything to deter them. But the truth is that we're all in danger."

I studied the crowd, their weary postures and disbelieving looks. "The best thing for newsouls—and anyone who wants to help them—is to get out of Heart."

"We'll have to go *very* far to avoid the eruption," Orrin said. "If the caldera does erupt, Range will be nothing more than a hole in the ground. Everything surrounding Range will be covered in ash as high as Ana. Beyond that, there will be yet more ash. The air will be toxic across most of the continent, and ash in the atmosphere will drop the world's temperature. Animals will die, and crops won't grow."

"How far away will people have to go to be safe?" I thought of the globe and how *big* the world had seemed, not half an hour ago.

Orrin shook his head. "Everywhere will be affected some-how, but the farther we travel, the better our chances of survival."

"Both from the eruption *and* Deborl." I swallowed hard. "Please consider leaving Heart soon."

"This gives me a good place to lead into the next bad news," Stef said. "It seems Sam and Ana weren't the only target tonight. Every Councilor who approved the newsoul protection laws has been killed. Frase, Antha, Finn, Sine: they're all dead."

5
PHOENIX

"THEY'RE DEAD?" I lurched to my feet, SED tumbling off my lap. "No—"

Everyone was speaking at once, outrage and grief flooding the room in torrents. People shouted, "Deborl will pay!" and "We need to call the guards!" Several people pulled out their SEDs, but Stef lifted her voice.

"Stop!"

Everyone went silent.

"Here's the truth of the matter." Stef looked around the room. "We don't know who's involved with Deborl. He and the others escaped prison during the earthquake, that much we do know, but how? Did something shift and free them? Did they do it on their own? Or did someone help them, knowing the earthquake and eruptions would be the perfect cover?"

"No one can predict earthquakes," Moriah said.

"Deborl might be able to." I cleared my throat. "He replaced Meuric as Janan's Hallow—Janan's representative—and since the earthquake was connected to Janan's ascension, Deborl might have known something would happen. When friends visited him in prison, he'd have been able to warn them and ask for assistance."

Stef nodded. "But *how* he did it isn't as important as the fact that he *did* escape. I asked all of you to come here for one of two reasons: either Deborl is an immediate threat to you, or there's no question where your loyalties lie. But everyone else? We don't know. We have to assume they're with Deborl."

Forty people against the world.

They began muttering among themselves, and I caught Sam's eye. He flashed a sad smile, like he knew I thought this was hopeless.

"So what do we do?" Lorin asked. "We won't change everyone's minds about newsouls, or siding with Deborl. Not even if we can find proof that he killed half the Council. He'll convince them he did the right thing."

"Like I said, we leave." I bent to pick up my SED, and put it into my pocket as I sat. "I've already been exiled." Did that still stand if half the Council was dead? "I want newsouls to leave, too, for their protection. As for the rest of you? You can stay, or you can go with the newsouls. They'll need your help." Assuming they could travel far enough from Range in the event of an eruption. If the only way to stop the eruption was to stop Janan, then the future looked very bleak. But I would try, even if it killed me. "The safest thing for everyone—newsouls and oldsouls alike—is to go far, far away."

"Then we all go—where?" Lidea asked.

I shook my head. "Talk with Whit and Orrin about where the safest place will be. Far away. That's all I can guess." I pressed my mouth into a line and glanced at Sam, who just looked sad. "There's something else I have to do, so I won't be going with you. Not the whole way, at any rate."

"Where Ana leads, I follow." Sam managed a half smile.

"I'm going with Ana and Sam, too." There was a deeper meaning in Stef's words. She was the only one other than Sam and me who knew what Janan was, and what he did to newsouls. The time she'd spent inside the temple had opened her mind, shattering the memory magic that had kept her ignorant for five thousand years.

"I— I'll go, too." Sarit met my gaze. "I'm not completely sure what's going on, but I want to be part of this."

"Thank you." Maybe it shouldn't have relieved me to know Sarit and Stef were coming on what would no doubt be a dangerous mission, but it did. Stef was Sam's best friend, and Sarit was mine. They would help. They would make the journey more bearable.

"I'll go along, too." Whit looked at his hands. "Maybe an archivist will be useful."

"You will." If I managed to get the temple books again— and I had to try before I left—Whit might be able to help translate.

"I . . ." Orrin dithered, looking between Geral and Whit.

"You'll go with Geral," Whit said. "And Ariana. They need you."

Orrin nodded.

"I'm going to stay," Armande said. "Someone needs to stay here and keep an eye on Deborl."

Stef nodded, but from the edge of my sight, I caught Sam looking down. Armande was his father in this life, and they were close friends as well. He'd lost Councilor Sine, and now he was losing Armande.

"I'm sorry." Armande didn't look at Sam or meet anyone's eyes. "It sounds cowardly that I don't want to go, but—"

"It's not cowardly," I said. "It's brave. It's going to be dangerous here. You'll have to hide. There will be constant earthquakes. You won't even be able to stay at home or open your pastry stall, because Deborl knows we're friends."

Armande nodded. "I understand."

"Then it's settled," Stef said. "Everyone but Armande leaves."

44

"What about Emil?" Whit asked. "He should come, too."

Emil the Soul Teller wasn't in the library.

Stef shook her head. "No one else. We don't know who might be working with Deborl."

"Emil wouldn't. And neither would Darce. There are lots of people we should take." Whit stood and faced Stef. "We can't leave them behind."

"I agree with Whit," Orrin said.

"Of course you do." Stef rolled her eyes. "No, we've taken a chance on people before. Anyone remember what Wend did after Ana invited him to our meeting about newsoul rights? He told Deborl about our plans. Together they killed two pregnant women, caused another to miscarry, and almost killed two more. Including Geral."

Lidea, formerly Wend's partner, dropped her head like his actions were somehow her fault.

"Stef's right," Sam said. "We can't trust anyone else. We'll all be leaving behind people we care about, but the risks are too high. If Deborl stops us from leaving, that's the end of it."

"Security over friendship?" Orrin asked. "Is that it?"

A few other people spoke up, arguing Stef's fears or Whit's anger. Their voices crowded the library, crescendoing into shouts as they struggled to make their opinions heard.

I surged to my feet. "Stop!"

The room went quiet.

"I agree with Stef and Sam. We've already seen what happens when we're betrayed, and I won't risk the newsouls' safety. I can't."

Sam gave me a small nod, and Whit and Orrin slumped in their seats. "When did you lose faith in people, Ana?" Whit asked.

It was amazing he ever thought I'd had any, considering all I'd been through with Li and everyone who'd fought my entrance into Heart. People kept *doing things* to reinforce my aversion to trusting them.

"I have faith in you," I said to Whit. "And Orrin. And Sam and Stef and Sarit and everyone else in this room. But I have to consider what's best for the newsouls. If we don't protect them, no one will. Perhaps other friendly people, like Emil and Darce, will announce themselves after we've gone. Armande can send them after us, or they can stay here and try to form some kind of resistance. But the newsouls need to leave *now*, while there's still a chance they can survive the eruption."

Orrin glanced at Geral, and their baby in her arms. No one else said anything.

"We'll work out the logistics," I said, as though the argument had never happened. "I'll let you know when to be ready. Pack what you can, but do it quickly and secretly. We'll all leave at the same time. Deborl doesn't want me to leave Heart." He'd campaigned hard for my exile, but now it seemed he preferred I were dead. "I doubt he'll be happy with any of you leaving, either."

Everyone nodded and began writing lists of supplies on their SEDs, discussing who would bring what and where they might be the safest when the caldera erupted.

When Rin got up to look at Sam's hand, I slipped from the gathering and found my way to the large doors that led to the rest of the Councilhouse. Without thinking about where I was going, I wandered through the halls until I landed in front of my favorite painting.

It might have been a large eagle, except the feathers seemed made of flame. Ash from its pyre shone with sparks, and the lush jungle around the bird had dimmed in its light. In spite of the fire-bright bird, there was no smoke.

The painting was of a phoenix, or of someone's memory of how the phoenix had appeared, because the beast on canvas was too beautiful to be real.

Once, I'd asked Sam if he'd ever seen a phoenix. He'd said no, which disappointed me. He was so old. He'd seen and accomplished so much. I couldn't imagine how he hadn't managed to see even one phoenix in his five millennia.

Cris had talked about phoenixes in the temple, before he'd fought Janan. He'd said phoenixes had imprisoned Janan in a tower, though not what Janan had done to deserve such a punishment. Meuric had also mentioned phoenixes. He'd said someone had cursed the sylph, and he thought phoenixes were behind it.

What had *happened* five thousand years ago?

I hoped the answers would be in the temple books. I just had to get them back. And translate them.

"Do you think phoenixes remember their past lives like we do?" Sarit's voice behind me made me jump. "Sorry." She stood next to me and looped one arm around my waist. "I saw you walk out."

"It's okay." I leaned my head on her shoulder. "I just needed some time to think. So much has happened tonight."

She nodded, admiring the phoenix painting with me.

"I asked Sam that question once." I turned my face up to the painting again. "He said there's no reason to believe they don't remember every lifetime."

"I hope you'll be reincarnated, too." She squeezed me. "Even if Range erupts and we die, there will be a lot of people far away. It might take a long time, but eventually we'll all come back."

I lowered my eyes. "Sarit."

She waited.

The truth crowded my throat. I almost told her what I'd learned in the temple, but I couldn't take the pity right now. "If Janan ascends, do you think he'd keep reincarnating everyone?"

"Maybe." She sounded hopeful. "I guess it depends why he's returning. To rule? He'd want people he could rule."

"Meuric told me he needed a special key to live once Janan ascended. It seems like if you don't have the key, you don't live." In the temple, Cris and Stef hadn't thought Janan would reincarnate people, either. Since their memory magic was broken, and Meuric had never been subject to it, their prediction seemed the likely outcome to me.

"Oh."

"You know that I'm trying to stop Janan from ascending, right?"

"Of course. Stopping him means stopping the eruption. But . . . What about reincarnation? Will his death stop reincarnation?"

I nodded. "It stopped during Templedark."

"Yeah, it did." Sarit shuddered, and her tone grew husky with grief. "So either way—it ends. No matter what happens next, this will be our final lifetime."

"There's a cost to reincarnation," I said.

She looked at me, concern darkening her face. "What is it?"

When I'd told Sam, the truth had nearly destroyed him. And when Stef and Cris remembered—

Stef had been unusually nice to me ever since, and Cris had sacrificed himself to save me. I didn't want to hurt Sarit, but she deserved to know the truth. Everyone did. And maybe she would remember. Maybe I could help break her memory magic, like I had Sam's.

"Newsouls." The word almost choked me. "Whenever someone is reborn, Janan takes a newsoul."

"And does what?"

I closed my eyes and repeated what Meuric told me in the temple. "They're being eaten."

"Oh. Oh, Ana." Her voice broke.

"Instead of newsouls being born, Janan takes the souls' power and reincarnates an oldsoul. It worked like that for five thousand years, until Menehem was experimenting in the market field one night, while Ciana was dying."

"The first Templedark," she whispered.

"Janan wasn't able to catch her soul, because he was asleep. So years later, I arrived in her place." The first, but not the only. Not anymore.

"Menehem did the same thing last year."

"Yes. Both to allow more newsouls to be born, and because he wanted to see if it was possible to stop Janan. He was just curious."

She squeezed her eyes shut, a frown pulling on her mouth. "And because of his actions, so many souls are gone forever."

And new ones would replace them.

"This is all just so—so *horrible*. None of it's fair." She hugged herself and stared at the ceiling, tears sparkling in the corners of her eyes. Black hair cascaded down her back in inky tendrils. "Not everyone will believe that Janan will stop reincarnating us after he ascends."

I waited, but she didn't say what she believed.

"All those people will see your actions as a choice: a choice between oldsouls and newsouls. So." She lowered her voice. "If you let Janan ascend, he'd keep reincarnating the rest of us. But he'd keep consuming newsouls."

"And if I stop him," I said, "then newsouls are born, but people I love won't be reincarnated after they die."

"Which means you decide newsouls. Over me. Over your other friends. Over Sam."

"I wish this wasn't my decision, but it seems it's been given to me anyway," I said after a minute. "I didn't ask for this responsibility."

"I can't imagine having to make that choice."

I was on the edge of admitting the rest of the truth, that everyone in Heart had agreed to the exchange knowing what would happen, but Sarit was already crying.

I kept my mouth shut. I hadn't told anyone, not even Sam. It was too much. It would break them.

The only ones who knew were Stef and Cris. Stef was humiliated, and Cris was a sylph.

Sarit didn't need to know.

She let out a long sigh. "I changed my mind. I'm staying with Armande."

My stomach dropped. "What? Why?" She was supposed to come with me. She was my best friend. She'd *said* she was coming with me. "Is it because of what I just told you?"

"No." She pressed her mouth into a line. "Maybe. But the truth is, I'm not good at trekking through the wilderness. I would, for you, but when Armande said he was staying, I realized I should, too. I don't want him to be alone. Besides, I'm good at getting information. I'll be useful to you here."

She *would* be useful here. That didn't mean I *wanted* her to stay.

Maybe I shouldn't have told her about Janan. Maybe it was better to keep these things a secret.

We stood together for a moment longer, then she squeezed my hand and left the hall.

I stayed in the hall, staring at the phoenix painting and fiercely wishing my life were different. Better. I wished for a lifetime with Sam and my friends, a lifetime with music. Wasn't that how life should be?

"I wish I were a phoenix," I said to the empty hallway.

Soon it would be dawn. Yawning, I trudged back to the library and found they'd turned off all the lights but one. Several people had left, but a few were dozing in chairs, or had taken blankets into small alcoves. Sam was reclined in the chair he'd taken earlier, a blanket draped across his legs.

I didn't see Geral and Orrin anywhere—they were probably somewhere else in the library with the baby—and no one else was sleeping curled up with anyone. Well, too bad if

I made them uncomfortable. I'd been promised cuddling with Sam, and I was going to have it. Right now.

After kicking off my shoes and grabbing a spare blanket, I turned off the lamp and found Sam in the dark. No one said anything as I nudged him to one side of the chair and curled in with him. With the blankets over us, he wrapped one arm around my waist, and we adjusted until we found a comfortable position.

"Remember when you said you wanted to move into the library?" Sam murmured by my ear.

"I didn't mean like this."

He kissed my neck, all warmth and pressure. "Where'd you go?"

"To look at the phoenix painting."

"Sarit followed." When I didn't respond, he added, "Did she help?"

"She said she's staying here with Armande. That she changed her mind."

"I'm sorry," he whispered. "Did she say why?"

I closed my eyes and found his good hand, tangled our fingers together. "I told her the truth about newsouls." Part of the truth. If I'd told her the rest, how would she have reacted? Her decision strengthened my resolve to keep the oldsouls' choice to myself.

"She deserves to know," he said. I couldn't find a response that wasn't selfish or whiny, so I kept my mouth shut.

I listened to others shifting in their chairs, muffled voices coming from behind the walls made of bookcases. As dawn crept through the library, I dozed half on Sam's lap, half on the chair. It wasn't comfortable, but I didn't move. I needed to be close to him.

When I awoke hours later, still wrapped in Sam's arms, most everyone had gone. A note from Stef waited pinned under a lamp, saying we'd be leaving not tomorrow, but tonight.

Because tonight, we were stealing back the temple books and Menehem's research.

6

ARCHIVES

"SO THAT'S OUR plan?" It sounded too straightforward and easy to me, but what did I know? I'd never broken into a secure room of the Councilhouse before.

"Do you have a better plan? Get some rest before tonight. You'll need it." Stef gestured toward her sofa, which was shoved next to a small piano against one wall. Her parlor was cluttered, holding dozens of bookcases and only a few places to sit. Where Sam's parlor had taken up most of his first floor, Stef had devoted only a small space for company. The rest was filled up with machines in various stages of completion. Stef didn't get a lot of visitors, but that was by choice. She preferred going out.

When she climbed the narrow stairs and vanished, I

glanced at Sam, who leaned in the doorway with his arms crossed and a worn expression on his face. "Well." I nodded toward our bags piled up in a corner. "At least the most boring part is already done."

A smile tipped the edges of his mouth upward. "Stef has really taken charge, hasn't she?"

It was a relief. From the library, she'd dragged us to Sam's house and forced us to pack as quickly as possible. Then, as we set up motion sensors and alarms outside Stef's house, she'd explained her plan and everything we needed to do. Whit and Orrin were coordinating with the rest of the group, ensuring that everyone was protected as they moved through the city.

News of the Councilors' deaths had spread quickly.

Deborl's friends—those who hadn't been imprisoned for the last week—were creating rumors about newsouls being responsible for the murders, as well as the earthquake and eruptions last night. If everyone would just band together to rid Heart of newsouls, everything would go back to how it had been. . . .

Sam turned and gazed at the piano, flexing his hand in his bandage. "This is possibly my last time with a piano, and I can't even play it."

"I'll play the left hand." We squeezed onto the bench together, his leg resting against mine. I leaned into him and inhaled the scent of soap and clean clothes. "What do you want to play?"

He twisted and met my eyes, something warm and seductive in his. "Just play."

I stretched my hand over the keys and played a major chord. The music resonated through the house and burrowed inside me like hope. This piano had a smaller sound and a thinner bass than Sam's, but it was still beautiful in its way. And it was a piano. I'd missed playing the piano.

Sam brushed a kiss across my forehead, finding a middle note to match mine. His left hand tightened a little over my hip, as though it hurt worse to *not* use it. He played four notes: three moving lower, and one higher. "I sent 'Ana Incarnate' with Orrin."

I looked up. We were so close now, his breath rustled my hair across my cheek.

"While you were looking at the painting, Orrin asked if there was any music I wanted him to take when he goes with the others."

"An archivist until the end, hmm?"

Sam nodded. "He understands how I feel about my music collection. It's the same way he feels about his library. He and Whit have spent so many lifetimes building it."

Like Sam had spent so many lifetimes writing music. Would any of it survive Soul Night?

"Most of the library archives have been digitalized, so he can easily take all that. But he was letting himself take one physical piece, too. One physical piece of our history, just in case they do survive. He wanted the newsouls to have something to pass on to future generations."

My throat tightened. "Isn't most of your music scanned into the digital archives?"

"Yes, and Stef sent it to all our SEDs." Sam played the next few notes of "Ana Incarnate." "But he understands what the physical thing means to me."

"And out of all the music, you gave him mine?" There were so many others he could have asked Orrin to save. Phoenix Symphony. "Blue Rose Serenade." "The Dance of Light," or any of the other compositions dedicated to the names of years.

"It's the most important to me." He kissed me, just a brush of lips on lips. "After Li destroyed the original, we worked together rewriting the music."

"I remember." I could hardly speak around the tangle of emotions. Sam had been arrested, and Li had thrown the music into a fire. I'd tried to save it, but most of it was too burnt. When Sam had finally been exonerated and I moved in with him again, we'd spent a month rewriting "Ana Incarnate," the waltz he'd written for me. And we hadn't stopped there. He'd insisted we transcribe it for flute, too, and later he'd presented me with a flute of my very own.

"No matter what happens, I want that piece of music to live. When people hear it, I want them to think about what we tried to do, regardless of whether we succeed. And I want them to know that without you, Ana Incarnate, whatever

Janan had planned would have just happened without opposition. You opened our eyes. I want that legacy to continue."

"Oh." I could hardly breathe. Once again, Sam had made me into something more important than I really was. "I don't know what to say."

He gave a wry smile and let his fingers dance across the piano keys. "You don't have to say anything. Just play."

Music flowed through the small parlor, like a river rushing around rocks and trees. While Sam played half-familiar melodies and whispers of something new, I found chords and countermelodies. Anguish flashed through Sam's expression a couple of times. His piano was gone. His flute, violin, clarinet: all gone. We'd packed my flute—it would journey wherever we did—but the wound created by the loss of the others, it was still gaping.

We played until nightfall, when Stef came downstairs and we ate a small dinner of chicken and vegetables. I savored everything; it might be one of the last times we had hot, fresh food.

At midnight, our SEDs beeped in unison, and slowly, I untangled myself from Sam's arms and legs. We'd fallen asleep on the sofa, music still heavy inside of us, but now it was time to let everything go. Home. Heart. Relative peace.

I switched my SED to silent and double-checked that my knife was in my coat pocket.

"We'll leave our bags," Stef said, hitching an empty back-pack over one shoulder. "Whit and a couple others will come to get them. We need to grab the books and research, and we'll meet them at the east guard station. There will be vehicles enough for all of us. Hopefully we'll be far away from Heart before Deborl ever realizes we're gone."

It was the same plan she'd announced earlier. I nodded.

Outside, flecks of snow stung my face as I pulled up my hood and checked my SED. The program Stef had loaded earlier popped up, reporting a cluster of small earthquakes I hadn't felt. Then, conscious that the SED light might attract the wrong kind of attention, I shoved the device into my pocket and took Sam's hand, letting him guide me through the dark. The only light was the temple, still blazing unnaturally bright.

Our footsteps crunched on the thin snowfall, and a breeze hissed through the evergreens. "Here's what will happen," Stef said. "I've adjusted the security cameras in the Councilhouse so they won't record us. Getting caught won't matter for you, Ana, since they've already exiled you, but it does for Sam and me."

How much, though? The majority of the Council had been killed.

How long would they argue about what to do before they took action against newsouls or accepted Deborl back into the Council? What if they made him *Speaker*? I shuddered.

"The other thing is the soul-scanners." Stef turned us down another path. "I took a peek into the scanner logs. It looks like several Councilors went into one of the private archive rooms while you and I were stuck in the temple, and then again the other day after you had the meeting with them."

The meeting where they'd kicked me out of Heart. "They had the temple books and research with them."

"Exactly. It seems to me they must have been fetching something important from that room, like books or research. Maybe even the key. Unfortunately, that scanner is programmed to let only Councilors through that door."

"Fortunately," Sam said, his tone a smile, "we have you."

"You do." It sounded like she was grinning. "No one on the Council ever realized I *always* leave myself a secondary entry code for every building in Heart. I guess—" She stumbled over the words. "I guess they never will now."

Grief twisted in my chest, and I couldn't respond. Sine's attitude toward me had changed once she became Speaker, but she'd still been more a friend than not.

Was there anyone left who would publicly oppose Deborl after what he'd done? Anyone who might be brave enough to stand up to him—Sarit and Armande excepted—was going with us tonight.

Stef was quiet for a while. She'd been very selective about the people she'd invited to the library earlier. She'd probably

61

left behind some of her friends, because she wasn't sure she could trust them.

Stef had chosen. She'd chosen me.

Humbled, I followed all the way to the market field, keeping an eye out for anyone. But the way was clear, and I heard nothing but the wind. Snow smothered sounds, making the world unearthly still. Templelight reflected off the snow; the market field was bright.

"Try not to think about it," Sam murmured.

"Think about what?" I huddled inside my layers of wool and silk. My hood blocked my peripheral vision; I could see only straight ahead.

"The risks and consequences. Where we're going after. Just focus on getting through this."

I opened my mouth to argue that I hadn't been worried about this part, but reconsidered. Though the research and books had belonged to me before Deborl took them, reclaiming them now still felt a little like stealing.

"So I take it you've broken into a lot of private archive rooms?" I asked.

Snow quieted his reply, keeping it from carrying. "I admit to nothing, except that Stef is a bad influence."

I snorted. "You can't fool me. I know better than to assume it's all Stef corrupting you."

"But you know her well enough to realize that most of the trouble I've gotten into is her fault, right?" He flashed me a look of boyish innocence.

"Right, of course." I kept my tone dubious, though conceded the point. Without Stef dragging Sam into trouble, he probably would stay at home, composing and practicing all day.

Now that I thought about it, Sam definitely attracted a type.

Stef pouted. "You two are going to ruin my good name."

"Oh, it was ruined a long time ago." Sam grinned and gave her a sideways hug.

We scanned the bright area once more before taking off at a trot, crossing the cobblestone market field. Our footfalls suddenly seemed so loud.

But no one caught us, and soon Sam dragged open the library door and ushered me inside after Stef. She had a pistol out.

The library was dim and quiet. I strained my ears but couldn't hear anything suspicious. No floorboards creaking. No hiss of clothes that didn't belong. Just the three of us.

We crept through the long hallway. It was unlikely anyone was working this late, but who knew about Deborl's people.

What if Deborl had gotten to the research and books already?

Worries nipped at my heels as we traveled through the quiet hall.

"This is it." Stef pulled a screwdriver from her pocket and

used it to pry open the soul-scanner cover. "Give me just a second." She replaced the screwdriver and removed a slender cord, which she connected to her SED and a port inside the scanner. After a moment of shifting functions, she tapped the SED screen and the scanner beeped. The door unlocked.

"Nice job." Sam pulled the door open before it locked again.

"I know." She shut the scanner and breezed into the room. I followed, and the lights turned on as the door swung closed behind us.

Rows of cupboards filled the rectangular room, hundreds of them. There wasn't even room for a table, just counters along the perimeter.

"Let's get started." I strode to the far end and began opening cupboards. Some were empty, but most had old documents or artifacts stored in vacuum-sealed glass boxes. "What is this?" I pointed at a stick with a feather tied to one end. "An arrow?" I'd seen drawings of them, but no one used those things anymore. Laser pistols were far less messy when it came to killing from a distance.

"Some of our earliest inventions, or things we found in the area when we first settled." Stef shrugged. "It's all useless junk now, but the Council is determined to keep it."

"Because Whit and Orrin are determined to keep it," Sam said. "At first they stored those things in the library where everyone could look at them, but a few people never understood the point of sealing them to slow the decay, so the containers kept getting opened. Orrin had them moved here."

"Ah." I thought it was nice they'd kept these things. It would have been nicer if I'd had time to look through everything, but since I was in a hurry, I simply tried to take in as many details as I could while sifting through piles of stuff. At last, I opened a door to find a stack of familiar leather spines and a large envelope filled with notebooks and diaries. "Here's everything."

Well, almost everything. As I slid the items across the counter to Sam and Stef, I didn't see the key to the temple.

"Have you seen the key anywhere else?" I asked, checking the cupboard below and beside the one where I'd found the books, but it wasn't there.

We looked around for a while longer, until finally Stef said, "We have to go. Whit and the others are ready."

I didn't like leaving the key behind, not that it would do us any good outside of Range. But if we had it, that would mean Deborl didn't.

Sam shrugged on the backpack, and we left the room.

We moved through the halls as quickly as possible. Outside, the layer of snow on the ground shone with temple-light, and the air glowed misty white. We headed around the side of the Councilhouse and rounded the immense temple. Having a vehicle wait for us at the Councilhouse would have been faster, but would draw attention. Deborl would surely notice. As long as we were sneaky, we could reach the guard station without incident.

Light still blazed from the white temple, so unnaturally bright ever since the Year of Souls began. It made me itch all over.

By the time we reached the guard station, a large building tucked into the city wall, I was shivering with cold and damp.

Stef pulled open the door, letting a rectangle of light fall onto the snowy road, and a figure emerged from around the corner of the building.

A blue beam of light shot toward us.

"Watch out!" I shoved Stef inside the guard station and hurried to follow, but the stink of singed wool chased me. The laser had been aimed at my head.

Sam grabbed my wrist and dragged me inside.

The shooter stepped into the light.

Deborl.

7

COMPASSION

I SLAMMED THE door, locked the bolt, and spun around to find everyone gathered around ten black vehicles. "It's Deborl." My voice shook, but the words rang throughout the brightly lit guard station.

Stef swore and turned to the crowd. "Get ready to open the gate, but don't leave until we know it's safe. He could have shooters on the roof."

People rushed into action as something thumped on the city-side door. Shouts rang throughout the guard station, orders and cries for help. The newsouls wailed at the sudden commotion.

Stef shoved a laser pistol into my hand. "Shoot anyone who comes through that door." She grabbed Sam's elbow and dragged him deeper into the guard station.

I clutched the pistol in both hands, staring at the rattling door for a few agonizing minutes before I realized there was no one there to shoot. Not unless I wanted to burn holes in the wood. Hands trembling, I shoved the pistol into my coat pocket and searched for something to block the door with. A desk or chair. Anything.

But guard stations were sparsely furnished. There was an armory—no doubt raided already by Whit and Orrin—and a stable for horses. Nothing useful there, but—

"We can block the door with bales of hay." There were at least five other people by this door. We didn't all need to be here. I turned to Aril, who stood near me. "Will you help?"

She looked up. "Bales of hay? Good idea." She grabbed Thleen—a wildlife expert I'd only recently met—and we ran through a short, dark passageway and into the stables.

"Careful," Thleen said. "There's another entrance on the far side, where they let horses out to exercise."

We slowed to a walk, listening as we came to a long row of stables. The din of our friends was behind us now. Ahead, there were only the sounds of horses snorting, shuffling hay around their stalls, and lapping water. The stables smelled warm and earthy, and a little like sweat.

"Bales are kept up there." Aril motioned to a rickety stair-case leading to a loft. Bits of hay floated down, but there was no wind, so why—

"Watch out!" I grabbed her arm and dragged her back into the passageway just as blue light flashed and a hole sizzled in the wall to my left.

Strangers appeared in the hayloft above the hall, lasers aimed. A handful leapt down to the floor level and shot toward the guard station.

My companions fired their weapons. Between shots, Thleen shoved me into a shallow alcove. My elbow slammed against the wooden wall, aching, and I looked up just in time to see her double over and clutch her leg.

But we weren't alone. Our people rushed through the passageway, firing pistols. Horses screamed, and the odor of burning wood filled the area. Both sides collided, all wild and chaotic.

"Ana!" Sam's voice rang above the cacophony. "Ana!"

I squeezed through the fighting, searching for Sam, but when I found my way back into the guard station, another group of Deborl's people surged into the main chamber. Blue targeting lights lit the room. Glass exploded in one of the vehicles, and screams crescendoed.

I shouldn't have left my post. Stef had put me by the door, and I'd left.

"There you are." Deborl's voice pierced the noise as he appeared in front of me, his laser aimed at my forehead. He was small, only my size and barely a year past his first quindec. He still had spindly arms and legs he hadn't quite grown into, and though he might have been attractive in an awkward way, his glare and cruel smile destroyed that. "Nosoul."

If I raised my pistol, he'd shoot. He'd shoot anyway. Words tumbled out of me. "We're just trying to get out of Heart, okay? You win. You can have the city. Newsouls are leaving."

He took two long strides and shoved me against the wall, his free hand around my throat. The edges of my vision fogged as I struggled to breathe, and my pistol slipped from my fingers. "I will kill every one of you," he said. His pistol pressed against my shoulder. "You're no threat to Janan. You aren't. But you're an annoyance to me."

First Meuric, now Deborl. Janan's Hallows needed so badly to convince themselves of my unimportance.

I jerked my knee up, between his legs. He stumbled backward, and the blue light from the pistol flashed. I gasped for breath as I dropped, fingers grasping for my pistol.

Beyond Deborl, the fighting had shifted, mostly in the passageway now, with my friends bottlenecked. They had us outnumbered, but we seemed to be winning anyway.

I gripped my pistol and stood just as Deborl righted himself, too. His face was still contorted with pain, and in his haste to stagger away from me, he'd dropped his pistol.

Pulse aching in my throat, I leveled my pistol at him and ordered myself to shoot.

Someone screamed near the exit.

Sam called my name again.

Deborl's people began to back off, though I couldn't understand why.

"Shoot," I whispered to myself. My hands shook on the pistol, and as Deborl recovered, he gave a long, slow smile, like he knew I was hoping someone else would come and save me from this choice. Stef shot people. Sam had, too. Why couldn't they come do this?

The blue targeting light flared from my pistol. I had only to press the button the rest of the way down.

Deborl reached for his weapon. I shifted my aim and shot his pistol before he could grab it. It spun for a moment, then burst into flames. Scraps of metal flew up, into Deborl's hand. He screamed and clutched his bleeding, heat-singed hand to himself. Cursing, he called a retreat and his people began running for the exit.

Slowly, I advanced on him, holding my pistol steady for the first time. "Give me the temple key."

He shifted away from the burning wreckage of his pistol. "I don't have it."

That was a lie. His coat had fallen open, revealing a slice of silver inside one of the interior pockets: the key. Maybe I couldn't make myself shoot him, but I could kick him.

I rammed the toe of my boot into his ribs, and when he fell over, gasping, I snatched the key. With his good hand, though, he grabbed my wrist and dragged me to the floor. I tightened my grip on the key, but my pistol spun away.

Deborl jammed his thumb against my arm. Fire raced through me, and I screamed.

I struggled to pry myself away, and he grabbed the key back. We fought, shouting curses at each other, and just as I was ready to give up, a boot collided with Deborl's head.

Sam hauled the former Councilor to his feet and retrieved the key. Fighting tears, I pressed my hand to my arm. I couldn't remember getting hurt, but something must have happened.

Before Sam could shift the key and pistol around in his good hand, Deborl squirmed away and followed his friends out the door, never giving Sam a chance to shoot.

Sam dropped to the floor next to me, good hand tight over the temple key. "Ana." He wrapped his arms around me as Deborl and his friends escaped, and our people filtered back into the guard station.

"Anid and Ariana?"

"They're safe." Sam's words were warm on my neck.

Relief poured through me, and I clung to Sam. "I'm sorry," I rasped. "I couldn't do it."

Two of ten vehicles had been damaged in the fight, so Orrin and Whit reorganized groups and supplies and removed the solar panels from the roofs to store inside other vehicles as backups. They'd need the extra electricity when they reached their destination.

Since Rin was the only medic in the group, she made quick evaluations of injuries, then had the most urgent cases helped into one vehicle, where she could treat them en route. Miraculously, no one had been killed, though someone had a broken leg, while another had been shot in the throat; the laser had cauterized the wound.

I climbed into one of the vehicles after Sam. I'd ridden in one just once that I could remember, and that had been when Meuric, Li, and a pair of guards came to arrest Sam after the rededication ceremony. That time, I'd been too angry to enjoy the luxury. This time, too much hurt, both my heart and my arm.

Stef drove. Orrin, Geral, and Ariana crowded in, too, and as the others pulled out of the guard station, we crept after them into the icy night.

Ariana cried, and Orrin and Geral could do nothing to console her. The rest of us cringed miserably as the wailing grew worse, rising every time the vehicle hit a bump—which was frequently. I slumped in my seat and sent a message to Sarit, letting her know that we'd made it out of Heart.

I wished we'd gotten a chance to say good-bye, but there'd been no time in all the last-minute rush to escape. I missed her already. Maybe we'd get to see each other again before Soul Night.

Sam helped me out of my coat, mindful of my injured arm, and applied burn cream. We had to put the bandage on together, since his left hand was immobile, thanks to Rin. Then we pulled a blanket over us. When he leaned against the door, I leaned against him.

"I didn't even realize he shot me," I whispered. "Not until he jammed his thumb into the burn." The wound throbbed, almost consuming my thoughts. I preferred the pain. I'd very nearly never felt pain again.

Sam spoke into my hair. "Adrenaline does that."

Outside, snow-covered trees slid past and mountains grew in the distance. I'd done a lot of walking in my life. From Purple Rose Cottage to Rangedge Lake to Sam's cabin to Heart. Later, from Heart to Purple Rose Cottage to Menehem's lab and back to Heart. I was used to journeys taking days.

Even though Stef kept complaining how slowly vehicles had to travel over the ice and uncertain road, this was so much faster than walking. It would have been luxurious if I weren't an exile. If we weren't fleeing for our lives.

We were all exiles.

I gazed out the window, looking through my reflection in the glass. In the north, illuminated by the templelight and silhouetted by starlight, I could just make out the dozens of obelisks beyond the city.

Templedark Memorial stood solemn and waiting, a silent testimony of our fragile existence. As much as I wanted to forget the days we spent in remembrance of darksouls, the sensations whirled up as we drove past. Wind in the trees, the scent of sulfur from nearby fumaroles, and the tolling of the bell rung seventy-two times. One peal for every darksoul.

Soon, Templedark Memorial faded from view. Trees huddled over us, and flakes of snow looked like tiny darts in the headlights. Beyond that, the whole world was very, very dark, and it seemed we were driving off the edge of it.

The baby fell asleep, and Geral and Orrin began speaking in low voices in the front. Sam held me in his left arm, injured hand resting on my hip, while he stroked my hair with his good hand. His touch was soothing, and finally we were getting away. We were alive.

"I couldn't do it, Sam."

His fingers paused over my cheek, then continued down in a warm trail. He didn't ask what I was talking about.

"I should have. I had a chance, and I hesitated. If I'd just acted, we wouldn't have to deal with him ever again. Whatever hate he spews in our absence, it's because I didn't just shoot him."

The vehicle slowed further and crawled over a lump in the road. The baby whimpered, and everyone tensed, but she didn't wake.

"No matter what Deborl does," Sam said, "his actions are his. You shouldn't accept any blame for what he chooses to do."

"But if I'd just done it—"

"No. He's still responsible for his actions."

"All right." That made me feel a little better, but I still should have done it. Neither Sam nor Stef would have hesitated.

"And either way," Sam murmured, "Janan would still be ascending on Soul Night. We'd still be escaping Heart, because Deborl isn't the only one to feel that way. If you'd done it, that might have—in others' eyes—proven every awful thing he said about you."

But still. The idea of never having to deal with Deborl again . . .

"Regardless." Sam's voice was warm and deep and filled with compassion. "I'm glad you didn't."

As the sun rose, Orrin pointed out bulges in the land that hadn't been there before. The road had buckled under the pressure, leaving cobblestones jutting up at strange angles. Everywhere, ice shone blinding-bright in the sunshine, in sheets or icicles or hoarfrost on trees.

No wonder we'd been forced to travel so slowly; at anything more than a crawl, we'd have slid off the road.

It wasn't until late afternoon that we came within sight of Menehem's lab, a colossal building of iron and ugliness. Stables and cisterns stood on one side of the structure. Snow coated the solar panels on top of the lab, but they could be swept clean with one of the extendable brushes Menehem had kept inside.

All eight vehicles formed a semicircle and engines quieted. Calm stole across the yard. Even the wind died. With the ice dressing the world in white, the front of Menehem's laboratory was as still as a painting.

"Are you ready?" Sam squeezed me. "Everyone's waiting for you."

He was right. Everyone in our vehicle was looking for me to make the first move. This had been my father's lab. He'd left it for me, as well as everything inside. Including the poison that would put Janan to sleep again, if we could produce enough.

I wasn't sure I liked the responsibility of this kind of power, the ability to stop reincarnation.

But reincarnation wasn't natural, and souls suffered for it. Didn't that mean I needed to right this wrong if I could? I couldn't ignore it. But this power, the existence of the poison being manufactured in that building, was too much for one person.

Just like the power of reincarnation was too great for Janan. He shouldn't get to decide who lived and who never lived. He took away their choices.

I stepped out of the vehicle, cold air nipping at my cheeks as I turned toward the building. The lab key turned in the lock. I typed in the pass code, and the machinery beeped. Only when the door swung open did others begin to join me outside, gathering babies and bags to lug toward the wide door.

"What is this place?" someone muttered, sharp on the winter evening. I'd forgotten we hadn't told everyone what was here.

Sam stepped alongside of me. "Ready?"

I flashed a tight smile, hoping he'd ignore my worry. "When we came here last autumn, there was a dead raccoon inside. So I'm a little nervous about what else might have crawled in during our absence."

He chuckled, and together we went inside.

Lights flickered on, illuminating dusty furniture. The front section of the lab held the living quarters: kitchen, bedroom, and a small walled-off washroom. Low humming emanated from the laboratory in the back, where the machine produced the poison that had twice put Janan to sleep.

Slowly, others filed inside and made themselves comfortable on the bed, sofa, and the floor. Soon, I'd have to tell them exactly what this place was, though some could probably guess its purpose.

And would I tell them that the machine was making poison right now? Sam had only told me the other night, before the earthquake.

"Now what?" Sam asked me as we finished helping bring in supplies. The others would stay here only a few days, just long enough to recover from their injuries.

"Now we hope the sylph come." I'd been certain they would be here waiting for me. They'd found me at Purple

Rose Cottage, and then followed me here when I decided I needed to study what my father had done to them.

As Sam and I helped the temporary residents of Menehem's lab clean the area and prepare an evening meal, I kept an eye on the forest outside. The sylph had to come. I needed to know what they wanted from me, and if they could help me stop Janan.

But when darkness fell, only natural shadows filled the woods.

8
POISON

MORNING DAWNED COLD and still, only a few flakes of snow spiraling down. But the vehicles were dusted with white, and the mountains looked like upside-down icicles. The frozen world made Heart and all our troubles seem far away, like a fading memory.

There were still no sylph, but I reminded myself they'd taken a while to come before. And Cris . . .

I gripped the windowsill and closed my eyes, suddenly back inside the skeleton chamber with Cris lying on the stone table, next to Janan's body. The walls glowed red, and the silver knife flashed as he plunged it into his own chest. White and wind filled the chamber, and it seemed the world had been ripped open. Now he was cursed. A shadow of himself. Incorporeal.

Soft, peaceful snoring brought me shivering back into the present, and I picked my way between the sleepers and headed into the lab.

I'd been in here only briefly last night. It had been dark, and I hadn't wanted to draw attention to what was going on.

Lots of metal bits and curiosities lurked in the back of the lab, most coated with dust and grime. The groaning machine that made poison was only the size of a bookcase, with a conveyer through the bottom, which pulled canisters under a spout, then pushed them onto the solid floor where they waited to be dealt with. When I'd come in last night, twenty big canisters huddled around the conveyer. I'd moved them aside and added a few empty ones to the "in" side.

Menehem had made a *lot* of extra canisters. But whatever his plans had been, death had delayed them.

Though the canisters were large, the metal was light-weight and they were filled with aerosol, so they weren't too heavy for me to carry. One by one, I lined them up by the door at the rear of the lab and draped a heavy cloth over them. The door was too big to open now; cold air would shoot in and wake everyone.

Menehem's notes indicated he'd taken six with him for Templedark. And according to the notes, Janan and the sylph developed a tolerance to the poison swiftly, but so far we had almost three times as much poison, and there was more coming.

Maybe it would be enough to stop Janan during Soul Night.

Finished, I sneaked back into the living area and crouched next to Sam. In sleep, his face was peaceful and soft. I touched his cheek and traced the contours of his jaw and neck. He smiled a little as he opened his eyes. "Ana."

I leaned down to kiss him, quickly because groans and rustling blankets indicated others were waking, as well. "Make sure the back door gets opened later so I can take the poison outside without everyone noticing."

He squinted and rubbed his face. "Why?"

"I want to hide it."

"From everyone?" Alert now, he pushed himself up and whispered by my ear. "Is there someone you don't trust?"

"No." I glanced at the people stretching in their sleeping bags and speaking to neighbors. "It's not that. I just don't think they'd understand. Not everyone. Someone—any of them—might get the wrong idea and destroy the poison." I didn't have a *plan* for the poison yet, but I wanted as many options as possible.

"Do you have to tell them what it is?"

I shrugged. "If they ask, I'll have to tell them the truth." These people were on my side because they didn't want newsouls to suffer. But that didn't mean they were willing to give up their own immortality for the possibility of more newsouls. They didn't know—wouldn't understand—that reincarnation was over anyway.

Sam looked dubious but didn't say anything else about it, and we spent the next hour assisting with breakfast while Aril and Lorin complained bitterly about Armande's absence.

"He'd be able to deal with this. Somehow." Lorin glanced over her shoulder at the dozens of people wandering around the living area. "And there's only one baking sheet. How are we supposed to feed all these people?"

"You'll manage," Sam said, putting on another pot of coffee. The morning passed quickly as Rin went around and treated injuries again, checking on my arm as well. While everyone was busy, I sneaked the canisters outside.

Taking them with us when we left was out of the question. Who knew where we'd travel? But I didn't want to leave them just sitting in the lab. If Deborl had looked at Menehem's research, he'd know where the lab was.

There was a wide, clear yard in front of the lab, but behind it was densely forested with spruce and pine and cottonwood trees. Rocks and boulders jutted everywhere. A deer path along a cliff face led to a shallow cave, its entrance mostly concealed by snow-covered brush. Perfect.

Two hours later, I had all the canisters tucked inside the cave, heavy blankets draped over them to insulate them from the cold. Thank goodness Menehem had kept so much junk in his lab.

When I returned, sweaty and gross, everyone was settled down and discussing where to go next. Sam lifted an eyebrow as I sat next to him, and I nodded, ignoring the conversation I had nothing to do with, in favor of thinking about where *we* might go next, and when I might get a chance to work on translating the temple books.

"Ana," Lidea said, "what is this building? How'd you know to take us here?"

I shifted and wanted to look to Sam or Stef for help, but everyone was waiting. I had to appear confident.

"This is Menehem's laboratory. It's where he disappeared to after I was born."

Dozens of faces turned to me, not hiding the revulsion and loathing at the mention of Menehem and his experiments.

"Is this where he started Templedark? Is this where he started killing our friends?" someone asked.

I resisted the urge to lower my eyes. "Before you say anything, let me tell you what happened.

"The Council told you that Menehem admitted responsibility for Templedark, but that's not the whole story. It starts almost twenty-five years ago, when he was looking for ways to control the sylph. One night, while he was experimenting in the market field, Ciana was dying in the hospital. He was working with a gas, and there was a minor explosion. Wind took the vapor toward the temple, and the temple went dark."

Everyone looked pale and sick. Lidea said, "What does that have to do with this place?" She squirmed, as though this air might be contaminated.

"Well, you know Ciana died when the temple was dark. And in the Year of Songs, I was born instead."

"The gas did it?" Whit asked.

I nodded. "Yes. Once he realized what he'd done, he left Heart to figure out the details. The mixture he'd been working with had been a mistake, one he wasn't sure how to reproduce. So he built this place, and eighteen years later, he had a breakthrough.

"He'd been working with sylph. I can show you footage, if you want. He documented everything. And one day, his mixture put all the sylph in the area to sleep."

A couple of people muttered, but mostly they just waited.

"He experimented on the sylph repeatedly, logging how long the poison affected them, the size of the doses—everything. He realized they quickly developed a tolerance for the poison, so it was useless as a weapon."

"And then," Orrin said, "he took the poison to Heart."

"Why are you calling it a poison?" Moriah asked. "It doesn't kill them, does it?"

Other people chimed in with more questions, but stopped when I held up my hands. "It doesn't kill them. They recover, and there seem to be no lasting effects. But they are put to sleep involuntarily." I shrugged. "If someone did that to me, I'd think of it as poison."

Moriah nodded, satisfied with that.

"As for what happened next, Orrin, you're right." I fidgeted with the hem of my shirt. "For reasons only Menehem will ever understand, he trapped dozens of sylph in eggs, then took them and a large quantity of the poison to Heart. He set the sylph free and delivered the poison. That night, dragons came too."

The lab was silent, except for the humming of the machine in the back.

"So." Moriah tilted her head. "The poison was intended as a weapon against the sylph, but it affected Janan too. Why? How? They aren't the same things."

I glanced at Sam, but he offered no answers. "I don't know," I said at last. "There's a connection between them, but I don't know what it is."

"And we're here because . . ." someone in the back asked.

"Because we're safe here." For now.

"What about the poison?" Lorin asked. "Is that still a danger?"

A danger. Not an option for stopping Janan. It was as I'd anticipated: they didn't mind the newsouls who already existed in their lives, but they weren't willing to risk their own immortality.

Maybe if they knew that oldsouls had been replacing

86

newsouls this whole time—not the other way around—they'd think differently. But even if I told them, they wouldn't remember. The memory magic would never let them.

I hated that. They'd *all* made the bargain for immortality. Every one of them had traded countless newsouls for their own reincarnation. And none of them could remember.

"The poison isn't a danger," I whispered, as though I hadn't just hidden twenty canisters full of it. "Menehem used an incredible amount on Janan the night of Templedark, and the sylph gained tolerance exponentially. If he isn't immune to it now, he's very near."

They nodded, mostly reassured. After a few more questions, we slid the cover off the video screen and prepared a few discs so they could witness Menehem's first success with putting sylph to sleep, and his first ideas on how to prove the existence of Janan.

Then, after convincing Rin to give me as much basic medical training as we could fit in, I pulled out the temple books and began the long process of translating the few symbols I knew.

Sam leaned over. "I thought you were going to tell them that I turned on the machine."

I cast my eyes down at the books and smoothed a bent corner of paper. "It's easier if they don't know."

I'd been attacked and betrayed too many times to trust anyone but our closest friends. People had been *killed* because

I'd trusted someone I shouldn't have, like Wend, and I wouldn't let that happen again. Not ever.

From now on, I'd tell everyone only what they needed to know, and when they needed to know it.

A few days later, Sam received a call. When he clicked off, he was pale. "That was Armande."

Everyone in the lab went quiet.

"Deborl has named himself Speaker. With the majority of the Council gone, that makes him the sole leader of Heart. He's sent Merton and a team of three dozen out of the city. Armande doesn't know what they're after or what direction they headed, but I think it's safe to assume they're looking for us.

"Meanwhile, Deborl has put several of his friends in charge of the guard, and all the entrances to Heart have been sealed. There's a citywide curfew, and anyone who stands up for newsouls is imprisoned."

No one spoke.

"It gets worse," Sam said. "Deborl has dispatched air drones, programmed to find us."

I used my hand to mark my place in the temple book on my lap. "Why send air drones if he's sent people too?" I shook that away. "Rather, why send people if he's sent air drones? That seems like a waste of time."

"Perhaps he has another goal for them." Whit glanced

west, toward Heart. "At any rate, we won't have to worry about Merton and the others for a while. We disabled all the other vehicles in Heart, and it will take them days to walk here in this weather, assuming they even know where we are. It's the drones we need to worry about."

"I may be able to reprogram those." Stef looked up from her SED. "Though I can't promise Deborl's people won't catch the changes. I'll monitor the program.

"I'm also sending the archive of maps to everyone's SEDs, so we ought to go over your route once more—and then you should leave. Everyone not staying with Ana needs to get as far away from Range as possible. Tonight."

That evening, the eight vehicles parked in front of the lab were gone. Only Sam, Stef, and Whit remained with me.

"Why don't we leave?" Whit asked, as we settled down for bed. "If Deborl is searching for us, why are we staying in one spot?"

"I'm waiting for someone." But when I stared out the window, Cris and the other sylph were nowhere to be seen.

9
PATH

NOW THAT THE others were gone, Menehem's lab was too quiet, and I spent all my time poring over the temple books and translations of symbols, hoping for a breakthrough. But if there was anything about how to stop Janan, I hadn't seen it yet.

"We need to consider moving on," Whit said one afternoon. "Every day we stay here is another day Deborl might find us."

"Especially since we'll have to walk." Sam flipped through his SED, checking for earthquakes and eruptions around Range. From beside him, I could see several red dots on the screen, but none of them were very large.

"And carry all our things." Stef looked up from reading

through Menehem's notes on building his machine.

"We're waiting for the sylph." I turned a page in the temple book and scribbled out a few more possible translations. "And Cris."

Whit cocked his head at me. "Wait, how will Cris be here? He died during the riot on market day."

I groaned and dropped my face into my hands. "Stef. Your turn."

She sighed. "You promise if we tell him enough, he'll start to remember?"

I nodded, face still buried in my hands. "It worked on Sam. The magic will crack and fade, but it takes time."

"I'm sitting right here," Whit muttered darkly.

"Cris is a sylph now." Stef headed for the kitchen area, an empty coffee mug in hand. "When Deborl trapped Cris, Ana, and me inside the temple, Cris sacrificed himself in order to free us."

"You were inside the temple?" Whit asked.

I slammed the temple book shut and grabbed my note-book. "This is what Cris told me: five thousand years ago, Janan was your leader. The leader of all the humans, as far as I can tell. He was just a man, nothing more. But he craved immortality, so he gathered a group of warriors and went hunting for the secrets of eternal life. Something big happened. I don't know what. I'm studying the books, trying to understand. Then Janan and his warriors were imprisoned in towers all across the world. When his followers—you—heard of his capture, they went to free him.

"They—you traveled until you reached an immense wall ringing a single tower. But when you tried to free him, he said the phoenixes had imprisoned him because he had succeeded in his quest: he'd discovered the secret to immortality."

"And then what?" Whit asked.

"Then . . ."

Stef lifted an eyebrow, a silent question. Did I want her to say it?

I shook my head. No. No one else needed to bear that guilt. And . . . it was easier if they didn't know.

Sam looked at me with a sudden and penetrating curiosity, as though he could tell I held back something important.

I averted my gaze and continued speaking. "Then Janan shed his mortal form. He became part of the temple, which was already infused with phoenix magic, and began the journey to immortality. *True* immortality, without the cycle of life and death and rebirth. He wanted you all to wait for him. He wanted to come back and rule you as he had before"—so he'd told them—"so he caused you to reincarnate."

Stef nodded. "We allowed Meuric to bind us in chains inside the temple, and then Janan became part of the temple. We were all bound to him."

From across the room, Sam's gaze was dark and heavy and grieving.

"Does that mean—" Whit glanced from me to Sam and back. "Oh. You'll never be reincarnated, will you?"

I shrugged and opened the temple book again. "It's not important."

"It is—" he started.

"It's not. There's nothing we can do about it, and even if we could change it, the cost is too great." I tried to focus on my work, but my vision was misty. No matter what happened, this was it for me. I had this one fleeting life.

I had to make the most of it.

"All right." Whit's voice was soft; he was only conceding because he wouldn't argue with a girl who'd live only once.

I didn't look up from the book, but I could feel everyone's stares. Their pity.

Sam's grief.

"It's not important," I repeated. "After Soul Night, no one is getting reincarnated anyway. Not even you. The next time someone dies, they're gone forever."

A heavy silence descended on the lab, this simple and terrifying truth a smothering snow. I should have said it more gently. They all knew the truth, but they probably didn't appreciate being reminded any more than I enjoyed being reminded about my newness.

After a moment, Sam took a seat across the table from me. "We keep talking about Janan ascending and returning and how it will destabilize the caldera enough that it erupts, but what does Janan's ascending actually mean? Will he stay here? Go somewhere else? Be corporeal or not? You said he doesn't have a mortal form anymore. Will he be just a soul flying around?"

"If you can say he even has a soul," I muttered, but Sam's words struck something else inside me. No mortal form. Just a soul flying around.

Like sylph?

"He was human once." Stef leaned against the wall, her arms crossed. "He must have had a soul at some point."

Less sure, but unwilling to argue, I turned back to Sam's question. "I don't know what will happen, or how. That's why I've been trying to translate these books."

"Then let's do that." Sam picked through my notebook, finding my potential translations of strings of symbols from the books. "This symbol means Heart, city, and prison?" He pointed at a circle with a dot inside.

I nodded. "That's my best guess. You've mentioned the wall in the north before."

Sam hesitated. "Yes. I remember the wall."

"Cris told me about another white wall in a jungle." I'd repeated this story to Sam already, and Stef knew it, but Whit hadn't heard it. "He said he was collecting plants and came across crumbling white stone. When he climbed on top of a tall piece, he realized the stone had once been a huge wall, which circled a collapsed tower. There was enough rubble around the tower to indicate it had once been as tall as the temple in the center of Heart."

"But there were no other buildings," Stef added. "It was like Heart, but without our homes and the Councilhouse, if you looked at it from above, it would look like a circle with a dot in the middle."

"Right. And I'm guessing they were all prisons, like the temple inside Heart originally was for Janan. Cris told us that all the warriors with Janan were imprisoned separately so they'd never join forces again. That also begins to explain why Heart is built over a caldera that size, even though it's entirely impractical."

"Why?" Whit asked.

"Because it was a prison. It was meant to deter people from coming to rescue him. The other prisons we know of are in the frozen north, and in the jungle where not even the water is safe to drink. Who knows where the others are?" None of my friends would be able to remember the locations, even if they'd seen them. Not without a lot of prodding and leading questions, and I could only offer leading questions if I had an idea of where to start. Like Sam's death. Or symbols Cris might have seen. "Maybe under the ocean, or in deserts, or high on a mountain where the air's so thin you can't breathe. They could be anywhere."

"To be fair to us, though, Heart didn't look dangerous at first." Stef frowned. "Except for the geysers and mud pools and fumaroles . . ."

I nodded. "You were on a quest to find your leader, anyway. You believed he'd been wrongly imprisoned, because that's what you were told."

"Who told us?" Whit asked.

"I'm not sure. Cris didn't mention." I frowned and tried to recall everything he'd said, but those hours in the temple were a blur. I'd been so afraid and depressed.

"And how'd we get the key?" Stef asked. "Someone must have taken it, because otherwise, Janan never could have gotten out to speak to us, and we never could have gotten in."

I doodled spirals in the margins of my notebook. "If phoenixes built the prisons, it seems likely they would have had the key, as well. Someone must have stolen it from them."

"That seems like a reasonable conclusion," Whit said, but I wondered how much of the conversation he was actually retaining. "Perhaps your books will give us the answers."

"That's my hope." I turned the page. The spiral of writing was easy to see now, and I'd gotten better at spotting the symbols I knew, without having to search for them. But it wasn't enough. Time was running out, and what if I deciphered the text only to realize it was a list of complicated instructions that I couldn't possibly complete before Soul Night?

What if the books only told me I was too late to stop Janan?

I couldn't think like that.

"Well, let's keep working for now." Sam turned my notebook toward me again. "Just tell us what you need us to do, and hopefully the sylph will show up soon. It took them about a week when we were here before."

"Thanks." But we'd been here a week and a half now. Either they'd come, or I'd misinterpreted their actions before, and they wanted nothing to do with us.

Shrill beeping jerked me from my slumber.

In his sleeping bag next to me, Sam squinted around the front room, looking just as confused as I felt. "What's that?" Whit echoed the question from his place on the sofa.

It was Stef's turn on the bed. We all looked up at her as SED light illuminated her face, making her skin eerily white. "We have to go." Her voice was rough with sleep, but something in her expression snapped. "We have to go. *Now.*"

Everyone scrambled up, elbows and knees thudding on the floor, and within five minutes, we'd swept our belongings into backpacks and rolled up our sleeping bags. When everything was ready, we turned off the lights and headed outside, leaving the soft thrum of the machine in the lab.

The night was crisp but motionless as we headed east down an overgrown path, continuing away from Heart.

Darkness made the unfamiliar ground difficult to navigate, but moonlight shone down, reflecting off ice and snow. Our breaths misted, reverse sylph.

When the lab was out of sight, I adjusted my winter clothes, which I'd thrown on too hastily, and took in the midnight surroundings. "What was that alarm, Stef?" My voice sounded so loud in the darkness.

"A warning that someone had overwritten my commands for the drones. Before, I could keep them away from the lab, searching other areas of Range. But someone else is in control now."

"Can't you take back control?" Whit asked.

"If I had more time, and a data console. My SED just isn't powerful enough."

"Stef's Everything Device isn't everything after all?" Whit teased.

Stef glared, and no one laughed.

"What about Orrin and the others?" Whit asked. "Will the drones be able to find them?"

Stef's nod was barely perceptible in the dark. "It's possible, but unlikely. They're far enough out of Range now. It was the lab we needed to worry about."

"And he'll find it," I added, "because he's seen Menehem's research. He wouldn't come out here himself, though. Not after the guard station."

"Right." Stef tapped her SED, bringing up a screen filled

with unfamiliar codes. "He doesn't know what's in there that we might use to fight back. Menehem has always made Deborl nervous."

Menehem had probably made a lot of people nervous.

Maybe that was part of what made me so frightening to others: not only was I a newsoul, I was Menehem's daughter.

We stopped to rest where the wide path dipped into a hollow, keeping us out of sight. Trees and mountains rose high around us, blocking most of the moonlight. It looked as if the path kept going for a ways beyond Range, but it wasn't maintained regularly. Mostly deer and other large fauna had been using it; tufts of fur had caught on brush, and hoof and paw prints stamped the snow.

There was little evidence of the caravan of exiles passing through, though when I bent, I found snapped blades of frozen grass and twigs, crushed into smeared vehicle tread marks. Time and weather would erase those, and the four of us would leave even fewer traces.

"We should get far enough away from the lab that the drones won't find us quickly," Whit said. His voice was harsh on the still night. "And we should get off the path, because won't that be the next guess? We left the lab and took the path?"

Stef nodded. "I don't like that it's so obvious."

I drifted along the edge of the path, searching for . . . something. I wasn't sure.

"What are you thinking?" Sam appeared beside me, a warm, dark presence that calmed and excited me. We'd had no time alone, except for the moments before sleep, and those had been exhausted moments, separated by our bedding and a small stretch of floor. We were just close enough that we could see each other and reach to touch, but no more. If we'd been closer, if he'd been holding me at night and I'd kissed him, I don't know that I would have ever stopped.

I turned my face to the stars. "What do you see?"

"The sky." He wrapped his arm around my waist, pulling himself close. "Lots and lots of sky."

"How often do labor drones clear this path?" We were outside of Range now, beyond where people regularly traveled. There was no reason for the path to be so clear. Even the trees above looked as though they'd been pushed aside recently, though not with the evenness of a labor drone. The fallen branches all had jagged edges, as though they'd been ripped from the trunks.

"Not very often." Sam lowered his voice. "I see what you mean."

"What lives this way? Trolls?"

"Yes."

And they traveled this way frequently enough to carve a path through the woods. "Do you think the others would have run into trolls?"

"I don't know." Sam tilted his head, listening. I listened,

too, to the soft voices on the trail, a pale breeze rustling pine trees, the clatter of some small creature high in cottonwood branches, and a pack of wolves howling in the distance. "I don't hear anything unusual."

"Me neither. Still, I agree with Stef and Whit. We need to get off the path."

We turned toward our friends again, but just as Sam began to speak, a deafening screech came from above.

Everyone looked up at once.

It was shaped like an eagle, but big enough to block out half the sky.

"What is that?" I whispered, dreading, feeling I already knew.

Sam grabbed my hand. "It's a roc."

With another terrible screech, the roc shifted its flight. It dove straight toward us.

10

OUTSIDE

"RUN!" SAM DRAGGED me toward the forest. We crashed through the underbrush as the roc keened and spread its wings wide.

Branches cracked. Ice clinked and clattered from above. Talons thumped on the ground behind us. Stef screamed, and I spun to look for her—catching a glimpse of broad brown wings and dark raptor eyes—but Sam jerked me back.

"Come on." His voice was rough, the order leaving no room for argument.

I stumbled after him, struggling to avoid getting caught in the brush. Rocks and branches and ice snagged at me, but I pushed on with renewed energy when the roc cried and thrashed through the woods. Tree trunks groaned, and huge talons reached after us.

On the ground, chasing prey through the woods, the roc had terrible coordination. Its talons knocked a small tree aside, and they left gouges in the earth as the roc withdrew. Sam and I pushed onward, climbing a small hill, darting around trees. Patches of snow made me slide, but I hauled myself up every time. The forest was quiet, aside from our passage. No birds or small animals made a sound as the roc struggled to reach us.

But its size hindered it now. It couldn't move through the forest, though surely it could hear our escape. Maybe even our gasping and my whimper as twigs scraped my face and hands.

Finally, Sam allowed us to stop. I bent over to catch my breath. My cheek stung, and a trail of blood leaked into the corner of my mouth, cold and coppery. I wiped it away and scanned the area for our friends. "Where are Stef and Whit?"

"They went to the other side of the path." Panting, Sam collapsed onto a large rock. He leaned over, head between his knees. His shoulders heaved. "The roc will follow us."

I collapsed next to him, hyperaware of the thrashing toward the path. The roc cawed and squeaked, and trees groaned under its wrath. More branches snapped, but it didn't seem like the roc was making progress. I saw only a shadow of movement in the snow-reflected moonlight, but it still seemed much too close for comfort.

"How long will it follow us?" Adrenaline made my head buzz, and I couldn't stop checking on the roc.

"Until it finds better prey." Sam searched his pockets until he found his SED. No alerts of messages from friends. "Will you find out if Stef and Whit are okay?"

I nodded and sent a message from my own SED. "How's your hand?"

"Better." He flexed it a little, wincing.

"As long as it's better." I stuffed my SED in my pocket. "What next? Do we keep walking? Try to sleep? They have the tent."

And the roc was *right there*. I wouldn't be able to sleep if I could hear it, though exhaustion nipped at the back of my thoughts.

"Keep walking. We'll head away from the roc; that way it doesn't draw anything else's attention. As long as we stay in the woods, it won't be able to reach us. Then we'll meet up with the others when the way is clear."

My SED chirped, and reading the message, I let out a soft chuckle. "Stef just sent those exact thoughts. They're not hurt."

"I'm glad."

I readjusted my belongings and made sure there were no holes or scratches in my clothes. "I'm ready." The sooner we left the roc behind, the better. Everyone had said leaving Range was dangerous, but I hadn't realized danger appeared as soon as one left. Menehem's lab was just beyond the edges of Range, close enough that there were still traps and the occasional drone patrol, so wiser creatures would stay away.

But already we'd walked down a troll path and been attacked by a roc. No wonder everyone stayed in Heart.

No wonder they'd all been so afraid of death when Janan offered them reincarnation.

We began walking, this time mindful of the brush and snow and ice. We were far enough away from the roc now that we didn't need to rush, and it would be foolish to risk getting injured out here. Rin's medical training hadn't been *that* thorough, and we'd only brought a few supplies.

Sounds of the roc's thrashing faded behind us, and mice and shrews began moving about the forest again. Probably heading back to their dens. Light touched the horizon, a dull red glow that was barely visible through the trees.

"They have the tent," I said again, when Sam yawned.

He kept his voice level as we hiked up a small hill. "We'll simply have to huddle in the same sleeping bag. For warmth. And so I don't accidentally lose you to the wilderness."

"You come up with the best plans."

He smiled, and we kept walking. The roc was either far behind us now, or had given up trying to force its way through the woods. The trees were still thick, so it wouldn't descend on us again, but I kept a wary eye on the sky as light bled between the trees and birds began singing to the dawn.

We walked parallel to the path, east and into the wilds outside Range. Small animals scurried through the forest, hiding as we passed, and everywhere there was evidence of larger mammals: tufts of fur on branches, fallen twigs, and piles of dung, which we managed to avoid, thanks to Sam's caution.

Ice shone on every surface, hoarfrost and glittering icicles, the forest's jewelry. I brushed my mittened fingers across ice crystals, listening to a few clink as they broke off. Winter, and talking about music with Sam, distracted me from my exhaustion for a while, but by midmorning, I couldn't ignore it anymore. We sent a message to Stef and told her we were taking a break. Hopefully we'd meet up again soon.

Sam and I settled near a fast-moving stream. I rinsed blood and dirt off my face and arms, then scrubbed my skin dry before crawling into Sam's sleeping bag with him.

The bag was warm relief after the frigid night and day. Sam had positioned the bag inside a shallow hollow among tree roots—an abandoned animal den, perhaps—so we were concealed on three sides. And Sam, being Sam, made sure he was between the exit and me, which meant that when he curled his body around mine, our burrow was deep and dark. His breathing was warmth on the back of my neck, and his hand rested on my hip.

"Are you comfortable?" he whispered.

"Yeah." My feet were squished against our backpacks, and we were using the other sleeping bag as an awkward pillow. And though the cloth was thick and soft, a root dug at my shoulder. I shifted toward Sam, and his breath hitched. "Very. Aren't you?"

His hand trailed up my side. "I wish we were at home."

"Me too." My hand slipped to my SED. "And I wish we had music, but I want to be able to hear in case anything happens." Who knew what else might appear on us, now that we were beyond the safety of Range?

"You can listen if you want." Sam kissed the back of my neck, making me shiver. It was amazing how he could make me want this huge and unnameable thing no matter where we were, and no matter the circumstances. "Listen if you want," he said again. "I'll let you know if anything happens outside. Just relax."

Relaxing seemed unlikely, but when I pulled out my SED and earpieces and closed my eyes, there was only music.

Warm sounds of the piano pulsed through me. Heavy. Familiar. And with Sam's presence behind me, soothing me, I drifted into dreamless sleep.

I jerked awake, darkness all around as the earth trembled.

Sam wasn't behind me. I flailed inside the sleeping bag, discovering that one of the backpacks was gone and night had fallen.

"Sam!" I scrambled outside as the earth shuddered again and dirt rained into the hollow. My SED continued playing an old sonata, even as I ripped the earpieces away from me and shoved the whole thing into my pocket.

The forest was dark, quiet except for the thumping in the ground. It wasn't like an earthquake—not this time—so it must have been something large moving nearby.

And I'd shouted.

I hunched, making myself smaller as I squinted in the darkness. Faint moonlight found its way through the forest canopy, but everything was still in shadows, and I couldn't detect any movement.

The ground shuddered under my knees, under my palms when I touched the dirt. The movement was long and sustained, not like a troll plodding down the path. This was something else, maybe vehicles rumbling nearby. Our friends should have been far away, so if the shudder in the earth was vehicles, was it drones or people?

Either way, they wouldn't be friendly.

I snatched the sleeping bags from the hollow and quickly rolled them up to fit over my backpack. There was no chance I'd find this tree again on my own.

But before I took off, I needed to find Sam. I called his SED, and he answered immediately. "What's wrong?"

"What's wrong?" I shook my head and peered through the

dark forest. "You're not here. That's what's wrong. Where are you?"

"I couldn't sleep, so I went to check on the path. The roc is gone. Flown off, I guess. I'm on my way back now. We can meet up with Stef and Whit soon."

The rumble in the earth was fading. "Did you see anything? I heard something. Like thunder, but—"

"I heard it." Sam paused, seeming to focus on something else—walking or climbing, probably—and dragged in a long breath. "I heard it, but I don't know what it was."

"Okay. Raise your flashlight in my direction. Maybe I can see it and start walking to you."

"Just a second."

While he was quiet, I peered through the forest. Faint light glimmered in the north. I secured my backpack and the sleeping bags and began picking my way around trees.

"Did you see it?" he asked.

"Yep." I ducked around trees and crumbling boulders and clicked off so I could use my SED as a flashlight; mine was in my backpack, and I didn't want to stop and remove it. Not with *something* out there. Frozen pine needles rustled and twigs snapped as we approached each other. "Next time," I said, huffing, "wake me up to tell me you're leaving. As far as I knew, something came by and ate you."

"Sorry." Sam hugged me and kissed my cheek. "Let's head

this way. There's a pond not far off. Stef and Whit are waiting for us there."

I nodded and crept through the woods with him. Being
outside Range made me jumpy. It seemed like anything could
happen. There were no traps in these woods, meant to capture or deter other dominant species, and no drone patrols.
This place was strange and wild, though hauntingly similar
to the forests of Range.

Vibrations traveled through the ground again, low and
steady. An odd scent rode the air, like animal sweat mixed
with pine and dirt. "Sam."

His nod was barely perceptible in the darkness, but it was
enough. He sensed it, too.

Maybe it was only a herd of deer or bison. There were
lots of large animals in and around Range. But as Sam and
I approached the pond he'd spoken of, the rumbling grew
louder, and a deep murmur filtered through the woods. Like
voices.

Hundreds of voices.

Sam and I glanced at each other. "The pond is just ahead,"
he murmured.

Lights danced through the trees, uneven and orange-red,
like fire. Chills prickled up my spine as we crept forward.

Sam turned off the flashlight so the glow wouldn't attract
attention, and a few minutes later, we halted on a small ridge

overlooking a valley where the pond waited. And there, we saw the source of the lights.

The roar of voices rolled across the water, where ripples glinted in the flickering illumination of hundreds of torches, revealing a thousand bodies. At first, I thought they were people on horseback. Then, as my eyes adjusted the dark figures resolved into more coherent shapes, I realized the people were too far in front of the horses to be riding them. And the "horses" had no heads.

"Centaurs." The word came out a breath, but Sam nodded. Even in the dim light, he looked pale.

"Stef said she and Whit are there." He pointed across the pond, toward a break in the trees where trolls had carved the path. "So we'll have to go around the herd."

This was what I'd felt in the ground earlier: a thousand centaurs heading toward the pond. They'd probably cut through the forest within sight of where I'd been sleeping. And I'd shouted Sam's name. I was unbelievably lucky they hadn't heard me.

"Do they really make clothes out of people's skin?" I whispered.

Sam just shuddered and guided me back into the forest.

"Maybe Stef and Whit could come here instead of us going there."

"We're heading that way anyway." Sam kept his voice low

and consulted the map on his SED.

We were only heading that way because it was away from Heart, not because that way necessarily had answers, or clues about where to find the sylph.

"I really want to know why all those centaurs are this far from their territory. Perhaps they've broken away from the main herd or they're picking a battle with trolls. . . ."

"Maybe they can sense the caldera is unstable." My SED showed at least five new earthquakes since the last time I'd checked. None of them were as large as the first, but some were sizable enough that people would notice. Centaurs' territory was south of Range, so they'd probably felt the big earthquake as the Year of Souls began.

"That seems likely." Sam pointed at the map. "We'll go down the hill this way, keeping to the woods. With luck, the wind won't shift. Centaurs have a powerful sense of smell." He glanced toward the herd and wrinkled his nose. "And powerful smells."

I stifled a panicked giggle. "Yes."

"Once we're off this ridge, we'll head toward the troll path here. We'll be visible when we're crossing, but if we keep far enough back, they shouldn't notice us. It looks like they're getting ready to stop for the night, and they can only see as well as humans in the dark."

"So no flashlights."

He nodded. "But once we're across the path, we'll be

fine. The rest of the way seems to have enough foliage to cover us."

"Okay, we'd better get going."

We picked our way down the ridge as quietly as possible, cringing every time a branch cracked or evergreen needles rustled. But if the centaurs noticed movement in the woods, they must have assumed we were one of the many nocturnal creatures that lived here.

Our progress was slow, especially without light, but we had time to be cautious, so we took it. Two hours later, we reached the path.

It was wide enough for two vehicles to drive side by side. That hadn't seemed so wide when we'd been walking on it yesterday, but now that we had to cross in full view of a herd of centaurs, we might as well have been crossing the Range caldera.

Sam tested the wind. It still carried the centaurs' stink and fractured voices. I couldn't make out their words, but it seemed unlikely they'd speak our language, anyway.

"We should crawl," I whispered. "So they don't see two tall creatures go walking by."

"One tall and one unusually short." He said it with a smile, but his humor was strained. "You're right. We'll crawl." He sighed and flexed his injured hand.

We adjusted our belongings and lowered ourselves to the ground. Frosty grass reached up to my elbows, blocking too much of my view—and not blocking enough. Though we were far back on the trail, around a bend to keep out of view, by the time we reached the center of the path, I could see the centaurs' fires and their silhouettes as they moved about the field. There were so many. They wouldn't have to worry about rocs swooping down on them.

The ground trembled under my palms, vibrations from all the movement to the east. Faintly, I saw startlingly graceful movements as a group of centaurs chased one another. They called out and laughed, their hooves beating the ground in rhythm.

They'd seemed awkward at first, so forward-heavy with their human halves in the front, but firelight glistened off muscular horse halves and sturdy legs. A pair of centaurs embraced. One reared up and spread his arms to the stars and moon and sky.

None of them *looked* like they were wearing human skin as clothing.

We'd been wrong about the sylph. Sort of. They *had* attacked people for thousands of years. They'd attacked me on my birthday last year, too. But there was something about them. They loved music. And now Cris was one.

What if we'd been wrong about centaurs?

Hoofbeats pounded on the ground, coming closer. Sam twisted to look back at me, and in the darkness, his eyes were wide. "Go," he mouthed. "Fast."

I scrambled across the path as quickly as I could, aching to get up and use my legs. But if they were coming our way, I didn't want to be seen.

The hoofbeats thumped and a high, thin voice shrieked.

I jerked my face up to find a young centaur staring down at me, wearing a shocked expression. Another stopped next to the first. They both screamed.

I screamed.

Sam reached back and grabbed my wrist, and together we lurched for the other side of the path, but the centaurs were following—

And then the ground shuddered. Not from the herd. No, this was from the opposite direction. One solid thud followed by another.

The young centaurs stared past Sam and me, and the herd went quiet.

A hush fell over the entire area as the thuds came louder, faster. Then Sam climbed all the way to his feet—making the young centaurs jump back—and dragged me into the woods.

"Troll!"

At once, the area turned loud with centaurs shouting and metal clashing. And when I glanced over my shoulder, the young centaurs were just standing in the middle of the path, staring up with their mouths wide open as a human-shaped beast three times my size came roaring toward the field. Ice and branches flew away from the troll's destructive passage.

"Wait!" I shook myself away from Sam and darted back to the path. The young centaurs—colts? children?—both snapped their attention to me. "Come on!" I had no idea if they understood me, but when I reached for them, one of the boys clasped his hand around my damp mitten, and we raced into the woods just as the troll thundered into the place where they'd been standing.

Sam opened his mouth, but shook his head and began running through the forest as cacophony erupted by the pond. Screams and roars spurred us through the woods. The children surged ahead, shoving branches and bushes out of the way. Sam and I hurried to keep up, but the dark forest was only brokenly lit with torches on the battlefield.

My SED buzzed in my pocket, but I couldn't answer it. I focused on jumping over the tangle of roots the centaurs jumped over. On ducking ice-white limbs. On putting one leg in front of the other.

Shouts filled the area. Then a thundering growl. And the world thudded hard as something dropped. I stumbled, but one of the centaur children reached back and took my arm until I was balanced and running on my own again.

"Ana! Sam!" Stef's voice came from just ahead. "There you are! I—"

Blue lights flared, targeting the young centaurs as we broke out into the open. The rest of the herd was far to our right, gathered around the fallen troll, so now it was just four humans and two scared centaur kids.

One of the boys screamed. The herd's attention shifted.

"No, don't!" I moved in front of the boys and held out my hands. They tried, unsuccessfully, to hide behind me. They were both much bigger than I was. "Don't shoot. They're just kids."

"They're *centaurs*." Whit kept his weapon up. No one else moved, either.

Sam stayed off to the side, looking between us. "Don't shoot Ana."

"They're just kids," I said again.

The herd of centaurs rumbled closer, swords and spears lifted and glinting with blood in torchlight. Suddenly, we were surrounded. All of us humans. The young centaurs.

Stef swung her laser pistol toward the approaching army, but there was no way she'd overcome a thousand centaurs.

One targeting light still aimed at the young centaurs. I didn't move from my position guarding them. And the other centaurs were deadly quiet as they appraised the situation.

No one moved. I could hardly breathe.

And then shadows appeared in the forest, falling toward the torchlight as they abandoned natural shadows. These were tall and thin, not attached to anything. They hmmed quietly, singing among themselves.

Gradually, the centaurs' attention shifted from us to the shadows approaching from the other side. Heat billowed across the cool space as one shadow pushed forward, ahead of the others. It paused near me, a slender black rose blossoming inside one of its tendrils before it shivered apart.

The sylph had come.

11

REUNION

HOPE KINDLED INSIDE me, then was smothered when, as one, the herd of centaurs lifted their weapons and screamed their rage to the sky. Ground shook under their pounding hooves as they ran to meet the sylph.

The sylph keened: awful, dissonant wailing. Shadows surged forth, sending waves of heat throughout the gathered humans and centaurs. What had been a midwinter night now became like summer as the sylph songs morphed into terrible cacophony.

The two young centaurs sobbed and dropped to the ground, clutching each other, clutching my legs. I tumbled down with them.

Sam and my friends cried out, but an insubstantial wall

of shadows forced itself between us, carefully not burning delicate human flesh. But they were going straight for the centaurs, who just wanted their children back.

"Stop!" I pulled myself up from the tangle of limbs.

When I tried to throw myself into the mass of shadows, one of the centaur boys grabbed my wrist and shook his head, a panicked look on his face.

I used my free hand to cover his knobby knuckles, sharp with the strength of his grip, and smiled a little. "It's okay." No idea if he understood, but when he released me, I turned and shouted, "Stop!" again.

The sylph and centaurs kept moving toward one another, and the centaurs were about to be boiled alive—

I sang one long, sustained note. The pitch fell, and my voice cracked with winter and nerves. Though Sam had given me a few tips on how to best project my voice, we'd never arranged real lessons. There'd never been time.

But the sylph nearest me shifted and turned at the sound of my voice, peeling itself from the mass of shadows. It hovered around me, waiting, matching my note.

If music were water, this would have been a ripple. The angry keening dropped, and the sylph all seemed to gasp and face me. They watched me, though they had no eyes, no faces. They were but tall shadows, with tendrils that flickered toward the sky as I fumbled to free my hands of mittens, then found my SED and searched through the music function.

I chose Phoenix Symphony. Some of the sylph already knew it, and it was one of my favorites.

The first chords rushed from the speakers like a waterfall, and I let my voice fade beneath the powerful sounds of the piano, violins, and thunderous bass.

I pushed the volume as high as it would go, so that every sylph heard. They halted just before they reached the line of centaurs, and the incredible heat faded to something more bearable.

Behind me, the centaur boys scrambled to their feet. One touched my shoulder, and his gaze fell on the SED clutched in my hands. The light from the screen illuminated his face, scratched from our run and his fall to the ground. But he smiled when his hand passed through the SED glow, and he said something I could neither hear clearly over the music, nor understand.

My SED screen flashed; on the other side of the sylph swarm, Sam had synced his SED with mine. Phoenix Symphony played all around.

The boys needed to return to their people. The centaurs just wanted them back. That was why they were here. And surely the sylph wouldn't let the centaurs hurt me, if they tried.

I put my SED in my pocket, speaker facing up so the music remained loud and clear, then reached up to take each centaur boy's hand. Together, we walked around the sylph, which sang and danced along with the music, though still watchful, as though waiting for the centaurs to attack again.

We broke through the line of shadows and found the centaur herd almost motionless. Their eyes narrowed, but that was all.

One of the centaur women crashed through the herd, her arms wide. The boys leapt out into the thin strip of land between us and bounded to her, and sylph fanned around me, including me in their line as they sang melodies and countermelodies of the first movement of Phoenix Symphony.

The boys hugged the woman—their mother?—and the lead warriors of the herd seemed to look over my group. Four humans armed with only lasers and music, and dozens of sylph.

The shadows coiling around me must have been the deciding factor. One of the leaders turned and shouted some kind of order, and the herd began moving away, their hooves like thunder in the ground.

One of the centaur boys ran back, though. He stopped midway between our groups and called out something as he pointed southeast. Showing me where they were going. Then, in a high and eerily beautiful voice, he sang along with a measure of melody as it flowed from the SED, and from the sylph.

Only a moment later, he was gone, lost among the other centaurs.

122

The music swelled, and I turned back to Sam and the others. Sylph parted, forming a clear path.

As I headed for Sam at the other end of the dark tunnel, tendrils of shadow snaked out and wrapped around my wrist or touched my hair. But the tendrils were incorporeal. I felt nothing but warmth where they touched me.

Sylph song surrounded me, layers of harmony in otherworldly wailing and whispering. A few sylph swayed, as though lost in music.

"Are you okay?" Sam reached for me, and our SEDs were muffled as we hugged.

"I'm fine." I pulled back, relieved to be reunited with my friends. "They were just scared children. They were new. Like me." My smile felt forced as I gazed from Stef to Whit. These were my friends. They'd agreed to come on this incredible and possibly futile journey with me. But they were oldsouls. They'd never truly understand the connection I felt with other newsouls, even if the newsouls were centaurs.

"We're just glad you're safe." Whit gazed beyond me at the sea of sylph still fluttering with the music, singing along with the parts they knew. "And I see you found the sylph." His voice was raspy, wary.

I shook my head and lowered the volume of my SED, but didn't turn off the music as the second movement began to play. "They found us."

"They seem to really like you." He frowned, and I tried

to imagine how strange the whole situation must appear. Centaurs retreating in the background. Sylph curling up around me like shadowy cloaks. "Which one is"—he seemed to struggle with the memory and knowledge—"Cris?"

I glanced over my shoulder, but I couldn't tell the sylph apart. They were all just pillars of darkness.

One sylph moved forward to stand beside me.

"Cris."

He twitched a little, almost like a nod, and a black rose bloomed around him.

"Oh, Cris." Stef reached out, and her voice broke.

I bit my lip. "That movement earlier. It was a nod?"

He did the same thing.

"And what means no?"

The shadow twisted, just the upper half. Like a head shake, only the smoke resettled and he hadn't twisted back. Unnerving.

"Okay." I didn't know what else to say. Great, we could ask yes and no questions, but I didn't want to ask if he was miserable like this, if he hurt, or if he blamed me. I didn't want to know the answers in case they were yes.

"These other sylph won't harm us?" Whit asked.

Cris shook his head, even as the rest of the swarm circled us, radiating heat to ward off the cold night. They'd stopped singing.

"Now that we've joined with the sylph," Whit said, gazing

around at the ring of darkness, "what do we do?"

I wasn't sure. I'd wanted to find them, be able to ask questions. And now I could. But I hadn't thought about much beyond that. I had goals, but no idea how to complete them. "First thing," I said, turning to Cris. "We need somewhere safe to hide. Most of the Council has been killed. Deborl is in control of the city. He's searching for us. Sarit and Armande stayed behind to keep us informed." My heart ached at the thought of Sarit, but I'd call her later. She'd never believe it when I told her about tonight.

Cris nodded.

"Second thing." I glanced southeast. "We sent a group of about forty people that way, to get them away from Deborl and an eruption. That way they have a chance."

Cris nodded again, and the other sylph all leaned in, listening.

"Can a few of you catch up with them and protect them? We'll call and make sure they know you're coming, so they won't try to trap you. But they don't have much in the way of protection. A few sylph would help a lot."

The sylph hummed and sang among themselves for a minute, and then four broke away and darted southeast. They were frighteningly quick, almost like real shadows when someone turned on a light.

"Thank you," I whispered as the sylph closed the circle in tighter, and my friends pressed closer together. "The third thing is this: I need to learn, and I was hoping you would be able to help. We have only a short time, so the sooner I figure out how to read these books and understand what happened five thousand years ago, the sooner I can get started on my plan."

The sylph waited, undulating darkly under the moonlight.

I made my voice strong. "I want to stop Janan from ascending."

Night shattered as every sylph cried out in triumph.

The sylph led us to a cave at the base of a mountain, with a stream running through its center. Wind blew in, and the stone was cold and hard, but when sylph lined up around the perimeter, warmth radiated through the walls and ground.

With lamps brightening the gloom and our sleeping bags folded up to sit on, the cave wasn't so bad.

"I bet the stream floods in the spring," Stef said, looking up from her SED. "Not that we'll be here that long. I have an update from Armande, by the way."

We all leaned in, and one of the sylph broke away from the others.

"Cris." I scooted closer to Sam to make room between Whit and me, and though Whit's smile was more strained than welcoming, he edged toward Stef and patted the place beside him. "Sit with us," I said.

Cris hesitated, seeming to look between the other sylph

and us, all gathered around a bright lamp and things we'd brought from Heart. He wasn't sure what to do. Sit with people who'd hated sylph for five thousand years, or stay with his new people. Suddenly, I felt rotten for asking him to choose.

The others were all waiting, too, watching Cris to see what he'd do.

"Why don't you all come closer?"

Stef and Whit cringed, even as they nodded, and Sam went pale. It was hard to accept that while sylph were frightening, they wouldn't hurt us.

But what about the sylph that had chased me on my birthday last year? Or burned my hands?

I'd have to ask Cris later.

None of the sylph moved to accept my invitation. "Come on," I said. "We're allies. We have friends in common. We have goals in common." At least, it seemed like the sylph wanted me to stop Janan, if their singing earlier was any indication.

Gradually, the sylph eased toward us, keeping their heat low and their songs quiet. They left a good distance between us, but this was an improvement. I tried to smile at them.

Stef cleared her throat, and everyone's attention shifted back to her. "Armande reports the curfew is tighter than ever. Several people have been imprisoned for disobeying. Even more have been imprisoned for skipping morning gatherings around the temple. Deborl insists they make amends for centuries of ignoring Janan. They've started building something inside the city, as well, but no one is sure what it is, just that they're all to contribute. Some people have been sent to mine or refine more materials."

"So even regular jobs are suspended?" Whit asked. "For whatever it is they're building?"

Stef nodded. "It's in the industrial quarter. It looks like they're using the geothermal energy lines for something. And many of the warehouses have been destroyed. There's a picture." She turned the SED to share it with the rest of us.

As she'd said, a large section of the industrial quarter had been seized and razed. Where there had once been warehouses, now only a few odd buildings and skeletal tubes remained. Some of those were water lines or sewer lines, while others were for power generation. Along the far edge of the quarter, the textile mill, pottery workshop, and forgers were still standing. For now.

Whatever they were building, it wasn't far along enough for us to guess its purpose. Something wide and flat, though that could simply be the foundation for something bigger, especially if they were gathering more materials.

"Just because we don't know what it is," Sam said, "doesn't mean we don't know what it's for in the end."

"Janan." Stef nodded. "No doubt it's to benefit him."

"There's so much we still need to know," Whit said. "Which means we need to get back to those books. Ana?"

128

"I'm ready." I glanced at Cris—or the sylph I thought was Cris. "Did you happen to learn how to read these books when you became a sylph?"

Cris hummed and trilled, almost like a chuckle as he shook his head. But before I could be disappointed, he twitched, and another sylph came forward.

I struggled for a pronoun. I'd always thought of sylph as genderless *its*, but it seemed rude to say that to . . . not their faces, since they didn't have faces, but . . . Ugh. I addressed the new sylph. "You can help me translate the symbols from the books?"

The sylph nodded, mostly a vertical rolling of smoke.

"Great." It would be a long night if we had to ask yes and no questions about the meanings of words, though. Still, we could start with confirming the words we already had. "Whit?"

He stood and headed for my bag, where I kept the temple books. "The sooner we get this done, the sooner we're not living in a cave."

Sam leaned toward me—and the sylph. "He misses the library."

I sighed. "I do, too. All the books. The well-lit reading areas."

"The chairs." Stef swooned dramatically. "I miss chairs. My legs are tired after all this walking."

Cris whistled, like bragging he didn't have sore legs.

"Ready?" Whit handed everyone books and notebooks, and we all got to work. Sylph floated around as we went through pages, confirming or attempting to correct our translations. It was difficult, trying to understand the sylph, but as the night deepened, I began catching on to their movements more quickly, and their trills and hmms, the moods conveyed by their pitch and the notes they sang.

When I glanced at Sam to see if he'd begun understanding the sylph, he smiled.

At the end of the session, when everyone was yawning and curling up in their sleeping bags and most of the sylph had retreated around the cave to keep it warm, I found Cris.

"Thank you for your help."

He nodded.

"Did you know we were looking for you?"

Yes.

"Do the other sylph know what happened five thousand years ago? How they became sylph?"

Yes. An emphatic yes.

"Did phoenixes curse them?" Meuric had believed phoenixes were responsible, but Meuric had also been in a lot of pain.

Yes.

Phoenixes. They were connected to so much, but no one had seen one in centuries. "Will you be able to tell me what happened? Or the books?"

Yes, and yes.

"Were any of these sylph responsible for chasing me last year? Or burning my hands?"

Cris nodded, hesitantly, and then there was something like an apology, or an excuse. I couldn't quite understand the way his voice rose and fell, and he cut off whatever he was trying to say with a soft, frustrated keening.

"It's okay." I held out my hand for him and tried to smile. "I know you won't let them hurt us."

He hummed irritably.

"Or they wouldn't anyway."

He nodded.

"I know you're here to help."

Cris surged forward, shadowy tendrils winding around my forearms as he tried so hard to express something. I could almost catch it. Almost.

-We are your army.-

12

CHOICE

THERE WEREN'T WORDS, really. It more like a mel-ody, a song with lyrics half-remembered. It was the notion of words, the way music tugged inside me and made ideas bubble up from a deep and forgotten place.

A spiral of shock kept me from responding. Sylph could *speak*. They loved music. They had language. How, in thou-sands of years of people running from the sylph, had no one ever noticed the sylph *communicated*?

Cris shifted, and his song sounded like a question. Like, -Do you understand me?-

"Yes," I whispered. "I think so."

Cris wringed himself into tight coils of shadow, then zipped from the cave faster than my eyes could follow.

"Wait." But he was already gone. Everyone else was fast asleep. I almost left the cave to follow the sylph, but after the roc, the centaurs and troll, and the sylph's arrival, I wanted to sleep for a week.

The lamps were all low, and Sam had chosen a dark corner to put our sleeping bags, where we were sort of alone.

I peeled off my shoes and coat, then crawled into my sleeping bag, edging closer to Sam, who was passed out, his dark hair fallen over his face. He looked so relaxed, all the lines of stressed erased as he dreamed. And when I caressed his cheek, my fingers pale over his tanned skin, he sighed and pulled into my touch.

With a heavy yawn, I pulled out my SED and took it inside my sleeping bag to hide the glow under the layers of wool and silk. I sent a message to Orrin, letting him know we were all safe here.

Have the sylph we sent arrived?

He was either up very late, or very early, because my SED buzzed with a reply.

*Yes. Everyone was afraid, but the sylph just float around
the camp perimeter.*

They'll keep you warm, too, if you let them.

That's probably too much to ask most of us.

A few minutes later, he said he had to go, so I put in my earpieces and listened to music while playing around with maps of the land around Range, wondering what to do next.

We couldn't go back to Menehem's lab until we had a plan. We wouldn't have a good plan until we'd learned everything we could from the books—and the sylph.

We had sylph.

We had the poison.

We had four people who wouldn't give up.

There had to be a way to stop Janan from ascending.

I drifted to sleep, walking dreams of fire from the earth and sky, and shadows flooding the world. I dreamt of birth and death and rebirth, and the overwhelming sorrow of one fleeting life.

My body felt sluggish when I awoke, but the scent of searing meat drew me out of my sleeping bag to find Stef on the other side of the cave, teaching a sylph how to cook.

"All right," I said, mostly to myself as I ran my fingers through my hair, all wild with sleep. Sam and Whit were gone. "How soon for breakfast?"

"Not much longer." She adjusted her baking sheet on a rock. There was no fire under it, just a sylph coiled around the metal, which glowed red. "And you mean late lunch. Everyone slept most of the day. The others went outside to catch a few more meals before the snow hits. Would you mind fetching them?"

I dragged on my boots and hauled our lanterns and solar batteries outside to charge while there was still light.

Clouds blanketed the sky and the cold air prickled against

134

my face, but it didn't look like the storm would be bad. A light snowfall. It would cover our tracks.

Instead of wandering the woods to find Sam and Whit, I sent a SED message and waited by a stream, absorbing what sunlight I could, too. The last couple of days had ruined my sleeping schedule. All this being awake in the middle of the night.

After the others returned and we all ate, I took Sam outside and brought my flute and a lantern. It wasn't dark yet, but under the forest canopy, the animal paths were dim and difficult to see.

"The cold weather will just make you sharp." He glanced at the woods. "And the sound may frighten lunch away from our snares."

"Then let's go this way." I led him in the opposite direction he'd come from earlier. "I wanted to ask you something. About the sylph."

We'd left them in the cave, too. Sam and I were alone. "Okay," he said.

"I keep imagining I hear words, almost." I glanced up at him, but he was just staring into the forest as we walked. "Last night, I was talking to Cris, and I could have sworn he said something back. Then he just vanished."

Sam was quiet for a while, but as we descended a rocky slope, he said, "I thought I must have been imagining it. I knew I was hearing emotions while they sang, but every now and then I thought I heard words. Or—something like words. Something that made me think of words."

"Exactly. That's exactly what I heard." I slipped my mittened hand into his glove, relieved. "Cris said they're my army."

"Your army." His tone was all awe.

"I know. It seems crazy to me, too."

A sort of reverence filled his words, low and hopeful. "Is it really that strange? The way they follow you, the way they protect you. They've been acting like your army since the first time we saw them at the lab. They were guarding you."

"I want to know why."

"Me too." He scanned the bank of a shallow stream and guided me toward a rock, big enough for both of us to sit on. "There's a lot we need to ask the sylph."

That was for sure. And not at all a statement I ever thought I'd hear coming from anyone's mouth. Just a few months ago, we'd been wondering why they kept following me, and whether they were going to burn us up in our sleep. And now Cris was one of them. Now we were *relying* on the sylph.

"Thank you." I held my flute case against my chest and waited as Sam swept snow off the rock and sat. I perched next to him and placed my flute across my lap, keeping as close to him as I could without sitting on him.

"For what?" He wrapped his arm around me and set down the lantern, illuminating our boots, water bubbling over

136

pebbles, and pine needles. His leg pressed against mine.

"For understanding about the sylph. And not thinking I was crazy with the centaurs. I know everyone must have some history with them, but these—"

Sam turned and rested his other hand on my knee. His fingers curled around, and I could feel the heat of him even through the layers of cloth between us. "I trust you. You see the world differently from the rest of us, and I want to learn to see the world that way, too. You challenge us, inspire us. You inspire *me*. We were wrong about sylph. Maybe we were wrong about centaurs."

I ducked my head, hiding a blush. "Maybe you weren't wrong about sylph at first. Like you said, they do seem to like me. And their liking me doesn't change thousands of years of violence between you all."

He gave a weary chuckle. "You have good instincts. You're right to question things, even when you've heard all our stories. If you hadn't questioned reincarnation, we'd still be in Heart with no idea why Deborl had taken over the city, or what we were being made to build."

"We might be happier not knowing." That sounded like we weren't happy now. But were we? I was happy *with him*, but all this getting shot at, dodging explosions, hiding in caves—that certainly didn't make me happy.

"We'd have problems no matter what, Ana."

"Oh." That sounded even worse than what I'd said, but he

was probably right. I could cause trouble by just breathing.

"No life is perfect. There's always something that hurts, but it's important to appreciate the good things, too." He kissed my cheek, breathing warmth over me. "If it wasn't the end of the world, it'd be something else. Maybe not this big or terrible, but there are always events in life that can make you unhappy if you let them."

"Thinking about the end of the world makes me unhappy. I don't think that's just because I'm letting it."

He laughed. "It makes me unhappy, too. All I'm saying—"

"I get it." I only sort of got it, but he didn't need to keep trying. "You make me happy, though." It seemed vitally important that he know. I tilted my face toward his, all warm shadows in the winter gloom. "No matter what else is going on, you make me happy. And I want to let you make me happy. I'm not always very good at it." My breath felt heavier, misted the space between us.

Music had always been my comfort, and Sam before I knew him. His compositions, his playing, his singing. But that happiness had been distant. Someone else's life. I'd imagined a world away from Purple Rose Cottage, but it was the faraway imagining, knowing it would never be my life.

And then it *was* mine. Sam came, giving me music and happiness of my own. The life I'd always wanted suddenly happened, and trying to fit that with my old life was proving more difficult than I'd anticipated.

I kept expecting to wake up.

Like he understood everything I hadn't said, Sam kissed me. His mouth was warm and gentle, and his fingers soft against the back of my neck. "I wish I could give you all the time you needed to get used to happiness. Lifetimes, if necessary. I'd wait eternity for you to figure it out."

We didn't have eternity. I hoped I didn't need that long, anyway. I'd feel really stupid.

"You make me happy, too." He kissed my lips. My nose. My chin. My forehead. "You make me feel—everything."

My heart beat triple time when he kissed me again. With him, I could be happy forever.

Or at least for the single life I'd been given.

I drew back. "What if Janan actually were going to keep reincarnating people?"

Sam said nothing, but his silence was telling. He didn't want to die. No one did. Because what happened after? Where did you go when you died forever? What did you do?

"Right before the rededication ceremony last year, you and Stef were talking about choices. You said you were glad you didn't have to choose between Ciana and me, because how could anyone choose between two people they care about? You told me later that if you had a choice, if what you wanted counted for anything, you'd have chosen me."

"I still mean that. I will always choose you."

"I believe you." I closed my eyes and let him embrace me, trying not to think about what he and the others had decided five thousand years ago, that they'd willingly exchanged newsouls for their immortality.

Five thousand years ago, they'd all chosen themselves.

"Sarit thinks Janan will keep reincarnating oldsouls because he'll want people to rule over. What's the point of being powerful and immortal if you're all alone?"

Sam nodded. "I suppose anything is possible, but like Stef and Cris said: Janan wouldn't share power."

"But Meuric was desperate for the key. He said he needed the key to survive."

"He was also crazy when he said that, wasn't he? From pain? And being terrified of Janan? He'd been trapped in the temple for months." Sam didn't sound sorry for Meuric, but the knowledge of what I'd sentenced the former Speaker to was heavy. "Maybe," Sam went on, "all he meant was that Janan would kill him if he didn't have the key, because he'd have failed. Or if he had the key, Janan would heal him. Who knows what he thought would happen?"

I stared at my boots, sorting out thoughts and feelings, and how to ask for help without letting him see how torn my insides really were. "What would you do?" I whispered. "Only a few of us really understand that Janan isn't going to keep reincarnating people once he ascends. Sarit said everyone else will see my actions as a choice between old-souls and newsouls."

"And?"

"What if it were a choice? What would you do?"

Only the burble of water over rocks answered. Sam stared into the dim forest as snow began drifting through the skeletal branches above.

"I'm not testing you," I said at last. "I'm not looking for a certain answer. I wouldn't want to be responsible for reincarnation or whether someone gets to live. You've lived so long, though. I was hoping you might have some wisdom to share."

"I know your question wasn't a test. I was just thinking about it." He caressed my cheek, and his gloved fingertips came to rest under my chin. Soft wool brushed my skin, almost a kiss, and Sam leaned so close until all I could see were his eyes. His voice was low and rough. "I would choose you. Every time. No matter what."

My heart thumped, suddenly feeling too big for my ribs to cage it.

"That's probably a very selfish answer," he went on, "but it's the truth. When I consider the potential consequences of any scenario, I ask what would become of you, and could we be together? Any result that doesn't involve at least one very long life with you isn't an option for me. I've lived a hundred lifetimes, Ana. I've loved before, been lonely, ached for what I couldn't have. I've always made sure to fill every lifetime with what I can, because I've seen others grow complacent and weary. I've seen them move from living to existing. I've been tempted down that path myself, because it sometimes looks easier than this constant caring and trying to grow and change and be more than I am.

"I've also lived long enough to understand that there are few things more important than being with the people you care about most. And that's you, Ana. What good is reincarnation if I don't have you? What good is stopping Janan if I don't have you? Whatever it took, whatever choice I needed to make to keep us together—that's what I would choose."

Before I could find any kind of response, Sam's mouth was on mine and the world fell away. He kissed me, making the tingle in my stomach brighten into a flutter and pulse. I kissed him with everything in me, and his hands were on my face, pushing back my hood, combing through my hair. He kissed my throat and tugged at the collar of my coat as though to reach my shoulder, too.

I ached for him. I ached for his touches, his kisses, for lifetimes of loving him.

Heat surged through me as Sam laid me back, cradling my head and the small of my back until I was lying on the flat of the rock, hair spilling everywhere. He leaned over me, caressing my face, my sides, my hips, and when our eyes met, there was something raw and bare in them. Yearning. Desire.

Was that what he saw in my eyes, too?

A deer crashed through the forest and Sam's breath heaved, white mist on the air as he glanced around, seeming to remember we were outside. "Five minutes alone and I'm already trying to undress you." He touched my stomach, shooting sparks through me, and nodded to where my coat hung open around me.

I struggled to catch my breath. "It's been more like fifteen or twenty minutes." I shivered, both from his touch and the icy air. "And if it weren't so cold, and we weren't outside, I'd encourage this."

Sam zipped up my coat for me. "I suddenly find myself very bitter about the weather, the fact that we're stuck out in it if we want to be alone, and this entire situation in general. There are so many other things we could be doing instead."

I didn't move from where I was lying on the rock, even though cold radiated through my coat, chilling my back. My body still hummed with his touch, the ache he'd awakened inside me. "*Very* bitter." First chance we got, though, I would take it. Somewhere alone, inside, and warm. And minus the rock.

While we watched snow spiral down into the stream, I thought about his words, what he'd said, how any decision for him would come down to whether he could be with the person he loved. With me.

What an amazing feeling.

"Did you bring your flute for the sylph?" he asked, after a few minutes of silence.

"Yeah." I pushed myself up. "I thought they might like it if you played."

"Me?" He held the flute case gently, reverently.

"You haven't played for me in weeks. I'm sure you need to practice."

He chuckled and pulled the flute from the case, making the length of silver seem so small and delicate. He held the flute like a precious thing.

"Is your hand up for it?" I asked.

He nodded.

"Then play for me." I scooted over to give him elbow room. "Play for the sylph. I haven't yet found a song they don't like."

"Songs have words," he muttered automatically, his breath hissing over the mouthpiece. He warmed up with a series of long notes, scales, and rhythm exercises, and then he readied to play.

Gurgling water provided percussion, and the susurrus of wind made harmony. Sam gave nature a moment before he started with a low note, a haunting vibrato, and a deep melody that might have been something I'd dreamt.

Whenever the world shifted, his music did, too. A splash downstream lightened the mood, and the tune turned hopeful; a wolf howling eastward brought back the haunting tones.

Gusts of wind seemed menacing, the way he played. When I closed my eyes, I wasn't sure who led the music: Sam or nature. It seemed like he might be conducting all of it, even the breeze and falling snow. And when my throat vibrated with humming countermelody, I was ready to believe Sam had some kind of magic.

I didn't know the music, though my heart ached with it, and anticipated the next note even though I shouldn't have known.

Only when unearthly moaning joined in did I startle back into myself. Sam ceased playing, as though he'd reached the end of the melody anyway, like the sylph had arrived just on time, just how he'd intended.

"That was amazing," I whispered.

Sam said nothing about it, as though he spontaneously composed music with nature all the time.

Heat spread around the area. Snow sizzled as it drifted through sylph, and the creek steamed where a few sylph had to crowd in. Funny, only a minute ago it had been so cold I couldn't feel my ears.

One sylph floated toward us, eerie in the deepening gloom, and identified himself with a black rose.

Seeing Cris like this made my stomach clench. He was nothing like the tall young man I'd met at Purple Rose Cottage only a few months ago. He'd been all sharp angles and big smiles. He'd built greenhouses to grow roses all year around, cared for squirrels and chipmunks, creatures others would call pests.

He'd saved Stef and me.

He didn't have eyes to meet, but I turned up my chin and tried anyway. "I understood what you were saying last night."

All the sylph hummed hopefully.

"We want to hear everything," Sam said. "Starting with what you told Ana last night. That you're her army. Why? How?"

I frowned at him. There were more important things to ask the sylph—but maybe not to him.

Their song made me think of winter, cold and running and leaping. Trills and whistles, urging sounds like deceptively pleasant nightmares. The sylph songs smothered the night; not even the creek dared interrupt.

It took some sorting out to understand them. It wasn't easy, though I was learning.

"One at a time." My voice seemed harsh after the dulcet sylph songs. "Speak one at a time. I can't understand all of you at once."

Cris hmmed and came forward. -I was gone for so long because I was searching for the others.-

At last. Communication. "You brought them all together to be my army?"

He nodded. -When I left Heart, a few sylph found me. They

146

befriended me, and I told them everything I knew. They told me they'd been watching you your entire life. They've been waiting for you.-

"Waiting for me to do what?" I stared at my knees. I couldn't look at Cris and the others. Even now, I sensed them watching me.

-To stop Janan.-

13

BEFORE

WHAT MADE THEM think I could do anything?

-For a long time, sylph hoped you would come. They hoped you would see the truth about Janan. After thousands of years, many gave up that belief, but when they discovered you in Purple Rose Cottage, the news spread to all the sylph.-

"I don't understand."

-Phoenixes cursed the sylph. The only way to break the curse is to stop Janan from ascending. However, sylph are incapable of doing this on their own.-

"That doesn't seem like a very fair curse."

Cris trilled, like a laugh, and the others burned a little hotter. -No. But the phoenixes told them about the possibility of a newsoul, someone who *could* break the curse by stopping

Janan. And all the sylph swore they would do anything to find this soul, keep it safe. They would do anything necessary to gain their redemption.-

Redemption. A theory tugged at me, but I'd think about it later.

-When you were an infant, all the sylph traps were removed from Purple Rose Cottage.-

Sam and I exchanged glances. "Li did it?" he asked. "Hoping Ana would 'accidentally' be killed by a sylph?"

Shadows rippled. Nods.

-But they knew you were different. They protected you. They kept your room warm in the winter, and siphoned out heat in the summer. They sang you to sleep when you cried.-

It seemed crazy, but Cris wouldn't lie to me, and I had frequently dreamt of warm shadows. Maybe they hadn't been dreams, after all.

"What about the attack on her birthday?" Sam asked. "And the day after, when a sylph burned her hands?"

-The sylph wanted to communicate. They saw Ana leave the cottage, saw that she was leaving for good. They thought she was ready to help stop Janan, so they followed and tried to sing with her. Instead she got scared and ran. If they'd wanted to hurt her, they would have done it while she was sleeping.-

"But they chased me."

Cris shrank a little. -They got excited. After you threw

yourself off a cliff to escape, they realized you'd been frightened. So the next day, they sent only one sylph. But then you wanted revenge and tried to trap their messenger, who was afraid of you by then. The intent was never to burn you. It was an accident.-

The song sounded pleading, but too easily I could remember running between trees and dodging brush. Nearly a year later, I could still feel my heart pounding with the terror, and still feel the inferno in my hands where they'd been burned.

It had been a long and awful recovery, and I'd spent months terrified of sylph. I'd worried they were after me, like dragons seemed to focus on Sam.

And all along they'd wanted to be my friend? They'd wanted me to save *them*?

"Is that why sylph allowed Menehem to experiment on them for so long?" I knotted my fingers together. "And why they chose not to burn him the day he discovered the poison? Because they wanted him to keep working?"

The shadows rippled again. Assent.

"Did it hurt?" The question was out before I realized.

A shudder ran through the ranks of sylph.

My voice thinned, barely a voice at all. "I'm sorry."

One by one, sylph leaned close, brushed dry heat across my face. Nothing burned. It felt only like walking into a summer-baked room, sunlight all around.

Melancholy whispers made me think of leagues and leagues of golden sand, wind-rippled dunes like snowdrifts. They gave me images of turquoise water and heat-shimmering air, strange trees with wide fronds and peeling bark. Lizards scampered everywhere, giant turtles, flocks of white birds screeching. Sylph voices rushed and hissed like waves on the beach.

When they pulled back, I sighed and shivered. I wasn't sure what that had been. A gift, maybe? But now that it was over, the cold air snaked in, even through the sylph.

"What else can you tell us?" I asked Cris.

He rippled in a way that might have been a shrug. -The books you're trying to read are phoenix books. The others can help you with possible translations for symbols, but deciphering what the books actually say—that's up to you.-

"And the phoenixes? You said they saw the possibility of me. How?"

-Phoenixes don't experience time like we do. They see things all at once. They see possibilities.-

"They see the future?"

Cris gave a frustrated keen. -No. They see possibilities. Like you can see water in the creek. It's always moving. You can see what it's doing right now. Perhaps it will trickle into the ground later, or evaporate, or join a larger stream. Even if you knew the course of the stream, there's still a possibility of something outside happening to the water, like being lapped up by an animal. There are a hundred possibilities. Phoenixes see those.-

It still only made half sense to me, but I nodded.

Sam frowned. "It sounds as if these phoenixes are very powerful. They see possibilities, they curse sylph, they can build prisons to hold Janan and his allies—"

All the sylph hissed and grew hot, but Cris didn't explain their reaction. I had suspicions, though.

Sam said more carefully, "If the phoenixes have all this power and they want Janan to fail, why don't they help? Why leave it up to sylph and one newsoul?"

Cris shivered, black roses blooming around him. -Redemption must be earned. If we want it, we will work for it, even though we can never obtain it on our own. To succeed, we need Ana's willing help. And your help, Dossam.-

Chills swept through me. "And the phoenixes?"

-They don't *need* Janan to be stopped, any more than the earth needs the moon to orbit it. The world would change without the moon, but the earth would still exist.-

I nodded, still filled with so many questions, trying to absorb so much information. I didn't even know where to start.

Brush snapped nearby, and a wolf howled in the south.

"We should head back in." Sam wrapped an arm around me. "The others will wonder where we are." He placed the

152

flute back inside its case, and sylph songs faded into the night as all but one sylph vanished back into the forest.

Cris stayed with us as we headed back to the cave, our path illuminated by the lantern Sam had brought along. Snow fell more quickly now, dimming the world beyond our little circle of light.

Back inside the cave, Whit and Stef were going over our notes on the temple books. A pile of dead rabbits lay in the corner, waiting to be dried.

I draped a cloth over the carnage. "You had a lot of luck with the snares?" We wouldn't starve, at least.

Whit shook his head. "We took the sylph hunting. They'd find a rabbit, chase it, kill it quickly, and we'd fetch it."

"They hunt *and* they cook. Who knew sylph were so useful?" I sat down beside Stef and Whit and looked over the notes they'd taken, but nothing new stood out. "Have any of you ever been to the ocean?" I asked.

"Lots of times," Whit said. "It's beautiful, but it can be dangerous."

"How?" The paintings I'd seen had been gorgeous, and that glimpse the sylph gave me had made the ocean seem like another world.

"Once, a bunch of us built a ship to take us to different islands and continents. We wanted to explore. But we got lost in the middle of the sea. This was before we really understood how *big* the ocean is and how easy it would be to get lost, so we hadn't done enough preparation. Fortunately, we had machines to strip the salt from the water and make it potable."

"Salt in the water?" I gagged. "Sounds disgusting."

Behind Whit, Stef gave a very serious nod.

Whit went on. "Even being lost with no idea where to go—that was okay. Then a kraken found us, ripped the ship into five pieces, and started eating it. I was lucky enough not to be eaten alive. I guess. It might have been faster than drowning, now that I think of it."

I shuddered, trying not to think about all the times I'd nearly been in similar positions. If not for Menehem's experiment, Janan would have consumed me before I was ever born. And then I'd nearly drowned in Rangedge Lake.

"This isn't too much for you, is it?" Whit frowned at me.

"No. I was just remembering something else."

Sam touched my hand. "The ocean can be beautiful, though. Most of the time it's beautiful."

Whit nodded. "And there are lots of oceans. Some cold, some warm. Some, the water is so blue it doesn't look real. And I love the sound of waves on rocks or sand. . . ." His memory ran away with him.

How long did it take for someone to grow that somewhen-else look? One lifetime? Two? How easy was it for someone to fall back in time and lose all sense of the present?

I couldn't imagine. The present pressed around me, harsh and sharp and real.

Over the next week, I translated more symbols with the sylph's help.

Getting new meanings for different symbols was easy now. The sylph knew several words for every symbol and knew how different modifiers worked, but they couldn't always tell me what meaning a symbol had in specific context. So a sentence could read "People approached the city," or it could read "Humans attacked the prison." Or something else entirely.

But after days of going through a promising section of text, I'd found a translation that confirmed my fears. After lunch one afternoon, I passed my notebook to Stef for her opinion.

Chatter quieted as she read, and a few sylph skittered from the cave. Cris stayed, identifiable by his shadow rose.

After a little while, everyone waiting and watching Stef, she handed back my notebook, her tone sober. "That looks right to me."

"Thanks." I accepted the notebook and flipped back to the beginning of the story. "Then I guess if everyone is ready to know . . ."

"We are." Whit set our dirty dishes aside and cleaned his hands. "Then maybe we can move on from this cave."

I nodded. We'd move on, but I doubted he'd like where I was thinking about going. "Get comfortable." As I spoke, I adjusted my sleeping bag so I could lean against the wall, my notebook on my knees. Cris hovered nearby, while Sam sat cross-legged beside me. I offered him my free hand, and he held it in his lap, tracing the outline of my fingers.

The memory magic on Whit was cracked and fading, though he wasn't completely free of it yet. It took time. But Sam and Stef would remember everything I was about to tell them, and the more we reminded Whit, the better chance he'd have of recalling it later.

"First, I need to tell you what these books are. They're history, but as Meuric said, no one wrote them. They're simply written. I don't know when, or how, but this one"—I reached to open one of the books—"talks about my birth."

Whit snatched up the book as though to read it right now.

"How is that possible?" Sam leaned over to look at the book with Whit, but frowned and sat back when he couldn't read anything.

"No one wrote the books. They're written as history happens. But they do belong to phoenixes. They were stolen, along with the temple key." I shook my head. "I'm getting ahead of myself. I'll start with what you've been forced to forget.

"Before your time, the old world passed away. A new age dawned with cataclysmic events and the rising of creatures that

156

had once been legend. Dragons, trolls, rocs, centaurs—and phoenixes. Humans perished by the millions during earthquakes and volcanic eruptions all over the world. Hurricanes washed the earth clean. Only a small number of people survived the destruction, and it wasn't long before they would fall, too. That's when all this starts."

"There were humans before?" Whit asked.

"Lots of humans, it seems."

"Then they'd have had their own society. Technological advancements. Ideas and dreams and *culture*. What happened to all of it? How could none of that have survived?"

"Surely a lot of that world did survive." I couldn't stop my pitying look. "But Janan wanted you to believe he created you. Why would he have allowed a previous society's culture to stay? He erased it from your minds, just like he erased so many other things. But when you had flashes of inspiration or ideas for inventions, maybe some of what you'd learned in your very first lifetime leaked through the memory magic."

"So our inventions." Stef glanced at her SED, my flute, our lanterns. "None of what we thought was ours is *ours*."

My throat tightened, but I didn't know what to say. I didn't know if she was right or— Or what. The books didn't tell me.

Sam touched my leg. "What happened next?"

I eyed my notes. "The cataclysm was before phoenixes began recording history, so whatever incited it is a mystery. We may never know. It's not important, anyway. Only how people reacted to it." I found my place again. "Humanity dwindled as the other dominant species carved out territories across the world. After a hundred or more years of living with the constant threat of extinction, a new leader was born."

"You should probably mention that people weren't reincarnated." Stef glanced around the group. "People just lived and died, like everything else."

"That's how the population grew smaller." I smiled at her. "Thanks."

She ducked her head.

"Anyway, this new leader's name was Janan. He was strong and had plans to lead his people not just beyond their current problem—always getting slaughtered by the various creatures living around their small territory—but into a greater way of living: never dying. He saw how phoenixes rose from their own ashes, and was jealous. So he took dozens of his best warriors, and they went hunting a phoenix to discover the method of its immortality.

"They caught one and demanded answers, but the phoenix couldn't tell them." My voice broke. "So they hurt it and demanded again, but still the phoenix told them nothing. As they tortured the phoenix, its blood began leaking onto them, changing them. They didn't realize it, though."

Stef and Whit stared at their hands, and Sam had his eyes closed, as though seeing everything in his head. Sylph songs quieted.

"Soon, other phoenixes arrived to save their comrade. They were furious, but they didn't kill the attackers. If a phoenix takes a life, it would cost their cycle of birth and death. Instead, to punish the attackers, they conjured tower prisons in the most dangerous places in the world, like jungles or deserts or over immense volcanoes. Inside the towers, the attackers wouldn't starve or die of thirst. They'd get what they wanted—immortality—and they'd be alone for the rest of their eternal lives. Because the phoenixes separated all the attackers so they couldn't conspire again.

"The towers were empty. They had no doors. Only a special key could affect the stone." I glanced at Sam, who pulled the temple key from his pocket. It glittered in the faint light of lanterns.

"That's the key?" Whit asked.

I nodded.

"How did we get it?"

I turned back to my notebook. "Meuric stole it. He was there when Janan and the others attacked the phoenix, and when the phoenixes took everyone away. But he didn't take part in the attack himself; he hung back in the forest, hidden. When he returned to everyone else, he told them only that Janan and the warriors had been captured and imprisoned by phoenixes—not what they'd done to deserve it. He sent a party to steal the key, and they brought back not only the key, but a pile of books, as well."

"These?" Whit asked, touching the leather spine of the book nearest him, and I imagined he was wondering if he'd been the one to grab the books. Maybe he and Orrin had decided together to take the books. The beginnings of their library, later locked away for five thousand years.

"Those books," I confirmed. "Many people were lost in the attempt to steal the key, but when the survivors brought it back to Meuric, they had what they needed to free Janan. They went after him, and found an enormous wall circling a seemingly infinitely high tower.

"But inside the tower, Janan had been learning about the magic leeched from the phoenix, and he realized there was a way to achieve immortality after all. Like Meuric, he didn't tell everyone the truth about what he and his warriors had done. He said only that he'd learned the secret to immortality, and the phoenixes had grown jealous and locked him away for it.

"He wasn't going to let the phoenixes stop him from becoming immortal. Now that he understood how it could be achieved, he'd do anything to get it. He would begin with himself, and when that worked, he swore he would do the same for everyone else. In the meantime, he would reincarnate everyone, exchanging their souls with new souls. Everyone would perpetually reincarnate; no one else would be born because he could only reincarnate you."

Sam jerked his head up and stared at me. Stef shot me a warning look. But before anyone could ask, I pressed on.

"Janan said the key to the phoenixes' immortality was a death of their own making. After everyone was secured in chains, tied to him forever, he took the knife he'd used to harm the phoenix, still with its golden blood on the blade, and plunged it into his own chest. He shed his mortal form and became part of the tower, which was already half-alive with phoenix magic. And everyone inside the tower was bound to Janan.

"They reappeared outside the prison wall as adults, with no memory of what had just happened. Only Meuric remembered. He was meant to encourage people to worship Janan and prepare for Janan's return. When they went inside the prison wall again, there were houses everywhere. The prison had been transformed into a city."

Whit frowned. "But I thought there was a big fight over who would live in the city. . . ."

I nodded. "There might have been. I imagine everything was chaotic and strange then. The book doesn't go into detail about that."

"What happened to the others?" Sam asked. "The people Janan took to find the phoenix."

I glanced at Cris, at the other sylph hovering around the cave with us. Several of them moaned and curled in on themselves.

"No." Whit shook his head. "That's not possible. Because Cris—"

"It's the truth." I raised an eyebrow at the sylph, and several of them nodded, odd little twitches. "What happened with Cris was unprecedented, but the others were cursed by phoenixes. They repented. They wanted forgiveness. Phoenixes didn't trust them exactly, but they'd seen what Janan was trying to do. They gave the prisoners a chance at redemption.

"They had every prisoner do as Janan had done. They drove their own weapons into their chests—the weapons still covered in phoenix blood. The prisoners shed their mortal forms, but they had no one bound to them, no physical ties to their towers. They soon emerged as sylph: bodiless souls of shadow and fire."

"That doesn't sound like a chance at redemption," Whit muttered.

"Redemption comes when they stop Janan from ascending."

"How were they expected to do that?" Stef sounded indignant. "They were just going along with what Janan ordered. It could have been any of us he'd dragged along. Any of us—" Her voice broke, and she balled in on herself. Sam leaned over to hug her, and everyone was quiet for a minute.

"What about Cris?" Whit's voice was hoarse.

I couldn't look at the sylph next to me. "He was trapped like this because he performed the same ritual the others had. None of us realized what would happen after."

Cris murmured a song, as if reminding me his plight

wasn't my fault, but . . . I could have done something. I could have made him wait. I could have insisted.

I should have.

Sam's tone was all caution. "Earlier, you said Janan talked about exchanging souls. Does that mean we knew?" He faced me, expression torn.

He wasn't supposed to figure it out.

"Did we *know*, Ana?" Sam's voice dipped low and dangerous. "How long have you known that we agreed to the exchange? How long have you known we agreed to let new-souls be *eaten* so we could live forever? How long have you been hiding it from me?" There, at the end, the words caught and grief showed through.

I whispered, "Since Stef, Cris, and I were in the temple."

He turned to Stef, naked betrayal in his posture. "You knew, too?"

She gave a single nod.

Without another word, Sam got up and left.

14

BETRAYAL

I STARTED TO go after Sam, but Stef shook her head. "Give him some time."

My knees hit my sleeping bag and I slumped over the notebook, pages still open and glaring with the truth. He wasn't supposed to know. Not ever. "How long?"

Stef shrugged and seemed to struggle for words as Whit frowned and looked like he wanted to follow Sam outside.

"I didn't want anyone to feel guilty." It was the truth, but my words were hollow, because there was another, stronger truth: I hadn't wanted to deal with their guilt and grief. Already, the stress of what we had to do was overwhelming. "Besides, I know why you made the decision. I understand."

Whit scowled up at me. "Why?"

"You were scared." I couldn't raise my voice above a whisper. "You were in a strange and frightening land, and Janan offered you a way to come back if you died."

"Many of us were more afraid of Janan than we were the rest of the world," Stef added quietly. "He'd angered *phoenixes*. He'd done something so huge that phoenixes stepped in to punish him. Whether or not we knew the truth of what happened, we knew it had to be bigger than we were, and that meant Janan was, too. So we agreed because it seemed like he could protect us or destroy us. We made a decision based on fear."

"And it seemed like newsouls would never even know what they missed." I tried not to think about the non-voice I'd heard in the temple once, or the weepers: newsouls.

"It doesn't matter if they didn't know what they were missing," Whit said. "We knew. We knew what Janan would do to them. We made that decision."

Awkward silence filled the cave, and after a while, Whit went out after Sam, a spare coat slung over his arm.

Stef glared at me. "If you're going to be so bad at keeping secrets, you need to figure out a more delicate way of revealing them." She turned away and bent over her SED.

Now everyone was angry with me. Stef, because I'd told the others, and Sam and Whit because I hadn't told them before. I probably deserved to be left alone.

But even as I leaned my forehead on my knees, Cris curled up next to me, a companionable warmth.

"Thanks," I mumbled, and he gave a quiet hum. I hated Sam being mad at me, but what I had to do next would make it worse.

With a tired sigh, I grabbed my SED and shifted to the map, trying to work out time and distances.

After an hour, Sam and Whit returned to the cave. Stef and I both looked up expectantly.

"Ana," Sam started, but I stood and shook my head.

"You might as well just sit and listen to what I have to say. None of you are going to like it."

Sam's dark eyes narrowed, but he leaned against the wall, next to Whit. Stef gave me a wary look, and Cris lingered in the corner, invisible among the shadows.

I begged my voice not to shake. "This is my plan. It's going to sound rash, but unless any of you have better ideas, it's the only plan we've got." Dread coiled in my stomach as my friends' expressions grew more and more skeptical. "We get the dragons to help us."

Sam turned ash pale. Stef glared like she was ready to kill me, while Whit just looked stricken and like he hoped maybe this was a joke.

If only that were true.

Cris gave a small, disbelieving trill. Everyone's eyes darted toward him, but no one spoke. They just waited for me to explain myself.

"It sounds horrible, but hear me out. The dragons have— They might have— I read in the books—" The words tumbled from me, tripping and bumping one another. Everything came out in the wrong order.

I stopped, swallowed hard, and tried again.

"For thousands of years, dragons have come down from the north. Every time, they attack the temple. The day they flew in during a market, I remember seeing them come straight for the temple, ignoring everything else, even the people attacking them. I remember wondering, why? Why would they willingly sacrifice themselves to destroy a building?

"Now I think they're not attacking the building. They're attacking Janan. I know everyone else feels calm and peaceful when they look at the temple, like they're safe, but since the first time I saw it, the temple has made me feel awful. Like I need to shrink up. Like something is watching me and doesn't like me. And I thought that was just because so many people were watching me and not liking me, but then I realized Janan was real. Then I found out that if not for Menehem's experiment, Janan would have—"

Sam jerked his head up, his gaze so black and anguished I hardly recognized him. He looked a little wild, like he'd give anything to make me stop talking.

"The dragons tried to destroy the temple that day. Then, during Templedark, they brought more and attacked people, too, but lots of dragons still went straight at the temple. While it was dark, they cracked the stone open. They wrapped themselves around the temple, squeezed and clawed, and *broke it.*"

After a moment of awkward humming, Cris said, -That only happened because of Menehem's poison.-

"I know it sounds like a terrible idea, and maybe it is, but there's more to my plan." Why couldn't I stop talking? But the words kept rushing out, like a waterfall. I looked at Stef and Whit. "I have more of the poison Menehem used. While we were at the lab, I hid the poison so no one would find it. If we can convince the dragons they'll have a shot at destroying the temple—"

Stef shook her head. "Do you hear yourself? You just said 'convince the dragons.' What makes you think that's possible?"

My throat constricted, making my words come out like squeaks. "The centaurs—"

She shook her head again. "They didn't understand anything you said. You had two of their children and an army of sylph behind you. They didn't kill us because nothing can hurt a sylph."

Cris keened softly.

Stef ignored him. "The centaurs don't want to be your

friends, Ana. If they'd found you without an army of sylph, they would have destroyed you. They would have destroyed all of us if Cris hadn't arrived. And dragons, Ana. *Dragons.*" She touched Sam's shoulder, anguish flashing across her face as he jerked away. "How can you ask that of Sam? You know what happens. How can you ask him to die?"

I looked at Sam, all the fire pouring out of me. I knew about the dragons. I knew about the thirty dragon deaths, and the way he'd been after the dragons attacked the market that day. I remembered the terror in his eyes, and the way he'd steadily grown distant and darker.

He had that look again. Fear. Horror.

Resignation.

His voice was deep, soft. "She's not asking me to do anything she's not willing to do herself."

Everyone looked from Sam to me, though Sam continued speaking.

"Ana doesn't expect to live through this, either. She's been waiting to die this entire time."

I stared at my feet.

Sam's voice turned raw. "She has this one life, and she's willing to risk it so others might live. We all came along for a greater cause, knowing we might sacrifice our lives. Knowing we won't be reincarnated if we succeed in stopping Janan's ascension. After living for five thousand years, suddenly stopping is such a terrifying concept."

Where did they go? What did they do? Surely the soul lived on.

"But Ana has only had eighteen years." His voice tightened. "Nineteen."

Today was my birthday. I'd forgotten.

"No matter what happens, there's no reincarnation for her. If she's willing to sacrifice the rest of her life for this, I can, too. She's not asking for anything outrageous. She's asking us to atone for what we've already done."

I hadn't thought of it like that. "I'm not trying to force you into going out of guilt—"

Sam shook his head, and for a moment a there was a look in his eyes I couldn't identify, but it broke my heart. Then he was hard again. Distant again. "You don't have to use guilt against us. If you're going north, then we all go. We can't stay behind, can we? There's no catching up with the other group. And there's no surviving on our own."

So they'd join me not because they loved me or believed I was right, but because there was nowhere else to go. And because they believed they owed newsouls their lives.

They were angry with me. All of them. Even Sam.

Especially Sam.

"So that's your plan?" Stef said. "Menehem's poison, dragons, and optimism?"

It sounded so stupid when she said it, but I wouldn't give

in. "The dragons will listen to me."

"Why?" She scowled. "Because you have sylph friends? Because you're the newsoul? Surely you realize that nothing else out there—sylph aside—cares what you are. They can't even tell the difference."

"I'll find a way." I would. I had to.

Stef leveled her gaze on me. "Is that before or after they eat Sam?"

Her words were knives in my heart. "I won't let anything hurt him." Though when I met his eyes, I could see it was already too late.

"Even if you find a way to convince them, what next? You'll just set your poison out, put Janan to sleep, and let the dragons rampage through Heart?" Stef threw up her hands in mock surprise. "Oh, I know why that sounds so familiar. That's exactly what Menehem did."

"I'm *not* like Menehem," I hissed. "I'll tell the dragons not to hurt people. And we can warn people to stay away from the temple while the dragons—"

"Rip it apart?" She advanced on me. "Do you think that's going to work? Tear apart the temple, and Janan can't ascend?"

My eyes stung with tears, but I wouldn't cry. I *wouldn't*. "I wasn't finished."

"What else?" Whit asked.

"I read something about dragons in the books. Something

that might help us." I took a deep, steadying breath. "The dragons have a weapon."

The cave went so quiet I could hear the sound of snowfall.

"More than their teeth and talons?" Stef muttered darkly. "More than their acid?"

"Yes."

Sam closed his eyes.

I tried not to look at him. Or any of them. I tried to focus on the shadows shifting on the wall, but I couldn't ignore Sam's wretched expression. "Yes, another weapon. I'm still working on translating the symbols, but it seems like this weapon is something they revere. Something that's important to them."

"And you think what?" Stef's voice was a dagger. "You think they'll just give you the weapon? Or use it because you ask them to? They're not part of your army."

I pressed my mouth into a line.

"And even if they do have a weapon, why haven't they used it before now?"

"Because they're trying to use it on Janan inside the temple?" That hadn't been meant as a question, but my voice defied me and lifted at the end. "Look, maybe I'm wrong about the weapon. And the dragons. But do you have a better plan? Do you have *any* plan? You got us out of Heart and you've kept us safe from drones, and I can't thank you enough for that, but what now, Stef? The rest is up to me." I glanced at Cris and the other sylph shifting into the natural shadows of the cave, as though trying to avoid notice. "I don't know if it will work. I don't know if *anything* will work. I have to try, though."

No one spoke, though Sam's betrayed expression, Whit's obvious confusion, and Stef's hostility said everything.

My voice was hoarse as I grabbed my coat. "We leave tomorrow."

This time, I was the one to leave the cave.

I wandered through the twilight forest, sorrow curled up inside my chest. The sadness was lodged so firmly I could hardly breathe, hardly think. Only as light bled from the world did I realize I'd forgotten a flashlight and my SED, and the only ones who might come looking for me were shadows.

The moon hung somewhere above, but it was dark tonight. I could see the outlines of trees, thanks to starlight, but soon I was lost, shivering inside my coat, which suddenly seemed inadequate. Ice crunched under my boots and broke off against my sleeves as I brushed past.

In the dark, shivering and aching with misery, I swept snow off a boulder and slumped onto the stone. My butt froze instantly, but after everything, I was too tired to care. I was too tired to keep picking my way through the dark.

It was my nineteenth birthday.

A year ago today, I'd left Li at Purple Rose Cottage and set out to find my place in the world. Instead, I'd been chased by sylph—sylph that had evidently been trying to befriend me—and jumped into Rangedge Lake, where Sam rescued me. When I closed my eyes and sent my thoughts back in time, I could still feel the ache in my chest and the blackness swarming in my head as consciousness faded.

I could still feel Sam's arms wrap around me, feel him blow air into me, feel the cold wind on my wet skin as I saw him above me, smiling.

He'd brought me back to life.

And now I would take him to his death.

I bent over my knees and sobbed myself raw, coming back to the present when the shivers got too much. I grew hyperaware of every sound in the woods: a breeze rattling branches and rustling pine needles, birds settling into nests, and a low and melancholy moan.

Sylph.

I licked moisture back into my cold-chapped lips and tried not to let my voice shake too hard. "Cris?" It could have been any of the other sylph, too, but I didn't know their names, or if they even had names anymore.

Heat flowed around me, making my skin prickle. The sylph hummed quietly beside me. -This way.-

I couldn't see where we were going. I followed the warmth, frustratingly slow because any time we turned or went around something, I had to test the air. But I was relieved to have been found, and by someone who could thaw me to the core.

Twigs cracked beneath my boots as I followed, and somewhere in the darkness, small animals scurried away. At last, I caught the faint light that looked as though it shone from around a corner. The cave. Usually at night, sylph lined up at the exit, absorbing the light so anyone—or any creatures—wandering past wouldn't see it.

"Thank you for finding me," I murmured to the sylph, then headed inside. When I squinted through the dim light, everyone appeared to be sleeping in their bags. No one stirred as I pulled off my snow-dusted coat and boots and shoved them in a corner, but when I searched for my sleeping bag and found it near Sam's—though not as near as it had been earlier—I caught the whites of his eyes in lantern light when he blinked.

I paused, crouched by my sleeping bag. I'd been ready to slide it away from him so I wouldn't forget when I first woke up in the morning.

But our eyes met, and for a moment I hoped he'd say something or open his sleeping bag in invitation. We'd had fights before, and reconciling kisses were always sweet. Instead, he gave a slight nod—acknowledgment of my return—and closed his eyes.

Heart still aching, I dragged my sleeping bag away

from his, crawled inside, and stared into the darkness until morning.

When the sun rose, we left the cave and headed north.

To where dragons lived.

15

SOLITUDE

THERE WAS NO music for a long time. Not from Sam or the sylph, and not from the woods that shielded us from the bitter wind. The farther we traveled, the closer and taller the trees seemed, as if they held secrets between their branches and guarded them fiercely. With few small mammals in the underbrush and even fewer birds calling in the trees, the world began to look very lonely.

My boots crunched paths on the ice-crusted ground. The crackle was sharp and startling, but the others never glanced back.

Our progress was abysmal. After two and a half weeks, we were barely halfway to our destination, though we'd had to pause for a few days after eating something that shouldn't have been eaten. Still, we should have been farther.

It was the most miserable time of my life, relieved only by evening SED calls with Sarit.

Outside the tent, I listened to Sarit tell me about the curfews and who'd been imprisoned for resisting Deborl or expressing concern about newsouls.

"It was Emil this time," she said.

"The Soul Teller from Anid's birth?"

"Yes." She sighed, and it sounded like she was trying not to cry. "Everyone is so afraid here. With the earthquakes and storms, people are terrified."

I knew. She said the same thing every day.

"Armande said to tell you hello, and that he hopes you're eating enough. He keeps saying he should have gone with you to make sure you're properly fed."

"I wish you were both here." Except I didn't want them to be angry with me, too. I hadn't told Sarit the secret I'd revealed, only that they knew something and it had changed everything. She did know where we were heading, though.

"How are things going with you?"

"Sam still mostly talks to Whit."

"And Stef?"

"Still upset with me." I closed my eyes as snow began to fall. "They aren't mean to me. They don't *ignore* me. But they're all different toward me."

"Are you being different toward them, now that they know?"

I shrugged, even though she couldn't see it.

"I'll take your silence as a yes." Sarit sighed. "You can't expect things not to change. Give them time to adjust."

"You're right."

"Of course I am."

"But Sam—"

"You know what you're asking of him. It's probably taking everything he's got just to keep functioning. You remember how he was after the market attack last year. This is worse than that." Her voice crackled as the SED signal grew weaker. "I know this must be hard, especially after the way Li treated you, but they don't mean the silence the same way she did. Why don't you try talking to them?"

"About what? The longer we go like this, the more awkward it gets."

"Music? Food? How much you hate the cold? I don't know, Ana. They're just as miserable as you are. Don't wait for them to be friendly with you first. But if you won't take action, I can't help you." Something crashed in the background, and she swore. "Sorry, Ana. Armande needs me. Earthquake." She clicked off before I could say good-bye.

I sat outside, watching snow gather on my mittens and SED. Our goal wasn't the dragons' land, exactly. The library had information on dragons and their habitat, of course, so we knew roughly where they lived, but I didn't need to go quite that far north.

In his previous lifetime, Sam had come across an immense white wall, like Heart's city wall. There, dragons had discovered him and killed him.

That was my goal, because we knew dragons patrolled that area, and there was built-in shelter on one side. At first, I'd been afraid I would have to ask Sam to remember details about his trip north, or that I'd have to see if he'd recorded any details in a diary—and if that diary had been scanned into the library's digital archives—but the sylph ended up saving me again.

They knew where the other prisons were.

Of *course* they knew.

So the sylph led us north, through the forest of elms and pines and spruces, and though Cris assured us we were getting closer, it seemed we'd be "almost there" forever.

We'd been in the wilderness so long, Heart, Janan, and everything we were working toward seemed like another life.

"This is it," Stef said, walking up ahead with Whit. "This is the edge."

Whit checked the sky, all clouds and coming darkness. "Then we'll stop here for the night. Looks like it's about to get harder to travel."

Sam came up behind me, glancing at me from the corner of his eye. "The edge of what?" He spoke to Whit only, but Stef answered.

"Weren't you paying attention this morning?" She rolled her eyes. "Our SEDs are about to be disconnected from the others. We're too far out of Range."

Sam shook his head. "But they work farther south. And east and west."

Whit dropped his backpack and began unpacking the tent. "That's because people go those ways sometimes. They explore. There's food. Other things we can actually use."

"There are towers scattered across the continent," Stef said, "maintained by drones. They're what connect your SED to others when you're outside of Range. But up here, there's only forest and dragons. No one comes here." Her gaze darted toward me. "Except us, unfortunately."

She could hold a grudge for a *long* time.

"So no more calls or messages. Not after tonight." Whit frowned as he and Stef began putting together the tent.

No more Sarit was what it really meant.

"I'll gather dinner." At my words, the others only nodded.

Sylph flashed off into the woods while I dropped my backpack and dug through it for the canvas sack we used to carry dead animals.

Sam pulled water bottles and a smaller sack from his backpack, and Cris headed toward him. They usually filled up water together, and returned with what looked like clumps of dead grass, but actually tasted okay after being boiled and mixed with whatever kind of meat we got that night. Human or sylph, Cris was still the best at finding edible plants. I wished he'd go with me, though.

In the woods, sylph darted around, quickly burning squirrels, rabbits, and doves. I dropped the creatures into my sack one by one, and by the time I returned to the others, the tent was up and Sam and Cris were boiling water for dinner.

"Here you go." I placed the sack of animals by the pot, hoping. Waiting.

"Thanks." Sam didn't look up. "Stef's cooking."

"Okay." That was good, actually. Stef was a much better cook than the rest of us. But that wasn't what I'd been hoping to get from him. Maybe a smile. Or a complaint about the weather. I wished I could tell how much of his misery was aimed at me, and how much was everything piling on top of our search for dragons.

Sarit told me to try. I gathered my nerves. "Sam, I know I didn't tell you about the exchange, but I had a good reason—"

He shook his head. "I'm not ready to talk about that yet. I just can't."

The rejection stung. I turned away.

While the others took care of dinner, I retreated into the tent, pulling out my notebooks and the temple book. I'd discovered all sorts of interesting things over the last few weeks, but nothing the others would care about right now, so I kept them to myself.

I huddled in my corner of the tent and turned on the lantern, temple books spread around me. My notebook was almost full with all the translations and facts I'd collected.

I'd only been working a little while when Cris came into the tent and sidled up to me. -Anything new?- His presence made my corner of the tent wonderfully warm.

"I think I'm getting to a part that explains how the temple key works."

He nodded, just a flicker of shadow.

"When Meuric had me trapped in the temple, I pressed a lot of the engravings on the key."

-Hmm.-

I spent a few more minutes double-checking my translations before I went on. "All this would have been nice to know before I went in there. Okay, the symbols all do different things inside the temple. Horizontal lines make floors, and vertical lines make walls."

-The square creates doors.-

I nodded. "Inside or out, depending on whether you slide the one half inside the other. I was really lucky, making that happen before Templedark. If I hadn't done it before the poison took effect . . ."

-You would have escaped when the light came on again.-

But Sam, Stef, and so many others would be dead now.

Cris hummed soothingly. A tendril of darkness slipped around my wrist, over my hand, and between my fingers.

I closed my eyes and tried to pretend like shadows were enough. Like Sarit's voice on the SED was enough. But inside me, a hollow grew larger.

I tapped my pencil on my notebook where I'd drawn the silver box, and each of the symbols etched into the metal. "You'd think I would have guessed, having nearly been killed in one, but the circle creates pits inside the temple. The depth depends on how long you press the button, I think. It's hard to tell."

-And the diamond?-

"Turns things on their side. Or upside down." When Meuric had trapped me inside the temple, I'd witnessed everything flip over. There'd been a pit in the center of the room, and suddenly it had been crawling up the wall and over the ceiling like a spider. When I'd pushed Meuric beneath it, he'd fallen upward. "There are instructions for combining buttons to make stairs and things, but it's a little confusing."

-The temple is confusing.-

I leaned closer to him. "I'm sorry," I whispered. "I wish we'd found another way."

Roses bloomed in the shadows. -I'd do it again.-

My heart ached, and when I closed my eyes, all I could see was the knife in Cris's hands, the blade looking as though it had been dipped in gold as he plunged it into his chest. All

I could see was him sacrificing himself to save Stef and me. And now he was this. A shadow. A soul without substance.

Voices sounded, and footsteps thumped the ground. When the others walked in, Cris jerked away.

I dropped my face back to my studies, flipping through the books to scan for anything related to dragons. After I'd read through the library archives on my SED, I'd started on the temple books. Maybe they'd be able to tell me something we didn't already know about dragons. And if we were to meet dragons, I needed to know everything. So far, the most interesting thing I'd found was an ancient animosity between dragons and phoenixes. But that didn't help me, really.

"What I want," I muttered to Cris, "is to know more about the dragons' weapon." The books contained frustratingly little on the topic.

-I wish we'd been able to help more with possibilities for those symbols.- Cris sighed. -Let's go over the alternate translations tonight. Maybe we'll discover something new.-

I smiled at Cris, at his hope, but it was unlikely we'd have any revelations tonight. We'd already been over the passage a hundred thousand times.

They fight with the weapon that destroys all.

Or maybe *They love the instrument of consuming.*

Or even *They fear the tool that builds and destroys.*

Or none of those. With so many symbols possessing multiple meanings, it was impossible for me to guess what *these* symbols meant in *this* context.

"Three more earthquakes today," Stef said as she lit another lantern, pushing back the coming night. "And another hydrothermal eruption near Templedark Memorial."

I checked on my SED. The earthquakes had been large, but not as massive as that first one.

"It's getting bad there," Whit muttered.

"Anything from Orrin?" Stef asked.

"I got a message from him earlier. He said there's a fever going around, and they've had to stop traveling. Rin is treating everyone as best as she can, but it's difficult without access to the medicine she's used to."

"Are the newsouls okay?" The question was out before I realized.

Whit and Stef both looked up at me, as though they'd forgotten I was here. Sam sat near them, but not with; he just stared at his hands, miserable.

"The newsouls don't have the fever," Whit said after a hesitation. "They'll be fine. They're hard to hurt, like you."

He was wrong. All I did anymore was hurt.

Whit handed out bowls of soup. I took mine without comment, eating while I listened to Stef and Whit speculate about what kind of fever the others might have. And I watched Sam, hunched over his bowl and seeming deep in thought. When he contributed to the conversation, he seemed only half there.

Five minutes before Sarit usually called, I ducked outside and hid behind an evergreen tree. Through the sharp-smelling needles, I could see the tent and the light creeping around the edges of it, but I had a little privacy.

Snow drifted between the trees, making me shiver, but I didn't want to talk inside the tent. If I did, the others would be awkward and I'd just . . . I'd fall apart.

Her call came ten minutes late.

"Sarit." I sounded maybe a little too relieved. "I was worried you wouldn't be able to call. We're at the edge of the signal now. Tomorrow I won't be able to get you."

"Ana." Her voice was oddly low, sober. "Ana, what is everyone doing right now?"

"I—" I glanced through the veil of pine needles, but the tent flap was closed. I couldn't see anything. "Talking, I guess. I'm outside. They're inside. What's wrong?"

Her voice caught, as though she was trying not to cry. "Okay, I need you to go in there. I need you to talk to them for a minute."

"What's going on?" My chest constricted with worry. But I stood, shivering in the snowfall and clenching my mittened hand around my SED.

"Please. So I can tell you all at once."

"Okay." My dread for her news outweighed my dread of going into the tent again. Even so, the way Stef and Whit looked at me as I entered—and the way Sam didn't look at me—stung so much I wanted to turn and run back out. I closed the flap behind me and knelt. Cris shifted nearer to me. "Sarit needs to tell everyone something."

They looked at me now. Even Sam.

I balanced my SED on my knee and tapped the speaker function so they could all hear the way her breath caught and trembled. She was crying. "All right, Sarit." My voice was deeper now, too, filled with foreboding. "Go ahead."

"It's Armande," she said. "Deborl caught him after one of the earthquakes today. Armande is dead."

16
TOWER

THERE WASN'T MUCH to say after that. Stef and Whit asked a few questions, which Sarit answered as best she could. Sam just buried his face in his hands, motionless during the entire conversation.

I wanted to hold him, but when I touched his shoulder, he slumped as though the weight of my hand was too much.

"He's not coming back," Sam said. "He's gone forever."

He was right. For Armande, it no longer mattered whether we stopped Janan. Either way, Armande was a darksoul now.

"We learned what Deborl is having people build, though." Grief choked Sarit's voice. "It's a cage. An enormous cage, big enough to fit a baby troll inside."

"That's it?" Stef shook her head. "There were more parts

than just a floor, ceiling, and bars. That can't be all he's building."

"More importantly," Whit said, "what is he building it for?"

"I don't know." Sarit sounded young and alone and frightened. Armande had been like a father to all of us. He *was* Sam's father in this life.

When Stef and Whit were finished talking, Sarit said good-bye to them, and I sneaked outside once more with my SED. I didn't make it back to the tree, though. Just stopped halfway there, unable to control the tears coursing down my cheeks.

Armande was *gone*. I'd never again see him, hug him. He'd never again open his pastry stall in the market field and feed me muffin after muffin, as though terrified I wouldn't eat enough without his constant vigilance.

"What are you going to do?" My voice shook with grief and winter.

"I don't know." Our connection crackled, reminding me of the distance between us, reminding me we wouldn't be able to talk after tonight. "I don't know. A few people have tried standing up to Deborl, but most of them get put in prison. Maybe I can get them out. Or maybe . . . I don't know. I'll keep hiding. Keep up with what they're building. Maybe I can figure out what the rest of the parts are for. I just have no clue."

Everything in me ached for her. She was alone, hiding in Heart without anyone to console her or help her through this grief. "Just be safe," I whispered. "Do whatever it takes to be safe."

"I wish I were with you." Her voice trembled. "I wish I'd gone with you."

"Me too."

"I'll call you every night." Her voice caught on the words. She was trying to sound strong. "I'll call every night until you come back."

"And then you'll stop calling?"

She let out a strangled laugh. "Yeah, then I'll stop calling."

A few minutes later, we clicked off.

I stood outside, weeping in the snow until I heard everyone in the tent climb into their sleeping bags. Only when I was certain they were asleep did I sneak back in and shiver myself warm.

The next week was a thousand times lonelier than those before it.

Thunder cracked, startling everyone awake.

We hurried out of our sleeping bags and scrambled for the door to the tent, but the sky was clear and deep blue with coming dawn. Sylph hovered around our campsite, warming the air.

The thunder didn't return. Whit and Stef pushed back

inside the tent to start breakfast, but Sam remained by the door, glaring at the sky as if his life depended on it. The thunder hadn't been real thunder.

I wanted to reassure him somehow, but I had no words. Only the same awkwardness we'd carried since my birthday.

"Go inside with the others. I'll fill up the water bottles." Apparently, I couldn't manage reassurance. Just instructions and letting someone know where I'd be. After I'd wandered out on my birthday and Cris had come after me, Whit had pulled me aside and lectured me about telling people where I was going. If I insisted on going after dragons, then I'd best not get myself killed out of stupidity.

Sam looked at me. Sort of through me. He nodded. "If you see anything, come right back." There was a note of concern in his voice, but mostly he sounded hollow. He'd been worse since Armande died.

I put on my coat and boots and headed into the woods with an armful of empty water bottles. A few sylph trailed after me and hung close as I broke ice and filled the bottles in a fast-moving creek. While I worked, sylph dipped tendrils of shadow into the full bottles and boiled the water clean.

We were almost finished when thunder cracked again.

I glanced at Cris, my eyebrow raised, but he didn't move. The other sylph, too, remained motionless as the snap of leather wings came again.

Above, I saw only pine boughs, stark against the infinite blue.

And then, just to the east, a sinuous body flitted above the trees, darkening the fragmented sky.

I placed the last water bottle on the snowy ground. "Will one of you take me to see it?"

Cris dithered, and the other sylph hung back awkwardly.

"If you won't take me, I'll just go see it myself and possibly get lost again." I started walking, but after only a few steps, I turned and pointed at Cris. "*Don't* tell the others. I don't want them to scold me when I'm not even getting into trouble."

Sullenly, the sylph trailed after me as I followed the occasional crack of wings.

Cris sidled up next to me. -Consider yourself scolded.-

I smirked and swatted at him, but a knot in my chest loosened a little. Whether or not he agreed with my plan, Cris still liked me. He and the other sylph stuck closer to me than my real shadow.

At last, we came to a break in the woods, and a cliff overlooking a white valley. Trees huddled under the weight of snow, majestic and silent. Above the valley, three dragons flew.

Their serpentine bodies slithered through the air, gliding without sound until they flapped their wings, which stretched as wide as their bodies were long. A deceptively delicate network of bones and scales shone translucent when a dragon veered and twisted toward the rising sun.

I gasped and took a step back into the woods. The dragons were so *huge*. After a year, I'd forgotten how big they were. But seeing them fill the sky as they flew through the air, my heart stumbled on itself. Templedark was not far behind us. I'd seen too many dragons then, seen the way they spit acid on the fields of the agricultural quarter or tried to land atop the city wall. One had been leaning over Sam and Stef to kill them when I arrived.

I'd almost seen a dragon kill Sam.

My heart ached as I stared at the sky and lowered myself to my knees. I couldn't stand anymore. I couldn't *think* anymore. I could only watch as a dragon switched course and dove into the valley, its wings folded along its sides. The immense golden beast disappeared into the forest for a heartbeat, then erupted a short ways beyond with a deer in its jaws. Ice and snow and branches sprayed behind it, having been caught up in the dragon's path.

"Oh, Cris." My words were hardly a breath. Just mist on the frigid air. "How am I supposed to even get close enough to one to speak to it?"

Cris curled around me, warm but silent. He offered no advice.

I couldn't bring myself to move from this spot. Snow soaked through my layers of clothes, but Cris and the other sylph stuck close, keeping me from shivering.

Soon I'd have to go back to camp. To Sam, Stef, and Whit. And I would have to tell them that I'd seen dragons and I had no idea what to do now. The dragons were hunting in the forest below. They must have had keen eyes to see that deer. And unlike the roc, they had no trouble diving into the forest.

They could snatch us up, too.

"We're going to need extra cover," I whispered. "We definitely don't want to be caught in the open. Even in the forest, we'll need to avoid looking like food."

Cris nodded, trilling softly by my ear. -We will protect you.-

"Thank you." I lowered my eyes and didn't try to stop the tears, but what should have been a torrent came as only a trickle. I'd trekked through the cold woods before, gone hungry, been beaten, but I'd never felt like this. I'd never felt broken, like my spirit had split in two.

What hope was there? Stef had been right about the dragons. There was no chance of talking to them. They weren't *people*. They weren't sylph, who needed something from me, or centaurs, who'd been satisfied to have their children returned unharmed, and cowed by the presence of the sylph.

No, now we were in a huge winter forest, far, far from home and anything familiar. We'd taken weeks to get here, and for what purpose? There was no way I'd be able to convince the dragons to help us. What was I going to do? Shout from the cliff and ask for their assistance? Ask if I could borrow this mysterious weapon they had? They'd swoop in and eat me whole before I finished introducing myself.

And worse, I'd pushed away Sam with my secrets. It drove me crazy when he hid things from me and didn't tell me what was going on, so I should have *known*. Instead, I'd become a hypocrite. I'd hurt his feelings and dragged him into the land of his nightmares because I had a *plan*.

"I can't help you, Cris." My whisper came out rough, broken. "There's no way I'll be able to speak to the dragons. They won't destroy the temple for us. They won't use their weapon for us. They'll probably eat us. Janan will ascend and Range will erupt. Sylph will be cursed forever."

Only the crack of dragon wings answered.

"I wish you hadn't put your trust in me. I wish you had sided with the others to talk me out of this plan. We should never have come here. I made a mistake."

Cris hummed. -I believe in you.-

I sagged, too weary to hold myself up anymore. "I don't."

As I wiped tears off my cheeks, reflected sunlight caught my eye, drawing my attention north.

A white tower pierced the sky, brilliant and bright against the shadowed forest. Like the temple. And below it, a white stone wall ringed the tower, cutting through the forest like a knife.

It wasn't perfectly white like Janan's temple, though. Age and weather had dulled the shine of stone, and there were places the forest had toppled the wall, but this prison had certainly survived the millennia better than the one Cris had found in the jungle.

"We're almost there."

Cris nodded.

"It doesn't matter." I stood and brushed snow and slush off my clothes. There was no point to being here now. I'd seen the dragons. I'd seen the futility of my plan.

The sylph dried my clothes as I took one more look at the valley and the dragons moving farther away, still hunting in the forest. Their wings snapping the air grew distant.

I trudged back to where I'd left the water bottles, but there was only a shallow hole in the snow where they'd been. Someone had taken them.

"Did one of your friends go tattle on me?" I glared at Cris, who hummed with annoyance.

"It wasn't the sylph." Sam's voice came from not far off, just a few trees away. He peeled himself out of the shadows and stalked toward us. "You were gone a long time. We came looking, and some of the sylph indicated you'd gone off with Cris." He kept his voice low, even, but couldn't hide the lurking power in there, or the disappointment. His gaze darted to Cris, and he tilted his head.

Without comment, every sylph left the area.

Sam turned on me. "I told you to come back if you saw anything."

I prickled. "I didn't *see* anything. I *heard* something and went to investigate. I had Cris with me. He wouldn't let anything harm me." That last bit was meant as a barb—*Cris* still cared about me—but if Sam noticed my intent, he didn't react.

"What would Cris do if you got into trouble?" His dark eyes narrowed. "What if a dragon carried you off? Or you slipped and broke a bone? He can't catch you. He'd have to go find help, and you'd have to wait."

"It doesn't matter!" Shouting felt good. I didn't fight it. "Nothing happened. The point is, he was there. I didn't go alone. You're just angry I didn't run back and tell you."

"Is that what you think?" He advanced on me, expression hard and fists curled at his sides. "You think I only care about knowing where you are and what you're doing?"

I backed away, wary of the set of his shoulders and that dark look in his eyes. He looked like a creature barely contained.

I hated the way my voice shook. "You don't seem to care about much else lately." Not that I could blame him. My heel hit a tree trunk, then my shoulders and my spine. I'd backed away all I could. "You barely talk to me. You let Cris go out and find me the night I got lost."

"I *asked* him to find you."

"It was still dark." I tried to edge away, but Sam pressed his palms to the trunk on either side of me, caging me. I steeled my voice. "You don't speak to me. You barely look at me."

He was looking at me now. His face was so close we could kiss, and all his weight leaned toward me, making him seem bigger than he really was. "What do you want me to do?" he rasped. "Say it doesn't matter that you hid something so important from me? Say Armande's death isn't ripping me apart? Say I don't care that we're traveling back to the place I *died* so you can make friends with the things that killed me?"

"I know—" The words came out wispy and weak. "I know this is the last thing you want to do."

"But I'm here, Ana. For you. Because you said you believed this would work. But you can't expect me to be cheerful about it."

"I don't." I felt like I was hardening, like ice. Without the sylph nearby, cold nipped at my nose and cheeks. Even the heat of Sam's glare did nothing to warm me. "But you don't have to suffer alone."

That was the thing, though. He wasn't suffering alone. He had Stef and Whit, even if he was still upset with Stef for hiding the truth. She'd hidden it at my request. They both understood how awful this was for him in a way I would never be able to comprehend.

I wasn't worried about him suffering alone. I was worried

about my suffering. My loneliness.

Before he could see the shame in my eyes, I turned my head. My voice was pale and weak, almost snatched up by the wind cutting around trees. "I made a mistake. Lots of mistakes." Avoiding him was one of them. Sarit had told me to take action, but I'd been too afraid. I'd kept my distance and made little effort to comfort him when he needed it, too.

He didn't move. With my head turned aside, I could see only his forearm at my shoulder, and even with his coat on, I could see the strain and tremble where he held himself up.

"I shouldn't have hidden the truth from you, but I hoped you wouldn't have to know, because you shouldn't have to feel guilty about something you did five thousand years ago when you were young and scared."

"Of course I have to feel guilty." His tone softened. "Because of my decision, a hundred newsouls have been—" His breath caught. "It could have been you. I died shortly after Ciana. You and I were born only weeks apart. Everything was so close, *you* might have been the soul exchanged for my rebirth. You could have been one of those souls in the temple, paying for my selfish decision. I think about that every day. I think about it every time I look at you. How can I not feel guilty? How can anyone *live* under the weight of so much guilt?"

From the corner of my eye, he looked pained and passionate, like it took everything in him to stay together.

"You're trying to absolve me so I won't think about what

I've done. What we all did. You're trying to keep your friends good and blameless so we can continue on as we'd been before, but that's not going to work. Let us accept the blame for what we've done. Let us deal with that blame. It's not pleasant for any of us, but you can't—and shouldn't—try to stop it just because it makes you uncomfortable."

Without another word, he spun toward camp and vanished into the woods.

17
DEFIANCE

HE WAS RIGHT. I'd been making decisions based on what made me most comfortable.

Forcing them to come north with me. Not telling them the truth about reincarnation. Keeping my silence with the group. Avoiding Sam.

But now I knew what to do.

It was a terrible plan, but as I stood there with my spine against the tree, my breath misting on the frigid air where the heat of Sam's body had already dissipated, I knew it was the right plan.

My eyes closed and my face lifted to the treetops and sky beyond, I whispered, "Please," to nothing. To everything. To something greater than me. "Please let this be right."

Only the wind answered, howling through the valley and around the trees. Ice clattered and hoarfrost trembled. No wonder the phoenixes had built a prison this far north: dragons, freezing weather, and utter solitude.

I shivered and pushed toward camp again.

Inside the tent, Stef glanced up from the tray of rabbit jerky as she dropped the finished strips into a bag, but she didn't speak. The sylph assisting her hummed and twisted darkly, and Sam, with his knees pulled up to his chest, rested his forehead on his arms.

Unbidden, my mind conjured an image of the three of them in the temple's skeleton chamber, offering their wrists to Janan's Hallow. Silver chains clattered and gleamed. A million souls said yes to the exchange. A million souls traded countless lives for their own infinity.

My *friends* wore chains inside the temple.

I shook away the dark fancy as Whit met my eyes, offering a weak smile. "We need to get moving soon," he said. "We're already behind. Only four weeks until Soul Night."

"We should turn around." I startled at the sound of my voice, breathless and rough with chill. "We should return to Menehem's lab for the poison."

Sam looked up.

"Just . . . go back." While they stared at me, openmouthed, I retreated to my sleeping bag and pulled out my notebook, but Stef didn't give me a chance to get lost in my work.

She slammed her tray on the ground. "*Now* you realize what a stupid plan this was? *Now*, after we've come all this way?"

I spoke to my notebook, monotone. "I've put you in enough danger. And like Whit said, we have only four weeks before Soul Night. We don't have time to linger up here. We'll be more useful in Range."

"I can't believe this." Stef surged to her feet. "What about this *weapon* you were so convinced we needed?"

The dragons' weapon? I had no idea what it was. Or how I'd request an object I couldn't even describe. The temple books were next to useless on the subject, too.

"How long have you been thinking we should go back?" Stef went on. "One week? Two? You're right: we *could* do more in Range. We could have *been* doing more in Range. But you said you had a plan. Then you dragged us up here. And now you say it's time to turn around, having accomplished nothing but wasted time."

There was no way to respond to that, so I just frowned at my notebook and bit the insides of my cheeks. Still, my eyes prickled with tears and I had to turn my head away from everyone.

"Are you satisfied?" Stef's voice broke. "Are you *happy* that you've steered us so far off course?"

"Stop." Whit heaved a sigh and gathered an armful of lanterns and battery chargers. "Just stop. Yelling won't help." He took everything outside to let it charge in the sunlight.

Stef marched after him, and a moment later their voices came, arguing about the best way back to Range.

From behind the shield of my notebook, I caught Sam watching me from the corner of his eye. But I didn't acknowledge him, just lowered my eyes and began writing.

Sam had always believed in me. When I'd thought I was a nosoul, he'd insisted otherwise. He'd encouraged me until I believed, too. And when I'd thought there was no way I could help rewrite "Ana Incarnate" after Li had burned it in a fire, Sam had told me I could do anything. His belief had made me believe.

When he said he'd go anywhere with me, I'd suggested the moon and the bottom of the ocean. He'd liked that I thought big.

Now he was here with me. In the north. With dragons.

And my plan was too big, too wild. It was crazier than going to the moon.

I didn't blame him for not believing in me anymore. It hurt, but the truth was that he'd put up with a lot more than anyone would have expected. But his anger earlier and his silence now spun a thread of defiance in me.

I *would* reach the dragons. And I'd convince them to help.

The others spent the day discussing routes and gathering enough food to last a few days, because clouds threatened snow. Sylph helped wherever they could, but kept shooting me little whines of disappointment.

After supper, everyone found their sleeping bags and tucked themselves in for the night. Sam gave me a long, weary look, and I remembered again that he'd stopped believing in me.

"Get some rest," he whispered. "Tomorrow will be a long day."

As if they hadn't all been long. Yet still too short.

I burrowed into my sleeping bag, zipped it up all the way, and muffled my sobs with my mittens. How could this be so physically painful? We hadn't touched. We'd barely spoken. I wished myself back in time, back to the first moment I met him. If I could start over again, I'd open up to him immediately. I'd have kissed *him* in the kitchen, rather than being disappointed he hadn't kissed me. And after the masquerade, I'd have rushed him home before we could be attacked, then told him we'd be sharing a bedroom from now on.

But I wasn't back in time. I was now. In my stuffy sleeping bag with all my things packed and a short note to leave in my place. Well, all my things except for the temple books. They wouldn't help where I was going.

An hour later, the tent was filled with soft snores and deep breathing. I peeked my head out of my sleeping bag and checked, but no one stirred. Only the shadows shifted, their attention falling on me.

I pressed my finger to my lips. "Shh."

Cris floated toward me, curiosity in the way he writhed like flame, but he was soundless as I pulled out my letter and reread it one more time before leaving it by Sam.

My friends,

By the time you wake, I'll be gone. I hope you won't follow. It was selfish of me to ask you to come this far. This isn't your duty.

I don't know if I'll succeed, but I'm going to try to find answers, to find help. Someone told me he believed I could do anything, be anything I wanted because I'm new. He made me realize that one of my best qualities is not listening to what other people think I should do. He made me believe in myself.

If I have only one life, I'm not going to waste it. I'm going to fight for what I believe in. I believe in this.

I hope you can believe in me too.

I love you all,

Ana who Has Life

Quietly, I rolled my sleeping bag and strapped on my flute case, then secured my backpack over my shoulders. Cris and a handful of sylph followed me into the winter night, questions in their quiet songs.

-Where are you going?-

"To the prison," I whispered.

-We'll go with you.-

"Half of you stay with them. They'll still need sylph."

Cris bristled. -We are *your* army. We follow you.-

I crept away from the tent, careful where I placed my feet. My flashlight beam was weak, dimmed with the end of my scarf covering it. I didn't want anyone to wake and notice the light. "You're my army, so you'll follow my orders, right?"

A few of the sylph grumbled, but finally Cris nodded and handful of shadows peeled away, heading back for the tent.

After one last look at the tent and my friends inside, I walked north, uncovering my flashlight once there was a thick layer of trees behind me. "Is there an easy way down the cliff that will get me to the prison wall?"

A few sylph darted ahead to scout a path.

-Sam will be angry.- Cris stayed beside me, keeping me warm. Snow drifted through the forest, melting away in my sylph's heat.

"He'll live." I watched my step over a tangle of roots, listening hard for sounds of pursuit or animals in the forest. Dragons aside, other creatures were unlikely to bother me with sylph so near, but Sam had been right when he said I could fall or get hurt, and sylph wouldn't be able to help. I had to be careful.

I could go back. I could sneak into the tent, crumple up the letter, and go to sleep. No one would ever know, except for the sylph, and they would keep my secret.

But I pressed on through the deepening night, following the sylph to a snowy path. My boot skidded, sending me to my butt and knocking the air out of me. I found my feet again, wincing at a new bruise as one of the sylph heated enough to dry my clothes.

"Can one of you—" I waved at the steep path that wound down the slope. It looked like a dragon path, all the branches above shredded and the ground littered with sticks and fallen evergreen needles, creating traps beneath the snow. "Melt it? Harden it?"

Sylph eased into a line, singing softly to one another. Steam rose around them, hot and hissing like a part of their melody. Heat billowed around me, smelling of ozone and ash; a trickle of sweat crawled down the back of my neck.

Within minutes, it was done. The sylph seemed to shake themselves as they returned to my side, only one or two leading me down the now-dry path.

"Thank you." I had my light, so I could see the twigs and leaves on the ground, but as we descended into the valley, they glowed red and then crumbled to ash when I stepped on them. The sylph were being careful with me.

-We're so close,- Cris sang. -I don't know if what you're trying will work, but we sylph love you for the effort. We'll do anything it takes to protect you.-

Ah, and we were going to see the dragons, so no wonder he'd wanted all the sylph.

I stretched out a hand for him, and tendrils of shadow wound around my wrist and up my forearm.

I took the hill carefully, testing rocks before I trusted my weight to them. Every step took me away from my friends and into danger, but an odd sense of peace pushed through me. I'd said in my letter to Sam and the others that I believed in what I was doing, and I did. This was right. I couldn't give up.

I only realized I was humming when the sylph began singing with me, eerie and unearthly sounds that echoed through the night. Our song lifted, warm and rich like honey as it filled the dragon path and ran down ahead of us.

Sylph undulated in the darkness, tendrils of shadow reaching for the snowy sky as they danced. When we found level ground, I twirled awkwardly in my heavy backpack and all the sylph gathered around, burning with joy. They coiled around one another, around me as though I were one of them, and all of the sylph made flowers bloom. I danced through a garden of shadow roses.

The companionship I'd been missing over the last weeks built around me, built inside me.

A year ago—it felt like a thousand years ago—I'd trapped a sylph inside an egg and burned my hands. When they healed, the rose thorn scars I'd worn most of my life had vanished. The scars never would have healed without the sylph fire. Only the ruin had allowed new, healthy skin to grow over.

Like a phoenix bursting into flame and a rain of sparks before being reborn in its own ashes, it had taken burning up in my own misery for me to realize I didn't *need* other people to believe in me before I could do something.

I had to believe in myself.

Hopefully I would see my friends again and be able to explain that.

The singing faded and sylph burned around me, happier than I'd seen them in weeks. Shadows caressed my hands and arms, and Cris said, -Thank you,- as we continued on our journey.

I'd been so lost in my own ragged emotions, I hadn't even noticed their sadness. They'd missed the music, too.

I wouldn't ignore them again.

The sylph led me through the woods, melting snow where they thought I might have trouble finding traction. We crept through the forest for hours, strains of melody fluttering around like butterflies or leaves in autumn. Though exhausted, I felt oddly peaceful, considering I was in a dark and unfamiliar forest with a dozen burning shadows.

Only as morning light bled through the forest did I realize I'd been walking all night. My muscles ached, and my stomach felt hollow. I gathered up a handful of fresh snow and ate it, but it only helped a little.

One of the sylph flew off to find something for me to eat, and a few minutes later I was picking scorched feathers off a pigeon. It wasn't ideal, but a few bites too hot to taste, along with snow, helped immensely.

I was just about to sit and rest when morning reflected off white stone just through the trees.

A broken section of the wall.

I'd arrived.

18
RINGING

YESTERDAY THE DRAGONS had come in the morning. If I wanted to attract their attention, I needed to time everything perfectly.

Preferably *after* they'd found something to eat.

I tightened my backpack straps and tucked my flute case into my coat. A pile of rubble made a sort of stair; I scrambled up the steep incline, careful of slick spots and snow. When I reached a gap with too many loose rocks, I stretched for a low-hanging branch and climbed a spruce tree until I reached another decent section of the wall.

It took forever, and sylph kept stopping me so they could dry my way, but at last I reached the top of the wall.

Snow made the sky misty gray, but from up here, I could

see everything. Trees encroached on the prison, pushing through piles of weather-smoothed stone broken off the wall. I stood above them, the pines and spruces and maples, for a moment feeling like the tallest person in the world.

There was the cliff I'd found yesterday. It seemed awfully far away now, though it was probably only an hour's walk. I'd had to take the long way around, coming down the mountain in the dark.

Sam and the others would be waking soon, if they weren't already. I tried not to imagine their reaction to my letter.

Cold wind streaked across the wall, but sylph huddled around me, warming the air and absorbing the force of the wind to keep it from hitting so hard. The wall was plenty wide, but I couldn't risk falling. There were a few holes here and there; this wall—and the tower inside—didn't have Janan keeping it intact. The stone was ice cold and crumbling, with no heartbeat inside.

When I had a clear view of the frost-crusted forest, I drew my flute from its case and blew hot air into the mouthpiece to warm the metal. I wanted to remove the case and my backpack, since they were heavy and awkward, but I couldn't risk losing them. It seemed like if I put them down, they'd be gone. The sylph weren't corporeal; they were useless for carrying things.

I hadn't heard dragon thunder yet, but the gray clouds spat snow. A dragon could be hiding up there, easily.

My heart thudded against my ribs. What if they didn't come? What if they *did*?

"I don't know, Cris." My voice shook as I lifted my flute. "This is seeming too big again."

Cris hummed comfortingly, and shadows touched my hands, my cheeks.

Sylph formed a horseshoe around me, leaving everything ahead of me visible. I needed to be able to see and listen.

Wing beats cracked in the east, and I shivered.

Clouds rippled with serpentine bodies pushing closer. I breathed hot air into my flute, keeping the metal warm, getting my lungs used to the effort. I wouldn't have time to warm up like normal. Not unless dragons were impressed by scales and rhythm exercises.

I knelt and held as still as I could, waiting as the dragon thunder grew closer. Talons scraped the bottoms of clouds, shredding the vapor into ribbons. Immense wings scooped air, swirling snow in flurries across the sky.

A trio of dragons swept toward the forest, silent as they slithered over white treetops. Only the wind of their passing and the occasional clap of their wings gave auditory evidence of their presence.

From my perch, surrounded by sylph whose chief desire was to protect me, I could almost appreciate the beauty of these dragons. Sam once told me that the first time they'd seen dragons, everyone had stopped what they were doing and looked up. They'd been entranced.

Until the attack came.

I waited, heart pounding in my ears. What if they hated music? What if that was why they always attacked Sam?

Part of me wished he were here, because even though we'd been fighting, the way I missed him was an ache in my soul.

But most of me was glad I'd come alone, because I needed to prove to everyone—myself included—that I was right and I could do this on my own, and because I couldn't put Sam in this kind of danger. I almost had. It had nearly broken him.

"I can do this," I whispered as a dragon swooped into the forest. Trees splintered as it surged through, a streak of gold in snow-covered evergreens. The dragon came up with what looked like a small bear, and then swallowed it whole. The other two dragons dove into the same area, each emerging with another bear. They didn't even have a chance to roar before the dragons tossed them up and caught them, as though playing or showing off.

Was that it? Was that all they would eat? Dragons were huge. Surely they needed more. But they began moving eastward again, toward other hunting ground or home, I couldn't be sure. I needed to start now.

As I stood, sylph coiled around me, so hot that sweat trickled down my spine.

"I can do this." My breath wafted over the flute mouthpiece, making small hissing sounds. Sylph fluttered and began a deep, resonant hum. A chord, as though they were my accompaniment.

A high-pitched, terrified giggle escaped me. Then I set my mouth, pulled in a breath, and began to play.

Four notes. One, two, three climbing lower. Four jumped above, long and high and bittersweet. The first notes I'd ever played on a piano. The notes that began my waltz.

As one, the dragons veered off their course, turning back. Thunder cracked as they flapped their wings, but they made no other sound, gave no indication how they'd communicated.

Instincts urged me to run, hide. My backpack weighed me down, making my shoulders ache as I tried to hold my flute up at a right angle; Sam always made fun of the way I let my flute sag, reminding me I'd get a better sound if I held it up.

I moved away from playing the waltz, choosing something simpler instead: my minuet. It was the first thing I'd ever composed, a haunting little melody of my fears.

Music poured from my flute like silver silk, and the shadows around me caught on quickly, adjusting their voices to become the bass and countermelody. They lifted my flute's sound high above the treetops, carrying it eastward. My shadow orchestra. They listened to me, watched how I moved and where I sped and slowed, adjusting their songs to mine.

Thunder cracked again as the dragons grew nearer. Their wings seemed to dominate the sky, blocking the mountains and forest as they glided toward me. Their eyes were huge and bright and blue, and suddenly I felt very, very small. Like prey. Soon they would be upon me, able to gulp me down like one of those bears, or that deer yesterday.

When the minuet came to an end, I didn't stop playing. I repeated it, and the sylph continued their songs, though now they stretched out around me, wide and tall and just as terrifying as they'd been the night of my eighteenth birthday. As we spiraled through the music again, the sylph's voices grew louder, more intense.

Heavy wind pushed from the dragon wings. One of the sylph cut in front of me, absorbing most of the chill and rush, though my face ached with sudden cold and my flute's sound seemed sucked back into it for a breath.

The lead dragon opened its jaws wide, revealing four long fangs and a row of teeth, still wet with blood and matted brown fur. The stink of raw meat rolled across the wall, nearly choking me as I gasped for another breath to finish my minuet.

As I hit the last note again, the lead dragon reached me, its mouth wide open—

The sylph raised themselves in front of me, a wall of shadows burning phoenix-hot. Heat blasted my face, dry and ashy, and the dragon snatched itself away from me at the last second. It had been so close I could have touched its face. Only the stubborn need to appear strong kept me from staggering backward, away from the dragon and sylph.

Dragons roared in frustration, so loud and close my ears ached.

They wheeled around and snapped several more times, but the sylph continued to thwart them. Dark flames writhed around me, singing, blocking the worst of the wind from smothering me. They darted out to burn the dragons any time they approached too close.

"Dragons!" I shouted. "Can you understand me?"

I felt very foolish standing there, flute clutched to my chest, backpack weighing me down. My head throbbed with the rush of wind and noise, and blood and adrenaline racing through me. My whole body shook with fear and cold, but I held my ground.

One of the dragons spit a gob of acid. I started to run, but a sylph stretched up and the green fluid fizzled away, burning up like snow.

"Dragons!" I called again, trying desperately to ignore the volleys of acid they spit at me, and a sudden sharp ringing in my ears, from both the noise and the pressure headache building up. "Hey, acid breath!"

One of the sylph twitched like laughter as it burned away another glob of acid.

"Your scales are dull and your wings look like a moth-eaten blanket!"

The shrill ring in my ears stabbed so hard I almost doubled over, but I forced myself upright. All the research I'd ever seen on dragons indicated they respected power. If I fell over, I'd look weak. Like prey. I had to prove I wasn't.

"Your tails are stubby and your teeth are half-rotted. I've seen tadpoles scarier than you!"

Dragons swarmed around me, snapping and spitting, roaring as sylph foiled every attack.

I scooped up a fist-sized rock and hurled it at the nearest dragon as hard as I could. It dropped into the trees. "See this rock?" I threw another one, which followed a similar path. "This rock flies better than you!"

My aim was off. Way off. The ringing in my head made me sway, made my vision snap and sparkle around the edges. I staggered as I reached for another rock to lob at them, and now that I thought about it, if I was trying to make friends with the dragons, maybe I shouldn't throw rocks. I didn't like it when people threw rocks at me.

The roar and whine of dragons and sylph collided in my ears. My head felt filled with smoke, and the noxious fumes of burning acid poured inside me like poison.

My flute dripped from my fingers, just a silver smear in my vision. I stumbled as the cacophony of sylph and dragons faded, leaving only the shrill ring in my thoughts.

Lightning flared in my head, and the ringing coalesced into a voice.

<They break so easily.>

19
DETERMINATION

I AWOKE LYING at an uncomfortable angle over my backpack. Sunlight filtered through a sylph who leaned over me like a parasol. Warmth pressed around me, smelling faintly of ash and burned flesh.

Groaning, I pushed myself up onto my elbows and assessed my situation. It had stopped snowing, and the clouds had lifted. I was still on the wall. Sylph huddled around me. My flute lay next to my leg. Though it hadn't vanished, the ringing in my ears had subsided, taking my headache with it.

So far so good.

Low growling made the stone vibrate beneath me. The sylph heated, but didn't do anything to make me think I was in immediate danger. Nevertheless, it seemed likely there was a dragon behind me. I peeked and caught a glimpse of gold scales.

Great.

-They don't like you.- Cris sang quietly beside me, sending tendrils of shadow around me, as though he wanted to help me sit all the way up, but the shadow passed right through me. A small, frustrated keen pulled around him, but he smothered it quickly.

How often did he forget he wasn't corporeal anymore? I sat up and leaned toward him, missing the sharp-featured boy I'd met outside of Purple Rose Cottage, the way his smiles sometimes looked like a grimace, and the enthusiasm he'd shown when taking me around his greenhouse. He couldn't grow roses anymore. Not real ones.

I struggled to bring myself back to the present, and to the dragon behind me. The sylph made me feel safe, though. As long as I didn't pass out again. "I guess I deserve their dislike." I rubbed the side of my head where I'd hit the wall. A bruise pulsed under my skin, but I could see straight and focus on the way the wall stood white against the evergreens. The day was so clear and crisp after the snowfall. "I did throw rocks at the dragons and call them names."

-And you insulted their teeth, wings, tails. . . .- Cris wavered, and I could imagine him frowning at me.

"I know." Was the dragon behind me listening to our conversation? Could it understand us? "I got carried away. They

222

were trying to kill me." At least I hadn't pulled out my laser pistol.

-That's not how you make friends.-

I snorted. "I've never been very good at making friends." I picked up my flute and checked it for damage—it was fine—before I climbed to my feet. I wanted to be standing when I faced the dragon.

The ring of sylph around me parted as I found my footing, revealing deep blue eyes as big as my splayed hands. Its face was mostly jaws, topped by round nostrils, hung with fangs as long as my forearm. The dragon was stretched out, lying along the wall like a snake. It blocked my way down—unless I wanted to jump. Its huge wings were folded flat against the serpentine body, while one of its forelegs hung off the side of the wall, shredding a spruce tree as though it were fidgeting.

The other two dragons waited in the forest below, coiled around trees and rubble from the deteriorating wall. The woods were horribly silent. Nothing dared make a sound with dragons so nearby.

I met the lead dragon's eyes—one of its eyes, since they were so big and far apart—and decided to start with an apology. "I'm sorry I made fun of you and threw rocks at you."

Another low rumble carried through the stone beneath my boots.

"I really am sorry. I came here to talk to you."

The dragon only stared. Wind hissed through the trees,

and my sylph huddled closer to me, buzzing with some conversation they kept to themselves. I focused on the dragon in front of me. Its giant teeth. The eyes that didn't blink. It kept staring at me, the others too, as though waiting for something. Could they even understand me?

Suddenly I remembered a voice, a growled thought just before I passed out. I'd forgotten about it when I woke up, but now the words pressed on me. *They break so easily.*

It hadn't been a sylph song. There'd been no music in the words, no *idea* of words. Just thoughts that weren't mine.

Along with a mind-crushing headache.

"You said I break easily."

The dragon's eyes narrowed.

"I heard you. And"—I steeled myself—"I think you can understand me, too."

My ears rang, like the world suddenly gone silent, but I could still hear the wind and something far off, like animals chattering in the distance. I didn't look away from the dragon, though.

"I know you don't like humans." My voice trembled, no matter how I willed myself to be strong. I tried to tell myself it was no different from talking to a bird or squirrel in the woods. My childhood had been filled with attempted animal communication, since humans wouldn't talk to me. "Dragons have been flying to Heart for millennia, trying to break open the tower in the middle of the city."

The dragon growled again, and a word crackled in the back of my head. <Hate. Hate. Hate.>

I nodded. "Last year, you did break it. The tower cracked." I couldn't ignore the tower looming to my left. From here, I could see where trees were overcoming the stone, not as quickly and devastatingly as they had in the jungle Cris once told me about. Nevertheless, the structure would eventually topple.

I resisted the urge to look at my sylph and think about which one might have been imprisoned here five thousand years ago.

And the reason why.

They were on my side now, and they yearned for redemption.

I returned my attention to the dragon. "You may be asking yourself what was different about last year. Why you were able to affect the tower after trying unsuccessfully so long." Maybe saying their efforts had been futile before wasn't the best idea, but the dragon didn't react. "The answer is a type of poison. You see, there's a man who made himself part of the tower. He's been controlling it for the last five thousand years, along with the rest of the city. . . ."

The dragon yawned, its breath reeking of acid and dead bear.

Oh. Okay. I glanced at Cris for help, but he and the other sylph were distracted. I checked the forest but saw nothing unusual. Just lots of snow and trees and brilliant blue sky. Everything shimmered in the noon light. My stomach tightened, reminding me I'd had nothing but a skinny pigeon in what seemed like forever.

Acid Breath rumbled again, vibrating the wall so hard I staggered. The other two dragons peered at me, their eyes slitted as though they wanted to doze.

"Anyway." My voice came out high and panicky as the dragon shifted its head, so a long fang stood out right in front of me, bone white against shimmering gold scales. "It seems to me you're not much of a fan of the tower." Though they didn't seem to mind the one in their domain. "And I thought I'd let you know that I have the same poison that was used last year, and I'm going to use the poison again on the spring equinox."

The dragon lifted its head. <Why?>

Ah. At last.

I bit my cheeks to avoid smiling while I put together the next words. "Because that night, the man living inside the walls is going to ascend. He wants to be immortal. He's going to break free of the walls that have caged him for five thousand years. Already it's beginning. The earth is shifting."

The dragon lowered its head. <We don't care.>

"You should." I stepped forward, sylph fanning around me. "Because when it happens, the earth will crack open and fire will spit out. There's an enormous volcano under the city, powerful enough to make the surrounding lands boil. You're far away from the volcano, but not *that* far. Not far enough. Ash will rain all over your hunting grounds, smothering the plants and animals. This frozen land will be even colder and deadlier."

<Why do you want our help?> Acid Breath angled his face at me so that one of his eyes was an arm's length away, and the ringing in my ears intensified. <You hate us as much as we hate you.>

"I— I don't hate you." Though I certainly hated whatever dragons had killed Sam in previous generations. And maybe some of the dragons from Templedark, but several of those were dead. "I came because I thought you would like another chance to destroy the temple." And how did one bring up a mysterious weapon?

<It will only mend. Our journey will be futile, as you said, and humans will kill us. We aren't like you. We don't come back.> Acid Breath settled back onto the wall, jaw propped on one forefoot. <If our hunting grounds are destroyed, we will go somewhere else.>

This couldn't be it. I couldn't have come all this way, actually succeeded in speaking to dragons, only to be turned down.

An idea sparked in my mind. "What happens when Janan begins hunting dragons?"

Acid Breath rumbled, as did the others. <What?>

I nodded. "When Janan ascends, he's going to be immortal. Maybe unkillable. He stole a phoenix's magic and made himself like this. But before, five thousand years ago, he was the leader of a group of people—the people who live in the city right now. And considering how many times they've been killed by dragons, I'm sure Janan will want some kind of revenge."

It could happen. Maybe.

<He won't harm dragons. He cannot.>

"Are you sure?" Everything inside me twisted, numb from what I was about to say. In spite of what they'd done, I didn't want to hurt my sylph. It was the same as with Sam and all my other friends. They'd made a decision or followed orders, yes, but that was *five thousand years ago*. It hadn't been just another lifetime, it had been another world. They'd all changed. Their decisions from then didn't affect my love for them now. "Because five thousand years ago, Janan and his warriors trapped a phoenix."

The sylph shivered and whined.

<Phoenixes cannot be caught.>

"They can." I made my voice hard. "They can and they have been. You may think Janan won't or can't come after you, but if humans had menaced dragons for the last five thousand years, wouldn't you want revenge?"

Acid Breath lifted his head and looked at the others, and

the ringing in my ears intensified. I couldn't understand what they said to one another, but there was definitely something going on. Wings tensed. Words crackled around the edges of my thoughts, but the dialogue—what I could hear of it— didn't seem complete. There was something in the way they moved that added to the conversation—something I couldn't quite understand.

But the fragments I could hear—they were interesting.

<She wants us to destroy the temple.>

<And the song?>

<She doesn't have it. I don't see it in her.>

<Perhaps she hates the one with the song.>

<We should help.>

<We should destroy her before she destroys us.>

<She can't. She doesn't have the song.>

<Test it.>

Finally, the lead dragon turned back to me and settled on the wall. <Make a song for us again. Like you did earlier.>

"What?" I needed to ask them about the weapon the temple books had mentioned, and whether they could use it to fight Janan. But they were interested in a song?

The dragon growled, its anger rippling across the forest. <The song you made to lure us here. Make another one so we can hear.>

"Play my flute?" My words came out like squeaks as I lifted my flute, making the sylph stir with anticipation.

-Will the dragons help?- Cris asked me.

<Now!>

I stepped backward and held my flute to my chin.

The others began with a low hum that rolled across me, through me. I shifted my shoulders to readjust my backpack, still weighing me down, then played a few scales and arpeggios to warm up. The dragons grew still, watchful.

I had a few pieces memorized, having played them enough for my muscles to remember the melodies, so I let my fingers rest over the keys for only a moment before I decided on the music I'd played during the market day demonstration, right before I'd been captured and locked inside the temple. It was the music I'd written like a diary, keeping it to myself for months until I finally had the courage to show it to Sam.

The music started out slowly, melancholy. Sylph pooled their songs around it, matching the longing I played, the need for the unknown. Everything around me faded as the music took over, the sylph warmed me, and I pushed my heart into it. Gasping with a kiss. Awe at a fire-sky sunset. The amazing and humbling feeling of receiving love. My flute's sound soared across the valley, sweet and silver and filled with life.

Playing with sylph was nothing like playing with Sam. Both sylph and Sam understood music in a way I could only dream of, but where Sam played with immeasurable skill and deliberateness, sylph were free and wild. When they sang, they danced, and they burned with passion and joy.

Sound swirled through us, making my heart pound with fear and loneliness and exhaustion when I reached the section I'd written after learning of newsouls' fate. And then hope and desire when Sam took me home and revealed the parlor filled with roses, just because he'd wanted to see me smile.

As we pushed toward the end, I opened my eyes to find the dragons all looking . . . peaceful. Oddly happy, if one could assign a facial expression to dragons.

And as my gaze swept over the valley, I caught motion on the cliff where I'd stood yesterday. Three human-shaped figures and a dozen sylph, the latter of which echoed my music.

I dropped my flute to my side, banging it on my thigh. They hadn't left. They were still here. Sam was here.

And the dragons.

As the sylph finished singing, confused about why I'd stopped, I faced Acid Breath.

<What are you doing?>

I unzipped my coat enough to slide my flute into its case, still strapped diagonally across my chest. "Are you going to destroy the tower? Will you use your weapon to fight Janan?" Now that I'd seen the others across the valley, I itched to return to them, to tell them what I'd done. I also wanted to somehow put myself between the dragons and Sam, but they'd see around me. Over me. Maybe I could lure them away, or . . . I had no clue. "Tell me you're going to destroy the tower on the spring equinox, and I'll play all you like."

<Why did you stop?>

One of the other dragons lifted its head and looked toward the cliff, and buzzing in the back of my thoughts indicated they were discussing what had caught my attention. They knew why I'd stopped.

Sam.

I didn't think I was supposed to hear it, but one dragon murmured to another, <The one with the song.>

<We will stop the distraction.> That was meant for me, and with one graceful motion, Acid Breath dug his talons into the white stone as he crouched for flight. His wings spread wide, their wind almost knocking me off the wall.

"No!" I raced for him, as though I could stop a dragon. He was ready to fly off and leave me, ready to kill Sam while I was stranded here, helpless to do anything about it. I threw my arms around his foreleg just as he lifted into the air, sylph shrieking behind me.

We were flying.

Icy wind stung my face, poured down my throat. I gasped and clung to the dragon's leg as he lifted it and growled. His scales were cool and slick, almost slick enough to drop me. I wrapped my legs around his ankle—what I supposed would be his ankle—and tried not to think about hurtling through the sky. On a dragon.

The one with the song.

What song?

Acid Breath dragged his foot, skimming treetops, which whipped and caught at me. Pine needles smacked my legs and arms, slithering into my sleeves and coat collar. My hands ached from the cold and holding on, but as his wings cracked against the air again and I looked up, I found the cliff rushing at me.

The dragon hurled me to the ground, and the line of sylph that had formed around Sam, Stef, and Whit. I wrapped myself around my flute case as I rolled across rocks and dead grass. Sylph swarmed to surround me, and three pair of hands dragged me to my feet.

I didn't have time to thank them. I shucked off my backpack and pushed through the sylph.

"Stop!" I craned my neck as the trio of dragons pulled back as though to spit acid. "If you hurt them, I won't play for you anymore."

The dragons huffed, and an acrid stink washed over the ledge. They were standing in the forest below, heads held high enough to peer at us.

<The one with the song. He's here.>

<I see it.>

<She tricked us.>

<Kill her.>

"Ana—"

I glanced over my shoulder at Sam and held out a hand for

him to stay where he was behind the sylph. "Just stay," I said.

<She commands the one with the song.> The dragons' words came like smoke around the edges of my consciousness. Fragments I was only peripherally aware of.

I hardly recognized my own wind-torn voice anymore as I faced the dragons. "And maybe you don't care whether I play for you ever again. *I* don't care if I ever play for you again, honestly. But know this: if you hurt them, I will hunt you."

<Lies.>

"Not lies. I told you that Janan had warriors who hunted and captured a phoenix. Those warriors became sylph. They are with me now, my army and my armor, and I'm *sure* they remember how to capture something that doesn't want to be captured. If you hurt my friends, we will come for you and every other dragon in existence."

<The phoenix song. The one with the song.>

<We must destroy it.>

<She knows the one with the song. She will use the song against us.>

<If she wanted to, she would have.>

<Kill her to be safe.>

<She will use the song if we try. The one with the song will do it. See how he hovers.>

<But she wants the temple destroyed.>

The dragons' ringing intensified, filling my head like a

234

swarm of bees. I staggered and caught myself on a boulder, raw hands scraping on stone. Voices called my name and sylph closed around me, but I pulled myself up and glared at the dragons and summoned what was left of my voice.

"I. Will not. Give up."

Acid Breath blew a long stream of rancid air over the ledge, rustling trees and making sylph moan. Blue targeting lights flared, but I held up a hand again.

"Don't." I couldn't look behind me—I didn't have the energy—but the lights turned off. I focused on the dragons again. "Do you understand me?"

Acid Breath glanced beyond me as more heat pressed around. The sylph I'd left at the wall had arrived. Just a dozen sylph had fought them off before. Twice that number . . .

They weren't afraid of the sylph, though. They were afraid of something else. The phoenix song. The one with the song.

<Your friends will not be harmed.>

I nodded, carefully, so my thoughts wouldn't swim. "And will you destroy the tower on Soul Night? The spring equinox? Will you use your weapon?"

<We will decide. *You* have the one with the song. You refuse to let us destroy it, yet you ask us to destroy it. We will decide.>

Before I could respond, Acid Breath and the others pushed off the earth and into the sky. Trees cracked and fell under their power, and the cliff shuddered. Dragon thunder ripped, and I watched their receding forms as exhaustion and darkness overtook me.

But this time when I fell, there were hands to catch me.

20

CONNECTION

CONSCIOUSNESS RETURNED IN sharp fragments, like shards of glass and light. Warm water on my face and neck. Sips of thin soup. The scent of ozone. Voices that seemed as though they came from the other end of the earth.

A dark figure with his knees to his chest, face buried in his arms, shoulders hunched and heaving.

When awareness settled and stayed, I found myself wrapped inside my sleeping bag, wearing clean clothes and listening to a piano in one ear. My SED lay just outside my bedding, the wire of one earpiece twisting its way to me. The second earpiece played music at nothing.

"It's crooked." My voice rasped as though I'd been

screaming. Maybe it was just waking-up raspiness. "The music. It's crooked."

A quiet din I hadn't been aware of until now suddenly stopped, and someone gave a long, relieved sigh. Sam. "You did that. You said one earpiece was for you, one was for us, and when I suggested using the SED speakers for everyone, you said you didn't have time to argue."

"Oh." That did sound like me, but I didn't remember the discussion. I pulled the earpiece out, silencing the piano sonata, and pushed myself onto my elbow. My whole body was stiff and aching.

Whit and Stef were sitting on their sleeping bags, paused from tapping at their SEDs while they looked at me. A pot of soup sat near the open tent flap, steaming with a sylph coiled around it. Slanted light fell through the opening, making the gloom of the rest of the tent darker and deeper.

"Look who's finally awake," Whit said. "When I said you should get some rest, I didn't mean this much."

I made a face that might have been a smile.

Sam sat just beyond my SED, in the dark, so close I hadn't yet focused my eyes the right way to see him. But now I noted the folded paper in his hands, the slumped posture, the way he'd been right beside me when I awakened.

I sat up the rest of the way, ignoring the twinges of pain in my back and shoulders. "Sam." His name came out in a breath, sorrow and hope and longing all tangled up in three letters.

"Hey." His voice was soft, rough, and for a moment we looked at each other and there was nothing else in the world.

Light rippled in the corner of my eye as the others got up and left the tent. Even the sylph vanished, leaving Sam and me alone.

He swallowed hard and leaned toward me. "Ana, I'm so sorry. I don't know what else to say."

I rubbed sleep from my eyes and shimmied out of my sleeping bag. "Maybe start by telling me how long I was"— not unconscious, even if that was the truth—"asleep."

"Three days."

Three days. Time we didn't have to waste.

I pushed hair off my face, shifting questions in my mind. Who'd washed and dressed me? Were we still at the same camp? I couldn't tell without peeking outside, and the light hurt my eyes. "Have the dragons returned?"

What had they said? The one with the song? The phoenix song.

Sam shuddered. "No. They haven't come back."

"Okay." I didn't know where to go from there. I'd done the impossible. I'd spoken with dragons. I'd survived. I'd kept the dragons from attacking my friends because I was a very frightening tiny person with little regard for her own life.

A high, hysterical giggle slipped out. My voice sounded thin and weak in the shadows of the tent, but I couldn't stop it. After everything, I could do nothing but laugh to release the knot of tension in my chest.

Sam just watched me until the fit wore off. "Are you hungry?"

"Yes." My stomach felt hollow as I sat back, shoving hair away from my face again. I had vague memories of sipping thin broth, but before that, there'd just been the pigeon the sylph had cooked for me, and hours and hours of being awake and walking through the woods. "Oh yes."

He nodded and hurried to the pot of soup. "We haven't moved camp. We didn't want to disturb you." He returned and handed me a bowl with mostly broth, but a few chunks of some unfortunate forest creature, as well as what passed for vegetables when trapped in a winter forest.

I thanked him and sipped slowly, letting my stomach get used to the sensation of food again. It was bland, but filling, and too soon the bowl was empty. I set it aside; I'd get more, once I was confident I'd be able to hold this much.

"So, the note you left." He turned over the folded paper in his hands, and when he angled his head, I could see the worry line carved between his eyes, and the shadows beneath. Stubble darkened his chin and cheeks. "I read it."

Frantically, I tried to remember what I'd said. It seemed

240

I'd written that note a hundred years ago. So much had happened since.

"Is that how you feel? Selfish to have asked us to come? Like we don't believe in you?"

I should never have written that note.

"My feelings for you haven't changed. Did you think they had?" He stretched his hands toward me, but stopped halfway, as though he wasn't sure whether we were allowed to touch anymore. "Ana?"

No. Yes. "What did you expect me to think?"

He pressed his hands to his knees, and his gaze followed. "Ana," he said again, like a prayer. "Just because you want friends with you doesn't make you selfish. It makes you human. And even when we think something's an unwise idea, that doesn't mean we've stopped believing in you. I will *never* stop believing in you. What I said about believing you can do anything, be anything—I still think that. I still admire that you don't let others' limitations stop you. I love that about you. I love you."

Tears blurred my vision, catching on my lashes when I tried to blink them away.

Sam pushed himself forward, cupping my cheeks in his hands. Gently, he swept away my tears with his thumbs, and the way he looked at me was so sad and hopeful and intense, my heart ached with the desire just to be close to him. His

241

voice was husky when he spoke again. "I'm sorry that I made you feel like you needed to go the rest of the way alone."

All I could feel were his hands on my face, strong and warm and calloused from music.

Before Sam, I'd feared touch. My mother had only hit me, but Sam had shown me affection and comfort and pleasure. I *wanted* him to touch me. I'd grown to crave it, the way he held my hand or tucked a strand of hair behind my ear. The way he'd made me feel safe and connected, simply because he was close to me.

And these last weeks without—they'd felt like being locked away by myself. Alone.

"I was already alone, Sam."

He dropped his hands to his lap.

"Not physically. But for weeks everything inside of me was slowly unraveling, and not all of it was because of where we were going, what we've learned, and who we've lost. Some of me was unraveling because of you. Even though you were angry with me, and hurting just as much, I still wanted you."

His throat worked as he seemed to realize how far we'd pulled away from each other, and how we'd both been doing the pulling. "I wanted you, too." He drew a shuddering breath. "But every time I looked at you, I thought about what I did. What we all did. I thought about how it might have been your life exchanged for mine, and I couldn't bear it."

It almost had been my life.

"Is there a way to fix this?" he asked.

I lifted my eyes to his, meeting darkness and anguish. "Do you love me?"

He spoke without hesitation, without the usual line of thought between his eyes. "Infinitely."

"Then we can fix this."

"That's good." He closed his eyes, letting out a long breath. "That's really good."

I wanted to move closer to him, or for him to move closer to me, but it all seemed like moving too fast. I didn't want to risk breaking this tenuous truce. "There's something I need to tell you."

The one with the song.

He caught the shift in my tone, that we weren't talking about our relationship now, but something far bigger.

Though our relationship felt very big to me.

"The dragons." I hated talking to him about dragons. "I spoke to them."

"I saw." He was somewhen else for a moment. "I saw you on the wall. When I woke and found your note"—he tensed all over—"I saw that your things were gone, too. Your flute. Your SED. Your sleeping bag. Everything. I thought you weren't coming back."

"You were supposed to go home."

He snorted and shook his head. "No, I would never leave you. No matter how afraid I am of dragons, losing you scares me more." He shifted closer to me, just a little. Enough that our knees touched. "I woke the others and called out for you, hoping you hadn't gone far. Hoping you would hear."

"I left just after midnight. By the time the sun rose, I was already on top of the wall. I wouldn't have heard you calling in the forest." Maybe when he'd been on the cliff, though. I'd heard something I thought was forest animals, but now that I thought of it, the noises could have been voices.

Sam slid one hand forward and touched my ankle, all caution in his movements. "When we finally read your note again, it was obvious you meant to find the dragons, but not where you were going. So we kept searching and found the cliff, and when we looked north, we saw the dragon perched on the wall. And you were lying in front of it, sylph all around you."

His voice had deepened, heavy with the things he wasn't saying. I finished his thought. "You feared it had killed me."

"Yes." His voice was wretched. "Yes, I was certain. You were lying across your backpack. You looked broken. You weren't moving. I couldn't imagine how you were still alive."

I rubbed my head, still sensitive after the falls and the shriek of dragons' voices. If not for the sylph, I would have been dead.

"But then you got up, and I couldn't understand what you were saying, but I could hear your voice. I wanted to fly across the valley to you, even if it meant I had to face the dragon, too." He took a long breath. "Then you started playing your flute, and the sylph were singing with you. The sylph you'd left with us started singing, too. It was amazing. *You* were amazing."

I ducked my face to hide my blush.

"What happened to you on that wall?"

I took a long breath. "This is probably something everyone needs to hear, but I think I know what the dragons' weapon is. And why dragons always attack you."

His expression darkened. "Why?"

Haltingly, I rested my fingertips on his knuckles. His hand was still on my ankle, just barely. "Because they don't have the weapon. I mistranslated those lines in the book. You *are* the weapon."

I didn't feel well enough to explain everything twice, so Sam went to fetch the others. I ate another bowl of soup, a little more confident in my ability to keep it down. My muscles and bones still ached whenever I moved, but the movement *did* help.

While I ate and stretched, sylph came in, warming the air that had cooled in their absence. Cris trilled comfortingly as he dropped into the natural shadows with the other sylph, and I managed a smile.

"Did it hurt you?" I asked. "Absorbing the acid to protect me?"

Cris rippled, like a shrug. -Our powers seem limitless at first. We can absorb tremendous amounts of energy. But yes, like Menehem's poison hurt the others, the acid hurt. The pain fades and we recover, but too much at once might do irreparable damage.-

I lowered my eyes. "I'll try not to rush into danger from now on."

He trilled, a laugh. -Sure.-

"I mean it."

-We are your army. We'll protect you, no matter the pain or cost. That is all you need to concern yourself with.-

He meant it, too. They would do anything for me. I wasn't sure I liked the burden of their commitment and confidence. They believed I could help redeem them, but what if I couldn't? The thought of disappointing them was unbearable.

When Sam returned with Stef and Whit, they each gave me a long, appraising look and didn't comment when Sam sat near me. Not next to me. Not touching, as he had been. But near. It was enough for now.

"I'm glad you're back, Ana." Whit flashed a smile. "And unhurt."

"Me too." Stef glanced at Sam, then back to me. "I hear you have quite the story to tell."

Their attention was unnerving. We'd hardly spoken for weeks, even about Armande's death, and now everyone was watching me. Waiting. I wanted to look away while I told them about my trip to the prison wall, but I made sure to hold their gazes as I spoke of the climb, playing my minuet to lure the dragons, and the way the sylph had fought for me. I refused to look weak, or like I doubted my actions.

I'd spoken with dragons.

Maybe I *could* do anything.

Still, the story sounded crazy when I tried explaining the buzzing in my head, the way the sylph had been able to protect me from the volleys of acid, and the urge to jump onto the dragon's leg while it flew across the valley. "You saw the rest." I stopped there, not wanting to talk about how I must have looked, yelling and threatening the dragons. "Sam said they haven't been back at all. Not even to hunt?"

Stef shook her head. "A couple of sylph have been watching the valley just to be sure, but it looks like the dragons aren't coming back."

So the dragons had made a decision: no, they wouldn't help.

I eyed the tent flap, still open and letting in afternoon light. I could just see the edges of our lanterns and solar battery chargers, soaking in the light while it was available. Though we were only a few weeks from the spring equinox— Soul Night—winter kept a tight grip on the land. "I guess it's not like we expected dragons to agree to anything, anyway." The admission crushed my pride a little.

"They agreed not to attack us after you threatened them." Stef gave me a pointed look. "That's pretty impressive."

Whit looked up from writing down the last of my story. "Tell us more about the ringing. You said it grew so loud it knocked you out. I thought I heard something like that too."

I rubbed my ears and nodded. "I wasn't sure what it was at first, but it must have come from the dragons. They think at one another to communicate, and I was unlucky enough to start picking up on it. It got easier to understand them, like I just needed to practice, but . . ."

Sam leaned toward me and curled his hand over my knee. "They understood our language, it sounds like."

I hmmed. He was right. Centaurs hadn't understood us, and their upper halves were human. So why dragons? "Perhaps because their language is thought? Perhaps if I'd focused my thoughts as though I were *about* to speak, or speaking in my mind and not out loud, they would have understood it the same way, and what I say out loud is inconsequential."

Whit nodded and wrote more into his notebook. "That seems reasonable. When we speak aloud, we're organizing our thoughts and sharing them. Dragons may simply pick up on something we're doing unconsciously."

That made sense. "I think there's another level of their language, like we pick up on body movements and facial expressions as a sort of shorthand for what someone truly means." Having been raised with only Li as an example of this, I wasn't very good at picking up the subtler signals people gave, but at least I knew now what I was missing and could *try* to keep up. "But theirs also stands in for words they drop. I think."

"That's very interesting." Whit logged all of that as well. "I think we've learned more about dragons in the last twenty minutes than we did in the last twenty quindecs. All we needed was Ana to decide she can talk to anything."

"Apparently, I'm willing to try." I twisted my mouth into something like a smile.

"What made you decide to lure them with music?" Sam kept his voice low, like the question was only for the two of us, but the others looked interested, too.

"I'm not sure." I bit my lip. "It was the loudest sound I could make, but also, everything loves music. Humans, sylph, even the centaurs when I played Phoenix Symphony that night. One of the boys touched my SED and looked—I don't know—happy. Like he understood it." Sometimes I felt like everything understood music, or wanted to.

A smile twitched at the corner of Sam's mouth. "I miss playing music."

"You can borrow my flute."

"Ana," Stef said, "you told Sam you know why the dragons attack him?"

The one with the song.

"I *think* I know."

Sam paled, and I couldn't imagine what was going through his head.

"When they asked me to play for them again, they had another conversation among themselves. One was worried I had 'the song.' Another said he couldn't see it in me." I shook my head, trying to recall exactly how the dragons had worded it, but my headache had been so powerful. The way my ears rang had made it hard to focus. "They were testing me. And then when they noticed you all on the cliff, one said, 'The one with the song,' and they all got worried. They could see it in *you*. They tried to lie to me then, saying they were getting rid of my distraction so I would play for them more, but—"

"But they came to kill me." Sam's voice was low and terribly even. "I'm the one with the song."

I nodded.

"I thought they liked music." Whit studied him. "Why kill Sam if they like music?"

"Because of what song he has. The song is the weapon. I mistranslated the symbols from the books. I thought it was a weapon they possessed, but it's not. It's a weapon they're terribly afraid of."

Whit snorted. "And that's Sam."

We all looked at Sam, who sat hugging his knees and biting his lip. Stubble darkened his chin, and black hair breezed above his eyes. "I don't feel like a weapon," he said after a minute.

"You don't look like one either," Whit replied.

I rubbed my temples, trying to piece together all their clues. "The weapon is the phoenix song. They were afraid Sam would use it against them."

"What's the phoenix song?" Whit looked at Sam, who shook his head and seemed lost.

"The only music I have involving phoenixes is Phoenix Symphony, but I wrote that long after dragons started making my death their priority." Sam shoved his fingers through his hair. "Unless dragons can see possibilities of the future like phoenixes, I don't think that's the phoenix song they're worried about."

"They're convinced the phoenix song can destroy them," I said. "One at a time. All at once. I don't know. It seems to me they should be more concerned about actual phoenixes coming around and singing at them." But real phoenixes didn't kill, so maybe they weren't a danger after all. "Phoenixes don't exactly travel far from their jungles, though, do they?"

One of the sylph shook its head. Cris. -The last time phoenixes emerged from their jungle was to curse the sylph.-

"Five thousand years ago," Stef muttered. "So it's not Phoenix Symphony, and they're not worried about actual phoenixes. Because actual phoenixes aren't a danger. But anyone else who knows the song is in trouble."

"And that's me," Sam said.

I touched his hand. "That doesn't seem fair." Not that the dragons appeared to care much about fair anyway.

Something else the dragons had said, though, about my asking them not to destroy Sam, but also asking them to do it . . .

The thought flew away.

"I wish I could say it makes me feel better to know I have the power to destroy dragons." Sam grabbed his water bottle and turned it in his hands. "I'd feel better if I had any idea what this phoenix song actually is and how to use it."

"Would you use it?" I asked. It was strange, imagining Sam going out and singing at dragons until they were no more. The Sam I knew wasn't that callous. He'd applauded my compassion when I couldn't kill Deborl—though I had no doubt he would have shot Deborl if he'd been given the chance. Not after seeing him the night of the earthquake, when Mat had attacked us in the washroom. Sam had killed him and others. There was a darker side to Sam than the one I knew. There were thousands of years to Sam. I'd never know all of him. But he wasn't a murderer.

"I don't know," he said at last.

"Well, I hate to be the one to bring it up." Stef's expression was hard. "But in spite of Ana's success in speaking to the dragons, I don't think they're going to help us."

"Me neither," I said.

"What's our next step?"

No one looked at me.

I looked at my hands.

Very slowly, Sam said, "What if we did know the phoenix song?"

The tent went quiet.

"Rather, what if"—Sam set his water bottle on the ground in front of him—"we let the dragons believe we know it in order to persuade them to help us with Ana's original plan: use the poison, get the dragons to destroy the temple, and hopefully keep Janan from ever having a chance to ascend."

I didn't like that *hopefully* in there. It still sounded so unlikely, though it wasn't as if anyone else had other suggestions. And now Sam was thinking up ways to make my idea happen again.

I wasn't sure how I felt about that. Relieved, because he believed in me? Horrified, because he'd risk his life pretending he knew something he didn't? What if Acid Breath called his bluff?

"No," I whispered.

Everyone looked at me.

"For one, we'd have to go after the dragons. They haven't returned here. They can make the trip much more quickly than we can. We won't have time to get back to Menehem's lab and the poison if we have to go searching for dragons, too. Already, we'll have to hike extra hours to get there in time.

"The second thing is, even if we do go after them, who's to say the wrong dragons won't find us and kill us on sight? The sylph can protect us, but not forever. We'll have to keep moving and keep looking for Acid Breath and his friends.

"And the third thing is that Sam is not consciously aware of the phoenix song, so it's useless. I don't want to make threats with a weapon we don't know how to use. They believed me when I threatened them the other day, and they left. That will have to be enough. I won't risk it again." I dropped my voice. "I won't risk you all again."

The tent was silent for a minute, and Sam just looked at me, something indecipherable in his expression. "Then what do we do?"

"We came here looking for both help and a weapon. We're not getting help. The dragons have made that very clear. But we did learn that the weapon we've been seeking has been with us all along. Sam might not know it right now, but maybe we can find a way to use it against Janan."

"Which was what you originally wanted to do," Sam said. "Use the weapon to fight Janan."

I nodded. "We go back to Menehem's lab, gather the poison, and return to Heart. Sarit can help us get inside." If she was still alive. "We destroy the cage Deborl is building, and anything else that looks important to Janan's ascension. We do whatever we must to wreck things. On the way, we learn as much about the phoenix song as possible and hope we can actually use it."

Sam folded his hands. "All right. Then we head back tomorrow. Unless there are any other ideas?"

Stef and Whit glanced at each other but shook their heads.

In the morning, we packed our things and began the long journey back to Range.

21
NIGHTS

WE WEREN'T GOING to make it back to Heart in time.

A snowstorm smothered the world with white powder and wind, and though we trudged through it whenever possible, we had only twelve days before Soul Night. We'd have to hike extra, but even that wouldn't be enough.

Twelve days.

It was well after dark when we stopped to set up camp. "I wish I'd been able to test the temple key on the prison." I grabbed my food sack as sylph darted into the woods to hunt.

Whit looked suspicious as he and Stef put the tent together by lantern light. "Why?"

Stef let out a breathy chuckle. "Scientific curiosity. She gets it from Menehem."

"I like to think I get it from being me." I put no bite into my words, but I met her eyes. She needed to know I was serious. "Curiosity is just part of who I am. Like music."

"All right." She flashed a smile, but it was awkward and vanished quickly. Our relationship hadn't recovered, not wholly. They talked to me now, and every night Sam moved his sleeping bag closer to mine, but even the most minor disagreement strained conversations.

"I just wonder about things. The other towers have all fallen into ruin without anyone living inside them. Janan is the only thing keeping the one in Heart intact. But it seems like if phoenixes made the towers, they should last forever, right?"

Stef shrugged. "Perhaps they would have stayed forever, had the sylph not been released." She bent and tied the last of the walls to the tent. "Better go pick up our dinner. I'll be ready to cook soon."

At her dismissal, I hunched my shoulders and followed Cris into the forest, the beam of my flashlight illuminating the snowy world. By now, the other sylph had probably caught plenty of food, so I put in my SED earpieces and flipped to Phoenix Symphony.

I'd listened to the entire symphony a dozen times over the last week, and discussed it with Sam, but so far we'd heard nothing unusual in the music. The four of us even retranslated the passage I'd found about the weapon, but while that was interesting, it was not particularly descriptive of the weapon's nature or purpose.

Our latest translation was *Dragons fear the instrument of life and death*. Or the *song of the phoenix*.

I grabbed a burned rabbit and dropped it in my bag, humming the flutes' melody of the symphony's fourth movement. It was a faster-paced, majestic-sounding movement, one of my favorite parts, which always made my heart swell up with fierce joy.

A hand closed over my shoulder. I jumped and spun to find Sam watching me with an amused smile. A lantern swung by his side. "Are you honestly not tired of that yet?"

I shrugged and pulled out my earpieces. "I don't anticipate ever being tired of it, but if that happens, I'll let you know."

"I do have other pieces. Some better than that one."

"This is the first piece of your music I ever heard. It will always be my favorite." I paused by a fallen tree, whose death had given way to new life. Smaller plants huddled in the ground, waiting for springtime. "Besides, if there's a clue about the phoenix song, surely it's in the song you named after them."

"Songs have words," he said for the thousandth time as he placed his lantern on the ground. Shadows jumped up around his face as he looked at me askance, a weird little smile tugging at his mouth. "You say that just because it bugs me, don't you?"

I grinned and admitted nothing. "Then what about bird-song? Or songbirds? Are they singing words?"

"Who knows? Maybe birds have a language, too, like centaurs." He said it teasingly, but when I straightened and our eyes met, challenge snapped between us.

"Could it be something small?" I rested the sack on the ground and tried to shape my thoughts into words. "We were thinking it might be a whole song. The whole symphony. A whole sonata. But what if it's something small, something so tiny you don't even realize it's there?"

"Because birdsong is usually short, or a repeated series of notes."

"And phoenixes are birds."

Sam seized my upper arms, pulled me close, and kissed me so hard I'd have fallen over if he hadn't been holding me up. I gasped and shifted my weight closer to him, but just as I started to kiss him back, my SED chimed with a call.

We pulled apart as I fumbled for my SED, both of us eyeing each other like we weren't sure kissing was okay again. We hadn't yet, not since my birthday, like we were both waiting for the other to make the first move.

Now he had.

My SED chimed again. I answered, breathless. "Sarit?"

"Oh finally." Relief filled her tone. "You're there."

I checked the signal strength. "Barely," I said, handing one earpiece to Sam so he could listen, too. "I didn't think we were yet. Are you okay? What's going on?" It was later than she usually called. Much later.

"Yeah, I'm fine now. There was just—" She hesitated. "You aren't going to believe this."

I met Sam's eyes, dropped my gaze to his lips. He was standing so close still, so that we could both talk to Sarit. "I'll believe anything right now," I whispered.

"Three dragons just flew over Heart."

"Just now?" Sam looked up, like he'd be able to see them from where we stood.

"Is that Sam?" Hope tinged Sarit's voice. "I guess you're talking again. That's good. Yes, just now. They circled the temple and then flew north again."

"They didn't attack?" I could hardly believe what she was saying.

"They didn't. They were in and out so quickly there was no time to send up the air drones." She sounded like she couldn't believe it, either. "Have you seen any dragons?"

I made something between a squeak and a hysterical laugh.

"Ana has." Sam's voice was low and serious. "But it's more than we can explain right now. We might be on the verge of a discovery. We'll let you know if it comes to anything."

"We're on our way back to Menehem's lab," I added. "Then back to Heart, so we'll need to start thinking about ways to get into the city without Deborl noticing." We'd have to run to get there. I didn't see how we could make it, but we'd keep trying. We all agreed on that.

"Oh, guys. Deborl is worse than ever. People are being interrogated about where you are. No one knows, of course, but that doesn't stop Deborl from asking. His people have wholly taken over the guard. Everyone is recruited for it. If they don't help with his cage, they're in the guard now. He keeps talking about his friend Merton, too, and where they all went. I don't know what Deborl sent Merton after, but I guess it wasn't you. Whatever it is, Deborl makes it sound like it's even *more* important than you."

"I wish we knew what he's after. What else is going on?" The Heart I knew seemed so long ago.

"The cage is almost complete. The bars are electrified, and the whole thing is set off the ground. I'll send a picture." She paused to take a breath, and my SED beeped as the image arrived. "There have been earthquakes every day. Animals are leaving the forest around Heart, and Midrange Lake is nearly dry. It's falling apart. All of it."

I closed my eyes against the dark woods, my sylph all around. It seemed wrong to stand in such peace while everything at home was in ruins.

"The obelisks in Templedark Memorial have collapsed. Deborl says it's a sign that Janan is punishing us." She choked on a sob. "I wish you were here. I miss you. And I miss Armande. I'm going crazy by myself."

"I'm sorry, Sarit." Sam spoke with her a moment more,

calming her. Then he said, "We'll be home soon," and clicked off.

I picked up the sack of dinner. "The others will be wondering where we are."

He seemed reluctant to move away from me, but he nodded. "You're right, and Stef gets cranky when she's hungry. I'll help you with the rest."

We worked together without speaking, but I watched him from the corner of my eye. When he caught me, he offered a shy, hopeful smile. Relief warmed through me.

"Birdsong, hmm?" He shoved a strand of hair off his face, tucked it into his hood. "That gives us a lot to think about."

"We'll have to listen to all of your music to figure out if there's anything you do over and over."

"Like what?"

"Like rhythms or harmonies that appear in your music a lot." I shook my head. "Or something else, even. I suppose you'd have noticed already if you used the same theme in multiple pieces."

He frowned. "I like to think I would have."

"Maybe it's something in your preferred instruments. Or even just the way you play music, and nothing to do with what you've composed."

"This could take years."

Which we didn't have. "But if dragons are afraid of it, it's worth understanding."

Sam nodded and lifted the bag. "We're finished here."

It was almost midnight by the time we ducked inside the tent. Stef had water boiling, and Whit was paging through the temple books and my notes translating different sections.

"Took you long enough," Stef muttered.

"Sarit called." Sam crouched next to her, and while they skinned the rabbits, he told her about the conversation with Sarit.

"Ana." Whit looked up from his reading. "Come here a moment."

I collapsed next to Whit and the lantern, all my muscles aching. He flipped pages, back to the beginning of a notebook.

"I've been thinking about Menehem's research and your follow-up notes." He placed the notebook in front of me and took out one of Menehem's diaries. "I see here you were concerned about both the size and the delivery of the dose of poison to use against Janan." He pointed at one of my notes. "So I went to see what Menehem had done during Templedark."

"He had six of these big canisters of aerosol. We have at least twenty, and the machine has been on since we left, making more. We could have twenty-five."

"You said the sylph gained tolerance exponentially,

so considering the size of the Templedark dose, we might have enough to affect Janan for a little while. Ten minutes? Twenty?"

I didn't argue with his optimism.

"But in these notes, you're also concerned about the delivery. If I'm reading right, Menehem had his canisters set up on a timer. They were positioned around the temple, and when he was ready, he remotely opened the canisters in order to prolong the exposure. To help compensate for the tolerance, he did one, then two, then the final three."

"That's right."

"I think you were right to worry about an effective delivery. Will we be able to do anything like Menehem? We have twenty canisters. How can we release the poison so it has an immediate effect?"

"All at once."

"But then," Stef said, looking over as she finished dropping meat into the pot of water, "the effect wouldn't last. We'd get maybe a couple of minutes."

I shook my head. "We don't have enough to make it last. That's what we've been talking about. There's simply not enough."

As he finished washing his hands, Sam looked down and didn't say anything. He'd been the one to turn on the machine, hoping it would help.

"It's like a knife." My words drew Sam's gaze again. "It

may not be enough to destroy Janan, but if we time the poison to release at the right moment, it might hurt him. It might be just enough to give us time."

"To do what?" Stef's voice deepened and she crossed her arms, but it was because of fear, not anger. Soul Night was so close, and people we loved were dying. Forever. She was as afraid as I was. "If the temple is dark when Soul Night begins, is that it for Janan? Will he just go away then?"

That seemed unlikely. But would he be able to ascend? Maybe not. That might simply delay him, or everything might go back to how it was before. Newsouls included.

No, I had to find a permanent solution.

"There is one thing we can do that Menehem couldn't." I stood and fumbled through Sam's coat pockets until the corners of a box bumped my fingers.

"It's true," Sam muttered. "I'd never allow Menehem to poke around my clothes. What are you looking for?"

"This." I unzipped an interior pocket and removed the temple key. "Both times Menehem poisoned Janan, he did it from outside the temple. But *we* can release the poison inside."

"Will that make a difference?" Whit lifted his eyebrows.

"Maybe it will buy us one or two minutes more than if we used it outside." I started to put the key back into Sam's coat, but he caught my wrist and pressed the box against my chest.

"You keep it. I meant to give it back to you, anyway."

With a somber nod, I stashed the key inside my coat.

"If we use it inside the temple," Sam asked, "will we be able to get out?"

I dropped my voice. "I don't know." Again, I wished we'd had time to test the key on the tower in the north. Would the temple still respond to the key if Janan were unconscious?

Sam touched my hand. Snow began to fall, tapping the tent in a soft rhythm until all outside sound was smothered. "We did have a small breakthrough about the phoenix song," he told the others.

"Maybe." I didn't want to get their hopes up in case we were wrong. "We still need more information. I keep hoping the books will help." I glanced at the pile, but sleepiness tugged at the back of my thoughts. The books hadn't provided any new information during the time we'd been snowbound, and it was unlikely we'd find anything else before Soul Night.

While we ate, Sam repeated our conversation about bird-song and our guesses about the nature of the phoenix song.

"What's the next step?" Whit asked.

"I'm going to listen to as much of Sam's music as possible," I said.

"Oh *no.*" Whit clutched his chest. "How will you manage?"

I grinned. "I know, but to save the world, I'll do it. I'm also going to look at the scores on my SED if I can figure out how to do that and walk at the same time. I want to make note about any trends in style or instrumentation. All trends, really."

"So you'll need a volunteer to carry you back to Range, hmm?" Whit glanced at Sam. "You're looking a little scrawny lately. I'll carry Ana."

Sam snorted. "If anyone's carrying Ana—"

"I'm walking." I rolled my eyes. "I'll manage just fine. Thank you."

"I'm not burdened with youthful pride." Stef leaned back on her sleeping bag. "Feel free to carry me."

Whit chuckled and winked at me. "No, Stef, you may not have youthful pride anymore, but you certainly have every other kind of pride there is."

She threw a mitten at his head and for a few minutes, smiles and laughter filled our tent.

When the lanterns dimmed and Stef and Whit climbed into their sleeping bags, Sam crouched beside me.

"Ana, I was hoping . . ."

I bit my lip and nodded. "I was hoping, too."

The tension in his shoulders melted like ice in spring, and he arranged our sleeping bags so they were on top of each other, an extra layer of softness underneath as we both shimmied into the top one. I pressed my back against his chest.

"Are you comfortable?" His body curled around mine, solid and warm, and our legs tangled together. Our fingers knotted, his hand over both of mine.

"Yes." I closed my eyes and listened to the rhythm of his heartbeat, the way he tried not to breathe too hard, like breathing might ruin the moment. "Sam."

He kissed the back of my head.

"Sam." I wanted to turn around and press my body against his. I wanted to feel his skin beneath his clothes and push my fingers through his hair. I wanted things I could only imagine. But not unless we were alone. "I'm sorry about these last weeks. About the secrets I kept. About my wild ideas. I never wanted to hurt you."

"I know." He squeezed my hands, and our knuckles dug against my chest. "I didn't mean to hurt you, either. I got so lost in my own guilt and misery that I forgot what's most important."

"What's that?"

"Living. Loving. Making the most of our time together, no matter how short or long it will be."

I tugged my hands from his and pressed his palm flat against my heartbeat. After he'd saved me from Rangedge Lake, I'd awakened to find him like this, holding me close, warming me, though he didn't know who I was. *What* I was.

Now I traced the back of his splayed-out hand, feeling bones and knuckles and muscle, and when I released his hand, he didn't ask if I was sure. We both knew I was, or I wouldn't have invited him. He lingered over my heart a moment longer, breathing hard into my hair, and then slid his hand over the curves of my body, awakening in me a deep and wonderful ache.

Heavy layers of cloth muffled our breathing, his whispered love. We were cautious and quiet, but fires ignited within me and I'd never wished so hard that we were alone. I wanted to turn over and map out the lines of muscle on his body, too, but if I did, I never think about sleep again. And Sam seemed content—more than content—drawing patterns on my stomach, smoothing his palm over the slope of my hip, and turning my body into liquid. I'd never wanted anything so much as I wanted him to keep touching me.

When his movements shifted from sensual to sweet, and his breath turned soft and even behind me, warm on the back of my neck, I finally began to drift. Though I wasn't nearly ready to stop, sleep dragged at me, and this wasn't our only night. There were still a few more nights to fall asleep with his hands on my bare skin.

Halfway into a dream of sitting at the piano with Sam, thunder snapped me awake.

And a shrill ringing surged through my head.

22
FLIGHT

"DRAGONS!"

I struggled around Sam's arms and legs, shouting. He jerked awake, and on the other side of the tent, Stef and Whit were already out of their sleeping bags and lighting lanterns and finding pistols. Sylph poured from the tent, shrieking.

"Where are they?" Stef turned on her pistol, and the blue targeting beam shone across the tent. Lantern light caught her face, darkening the shadows around her eyes.

"I don't know." I tried to straighten my clothes as I stood. "I hear the sound. The ringing."

Wing thunder clapped again, and we all followed the sylph outside. Snowy rocks stung my bare feet, and the surrounding woods were black with shadows, both real and sylph. The sound of their moaning rose higher.

Above, dark shapes flew across the midnight sky. They circled us, as though looking for a place to land.

How had they *found* us?

"I have an idea." I dashed into the tent again and pulled my flute from its case. Sam grabbed me when I emerged again.

"What are you doing?"

"*You* are doing it." I pushed my flute into his hands. "They're afraid of you."

"Are you sure it's wise to threaten them like this?" he asked.

"They're armed. Now we are, too."

Trees snapped like twigs as dragons batted them aside. Rushing and cracking and chaos sounded. Birds squawked and flew away, calling out warnings. Animals in the forest skittered as trees fell and immense wings shadowed the earth.

I found one of the lanterns and turned the light as high as it would go.

<The one with the song is here.>

<They need us. They will not use the song against us.>

Sam, Stef, and Whit all screamed and clutched their heads against the ringing, but while it made my head throb, I kept on my feet. Maybe I was growing used to it.

Three dragons landed in front of us, wings tucked alongside them, blue eyes luminous. Immense talons dug gouges in the frozen earth. Snow dusted their scales. Their huge fangs shone in the lantern light.

I stepped forward, no coat and no boots, but sylph fanned around me like wings. "What do you want?"

<We have decided.>

They'd actually been considering helping? Huh. "And?" It took all my will, but I resisted the urge to look over my shoulder and check on my friends. Hearing the dragons speak for the first time was a painful experience.

<We have looked at your city. The tower shines even in daylight now. The evil inside grows stronger. Your people are enslaved to their own kind.>

I didn't move. Hardly breathed.

<The earth cracks itself apart. The steam vents have blown open wide enough for a dragon to nest inside. Your lake is gone. Only death lingers there now.>

Acid Breath's voice was huge, booming inside my head. Nodding made the world spin, but I managed to hold myself upright. "Yes." My voice seemed thin and weak, though aside from the sylph's soft moans, my friends' groaning, and the crack and patter of fallen trees settling, my voice was the only sound. "Yes, those things are happening because of what lives inside the temple."

<Many things live inside the temple, but the only one you want to destroy is the one you call Janan.>

"Yes." What else lived inside the temple? There was

nothing. Just endless mazes and horrors—and the skeleton chamber. But the skeletons didn't count as living, did they? "Why do dragons attack the temple?"

<To destroy the one with the song.>

I spun to find Sam clutching my flute to his chest, his eyes round and shadowed in the lantern light. He'd heard. The others—they were both looking up—had heard, too.

"All those attacks," Whit said, "to stop Sam?"

To stop Sam, who'd only just learned he had some kind of weapon, which he didn't even know how to wield.

Fleetingly, I considered telling the dragons he never intended to use the song against them, but they were unlikely to believe me, and if I wanted to keep them a little afraid of us, I needed something besides the sylph.

I focused on the dragons. "If you help us destroy the tower, the cycle of reincarnation will end. You won't have to fear the song anymore. Once Sam grows old and dies, it will be gone forever."

<We do not fear the song.>

I lifted an eyebrow, but one didn't just accuse a dragon of lying.

<If you know your cycle of reincarnation will end, and that the song will end with it, then we will help you destroy the tower.> Acid Breath glared at Sam, who was silent. Not moving. <If you will allow yourself to end, we will help you destroy the tower.>

And we wouldn't have to rely on a weapon we didn't know how to use. We'd just have to rely on *dragons.*

I glanced at Sam. This was his choice.

His voice came low and rough. "Destroy the tower."

<Good.> Acid Breath drew back and up, casting a disinterested glance over our campsite. <Gather your belongings.>

"Why?" I put my fists on my hips and glared up at the dragon, like I wasn't imagining how easily he could swallow me whole. As if the sylph knew my fears, they moved closer.

<Humans walk too slowly. We will take you where you need to go. Then we will return north and rally our army. Your tower will be nothing but rubble.>

Ride the dragons to Menehem's lab? *Ride the dragons?*

I glanced over my shoulder. Sam just stared blankly, while Stef and Whit seemed at a loss for words. Riding the dragons would get us there much more quickly, but then we'd have to trust them not to kill us.

Still, if they wanted to destroy the temple—and therefore the song they feared so much—they needed the poison only we could provide.

But Sam wouldn't be able to do this. There was no way he'd ride a dragon, even if it had good incentive not to drop him onto a mountain. We'd have to run all the way to Range.

"No," I said. "We'll walk."

"No. We'll never make it on our own." Sam strode forward and stopped beside me. His knuckles were white around my flute, but his voice was suddenly strong. "We accept your offer."

Acid Breath took us in for a long moment before nodding. It was a slow, heavy movement that looked foreign on his serpentine body. <Let us outline the terms of our agreement.>

I raised my voice. "Very well: you will not hurt any of my friends. Not now, and not after we destroy the tower. When the tower is destroyed, the cycle of reincarnation will end, and so will the threat of the phoenix song."

<Yes. The same must go for us. We will not harm you— or the one with the song—but you will not use your lights against us. You will not use your shadows against us. You will not use the song against us. If either side breaks these conditions, our agreement is off.>

And we could go back to trying to kill one another like normal. Great.

Acid Breath wasn't finished, though. <None of you will play music. Especially not him.> The dragon tipped his nose at Sam.

I turned toward Sam. "Are you sure about this?"

His expression was hard, his mouth set into a line. Stiffly, he handed my flute to me and said, "We agree to the conditions."

<As do we.> Acid Breath lowered his head again and a low, broken chatter started among the dragons.

<I knew they would.>

<Desperate.>

<Aren't we? Humans with that power, it's too dangerous. They could end us—>

<Hush.>

I pressed my flute to my chest, feeling the keys, the polish, the engravings on the silver, still sharp and new.

"Are we going now?" Whit asked, coming up behind us.

"I think so." Best to get there as quickly as possible and send the dragons on their way. I didn't think any of us would be able to sleep the rest of the night knowing there was a trio of dragons just outside our tent. "Stef, we'll need some kind of harness. We don't want to fall off."

She nodded. "I already have an idea."

Cris hovered around us. -We can't protect you in the air.-

"It's fine." I offered him my hand, and a tendril of shadow circled my fingers. "You can reach the lab quickly, right?"

-Yes.-

"Be there when we arrive. We'll be fine on the dragons. They need us."

-I don't trust them.-

"Me neither." I smiled, though the expression was grim. "But I trust they want the temple destroyed."

-They want the phoenix song destroyed. That just happens to be inside the tower.-

Sam lowered his eyes. "Let's hurry and get this over with."

While Stef worked on harnesses, I helped Whit take down the tent. Sam packed all our bags, constantly shooting worried looks at the dragons. His expression stayed dark, and shadows haunted his eyes.

Though humans had learned to make things fly generations ago—like air drones—most people held a strong belief that humans were born without wings for a reason. None of us were happy about this, but if we could get back to Heart early, that would make this worth it.

"I already rode a dragon over a valley." I tried to smile as I closed my flute case and double-checked the straps. "It will be fine."

"They dragged you through trees." Whit shook his head. "Orrin will never believe we're doing this."

"No one will." I couldn't even imagine Sarit's expression when we told her.

"*I* don't believe we're doing this." Stef held up two rope harnesses. "Now pay attention. All of you." She motioned at the dragons, too.

<What are those?> Acid Breath's words buzzed through my head, making the world spin for a moment. After this, I never wanted to speak to a dragon again.

"I've made two harnesses. They're to hold us secure. They'll go over the dragons' head and settle just above the wings. They shouldn't impede flight at all. There'll be two people to a dragon." She glanced at Sam and me. "I assume you'll want to fly together."

Sam nodded, never looking away from the ropes in Stef's hands.

"All right. There's also a ring here in the front for our backpacks. Since we'll be riding double, I don't want our bags to get in the way. They'll hang like pendants." She looked up at Acid Breath. "I assume you can handle that."

<Of course.>

Stef and Whit began putting the harnesses onto the dragons, their movements stiff and careful. Sylph ducked around them, keeping the air warm, keeping the dragons from moving too suddenly. Several times, Stef tugged on a harness and asked the dragon if it was comfortable or if it hurt, and for a moment it seemed strange that she'd put so much care into the comfort of a *dragon*, but she was right: if the harnesses were awkward to fly with, we were in danger.

When they were done, I told Acid Breath where we needed to go, trying to describe Menehem's lab as it might look from above. "There's a huge metal building, a clearing, lots of forest—"

<I have seen it.>

"Oh. Great. That makes it easier, doesn't it?" I tried to smile, but the dragon just glared at me.

Acid Breath held still while I climbed onto his back and

settled astride him. He hissed a little as Sam climbed on after me, muttering in the back of his mind, but nothing more.

Sam sat behind me, both of us bundled in coats and extra layers, and with blankets tied around us like a cocoon so we could share body heat. We pulled scarves over our faces like masks, and then he wrapped his arms around me. We wouldn't have sylph to keep us warm during the trip, and the dragon's scales were like chips of ice.

"Don't look down," Sam said, loudly enough for me to hear through my hood and three hats. "It's going to be dark, so you won't see anything, but it will be easier if you don't look."

"I'm not afraid of heights." I tried to snuggle closer to him, but we'd been so thoroughly secured I couldn't move. We were already seated as close as possible, anyway. All the layers just made it seem far.

"I know. But this height—it can still be overwhelming. It might make you dizzy or confused about how you're oriented, like when you're in water and you can't tell which way is up."

All this rambling was an attempt to put himself at ease, distract himself from what we were about to do. How did he even know what it would be like? Maybe he was guessing. Or maybe he remembered from dying, being thrashed around in a dragon's grip.

I wanted to double-check all our knots, but I doubted that would help his mood. Instead, I patted his knee. "When I was drowning in the lake, before you saved me"—he needed to remember his courage—"it was impossible to tell up from down. I wonder if it's easier to fly at night, when you can't see anything, or during the day, when you can see everything."

"Depends, I think." Sam hunched over me as muscles rippled and moved beneath us. "What's more frightening? The known or unknown?"

Most people would say the unknown. I wasn't sure what my answer was.

<We are ready.>

Indeed, Stef and Whit were strapped onto another dragon, their bags and the collapsed tent hanging from the bottom of the harness. It would sway, but Stef had done a good job securing everything tightly, so it would move very little.

Muscles coiled, fluttered against my legs and chest as I leaned over Acid Breath. From the corner of my eye, I could see enormous golden wings stretch out and shimmer in Stef's flashlight. A network of bones and veins stood out when light shone through the leathery appendage. I couldn't fathom how something so thin could be strong enough to lift an entire dragon, but during Templedark, I'd slid down a wing to escape a rooftop. The delicate flesh hadn't split under my weight, as I'd feared.

The wings rose up, swooshed down. Air caught in a bubble, giving us a heartbeat of weightlessness. In our cocoon of blankets, Sam's fingers jabbed against my clothes, against my ribs. I struggled to breathe evenly.

Thunder snapped as Acid Breath flapped his wings again. His body jerked lower—I bit back a yelp—and muscles bunched. <Hold tight,> he muttered in our heads, though there was nothing to hold on to but the blankets used as padding between us.

Wings beat faster, dragon thunder ripping through the air. He leapt, and my stomach dropped—

We thudded to the ground, trees crashing aside. He turned, galloped a few steps, flapped faster, and jumped again.

The air held us. Acid Breath's muscles flexed and moved, nothing at all like the smooth gait of a horse. His body twisted and bent, snakelike.

Then I couldn't think about that discomfort, only the sharp rise and the way he was suddenly vertical. I slid on the blanket, toward Sam. His grip on my ribs tightened, and something—his chin or forehead—dug against my back. I couldn't hear anything but the wings pounding on air.

We slid. Screaming, I reached forward, but my mittened hands glided along slick scales. No chance of holding on.

I had no clue how high we were, but with frigid air and snow stinging my eyes, stealing my breath, I easily imagined the terror of a free fall.

The blanket slid more. Faintly, I wondered if all the cloth wrapped around us would soften the blow when we hit the ground. Probably not.

Thunder and wind, my screams and Sam's, the shrieking

buzz of dragons' communication: the sounds deafened me, and my ears popped and popped as we rose higher. My head felt ready to explode as the pressure changed, and I couldn't breathe right. Thin, icy air rushed across my face, even when I ducked my head to let my hood take the brunt.

We hurtled into the sky, falling upward as fast as Acid Breath's wings would carry us.

We slipped. Ropes gouged my waist and legs. Sam pressed harder against me. Any moment now, the ropes would snap and we'd fall.

Our ascent eased, and Acid Breath was horizontal again.

I didn't know when I'd stopped screaming. Maybe whenever the air had stopped being heavy enough for proper breathing. Gasping, I waited for my heart to slow into a regular rhythm, and for my ears to stop aching. Sam shook against me; I trembled, too.

Acid Breath's wings thundered, and sharp air rushed against our faces, but we were still on his back, and that was what I cared about.

Sam's voice strained under the din of wings and air. "Are you okay?"

I tried to nod, but he wouldn't see it. Instead, I released my useless death grip on the blanket and touched his hand still on my ribs. My head still throbbed from the pressure— or not enough pressure—and my whole body felt like I'd lost a round with Rangedge Lake, but I was okay. As long as we never did that again.

Sam's grip relaxed as I sat up a little, letting my hood and our blanket cocoon hide the sight of wings, and the passage of blackness beneath and around us. I didn't want to see after all.

Movement behind me. Tugging on my coat and shirts. Hot skin slid against my waist and ribs, and the weight of Sam's head settled on my back. My heartbeat steadied with his palm on my skin. I couldn't stop the panic whenever Acid Breath dipped or changed directions, but this tactile reminder of Sam's presence helped.

We flew through snow clouds for hours, mostly gliding on a plane of air. The wind never ceased. For a while we listened to the dragons speak to one another, but the ringing in my ears was overwhelming, and the dragons seemed disinclined to converse much while we were on top of them. And with us around, in general. They seemed to fear we'd learn all their dragonish secrets.

I hoped Whit and Stef were faring better, but my thoughts shifted toward our inevitable descent, and what would happen when we finally reached Range.

The clouds moved northeast, away from us. Hours later, the sky turned indigo, and a brilliant line of gold light shot across the eastern horizon. The sun peeked from behind a ridge of mountains, illuminating the long curve of the earth.

Mountains pierced the sky, all snow and ice and frozen beauty. And in the west, a bright glow drew my gaze: the temple in the city of Heart.

As light flooded the white land, pouring between mountains and into valleys like rivers and lakes of pure gold, I found the cavities in the ground left behind from hydrothermal eruptions. It was difficult to see them from our distance, but the fact that I could see them at all—that they existed— was enough to be terrifying.

Sam shouted from behind me, "Do you see Templedark Memorial?"

I peered north of the city, but if Templedark Memorial existed anymore, it was too far for me to see. I shook my head and ducked as Acid Breath banked eastward.

It was midmorning by the time buzzing flared in my thoughts.

<This is the place.>

Going down was just as terrible as going up. The descent made us dip forward, and the impact of landing jarred every bone in my body, but then everything grew deliciously still and I imagined going to sleep in a real bed. Showering with hot water. Not living in a tent.

"Oh no." Sam swore quietly, making me look up.

Menehem's lab lay in ruins.

23
ALLIANCE

MOST OF THE building remained standing, though there were holes in the roof and a tree had fallen on it, leaving one end open to the elements. The cisterns were on the ground, a sheet of ice spreading around them. The solar panels had been damaged beyond repair, and unidentifiable bits of machinery spilled from the door.

"No," I breathed. "No, no." I fumbled for the straps of the harness, struggling to free myself from the ropes gouging into my midsection.

"Wait." Sam grabbed my hands and held me still. "Just wait. I'll get it."

When he released my hands and began unbuckling the harness, I just stared at the ruins of my father's lab and watched as sylph emerged from the forest. They gave a long, melancholy wail as they drifted through the ruins.

"Now." The harness loosened around me and I shoved the ropes off my shoulders and stomach, shoved aside the blankets, too. Hardly realizing what I was doing, I hopped onto Acid Breath's foreleg and slid down, then ran toward the wreckage.

Inside the building was even worse. There was the kitchen area where Sam and I had burned so many meals because we'd been kissing and lost track of time; now the contents of the cupboards lay scattered on the floor, crushed and spilling open.

There was the screen where I'd watched videos of my father experimenting on sylph; now it was cracked and hollowed out.

There was the sleeping area where Sam had sat next to me one afternoon and, for the first time, told me that he loved me; now the mattress was shredded, its foam and wool like snow on the floor.

In the back, the upper story had collapsed into the lab, crushing machines and crates filled with Menehem's clothes and old gear. The cracked screen of a data console shimmered in morning light, which shone through holes in the roof and the open mouth of the rear door.

"Ana?" Sam's voice made me turn to find him standing in the doorway, framed by light. "Are you okay?" He had our bags and my flute case, and behind him I could see Acid Breath peering suspiciously.

<Humans live in squalor,> he muttered to one of the other dragons.

"Yeah. No." I shook my head and tried to focus my thoughts around the exhaustion, the shock, and the constant ringing that came whenever dragons were near. "I wasn't expecting this. But of course Deborl destroyed the lab. Of course."

"There were earthquakes, too."

I motioned at the springs ripped from the mattress, the whole thing sliced open like a prize waited inside. "Some of this was deliberate. And there were drones."

Sam dropped our backpacks and laid the flute on top, his movements stiff under the dragon's scrutiny. "It's okay. Come back outside."

Even as he spoke, the building gave a low groan and shuddered. He was right. It wasn't safe to be in here, not after the earthquakes, too.

I trudged outside to find Stef and Whit off their dragon and removing the harnesses in silence. Buzzing filled my head as Acid Breath studied me.

<You said you had a poison. Was it stored here?>

"No." I gazed north, toward the cave where I'd hidden the twenty canisters. "I'm going to check on it, but it should be safe. The ones who did this wouldn't know where I hid the poison."

Acid Breath huffed. <Then our deal is still on. We will gather an army. Where will you be?>

I gazed around the ruins, snow and ice and metal shining in the sunlight. "Here for a little bit, but not long. Maybe a night or two. Then we'll return to the city. We can walk."

"And if Deborl left someone to watch for us?" Stef asked.

"We'll deal with them if it comes up."

Sam nudged me. "The canisters. How will we carry them?"

With four people and twenty canisters as big as my torso, it would be impossible. I'd hoped to have more, though. Twenty . . . I couldn't see how it would be enough.

Acid Breath narrowed his eyes. <Take me to the poison. We will leave it outside your city.>

That could work. "We'll have to get them into the city somehow."

Whit nodded. "And right now we don't even know how we'll get ourselves inside."

<When will Janan ascend? We can bring the canisters into the city when it begins.>

Sam, Stef, Whit, and I glanced at one another. "When does Soul Night officially begin?" I asked.

"Sundown." Sam's voice was low and sober. "Soul Night begins as soon as the sun sets."

Eleven more days.

<That is when we will have your canisters ready. Where

288

should we put them for now? Where should we bring them at sundown?> Acid Breath asked.

I glanced at the others for suggestions, but when no one spoke, I said, "For now, put them in Templedark Memorial. The field of black obelisks."

<They're all fallen.>

From the earthquakes. Yes. "I know. Put the canisters there, anyway. Can you do it at night so no one spots you?"

<They will hear us.>

"You can be quick, can't you?"

<Yes.> Acid Breath's voice grated in my head.

"Then you'll be fine. The darkness is so they won't see what you're doing. Most people in the city *want* Janan to ascend. They don't want us to use the poison against him, because they're afraid. They're terrified of the unknown— what happens if Janan *doesn't* ascend."

"They don't know what happens if he does, though," Whit said.

I nodded. "But someone they trust—Deborl—told them it will be good."

The dragon blinked slowly, and the other two swung their heads around to look at me. <Will the other humans try to kill us during the spring equinox?>

"Maybe." Or maybe they'd be too busy with Janan and whatever the cage was for.

<I suppose you don't want us to harm them, regardless?>

"That's what I'd prefer." Though if he wanted to drown Deborl in a glob of acid, I wouldn't mind.

The dragon's grumble vibrated the ground. <Where should we take the poison inside the city?>

I closed my eyes and thought about what places might be clear, what places would be easy for dragons to reach, while difficult for Deborl and his guards. "The Councilhouse roof. We can get into the temple from there, release the poison, and duck away quickly."

"And we'll fly onto the roof?" Whit asked. "Magically?"

"I'm sure Stef will come up with something."

Stef sighed and nodded. "Of course I will."

<That is acceptable to us. Take us to the poison.>

I motioned at Sam and the others to stay behind; they could start setting up camp. A handful of sylph came with us, melting snow and ice from our path.

<Are you sure you don't want us to carry you to the city? Your legs are so small. It will take you days to walk there on your own.>

"We can't just ride dragons up to the city," I muttered.

Besides, I wouldn't subject Sam to another dragon ride if I didn't have to. It seemed like we were safest if Sam and the dragons stayed far away from one another.

"Be careful with the canisters," I cautioned. "If they open before we're ready, we've lost. There's only one chance."

The dragons decided to wait until evening to take the canisters, but they stayed far out of our way the entire time they were in the area. We only heard them from a distance, crashing through trees and rumbling. Even the buzzing din of their dialogue was far away, allowing us to pick through the wreckage of the lab for a few hours in peace.

Little was salvageable. Stef found a few things she wanted to keep, and I found the canister that had been filling when we left the lab. There was nothing in it now—the poison had dispersed long ago—and there were no others lying around. So the lab had been destroyed shortly after we left.

I called Sarit to update her, and as evening fell, dragon thunder cracked the sky. We all went outside to watch Acid Breath and his friends take off, our hope clasped in their teeth and talons. Their bodies slithered through the air, scales reflecting the last rays of sunlight as they climbed higher and higher.

When they were out of sight, Sam's posture relaxed, and we both retreated into the tent where sylph warmed our sleeping bags and heated a pot of soup.

-Animals are leaving Range.- Cris's song was low, worried. The others hummed their concern, too.

They curled around us, closer than our own shadows, and in the heat I saw flashes of snow-choked forest with deer trails but no deer, trees with bird nests but no birds, and hollows with small animal dens but no small animals. Dry riverbeds, drained ponds with fish rotting in the bottom, and watering holes with prints stamped into the cracked mud. Hot springs were gone. Mud pools had hardened. Geysers hissed steam and nothing more.

-Range is falling apart. There will be little to eat until we reach Heart.-

And then there'd be whatever was in warehouses, no doubt closely rationed by Deborl. Sarit hadn't mentioned she was going hungry, so I hoped she was doing all right. Water, we could at least get in the form of melted snow.

"Thanks, Cris." Sam dropped to our sleeping bags and massaged his temples. Lines of weariness crossed his face, and circles darkened under his eyes. He needed a shower and shave. I couldn't imagine I looked much better. "I'm so glad the dragons are gone."

I sat next to him and rested my hand on his knee. "Me too. Though I'm relieved they're helping, even if it's because they're trying to get rid of you."

He winced. "It's hard to accept that for the last five thousand years, they've been coming to Heart to find out whether I'm still alive, and then kill me."

"Not just kill you, but destroy the place where your reincarnation happens. How do they *know* that?"

"I wish I knew."

"And furthermore, how do they identify you every lifetime? Acid Breath made it sound like he could see the song in you, but what does it look like? How does he know? And is he the only one?"

Sam opened his mouth, but I wasn't finished.

"He said they don't reincarnate, but do they live longer than humans? Why are they so afraid of the phoenix song? They've made your death a *priority* for thousands of years, and not only is that rude, it's just so *focused*. I just don't understand. And you know, if they didn't spend so much time trying to kill you, we might never have figured out that you have the phoenix song."

He gave a soft snort. "I can give you a few answers, but there's a lot we don't know about dragons, and probably never will.

"I hate not knowing the truth."

"That's one of the things I love most about you. Your endless quest for the truth." Sam wrapped his arm around my waist and hugged me close. "Well, they do live longer than humans. It appears that they're effectively immortal—until they're killed. There are a few we think are as old as Heart. Maybe older."

"Maybe that's why they're so afraid of the phoenix song." I glanced toward my flute case. "It seems to me those who think they'll never die are the most afraid of death."

"In some cases." He brushed a strand of hair off my face. "And sometimes we finally grow wise enough to understand life is a gift that can't—shouldn't—last forever."

"And the phoenix song . . . ends life?"

Sam shrugged. "I don't know. The translations from the book are all over the place. Builds and destroys. Life and death. Consumes. Or maybe it's none of those things."

Maybe it was all.

His mouth brushed my cheek, then he leaned forward to ladle bowls of soup for each of us. "You played your flute for the dragons twice. What did you play?"

"My songs."

He shot me a look. "They're not—"

"I know." I gave him the most innocent smile I could muster.

He chuckled and shook his head. "And hold your flute up straight while you're at it."

I grinned and accepted a bowl. "First I played my minuet. Then I played the one from the demonstration on market day."

"None of mine." Mostly he looked curious, but there was a tinge of hurt in his voice. "Why?"

"I wanted to do it on my own. With my music." It hadn't been completely on my own. The sylph had been there, as well as Sam's influence. "I just needed to do it myself, as much as I could."

"I understand." His mouth turned up in a half smile. "I was curious if they'd reacted to the music at all, if there was anything in it we could use to figure out the phoenix song."

294

"Whatever it is, it's not in my music. It's not in any of the parts you helped me clean up." I closed my eyes, remembering sitting at the piano with him, music resounding around the parlor until it overpowered all my senses and made my whole body vibrate with life. "I'll do what I said I would before: listen to your music and read the scores. Make note of any trends."

Stef and Whit came in while we were washing our faces. They both looked grim and exhausted.

"I've been intercepting a few messages from within Heart." Stef held up her SED. "Three dragons were sighted just north of the city, landing in Templedark Memorial. No one has mentioned canisters, but if anyone goes out there . . ."

"Maybe Acid Breath will think to hide them." My optimism sounded forced even to me.

"Maybe." Stef checked her SED again as she sat in front of the soup. "Guards have been on alert since the dragons flew over yesterday. They're worried about another attack. Usually it's a small attack followed by a much larger one, but these have broken the pattern. The same three dragons have come by twice and not attacked either time, so as you can imagine, Deborl is telling people everything they're afraid to hear."

Whit nodded and filled bowls for both him and Stef. "Deborl is saying the dragons are coming because of Janan's ascension—they want to stop him—but Janan will protect them."

"By now, of course," Stef went on, "everyone publicly opposed to Janan's ascension has left or been thrown in prison. So everyone Deborl is talking to is happy to listen to him, or too afraid not to."

How many people were opposed? Enough to be worth attempting to contact them? Or free them?

"Has there been any talk about what Deborl sent Merton to gather?" Sam asked.

Stef glanced at her SED and scowled. "Nothing about what it is, just that he's obtained the item and is on his way back to Heart. We'll be hearing more about whatever it is pretty soon, I assume."

Great. So whatever Janan needed to help him ascend, he had coming. "I wonder what it is."

"It sounds like he went a long way to get it—and lost five warriors while he was out—but that's all I can tell you."

"Well, there's not much point in staying here. Menehem's machine is broken. We're not getting any more poison. Is anyone opposed to heading back to Heart tomorrow?"

When everyone agreed, I pulled off my boots and outer clothes and got into my sleeping bag, leaving room for Sam. But I couldn't stay awake long enough to say good night. As soon as I settled on my pillow, I was asleep.

Over the next several days, we kept to the forest as much as possible, always looking up for air drones patrolling the roads in and out of Heart. The snow-covered trees were darkening, turning black where the ground beneath them grew hotter and cooked the roots. Everything was weirdly silent without birdsong and animals chattering and creeks bubbling just out of sight. The forest was dying around us.

Every night, we all went over the temple books, looking for anything about Janan, phoenixes, and dragons. Anything we didn't already know. Sam and I went over music, but so far nothing stood out. As for when we reached Heart, Sarit said she had a plan.

At last, the immense city wall rose above the woods. We were almost home, with time to spare, thanks to the dragons.

"This way," Stef said, and she led us toward Midrange Lake—or what was left of it.

Now the lake was a wide, sloping hole in the ground with decaying plants and animals at the bottom. The rotting stink rose up, almost unbearable when mixed with the sulfuric tinge that colored every breath in the center of Range. Everyone groaned and covered their faces with scarves, but that hardly seemed to help.

"The only good thing about the lake being drained," Stef said, "is that since there is no way into Heart from the surface, we can get into Heart from below. The wall only extends so far beneath the ground, which is the only thing that enabled us to build a sewer system and aqueducts from the lake. If the lake were full, we wouldn't be able to get into the city."

First, we had to descend into the pit of the lake.

"Do we go now?" I asked. Clouds hung low in the sky, heavy with the threat of more snow and another cold night. I couldn't see the position of the sun, but it felt late. We'd been walking for hours.

She nodded. "We might as well. We'll be in shadow. It will be harder for anyone to see us, and I don't want to go down there in the dark."

The sylph went first, forming a line of blackness down the bank. Brown plants flared bright and burned away as the sylph searched for the opening to the aqueduct.

"I sincerely hope this is big enough for us to walk through." I watched Whit and Stef start down after the sylph, then lowered myself until I found a foothold. Icy mud squished around my boot, and I wanted to be sick as I sank a little. The lake might have drained, but the earth was still damp and gross. The sylph's passage had only made it worse, warming the mud.

Sam shot me an amused look as he climbed after me. "It's pretty large. A million people consume a lot of water. Just be grateful she isn't taking us through the sewer."

I gagged and followed the others, my boots sucking and slurping as we descended into the bowl of the lake. Muddy walls rose all around.

Metal and shadow caught my eye ahead. A huge pipe protruded from the side of the lake, a thick grille and mesh over the front of it. Weeds dripped off the rusted hinges, then sizzled away as the sylph worked to burn off anything that might get in Stef's way. She already had her tools out.

The pipe was big enough for me to walk inside, but anyone taller—everyone else—would have to duck their heads or hunch. Finally. A real benefit to my lack of height. Of course, I would need a boost getting inside, since the bottom was at my waist.

"This is the intake pipe," Stef said, prying off the grille. Whit and Sam stepped in to help. "It pulls in water when the tank inside the industrial quarter is low. The water is strained for large particles here, but there's still a lot of cleaning to be done before we can drink it." She grunted, and the metal mesh followed the grille onto the bottom of the lake.

"Of course," Whit said, "all this is new within the last few thousand years. At one point, we drank straight from the lake. Then we got smart enough to carry the water in and boil it."

"Gross." I hid my flute case inside my coat and tightened my backpack straps, then let Sam and Whit boost me into the dark hole of the pipe. When I turned on the lantern Sam handed me, I saw only damp metal, algae, and lots of darkness beyond.

This would be the opposite of fun, but it would be better than trying to walk into the city through one of the arches. Leaving through a normal route hadn't gone very well, after all.

"Are you sure there's a way out of this?" I asked. "A way that's *not* one of the purification tanks, that is."

Stef grinned. "There's a hatch we use to put cleaning drones into the pipes. I swear I'll get you through this safely."

"Okay," I muttered, tapping Sarit a quick SED message to let her know to meet us. Then I helped the others in as best I could, and stood aside so Stef and Whit could lead. Sam followed behind me.

The pipe wasn't comfortable to walk inside. I'd never thought I minded small spaces before, but the walk underground took forever. We headed down, then up again, and I tried to recall all Stef's assurances that this was safe: they'd been careful to direct the pipe only where the ground was thick enough to support it, and coat it with heat-resistant material so that if something shifted, the pipe would be unaffected.

They must not have taken earthquake swarms into account, though, because several times, we had to stop and kick through piles of dirt where the pipe had cracked open. The air grew musty and hard to breathe, and my hair stuck to my head uncomfortably. Sweat pooled in my collarbone, snaking down my chest, down my spine. The sylph at the rear didn't help the heat, but at least they were quiet. The echo of their songs probably would have driven me to catch them all in sylph eggs.

"Is there water in the city?" I kept my voice low to keep it from carrying. Even so, the sound made me wince. "Since the lake is dry?"

"Yes." Stef's voice rasped against the walls of the pipe. "There are cisterns for rainwater and snow. The city is built for siege. Even with the lake drained, the population can live comfortably for five months. Much longer if we ration carefully."

That was good to know. I might get a shower after all.

Light grew ahead, off to one side. "This is it. Looks like Sarit already opened the hatch for us." After we climbed a small incline, Stef turned off her lantern and fastened it to her backpack. "Let's get out of here."

Cool air rushed in as she pushed the grate the rest of the way open, and at last we stepped into a small, dim room with powered-down labor drones sitting on shelves along the far side, and a handful of pipes crisscrossing the room with hatches leading in. The sylph hung back in the pipe, deep in the darkness. They'd come out when we reminded Sarit they were *our* army.

"Finally!" Sarit exploded from around the corner and stopped just short of hugging me. "You smell terrible."

"I feel disgusting, too."

She looked good, though, except for the dark smudges beneath her eyes, and the way her smile didn't quite fit right.

After losing Armande, she'd been alone. For a few weeks, she hadn't even had me, since the SED signal didn't reach as far north as we'd gone.

"I'm so glad you're back." Tears glimmered in Sarit's eyes as she smiled at everyone. "I can't say how much I missed you. But I'm not going to hug you until after you've all washed up. I have standards, you know."

"We missed you, too." I peeled hair off my forehead and gazed around the small room. It was good to be back inside solid walls, though the circumstances of our return could have been so much better. "Where have you been staying? How soon until I can shower?"

"Twenty minutes, if you run and get to the shower first. I've been rotating darksoul houses and industrial buildings. We're in the middle of the industrial quarter right now, in one of the few buildings still standing after they razed a bunch of warehouses and things. This one is still necessary." She shrugged. "I'm taking you to the textile mill. I had to pretend like I was Stef in order to rig some of the pipes into a shower, but it'll do if you're desperate."

"And we are." Whit laughed and headed for the door, but as soon as he pulled it open, a blue light shot in. Whit dropped over.

He was dead.

24
LOSS

I SCREAMED.

Sam and Stef drew their pistols and pushed their way to the door, keeping to the sides.

Another blue light shot in, but before Sam or Stef could duck outside, blackness surged from the pipe where we'd just come from, keening so loud my ears ached.

The sylph passed over Whit's body in the doorway, hotter as they moved outside. Though he'd been killed by a laser, leaving only a small hole in his forehead, the heat of sylph scorched his skin darker and darker, burning his clothes and hair and eyelashes.

Sarit screamed, her voice raw. Sam and Stef moved back as the sylph streamed outside, and within heartbeats, men and women cried out in pain. The stench of burning flesh flooded the room, mixing with the reek we'd carried in from the aqueduct and days of travel. Acid pushed up my throat; I doubled over and threw up.

Before I could spit and wipe my mouth, Sam grabbed my wrist and hauled me after him. Stef had Sarit.

"Let's *go*." Stef guided us over Whit's body.

His body.

He'd been alive a minute ago.

Now he was a charred husk.

"Come on!" Sam jerked me outside. It was dark, but there were enough lights in this quarter that I couldn't ignore the smoking bodies on the ground. Four of them, all burned to death by sylph.

I stumbled after Sam, my feet tripping over each other, over the hard ground.

Stef passed Sarit to Sam. "Get them to the mill. I'll take care of this."

Take care of this? There were bodies. Whit.

"Is that safe?" Sam asked.

"I'll make it safe." Stef's eyes were hard, angry.

Tears blinded me as I staggered after Sam, bumping against Sarit, who seemed just as disoriented and confused. Sylph flew around us, only half their usual number. The others must have stayed with Stef.

"This way." Sam's voice was rough as he dragged us

behind buildings to wait, listen, though I couldn't hear anything over the thud of my heartbeat, the hitch in my breath, and the gasp of Sarit's weeping.

For what seemed like hours, we started and stopped, hiding behind buildings, though the ragged sound of my breathing would surely give us away. Sylph pushed ahead and around, though only one knew the way to the textile mill, and I couldn't tell if Cris had stayed with us or Stef.

Or Whit.

He'd been killed, then burned up.

A door slammed, and after a sweep of the flashlight, Sam turned on the lights. Heavy curtains blocked the windows, keeping any passersby from noticing a glow.

"Shower?" Sam asked.

Sarit pointed across the main floor, toward a dark hall. Her voice was low, monotone. "Where they wash the wool. Just after—"

"I know where that is." Sam led me around a maze of machines, down the lit hallway, and entered a room with giant tubs. "Come on," he murmured, helping me remove my backpack, my flute case, and my coat.

I dropped onto the edge of a tub, vision blurring with tears. Sam tugged off my mud-caked boots and tossed them aside. They thumped loudly on the wooden floor. Then he pulled around a makeshift curtain and turned on the water. Hot and cold poured from holes in two different pipes above, pounding on the bottom of the tub.

"Time to get undressed." Sam helped me peel away a few layers of clothes, until I wore only my sweaty, stiff camisole and leggings. "In you go." He held my hand as I stepped, shaking, into the tub, and water thudded around me, hot and cold and hard from a pair of pipes in the ceiling.

I closed my eyes and let the water soak through me.

Whit was dead.

I'd seen him die.

We'd been laughing.

And then he was gone.

Deborl's people had been waiting for us.

They knew we were back.

When I opened my eyes, water still poured over my skin. Steam filled the room, and I couldn't tell how long I'd been standing under the broken pipes. A long time.

I found shampoo and soap on the edge of the tub, a washcloth. Other showerlike things. Sarit must have liked this place. It had water, and lots of soft things to nest in.

Still shaking, I peeled off my underclothes, clutching a pipe to keep from falling. Silk plopped at the bottom of the tub, where dirt and grime had turned to mud around the drain. I nudged the mud with my toes until it fell through.

I scrubbed as hard as I could, feeling like I'd never been so filthy in my life. My skin burned, raw and red by the time I stopped the water and stood dripping.

Sam had left the room a while ago, taking my backpack and flute with him, but a pile of fresh towels and clothes waited. I dried and dressed, fumbling to clean my mess so the next person to shower wouldn't have to. Sam still needed one. And Stef. And Whit. . . .

Not Whit.

I choked back a sob as I hurled my filthy clothes into another tub where Sarit must have been doing laundry; a heap of clothes already waited there.

When my hair was combed and braided and I caught a glimpse of myself in a fogged mirror, I looked skinny and pale. My cheeks were hollow and my collarbone jutted sharply, knifelike. The way short strands of hair clung to my forehead didn't help.

I chafed my towel over my skin one more time, then threw it in the laundry tub.

The hall was cool and dim. Low voices came from another room of the mill. I followed them past a storage room, another holding enormous machines with a wide conveyer and rollers at one end, with sharp pins sticking out of all the surfaces. Carders.

One room had machines with spindly arms and bobbins filled with spun yarn. Tufts of carded wool had long ago

307

settled on the floor like snow. Synthetic silk glimmered in the lights coming from the hall.

I found Sam and Sarit sitting on a bench in the weaving room, the giant looms half-warped with thread. Crates of fabric were stacked along the walls, some cloths dyed in brilliant hues, others in more subtle colors. None of these things looked like the smaller textile manufacturing machines I'd seen before. These were far less friendly, meant for production, but the whole building bore age and abandonment like a shroud.

As I entered, Sam looked up, dark and weary. "Do you want something to eat?"

"Thirsty." I walked around a loom and sat between him and Sarit. If Whit were here, he'd have teased me, asking how I could possibly be thirsty after all the water I'd just soaked up. But he wasn't. Whit would never be here again.

Sam handed me a bottle of water. The outside door opened, and he nodded at Stef as she walked inside, shadows trickling after her. "Want to shower next?"

She dropped her backpack and sleeping bag, then headed to the washroom without comment.

I leaned over my knees and tried not to think. A slender arm wrapped around me, and Sarit rested her cheek on my shoulder. "I know," she whispered. "I know it hurts."

Did she remember about Janan? That no one was getting reincarnated? Or could a death still carve out a hole in your heart, even if you thought they were coming back?

It had to hurt, no matter what. That was why Stef had once saved Sam's hat, after a dragon had killed him. And why Sam had saved me from drowning in Rangedge Lake. That was why people crowded into the rebirth room to welcome back old friends or lovers.

That was why the days after Templedark, and the memorial held in the north, had been so somber. They knew temporary loss, temporary death, and how it ached.

With Templedark, they knew permanent loss as well.

I leaned into Sarit's arms, grateful for her comfort. And deeply guilty for not being here when she lost Armande. Not that I could have magically transported myself to her side.

Soft moans came from around the room, and heat followed. Sylph.

Sarit tensed, but forced herself to relax after a moment.

"I've explained about the sylph," Sam said. "Cris is here. He and the others want to apologize for— You know."

For burning up Whit as they passed. I knew.

"And for what happened outside."

For leaving charred, smoking bodies. "They saved the rest of us." My voice was dry, aching.

"They swore to protect you," Sam said quietly. "They'll do anything it takes."

Because they thought I could stop Janan and redeem them, put an end to the punishment phoenixes had placed on them five thousand years ago. I knew that, too.

"What now?" I asked.

"I'll call Orrin and tell him about Whit. They've been best friends . . . forever."

"He needs to know," I agreed.

"And we do whatever it takes to stop Janan's ascension."

We had five days until Soul Night. That time was a gift.

"Maybe we can find allies," Sam continued. "We should start with Deborl's prisoners and find a way to free them." He kept his voice gentle. "Now that Sarit's not alone anymore, perhaps she can get some sleep."

A curtain of black hair trembled as Sarit nodded next to me. "I do miss sleep."

"Why don't you two catch up and get some rest?" Sam said. "I'll take a couple of sylph and check the area."

I looked up. "Check for what?"

Sam grabbed his pistol from the bench. "Anyone who might have followed us here. Sylph can stand guard, but I'd feel better if I looked."

He was a musician, not a warrior. But I didn't stop him from going outside, because he was also a soul with a deep sense of honor and need to protect.

When he was gone, Sarit hugged me tightly and stood up. "Let's find places for you to sleep. We've got lots of nice fabric. Do you want wool? Silk? Bison? Have some of everything." Her voice held a note of weary humor, like she'd asked me over to her house for the night and wanted to be a good host. "This place doesn't get used as much as it did before you came. Ciana was in charge of all this. While people still come here to weave and stock up before markets, it's just not as busy as it once was. Not since Ciana."

I nodded. The reminder of her absence must have hurt, especially for the people who were closest to her. Sam had been close to her.

"Anyway." Sarit opened a crate and rummaged through bolts of cloth. "It will be a nice change from your sleeping bag. We can make you a pallet as thick and soft as you want, almost like a real bed."

"That will be nice," I said, because she was trying so hard. "Where have you been sleeping?"

"In the storage room. No windows. Close to the washroom and tubs. It feels hidden." Her smile was strained. "There's a second door there to the other hall, so I can go out either way if someone sneaks up on me while I'm sleeping."

"Let's all sleep in there."

"I'd like that. It's been terrible, being alone." The bolt of fabric she held dropped when she pressed her hand over her mouth. "Sorry. I promised myself I wouldn't complain."

I hugged her as hard as I could. "It's okay. We're here now."

She trembled and whispered, "Thank you. After Armande— I was so glad when we could finally talk again. I didn't think I'd get to see you so soon, and I'm so, so grateful."

"We had to ride dragons."

"I'd have ridden a dragon and a roc to be able to see you again."

I pulled away and started unfolding bolts of woven wool. "How would you have convinced the roc?"

"Surely they like honey. Everything does. I would have bribed it with a whole jar of honey, even tied a bow around the lid."

"I'm sure that would have worked."

Together, we carried armfuls of our favorite colors into the storage room. It was filled with crates, so we arranged them into partitions for privacy.

"You and Sam are sharing, hmm?" She smiled a little.

I blushed. "Yeah. I mean, not . . . that. Yet. We were fighting."

She nodded. "I remember."

"We fought for a *long* time." It had seemed like forever, anyway. "We weren't talking or anything. And since then, we've been trying to ease back into everything, but we don't want to ease too much, because what if—" I couldn't say it.

"What if you don't succeed in stopping Janan?"

I sat on a crate. "Or what if we do, and everyone in Heart is so angry they toss us in prison for the rest of our lives?" That seemed like a very possible result of success, though definitely preferable to failure.

"Hmm. I bet you'd like some private time."

My cheeks ached with blushing. "Let's talk about something else. Anything else." Best friend or no, there were still things I wasn't comfortable discussing.

She flashed a smile and held up a brilliant blue fabric, the color of the sky on a summer day. "I think you should have this one. It matches your eyes."

We worked and chatted for a while, talking about anything that didn't hurt. Sylph came in to warm the room and lurk in the shadows, and soon Stef emerged from her shower, clean and with her hair done in a complicated braid. Sam returned from his mission and hurried to wash up. Soon, we were all comfortably settled in the storage room, sharing a small meal and stories.

And then the earth shook.

25
BURDEN

A DEEP RUMBLE traveled through the earth, shaking the floor, causing lights to flicker. In the other rooms, machinery clattered and banged. A wooden beam snapped.

My heart thundered as Sam grabbed me and held me under a doorway. Stef moved to the opposite door, while sylph flew through the mill, wailing as the earthquake intensified. Windows rattled and glass cracked, but Sarit just sat in her nest of blankets and waited for everything to stop moving.

"They happen a lot," she said when the world was silenced again. She stood up and straightened her clothes. "I'll make sure nothing is broken."

"We'll go with you." Sam left the doorway.

I grabbed our SEDs, and the four of us crept through the

hall, looking inside rooms for anything out of place.

A few machines had shifted over the floor and one of the looms had a cracked frame, but everything seemed well, otherwise.

I slipped my hand into Sam's as we followed Stef and Sarit around the mill, and Sarit pointed out all the things she'd done to keep the building from collapsing on her during earthquakes.

"They're getting worse," she said. "At first it was just one or two a day, nothing nearly as big as the one the night of the new year. But now we have four or five a day, and most of them are pretty strong. A while ago, Deborl sent people to dispose of all hazardous chemicals in the city; that way they don't accidentally spill."

I shuddered, trying not to imagine what kind of chemicals Menehem might have left in the city—chemicals that could eat through buildings and cause fires, and no doubt worse.

"Thank you," I whispered to Sam. "For earlier. For not panicking. For taking care of me when I did panic."

He kissed my hand.

"I don't know why I acted that way. It's not like I've never seen someone die before." I shuddered with the weight of memories. I'd seen Cris die in the temple. Li shot outside her own house. Menehem burned to death by sylph. Meuric falling apart on the Councilhouse steps—after I'd stabbed him in the eye and kicked him into a pit months before.

I'd seen too much death.

"Just because you've seen it before," Sam murmured, "doesn't mean it's easier to deal with the next time. Whit was your friend. A teacher. And considering all we've survived together, a lucky shot with a pistol . . ." He stared down at his socked feet.

"I miss Armande, too. I wish we could hear him complain about the state of the market field statues, or too many people skipping breakfast."

"He was going to start voice lessons."

"And teach me how to bake turnovers." I sighed and sat on a crate.

"It's scary," Sam said, "knowing they'll never come back. Knowing that one day—maybe in just a few days—that will be us, too."

I hugged myself. "We've lost so many friends in our quest to stop Janan's ascension. We have to stop him, no matter what. We have to make their sacrifices *matter*."

"We will."

High-pitched wailing broke the quiet as a sylph flew through the door, singeing the wood as it passed through. Everyone jumped, and I strained my ears to find meanings in the cacophony.

Other sylph swarmed around their fellow, humming and singing to console it.

At last, Cris broke free. -Merton has returned to the

city with his warriors. They've brought their prize. They're coming up South Avenue with it.-

Without speaking, we were all running back to the storage room, fumbling for boots and coats and scarves. Then, more quietly, we sneaked into the night, keeping to the shadows. Sylph concealed our presence as we moved west, toward South Avenue.

Lights shone across the road, reflecting snow and white stone houses in the southwestern residential quarter, though those were mostly hidden by trees. People filled the street, shivering in the cold weather. Above everything, the temple rose in the center of the city, blazing like a moon crashed to earth.

"This way," Sarit murmured. She took my hand and pulled me toward the pottery mill, a multistory building made of stone and wood. We entered through one of the small side doors, and she took us up a narrow staircase. "This leads to the roof, where we can watch. I try not to get lost in the crowd if I can help it."

The stairs creaked under the four of us, and the heat from the sylph made the closed space unbearable, but then she pushed open a hatch and brought down a ladder. Cold, fresh air blew in, and we all climbed onto the roof.

"Stay low," Sarit cautioned. "The templelight will give you away if you're not careful."

The dull roar of voices rose up as we crawled to the western edge of the roof. From here, I could see the four main avenues of the city, glowing under the light of the temple. The city wall stood bright white in a perfect circle, and from the Southern Arch, a brilliant lamp shone in on a large cluster of men and women wearing red from head to toe.

The group bore a litter on their shoulders, though whatever they carried on it was covered by a heavy black cloth, with ropes securing it. More supplies for the cage?

The cage itself stood right where Sarit had said: in the industrial quarter, where warehouses used to be. It was close to the market field—therefore close to the temple—and rose at least three stories into the air. Indeed, it looked big enough to hold a small troll, though the electric lines running into its base seemed unusual. Perhaps they wanted to shock whatever they were going to put inside it.

Whatever was being carried on that litter?

The procession made its way up South Avenue slowly. Their burden must have been heavy. Citizens of Heart followed behind them, their chatter loud and frenzied as they gathered in the market field. Focused lights blared down on the field as the red-clothed group called out a count, knelt, and then lowered the litter to the cobblestones.

The bundle trembled, but that might have been from the impact, not because it was alive. Or aware.

I sort of hoped it was dead, whatever it was.

"Can you hear what they're saying?" Stef murmured,

leaning closer as though a hand-width would make a difference. "I think that's Merton in the front."

Sure enough, the man in front was enormous, with wide shoulders and arms as big as both of my legs. Even from this distance, he was huge. As the crowd began to quiet down, I caught snatches of Merton's speech.

". . . months of travel . . . five dead . . . Janan's glorious return."

I shook my head. Sam seemed to be straining, too. Though we both had excellent hearing, Merton was just too far away.

"He's talking about their journey," Sam muttered. "But I can't tell where they went. Or what they brought back."

We all seemed to hold our breaths.

"Someone's saying they want to see it." Sam tilted his head, as though to hear better. "Merton is saying Deborl will reveal it only when Janan allows. I wonder how Deborl has been communicating with Janan while we have the key."

"He's probably just making things up," Stef said. "Though that cage is really specific."

"He could have Meuric's old diaries and plans," I said. Wind danced over our roof, making me shiver. "Meuric and Janan had lots of time to plan things, after all."

Stef made a noncommittal noise, and we all peered into the distance as a smaller figure emerged from around the side of the market field.

"Is that Deborl?" I whispered.

"I think so." Sarit scooted closer to me. "He's been hiding in the Councilhouse until he's ready to address everyone. He says he's in deep discussion with Janan, but he's been doing a lot of delegating. Like someone in charge of building the cage, though they're only given enough instructions for the next step, not the whole thing. Someone in charge of all the guards. And someone in charge of rationing food."

"It gives him the air of importance," Sam said. "Deborl likes to seem important."

Sarit snorted a little.

In the distance, Deborl walked around to the front of the litter and climbed onto the edge. It only brought him up a little higher; he was short, barely taller than me.

"Now what are they saying?" Sarit asked.

Sam shook his head. "I can't tell. Deborl's voice doesn't carry like Merton's."

We watched until the crowd began to disperse before we climbed off the roof and headed back to the mill. After assigning sylph to guard the building, we sent a few more to spy from shadows, and others to melt snow all over the city to help us avoid leaving tracks. Deborl already knew we were back in Heart, but that didn't mean we had to advertise our location.

"I'll start looking through SED messages and listening in on calls," Stef said. "Maybe someone will say something useful."

I nodded. "We've been doing a lot lately. Hiking across the world. Staying hidden in a locked-up city. It seems to me the best thing we can do until Soul Night is gather information, sabotage whatever we can, and go over every step of our plan for how to stop Janan from ascending on Soul Night."

I wanted to do as Sam had suggested as well: free the prisoners. They probably wouldn't help us, but it would annoy Deborl.

"And keep hiding." Sarit stayed at my side, feigning a smile, though her tone betrayed how desperately alone she'd been for the last months.

"Yes." I looped my arm with Sarit's. "And we'll be together."

"Look at your SEDs." The next afternoon, Stef reclined against a stack of crates in the storage room, blankets cushioning her against the splintering wood. "I've sent a keyword-recognition program to your devices. The basic searches are already installed: messages with our names or the words 'Janan,' 'cage,' or 'Soul Night' will be sent to you, and voice calls with those words will buzz your SED so you can listen."

Sam slouched and eyed his SED with distrust. "This thing is already confusing enough. You're making it worse."

"It's not Stef's *Everything* Device for no reason." She smirked and waved him closer so she could help him. "Look, it's not hard. There's a buzz coming in now. . . ."

"This will make spying on others a lot less tedious." I shifted through several tagged messages and glanced at Sarit, who was doing the same. "But no one seems to know what Merton brought back, only that it's important to Janan. And *I* had guessed that."

"Me too." Sarit put her SED in her pocket. "I was thinking about the people in prison. You and Sam were talking about freeing them, right?"

I nodded. "They probably won't want to help, but I want to *do* something. We can't sabotage much without hurting people, and we can't just tie up Deborl for a week; his house is too well guarded."

Sarit grinned. "I think I know a way to get them out, but we'd have to wait until right before dawn."

It didn't take much discussion before I was convinced, and we spent the remainder of the evening preparing and going over Sarit's plan until we were all confident we could pull it off.

Meanwhile, Stef kept an eye on her SED, monitoring calls and messages. We learned that people were afraid: afraid of Deborl and what he'd done to the city; afraid of Janan and what it would mean if he ascended, or didn't; and afraid of the rumors of the newsoul returning to Heart. What if she ruined everything?

Hah. Maybe they thought I had a real plan that didn't rely on dragons and poison and trapping myself inside the temple.

But it gave me a measure of satisfaction that people were afraid of Deborl and Janan. We couldn't rely on anyone to help us—they were more likely to betray us out of fear, like we'd argued with Whit and Orrin in the library—but it was a relief to know not everyone was ready to welcome Janan.

After a short rest, our SEDs beeped an hour after midnight, and we all dressed in red, the same color Deborl's guards wore. Our jackets and trousers weren't exactly like the guards' uniforms, but it was the best we could do with our limited resources and time; we were lucky to have all this cloth to begin with.

We left the textile mill, only a few sylph staying behind to guard it, and moved north toward the temple and Councilhouse. I tucked my hair into my cap as I followed Sam into the darkness.

Shadows pooled around us as we headed for South Avenue. We wouldn't be bothered unless someone got too close. Wearing the red laser pistols shoved into our waistbands, this was an opportunity to get a look around the city. As long as no one saw through our disguises.

As we came alongside the immense cage, I dared a glance. Templelight illuminated the bars and wires and troop of guards. Whatever Merton had brought back, it remained covered and unmoving.

"What do you think it is?" I muttered as Sam lifted a hand toward the guards around the cage. They waved back. For someone who spent most of his time writing music at home, he was alarmingly good at subterfuge. Stef was a *terrible* influence on him.

"I wish I knew." He hurried me along. Stef and Sarit would be waiting for us, since they'd gone straight to the market field. A big group would look suspicious, Sarit had said, because guards usually went in pairs. Since she'd been in the city the longest, I trusted her word.

After the dim road, the templelight was blinding as we crossed the market field to meet up with the others. We took a side door into the Councilhouse.

"Does it seem brighter to you?" Sam asked, shutting the door after a few sylph followed us in.

"It's been getting brighter these last couple of weeks," Sarit said.

Sam's voice grew heavy. "I wonder what it will look like on Soul Night."

The thought made me shiver. Four more days.

Sarit glanced down the hall, which was dark and quiet. Everyone was sleeping or wishing they were. She'd had lots of time to study the patterns and habits of guards, and while there was no time when it would be *easy* to sneak past everyone, the predawn hours provided the least resistance.

Shadows at our heels, we crept through the halls, straining to catch any sound of movement. Sarit's white-knuckled grip on her pistol never eased, but the building remained quiet, save the rumble and clatter of the world trembling beneath us.

Breaking into prison, it turned out, wasn't very difficult. Stef and Sam went in first, and after a few moments, they signaled Sarit and me to follow.

Three bodies slumped over a desk and chairs, clean burn holes in their temples. When I looked at Sam and Stef, they kept their eyes averted and motioned down a corridor. "That way," she said. "I'll unlock the cells from here."

I took Sarit's hand and dragged her with me. Sam and the sylph trailed after us, the latter keeping their heat low to avoid burning anything; we didn't want to leave evidence of their working with us.

Slumbering people crowded the cells, sleeping bags pressed against one another. There had to be a hundred people in this dark place of sweat and stench and hunger, with no empty floor space in any of the ten cells. They sighed and groaned in their sleep.

I turned on the lights.

Several people burrowed deeper into their sleeping bags, while others didn't move. A few pushed up onto their elbows and blinked around.

"Don't be alarmed," I said, conscious of the sylph around me like a cloak, and my friends walking up behind me. "We've come to free you."

"Is that Ana?" Whispers and mutters erupted throughout

the cells. A few shook others awake, and the prison grew loud with voices and rustling sleeping bags.

"The newsoul. She's back."

"She's going to get us all killed."

"Are those *sylph*?"

"Sylph!"

Within moments, every prisoner was on their feet and pressed as far back inside their cells as possible. One or two wept silently. Most just stared, terror in their eyes.

"Just like Menehem," breathed someone. "Come to kill us."

"I'm not here to hurt anyone!" My voice rang out over the cells. "We came to set you free. Stef is back there, ready to open your cells. But first I need you to know something."

The clamor of voices dulled, and gazes focused on me. I drew a few deep breaths to clear my head, but their fear and distrust was palpable.

"You've all been imprisoned for questioning Deborl, or refusing to follow his orders. Others have been killed." I met a man's grave eyes, and a woman's look of despair. "I know what you've suffered in the last few months.

"You know many of us left Heart and Range after the new year. Sarit and Armande stayed behind to watch and wait for our return. Because though I've been exiled, I swore I'd return and do everything I could to save Heart, the people here, and the people who left. I still intend to do that. Armande died at Deborl's hands several weeks ago, but Sarit was able to tell us what you've endured, and I'm here to tell you something: it will get worse."

"What do you mean?" someone asked, over the ripple of mutters. "I thought you were going to free us."

"I am here to free you." I straightened my shoulders and lifted my chin. "But Soul Night is coming, and Deborl is preparing for Janan's return. His ascension will trigger a series of massive eruptions. Whit"—his name caught in my throat, tangling with grief—"finished applying Rahel's seismic research to these signs, these earthquakes and dying plants and bulges in the land. There will be days and days of eruptions. The ash and pyroclasts will smother Heart and Range and all the surrounding lands. There will be nothing left."

"Do we all leave, then?" asked one of the boys, maybe a few years older than Sam and me. He kept eyeing the sylph, my silent, shadowy guardians.

I shook my head. "You can try, but you won't be able to outrun the eruption."

"Then what do we do?" asked a girl, a few years younger than me.

"I have a plan to keep Janan from returning—from ascending." I bit back revealing exactly what that plan was. Everyone already thought I was like Menehem. No need to give them more ammunition. "I'm going to do everything in my power to stop him, but I can't do it alone."

"What do you need?" The girl stepped forward, scraping

black hair from her face. "What can we do?"

"Where will everyone be when Soul Night begins?" I asked.

"By the cage," someone said. Others muttered agreement.

"All right. Then that's where I'm asking you to be, too. Disguise yourselves. Do whatever you must to keep from being caught until then, but I'll need you in that crowd. While Sam and I work, Stef and Sarit will be setting off distractions throughout the city, and we need people to point them out. We need to keep Deborl, Merton, and all of them away from what we're doing."

"And what *will* you be doing?" asked a man in the back of one of the cells.

I met his eyes, keeping mine hard and steady. "Doing anything I can to stop Janan from destroying everything."

"If we survive this," Sarit said, "maybe we'll be able to tell you everything Ana's done for Heart, oldsouls and newsouls alike. You wouldn't believe it now, but if we succeed, you will. If we succeed, you'll understand and believe what her friends already know: Ana can do anything."

I eyed her askance and frowned, but said nothing. They needed hope, and Sarit was giving it to them. Still, I wished she wouldn't use me as a vehicle for that hope. Yes, I'd do everything in my power to save Heart and the people I cared about, but my plan sounded crazy even to me. How was I supposed to succeed in this impossible task?

"Well," I said, "I'll certainly try."

Sam's hand curled around mine, and his thumb rubbed across my skin in a warm rhythm. He touched me all the time now, my hands or my hair or my back. The end of the world loomed nearer every moment, and time to touch each other was running out.

"And the sylph?" a girl asked. "How do they fit in?"

Black roses bloomed all around, and comforting heat enveloped the prison as the cell doors unlocked, then swung open. A trickle at first, and then the rest, the prisoners stepped out of their cells. They approached my sylph and me with only a little hesitation as I said, "They're my army."

26
BELIEF

"WE'RE GOING OUT for a few hours," Sarit said the last evening before Soul Night. The previous few days had been filled with planning and preparing and scattered napping, and all of us wore dark shadows under our eyes. "Stef has a few last-minute distractions she needs to check on. They involve fire."

I frowned. "You don't need our help?"

"Nope. It's a two-person job. You'll just get in our way." She kissed my cheek. "Get some rest. Or whatever." She turned quickly, but not before I caught the way she winked at Sam, and the sly look she and Stef shared as they left the storage room, then the mill. All the sylph followed.

"That was suspicious," I muttered, staring after them.

"Why did she wink at you?"

"No reason." Sam spoke a little too quickly.

Hmm. I narrowed my eyes. "And on the subject of suspicious, why do so many of my friends' names begin with an *S*?"

"It's a good letter." He stepped behind me and pulled the hair tie from the end of my braid, and gently began pulling the sections apart from the bottom up. Red spilled across my shoulders. I stopped moving and let him, relishing the feel of his fingertips on the back of my neck, down my shoulders. Even though we were alone, Sam kept his voice low. "But technically my name starts with a *D*."

"That's right. Dossam." I turned and looked up at him, my head dropped back so I could meet his eyes. "Maybe I should call you Dossam from now on. It's what I called you before we met."

"If I'd told you from the start that my name was Dossam, would you have been using my full name this whole time?" He rested his hands on my hips, watching me with dark eyes and genuine curiosity.

"I'm not sure." Dossam had always been my hero. The musician. The composer. He'd been a legend to me, almost not real. The boy I'd met in the woods had said his name was Sam. He'd saved me. Made me believe I was more than a nosoul. He'd been my friend, the first I ever had.

If *Dossam* had rescued me that night, rather than Sam, I'd probably never have bothered getting to know him beyond his music. I'd have tripped over myself, fumbling for any kind of coherent thought. I'd nearly ruined everything when I did find out who he was, and by then I'd already liked him for *him*.

"You're having a lot of thoughts." He released my hips and touched my chin, bringing our faces closer together when he leaned downward. "Good ones?"

"Maybe." I raised myself onto my toes and kissed him, just a soft brush of our lips.

His mouth curved into a smile, and the heat in his voice made me shiver. "I have to confess something. I asked them to give us some time alone.

"Maybe it's selfish to want time alone with you right now," he whispered, "but a year ago I promised to show you a thousand ways I love you. I thought we'd have more time. An entire lifetime."

I swallowed hard.

"Anyway," he said, "I wanted something special for tonight. I thought about taking you on the roof with a telescope, if we could find one. I would show you craters on the moon, other planets, and stars. But it's too bright out to risk it."

With the temple shining like the sun, we wouldn't have a good view of the sky anyway. "The idea is noted, though."

Sam took my hands. "You would have liked it."

"What did you have in mind instead?"

"Music?" He searched my eyes and squeezed my hands.

"I would give you everything if I could. Unfortunately, our options are limited right now."

I stood on my toes and kissed him, deeper than before. "Music is perfect."

He pulled away to dim the light until our world turned to dusk.

"Do you want to sit?" He glanced at a pile of blankets, rumpled from being used as a cushion.

"Yeah." My nerves caught and tangled with our *aloneness*. It was like fire, the way I wanted to be with him.

He settled on the blankets. Feeling bold, I sat so close my leg pressed against his, and he put his arms around my waist. His skin was hot against mine, even through our clothes.

"You choose what to listen to." I handed him an SED and watched as he scrolled through music. Titles flashed across the screen, pieces I'd heard only once, and pieces I loved so much they made my heart ache.

"Here." His voice was low, husky. "You'll like this one."

He chose a sonata called "Awakening." The piano began, its sound rich and warm as it surrounded me. Like air. Like blankets. Like Sam's arms. That was Sam's playing; I'd recognize it anywhere.

When the flute began to play, soft and low and mysterious, I shivered. "How are you playing both instruments at the same time?"

He gave a soft chuckle. "How can you tell they're both me?"

I twisted and raised my eyebrow. "Haven't you realized? I'll always know."

He smiled a little. "They were recorded separately. This recording was meant to be a test only, but I never got around to finding a partner for it."

"Ah." I let the music envelop me, growing sweeter, bolder, more seductive.

Though they were recorded separately, the flute and the piano blended together to make a new sound that flew through me. It was neither wholly flute nor wholly piano, but it made my heart soar higher than it had ever been. This sound, the way he played those instruments, was too lovely and strange to be real. I wanted to hold it inside of me forever, like I'd wanted the night he'd played my flute for the sylph, the night he'd seemed to conduct the orchestra of nature by simply holding an instrument.

When I looked at Sam, he seemed faraway, somewhen else. "What are you thinking?"

His face flushed. "Nothing. Sorry."

"No, tell me." I shifted so I could meet his eyes, and his hands breezed over my waist, as though he were afraid I'd fly off.

He breathed into my hair and held me tighter. "I've been having this dream since we returned to Range."

I waited.

"It's a little different every time, but in it, I'm always in a

334

forest listening for birdsong. I used to do that a lot. I liked to figure out ways to mimic their calls and try to understand what they meant. But in my dream, I hear something amazing. Not just a bird whistling, but a whole group of them singing with different voices, like an orchestra. Everything seems to join in the performance: the wind and water and leaves, the insects and mammals and birds. It's this beautiful, joyous music that's wild and unpredictable, but my heart feels like every note and beat is the most familiar thing in the world. It makes me feel like *home*, and every morning I wake up haunted by it. The emotions linger, but the music fades; I can't remember themes or melodies, no matter how much I try."

"That sounds frustrating."

"Incredibly." He sighed. "Now, after having the same dream so many times, it feels more like a memory of something long ago."

Maybe it was. "When Cris and Stef started to remember things in the temple, they said the memories were dreamlike. This could be more of Janan's memory magic shattering. And the way you describe the music . . ."

He looked up, hopeful.

"Remember when we went for a gardening lesson at Cris's house, and we both stopped to listen to the wind in the plants?"

"Yes." A sort of reminiscing sorrow stole his expression. "We both heard music."

I nodded. "And outside the cave, when you played the flute for the sylph? Did you notice anything about that?"

He seemed to search inside himself. "I don't know. Maybe."

"What you described before, about the music in your dream—that's what I heard that night. It seemed like you were conducting an entire symphony, like magic."

"You did? I— It felt special to me, but not like my dream. Not like *that*."

"I've heard it before, too. When you played 'Ana Incarnate' for the first time. I heard lightning and waves and wind. I heard . . . this force. This power that you play with."

His eyes met mine, dark and full of wonder. "Do you think that's it? The phoenix song?"

"Maybe." I smiled. "I think it could be."

"But we still don't know what it is, or how to do it on purpose. What use is it?"

It seemed to me he could call the music whenever he wanted, but I didn't want to pressure him. "We know it terrifies dragons. They think it can destroy them. It must be powerful. It *feels* powerful to me when I hear it."

He said nothing.

"To me, it sounded like life. The way the whole world seemed to join in, it made me feel alive."

"But dragons think it will destroy them."

"Maybe it depends who's using it, and why. The book said it was the song of life and death. Beginnings and endings.

They're all tied up together. It's the phoenix song. Expecting it to be as straightforward as a knife is a little unrealistic." I shrugged. "Why didn't you tell me about the dream before?"

"At first," he said, "I thought it was only a dream, and I didn't want to burden you with it. What we're doing tomorrow night is so much bigger than a half-remembered symphony."

"It's still important to me, if it's important to you."

He leaned his cheek on the crown of my head, his whisper a confession. "Even if we survive the ascension, what about the caldera? How can anyone survive Range erupting? How can anyone survive the ash cloud? It seems like no matter what we do, this is the end."

"If we stop Janan from ascending, the earth might settle, too. No eruption." No more earthquakes. Even now, I could feel a shudder in the ground, a constant reminder of the world's ability to open up.

"Then we could have this." He caught my hand in his, pressing it against his cheek. "A life together. And maybe it's only one, but we can fit a lot into one life."

"We've already done a lot. Flown on the backs of dragons. Discovered millennia-old secrets. Watched newsouls come into the world."

"Found each other at the masquerade." He kissed my fingertips.

"You knew who I was as soon as I arrived." I rolled my

eyes. "But *I* knew *you.*" When he'd shown me old photos, I'd known him in them, too.

"Maybe I knew you."

"Because I was wearing giant butterfly wings."

"That was a big clue, I'll admit."

"And I was probably the only person who didn't tell everyone else what they were going as."

He flashed a half smile. "Don't you want me to have known you immediately?"

"Oh, I do." I brushed my thumb over his cheekbone. "But I want it to be real. Not because you're a reasonably intelligent person who can recognize a short redhead when she's hiding her face. Besides, I know you don't believe in the matching souls stuff."

"You make me want to believe." He grew quiet.

Even if we lived through tomorrow night, I'd always look like me, even if I put on another costume. Besides, people didn't dedicate their souls to each other after only one life. A dedication of souls was supposed to be forever.

"I've decided," I whispered into the dimness. The sonata's final notes faded and another piece began, all warm lute strings and a clarinet.

"What's that?" His voice was heat, and his breath traced over the curves of my cheek. I never wanted to move.

"Everyone is terrified of the unknown. What happens after? Where do you go? What do you do?"

He gave a slight nod.

"I've decided what I think happens. Everyone is so busy being afraid, no one considers that what happens next might be good, too. Different. But not bad. Not something to be afraid of."

Sam kissed my cheek. "That sounds very wise."

"I don't want to be afraid of something that's inevitable. I don't want to go rushing toward it, because there are so many things I want to experience in life, but being terrified of something natural like that seems like a waste of energy."

"The pain that often accompanies death isn't very pleasant." He kept his voice low, thoughtful. "And pain often is a good reason to fear something. Fear is natural, too. It's what keeps us alive, sometimes."

I nodded. "I don't mean about not being afraid of everything that goes along with death. I'm still for avoiding it. I want to *live*. But as a whole thing. What happens next. What *really* happens next—rather than reincarnation bought with another's soul—doesn't have to be scary. I choose to believe it's another good thing. Like life. Another beginning. Only different."

"You have a beautiful way of thinking," he murmured, voice as sweet as the duet playing on the SED. He caressed my face, my throat, my shoulders, my arms. Everything melted under his touch, and the soft way he kissed me.

When I climbed onto his lap, our chests pressed together,

his kisses grew deeper and more passionate. His palms were hard against my spine, pulling me closer as he kissed my neck and shoulders and collarbone. He tugged my shirt askew and caressed the bare skin of my shoulder.

"I love you." His words pooled in the hollow of my throat. "I want to tell you a thousand times how much I love you."

I ran my fingers through his hair and turned his face up, leaned his head back, and kissed him. Soft black strands fell between my fingers, and his hands were up my shirt, palms flat on my back. My ribs. My waist.

My skin burned with our heat. I was melting into him.

Footsteps thundered through the mill, and light spilled across the storage room.

"Ana! Sam!" Sarit's voice was high and wild. Then she squeaked. "Oh. Oh no, I'm so sorry. I forgot. I can go away."

I scrambled off of Sam's lap, smoothing my clothes as my face ached with a blush. Sam pulled his knees to his chest and shifted uncomfortably.

"Oh, you guys." Sarit covered her face. "I'm *so* sorry. I can't believe I— Yeah. I'm going away."

"It's fine," Sam said, his tone clear that this was *not* fine. His clothes were crooked and his skin flushed. "Just tell us what's going on."

Sarit bit her lip, glancing between us.

"There are so many things I could say right now." Stef appeared behind Sarit, wearing an expression of awkward amusement. "I hope you both understand what a great effort it is for me to withhold comments."

"And we appreciate it." Sam's voice was tight.

My heart thudded—not in the fun way—and every bit of me burned with embarrassment. So much for having the whole night alone. "Maybe you should just tell us whatever you burst in here to say."

Sarit and Stef sobered as they exchanged glances. "We found out what's in the cage," Sarit said.

Sam looked up. I didn't move.

"It's a phoenix."

27

FLAMES

THE SPRING EQUINOX dawned cloudless and bright, with the whole world holding its breath. Even the constant rumble of earthquakes paused, leaving everything strangely silent and muted for the hours Sam and I moved throughout the mill, discussing our plans again, touching the supplies we'd carry tonight.

Using scraps she'd found in the nearby mills and factories, Stef had constructed gloves and boot covers that would help us scale the Councilhouse. She'd wanted to attempt making copies of the key, in case one of us was held back, but Sam wouldn't let her take it apart in case it wouldn't work again. Anyway, it seemed to me the key was imbued with magic, and despite all of Stef's talents, she'd never be able to replicate that.

Sylph trickled through the mill halls, moaning and singing anxiously.

-They don't like waiting for Soul Night,- Cris said. -They'd rather attack now.-

"There's nothing we can do now." I spoke quietly to keep from waking Stef and Sarit; they'd stayed up longer than Sam and I had, going out a couple more times to check that the mill was secure, and to set remote-activated diversions. "If we release the poison now"—which we didn't even have— "Janan would overcome it long before Soul Night started and we'd have wasted everything."

-They don't like trusting the dragons to bring the poison.-

It was a little late for us to worry about that. "We just have to trust that the dragons want Sam and his phoenix song destroyed. They'll help."

"That's not reassuring," Sam muttered.

-What if the dragons spot the phoenix and think we've betrayed them?-

I shook my head. "It's still covered. Deborl is supposed to unveil it only when Janan allows, right? So the dragons won't see it unless it wakes up and breaks free of its bonds."

What did Janan even want the phoenix *for*, though?

-What if-

"Stop." I held up my hands. "We're not going to do this. We're not going to second-guess everything at the last minute. We're not going to wish 'if only we had more time' or 'if only we had a better plan.' This is what we have. We need to make the most of it."

Cris started to drift away.

The last thing I wanted to do today was fight with my friends. I made my voice softer. "I know they're all worried. They're all counting on me to stop Janan so they can stop being sylph."

-I am, too.-

"I know." Again, I remembered Cris lying on the altar, the flash of silver as he raised the knife, the gold of the phoenix blood still marking the blade after five thousand years. It was my fault he was trapped like this. He'd chosen what he thought would be death. But this—as a sylph—no. For saving my life, he bore the same punishment as those who'd tortured a phoenix in their quest for immortality.

As much as I wanted to help them, free them from this existence, the idea of so many depending on me was staggering. I was only beginning to learn how to do things for myself. I'd done everything I could for newsouls, which hadn't turned out like I'd hoped, and now sylph needed me, too.

Another hour passed talking with Sam and Cris, trying to comfort one another, and encourage. But the sylph were right: waiting was the worst.

We were sitting in the weaving room when Sam looked up and scowled. "Did you hear—"

The door flew open. Daylight flooded the room, and all the sylph swarmed toward the door, heat billowing off them.

Sylph songs turned to screeches a heartbeat later. Brass objects skittered into the room. Sylph eggs. Lids open. My sylph poured into the eggs like smoke through a flue.

Crashing sounded from the storage room, then footsteps.

Sam and I scrambled for our pistols as a dozen people in bright red burst into the room. Half of them dove toward the sylph eggs, flipping the lids shut before the sylph could escape. From the others, blue targeting lights shone across the room and turned on Sam and me.

A sylph peeled away from the shadows, burning through wool and skin and tissue. The stink of cooking flesh filled the room as another guard withdrew a sylph egg, twisted it, and flipped open the lid. Cris darted toward the hall where Stef and Sarit were coming, their weapons ready.

Everything was chaos. I fired my pistol, not thinking about a person there, only that they'd come to kill us. Trap the sylph. Take the key.

People screamed as lasers threaded the room. Wood burned and cracked. Machinery came crashing to the floor, and the reek of smoke permeated the room.

Sam dragged me behind one of the burning looms, then pushed me down so we were both crouching. "First chance you get, grab your bag and get out of here. Don't wait for anyone."

"But—"

"No. You have the key. You know the plan. It must succeed, no matter what."

I clenched my jaw and peered through the flames, which licked across the old, polished wood of the fallen looms. The smoke caught in my throat, making me cough.

Stef and Sarit shot more guards, using a door in the hallway as a cover. Cris burned through people, struggling to open the eggs scattered across the floor, but he was incorporeal. He couldn't touch anything.

"We need to get the eggs open," I hissed.

Sam stood and shot the last guard before she could trap Cris.

The fire grew quickly, so we waited only a moment before the four of us crept from our hiding places and reached for the nearest eggs to free the sylph. Just as my hands closed around one of the brass devices, more guards poured into the room, targeting lights shining everywhere.

I flipped open the lid of my egg and let it go. Hot pain flared across my right arm as I grabbed for my pistol, but I ignored the sharp bloom of heat. My pistol was ready. I aimed at the door and shot. Someone dropped, clutching their burned leg. Around me, Sam, Stef, and Sarit were shooting too, though they had better aim.

A couple of sylph fluttered from their eggs, disoriented from being trapped for even a few minutes. But Cris rallied them and they dove in front of us, acting as shields, absorbing the laser blasts, as they had the acid from the dragons.

Smoke thickened in the room, searing my lungs. The fire licked the ceiling now, roaring as it grew. There was nowhere to hide.

With a sylph guarding me, I pushed forward and reached for another egg, but blue light—immediately followed by pain—shot across my fingers. I jumped back.

"Ana!" Sarit's voice pierced the cacophony of fire and screams and sylph song. Red marked her bare arms, and her face was flushed with heat and pain. She shook back the black tendrils of her hair as she hefted her pistol and shot another guard. "Get your bag and *go*."

Not without everyone else. I searched for Sam in the smoke-choked weaving room, but I couldn't find him or Stef. "Sam!" Smoke burned my lungs and made my voice crack. "Stef!"

One of the guards near me dropped, pistol burns crisscrossing his face. My sylph shield stretched as I bent to open another egg, but the heat of sylph and fire and pain made my head swim. I fumbled for the lid. My fingers caught with one another, feeling disconnected as the metal bit into them. My thoughts felt thin and faraway as I staggered toward the door and my bag there.

But I couldn't leave without my friends.

"Stef!" I couldn't see her. "Sam!" The smoke was too thick, and the fire too bright as it ate through the old wood of the mill, consuming walls and support beams and crates of woven fabric. My vision swam, fogging at the edges. When I searched for Sarit, she was gone, too.

Guards still flooded through the building, coming in from the door at the other end of the mill. Blue speared the smoke, aiming right at me, but my sylph caught the blast, then shifted around me where fire burned a loom. Heat poured *into* the sylph, smothering the fire a fraction before the sylph had to guard me again.

"Cris! Sarit!" My foot bumped something soft, and I stumbled over a body, the blackened corpse of a guard. I screamed and scrambled over him, toward the bags piled by the door.

Someone knocked me over as I reached for my backpack. My elbow and shoulder and head hit the floor, and the sudden pain shocked me back into alertness. I turned around and found a giant of a man bearing down on me.

Merton.

My sylph roared up between us, thick and black and burning. At the last second, Merton must have realized the sylph would block his shot. He turned and the blue targeting light beamed across the room, landing on Sam as he stumbled from the wreckage of a torched loom.

Stef shoved Sam aside.

Red and black welled up across her throat. A chunk of her hair seared off. Her eyes grew wide as she and Sam crashed to the floor.

My sylph surged up and wrapped itself around Merton. Three more shadows left their mostly dead targets and pooled over Merton, who screamed as his skin blistered and sloughed and blackened. The stench of burned flesh and hair overpowered the smoke. As Merton's screams fell into gasps and gurgles, I looked away. I didn't want to see him die.

Head spinning from the smoke and pain, I groped for my backpack and hauled it over my shoulders.

Bodies littered the floor, most of them burned beyond recognition. But the guards were gone. Either dead or dying. The fire still blazed, roaring across the weaving room and through to the other areas. I had to get out. But first I had to gather my friends.

"Sam." I coughed out his name as I staggered over corpses. "Stef. Sarit."

The sylph formed a line against the fire, absorbing what heat and flame they could to keep it from spreading, but it wouldn't be long before the building collapsed further.

Stef's eyes were wide and glassy. She wasn't moving, but she gasped a little. The burn on her throat made a heavy dark line, surrounded by red.

"No." I stumbled and dropped in front of her as Sam and Sarit approached, too. "Stef, come on. We've got to go."

She blinked, long and slow, and her eyes rolled toward me, though she seemed unfocused. Her mouth worked, but no sound came out.

Sam reached for her, stopped, reached again. Tears dripped down his face. "You're okay. We've got a lot of work to do, and we need you."

She closed her eyes and mouthed, "No."

Sarit leaned over and hugged me. Her voice was ragged as she spoke by my ear. "You have to go. Get Sam and go. I'll release the rest of the sylph and tell them to follow you."

Fire rushed around us, licking toward the door and the bags there.

"You have to come find us, too." I took Sarit's shoulders and held her at arm's length. "I'm not losing you. Come find us after you set the sylph free."

She glanced at her arms, speckled with burn marks. Her face, too, had dark bruises blooming, or smoke stains. I couldn't tell. "Okay." Her cough was deep and dry, and blood dotted her arm where she tried to cover her mouth. "You have to go. Promise you'll stop him."

"I promise." Tears ached around my eyes as I hugged her again, then touched Stef's cheek. Her skin was warm, but the heat wasn't from within her. It was the fire's. I searched for the words to tell her how much she meant to me, but nothing came. Nothing big or important enough. "I love you." The roar of the fire crushed my whisper.

Somewhere else in the mill, wood crashed to the floor, and flames rushed through the hall.

Sam was petting Stef's hair, repeating something that was lost in the cacophony. I wanted to let him stay with her, but Sarit glared at me and I grabbed his arm. "Let's go."

He struggled against me. "No."

Footsteps clomped through the mill. More guards. "Come on!"

Sylph flew through the fire, holding it back from us, but the fire grew and their numbers stayed the same.

Stef wasn't moving. I couldn't see her breathing. Sarit bent over her, sobbing, but when she looked at me, her eyes were fierce and demanding.

I hauled Sam to his feet, and we scrambled over burned bodies. His face was dark with rage and smoke as he accepted the backpack I thrust into his arms.

Ten guards emerged from the hallway, air masks over their faces. I leveled my pistol and shot, and one clutched his shoulder as he turned and saw me through the smoke. He aimed back at me, then dropped as blue light flashed from Sarit's pistol.

"*Go.*" Below her, Stef was dead. Behind her, a trio of sylph held back the fire. Everywhere lay bodies and sylph eggs.

I dug my free hand into Sam's coat and yanked him toward

the door. Smoke billowed after us as we emerged into the hot light of noon. People gathered, and a medical vehicle came toward the mill.

"Where do we go?" I asked Sam, but he was looking back at the smoke-filled doorway. He coughed and wiped his face, smearing tears and ash over his cheeks. He'd just lost his best friend. He wouldn't be able to help.

Avoid the people. They'd report us to Deborl.

That was a good first step.

Most of the people were westward, toward the main avenue, so I yanked Sam east, around the building. He ran with me, gasping and coughing. My breath was short and scratchy, and every time I looked over my shoulder, all I could see was the smoke pouring upward, a gray column against the clear sky and the intense light of the temple.

There were people, some pointing, some chasing. Some wore red, like the guards. I ran faster, though my backpack dragged at me and Sam seemed blind with tears and grief.

We ducked behind buildings, moving every which way. I tried to be smart about which paths we took, I wanted to be smart, but Stef's final sacrifice, Sarit's promise that she'd follow—

No.

Afternoon wore on as we ran along the edge of the industrial quarter, hiding in and behind anything available. Finally I found myself across East Avenue and in the northeastern residential quarter. A white house loomed above us. Evergreens huddled close to it. Dead vines and weeds littered the garden. The grass was long and brown. No one had been through here in a year, at least.

A darksoul home.

I glanced southward, toward the industrial quarter. The smoke had thinned, drifting across the sky like a memory. I couldn't hear sounds of pursuit. The world around me seemed silent and dead. Even Sam just stared blankly, whispering, "It should have been me. She saved me."

There was nothing I could do for his grief. Instead, I took his hand and guided him into the darksoul house before anyone came looking for us.

28

EQUINOX

THE DARKSOUL HOUSE was filthy, heavy with dust and neglect and age. I didn't know who'd lived here before, but only memories occupied this space now.

My lungs still felt choked with smoke as I helped Sam onto a musty sofa. He collapsed over his knees, face buried in his arms. His sobs were quiet, broken, so I pushed down my grief and moved through the house to make sure we were alone. Maybe there was something useful.

The house was laid out a lot like Sam's house, with a large portion of the first floor dedicated to art. Canvases covered the walls, while statues and wood carvings filled the main floor. Blankets protected the hardwood, though now the wool was tattered and gray.

In the kitchen, I found an old block of cheese. I cut off the mold and put the rest on a plate to take to Sam. There was bread on the counter, but it looked more like a compost pile than food.

I added a slab of dried venison to the plate and poured two cups of water. It wasn't much of a meal, but it was better than nothing.

"Start eating." I left the food by Sam and headed upstairs, where I found clean clothes inside cedar chests, and a cabinet full of painkillers and burn ointments. My arm and fingers throbbed where I'd been shot, but I'd been burned worse.

I took a few painkillers and brought some down to Sam, who was slowly cutting the cheese into slices.

"Here." I handed him a few pills and finished slicing.

We ate without conversation. The food tasted old, sort of dusty, but it was better than starving, and it gave me the energy to check the windows for signs of anyone after us.

"This was Vic's house," Sam said after a few minutes. "He built most of the statues around the market field and carved the relief on top of the Councilhouse. Lots of other things, too, but those were the projects everyone talked about."

"Is he the one who taught you carving?" Outside, the trees were white and motionless. "Like at your cottage and the shelves in your house?" Sam's graveyard had been filled with beautiful statues of animals and people playing music. Even the benches had been art. And inside, the wall of bookshelves had creatures of Range etched into the edges. Herons, bears, elk, wolves, shrikes.

"Yeah." Sam finished his water and stood. "He carved some of them, and taught me how to do it myself. I was never as good as him, and I had to be careful of my hands, but we became friends. I wanted you to learn from him, too."

I moved away from the window and took in Sam's wrecked appearance. Smoke stains clung to his shirt and trousers, and his hair hung in black mats. We both needed to shower, and there were enough of Vic's old clothes upstairs we could surely find something to fit.

"Come on." I motioned toward the stairway. "We've got a few hours."

While he showered, I checked outside again. Nothing. No sylph. No Sarit.

She'd said she would follow.

But she hadn't believed it. She'd known, then. She'd known she wouldn't make it.

I slumped to the end of the bed and checked for messages that wouldn't be there. Nothing from Stef. She was dead. Nothing from Sarit. She was dead, too.

My best friend was dead.

A sob burst from me as I fumbled for the message function on my SED. My thumbs slipped over the letters as I typed.

I miss you. I miss you. I can't believe you're gone and never coming back. I hate Janan and I hate Deborl. Even if I

stop Janan tonight, how will the world be right without
you? I wish you were still with me.

My chest ached as I sent the message she'd never receive.

Her image smiled at me from the screen. Sarit with her bees. Sarit and me, sitting in the market field with cups of coffee. Sarit dressed as an exotic bird for the masquerade last year.

Tears blurred the pictures, and I let my SED drop to my lap.

When Sam finished showering, I hurried to wash the stink off me, but there was no washing away the ache of loss. Sorrow saturated every bit of me like acid.

Dry and dressed, I found Sam sitting on the foot of the bed, listening to music.

"Let me treat your burns." I sat next to him, but he stopped me before I opened the tube.

"I don't want—" He touched my cheek and let his fingertips trail down my neck and shoulder, and suddenly I was too conscious of the way my borrowed clothes were too big and hung off my shoulders and hips. "Later," he said. "The burns aren't going anywhere."

The burn cream and other medical supplies dropped to the floor with soft thuds.

"I just want you. I want you forever, and I'm afraid—" His hands closed over mine. "I want a life with you. I'd give anything to go back and start this one over, to be reborn into

357

this lifetime. I wouldn't waste it. I'd find you sooner. I'd take you somewhere safe. I'd show you music and love and life every day so you were never alone, never afraid. If I could start over knowing what I know now—" He released a desperate laugh. "I know how this sounds."

"It's okay." My words were a breath, a gasp.

He squeezed my hands. "I'm afraid, Ana. I'm afraid, and I feel like if I don't kiss you right now, I'll break apart."

The music ended. Silence tugged through the room. All I could hear was Sam's shallow breathing. All I could feel was the pounding of my heartbeat.

He wanted this now? After everything that had happened? Before everything we were about to do? How could anyone—

No, I understood. A heavy desire for *him* wove through me. We'd lost so much, and we were about to lose even more. If we survived Soul Night, maybe we could have a life together.

But victory seemed an unattainable goal, and right now we had each other.

I wouldn't waste our chance by hesitating.

"You won't break apart," I said. "I won't let you." I watched his mouth, the curve of his lips and the creases and the gentle parting between from the way he might have been about to respond but couldn't seem to find words. The seconds spun longer as I caressed his cheeks and through his hair, all shaggy from weeks without cutting. Then I kissed him.

He let out a relieved groan and pulled me in, his mouth

warm and firm against mine. Jaw muscles worked beneath my palms. Stubble scraped my skin. I didn't care. I wanted only to drown in this kiss.

His hands slid down my sides and settled on my hips. I looped my arms around his shoulders and let him lay me onto my back, damp hair haloed around me. He kissed my throat and shoulders, gasped for breath over my collarbone.

I couldn't think. I could only feel the way his hands glided over my stomach and down my legs. Emotions caught up and tangled in my throat as he helped me out of my shirt and trousers, leaving only a thin silk camisole and leggings beneath. I shivered in the cool air.

"Is this all right?" he whispered. "If you don't want to, that's okay."

"I want to." I sat up and stretched to pull his shirt over his head. In the dim room, his skin was dark and I couldn't see the burns, just shadows and planes of muscle that shifted beneath my hands. "I've loved you my entire life. From the moment I first heard music, to when I saw your name inside a book, to the night you saved me from the water. No one has ever made me feel like you do: like I'm wanted; like I matter."

He kissed me, long and beautiful and desperate, and he didn't resist when I pulled him down on top of me, trying to draw him impossibly close.

But our lives were made of impossible things. I'd known him at the masquerade. We'd danced as though we'd been dancing for years and centuries and millennia. And when we'd kissed for the first time, we'd become a song with one breath, one voice, and infinite melodies. It was music, the way he touched me, the way our bodies fit together.

He caressed my ribs and hips and legs, then kissed trails of fire down my throat. The heat of his body over mine made me yearn for something deeper, but I let him set our pace as he kissed me, hungry and desperate, firm and fierce, and gentle as though I was the most precious thing in the world to him.

He drew off my camisole, making my whole body hum with anticipation and desire. The last of our clothes dropped to the floor with a soft *whumph.*

My heart filled up as he showed me a thousand ways he loved me, and in these glorious moments of peace, there was no fear or mourning or despair. There was only this boy. This body entwined with mine. This soul I'd always known.

Questions hovered in the gasp-filled inches between us, but I was too dizzy to think. I touched his face, his hair, smoothed back the black strands while I waited for him to say something. If we should say anything. A thread of awkwardness coiled inside me as the waiting grew longer.

Sam kissed me again, and in the dimness, he looked my age. Really my age, not the illusion of reincarnation. He looked like I felt: excited and hopeful, a little nervous. "I hope that was—"

360

"Wonderful." Did I speak too quickly? My voice was high and giddy. I hardly sounded like myself. "It was wonderful."

"Oh, good." Relief echoed in his words. "Good."

The idea of him being worried about it made me giggle, and then he laughed, too, until we couldn't breathe anymore and had to resort to shallow gasping that turned into kissing. I wanted this to go on forever.

But as my love deepened and spilled through me like music, pieces of me dreaded what would come next. We'd already lived through terrible things, terrible losses. And what happened tonight would only be worse.

Two hours before sunset, we took our things and started west, toward the temple and Councilhouse. I'd seen no sign of the sylph, but we couldn't wait. Using Stef's program, I'd tracked SED conversations about the fire and what was to happen tonight. Most people only speculated on how Janan would return, and what would happen with the phoenix trapped inside the cage.

Deborl had put out a warning about the escaped prisoners, as well as Sam and me, reminding everyone that I was an exile and Janan might not reward them if they didn't find and capture me. Or kill me. Killing was better.

I kept that to myself as Sam and I crept through the northeastern residential quarter, cutting through yards, hiding inside houses and behind trees whenever we heard voices.

The sun stretched lower toward the city wall, silhouetting the temple in the center of the city.

"Do you think the dragons will really come?" Sam asked.

"I think they will."

"Because they want me dead."

"They want the threat of the phoenix song gone."

"It's hard to believe this is something they're trying to destroy me for. Not just one lifetime, but all of them."

Mysterious as it was, the phoenix song was as much a part of him as his soul. A year ago, Councilor Sine had called music a "passion of the soul," which had resonated with me. After years of being called "nosoul," I'd still been accepting that I had a soul, and hearing that poetry or music or art could be tied to the soul had made me glow with happiness. But with Sam, it seemed music was literally part of him, something so intrinsic to his soul he'd be a wholly different person without it.

Yet he still didn't know how to use it.

Well, he wasn't a phoenix.

We came to the edge of the market field with an hour to spare. Our goal had been to get here early to give us time to wait on top of the Councilhouse for the dragons, but we hadn't anticipated all of Heart getting here early, too.

From behind heavy underbrush, we spied thousands of people in the market field, closing in on the industrial quarter where the cage was. Bright lights hung from poles, the white beams focused on the cage and the cloth-covered lump inside it. Could there really be a phoenix in there? It didn't look as if it had moved in the days since Merton had paraded it into the city—not that I had a good view from here.

"We have to cross the market field," Sam muttered.

"Yeah." Maybe we should have come much earlier, but then we'd have been waiting on the roof for hours, possibly getting seen. . . . "Let's go north, then around. Most people will be heading south, so we only need to wait for the market field to clear on that side before we climb up."

Sam's expression darkened, but he nodded and we crept north and east along the edge of the market field, hiding in brush and trees whenever voices came too close, but never forgetting that time was limited. If we were too late—

We wouldn't be too late.

As evening deepened, the temple seemed to shine brighter, a fallen star in the center of our city. *Their* city. I was an exile.

It seemed like forever before the flow of people on this side of the market field stopped. Their voices toward the industrial quarter were a low roar, and I could just hear someone speaking above the crowd.

"Janan, who gave us life!" The voice sounded like Deborl. "Janan, who gave us souls!"

A cheer rose up at his lies. They'd all been living and soul-filled long before Janan began reincarnating them. I wanted to believe there was *something* out there giving life and souls, but I *knew* it wasn't Janan.

"Let's go," I muttered to Sam, and together, we trotted across the market field. I strained my ears for any sounds besides ours, but I heard only the steady *thump, thump* of our boots hitting the cobblestones.

I checked over my shoulder, hyperaware and paranoid that someone was watching us, but I didn't see anyone in the gloaming, only shadows. The temple lit our path, too brilliant to look at directly. I kept my eyes down as we approached and veered toward the Councilhouse, which was fused to the temple.

Half an hour until sundown.

At the base of the Councilhouse, Sam and I pulled off our backpacks and removed Stef's last gift: gloves and boot covers.

We were going to scale the exterior wall of the Councilhouse.

The gloves and boot covers were inside out to keep the adhesive fresh, and to keep them from sticking to everything else we owned. As quickly as we could, we stepped into the boot covers and pulled on the gloves, carefully tightening all the straps so they wouldn't slip off.

"Ready?" I glanced at Sam.

He looked grim, but determined. "Yes."

I shouldered my backpack—awkwardly, thanks to the

gloves—and pressed my palm against the white stone wall. It stuck.

Giving it a little tug, the adhesive held, and I reached with my other hand, higher. I tugged, and it didn't come loose.

"It's working?" Sam balanced with his elbow on the wall, peeling his feet off the ground slowly. With only his toes on the cobbles, he jumped with his hands splayed out, smacked the wall, and hung like that until he pulled up his legs and pushed upward.

"It's working." I did the same as he had. It'd be the only boost we got. The adhesive held if jerked on, but would peel off quite readily. That meant we had to crawl up the side of the Councilhouse, as there were no outside stairs, and no roof access points from inside the building.

So we crawled, reaching and pushing and stretching ourselves higher until we came to the rooftop. White spread out ahead of us, and over the far edge I could just see the gathered crowd, all trying to get a peek at the cage. Was the cloth off the phoenix yet? Was the poor creature still alive?

The sun moved below the wall, making the sky look brilliant blue.

Ten minutes until sunset.

I tore off my sticky gloves and pulled my boots from the slip-ons. "Where are the dragons?" They should have been here by now. Already we wouldn't have the distractions that

Stef and Sarit had put together, since they had to be remotely activated and said remotes were still in the mill. Whatever was left of the mill . . .

"Maybe Acid Breath lied," Sam said. "Maybe they aren't coming."

Just then, a tremendous thunder burst through the sky. The crowd below was silenced. I held my breath and looked north.

From among the broken black obelisks, a hundred dragons took to the sky. Their wings shone brilliantly in the setting sun as they surged toward the temple.

Chaos erupted and screams sounded from below, but my heart lifted. The dragons had arrived.

Acid Breath landed, delivering the first canister of poison. He swung his head around to face Sam and me. <As promised, we will rip the tower from the earth.>

"Thanks." Such a small word, considering my heart felt ready to burst. I hadn't really believed that we could work with dragons, but we had. They'd come through.

Acid Breath roared and took off, his wings creating a wave of air that made me gasp for breath.

As the next dragon landed, I glanced at Sam. He was pale and sweating, and his knuckles were white where he gripped his laser pistol, but he was still functioning.

More of the dragon army dove toward the temple, delivering canisters of poison. Fifteen were here. Five to go.

Seven minutes until sunset.

I fumbled through my coat pocket for the key. I would create a door and open the canisters from the inside. Then—ideally—I would escape before the door shut and I was trapped as the dragons ripped the tower from the earth, as Acid Breath had said.

It was a simple plan. It had to work. But just as my fingers closed around the silver box, heat seared through my skin. I screamed and dropped the key. It skidded across the roof.

On the other side of the Councilhouse, Deborl stood with his laser pistol raised. How had he gotten up here?

I ran for the key, but lost sight of it when another dragon landed on the roof and delicately placed a canister of poison near the temple. Then it took off, the force of its wings on air making me stagger back. Sam grabbed for me, and we both tried to watch the place where we'd last seen the key as the long, gold body lifted and talons latched onto the temple.

The key had moved.

Deborl ran for it, and desperately, I wished I hadn't asked Acid Breath not to hurt the rest of the population. Either all humans looked alike to dragons and they thought Deborl was Whit, or the dragon leader had taken my request seriously.

I reached for my pistol as another dragon landed with a canister.

"Wait!" I shouted at the dragon. "Kill that one!"

But the cacophony of fear below was too loud. People ran for their weapons. Someone would release the air drones soon. When the dragon took off again, I aimed my pistol at Deborl, but he had moved, abandoning the key.

He stood by the canisters.

He'd guessed what we were doing, why we'd gone to Menehem's lab.

My SED beeped four minutes to Soul Night.

Sam and I both shifted our aims, but Deborl was already moving. He shot open two of the canisters. Aerosol spewed from the holes.

"No!" I screamed and ran toward him, like I could plug the holes with my hands, but another dragon landed and blocked my way. "It's too early!"

Sam was running with me, toward the dragon, toward the hissing canisters. Tears blurred my vision as I bent and grabbed the fallen key. The dragon took off. Sam and I staggered backward.

When the roof was clear of the dragon's tail, Sam surged ahead and shot Deborl. He had moved as soon as Sam's weapon was lifted, though. Only his arm was hit.

I tried to catch up, but another dragon arrived and placed its canister on the roof. I screamed and tried to get its attention, but the dragon's face turned up, and the ringing in my ears made me stagger.

<Finally. The song . . .>

When the dragon took off, I found Sam and Deborl wrestling on the other side of the roof. Their pistols had fallen away. They were hitting, kicking. I'd never seen Sam fight before, not like this. I couldn't tell if he was winning or not. He did have a size advantage, but Deborl was fast.

I raised my pistol to shoot Deborl, but my hands were shaking and I didn't trust my aim. I might hit Sam.

And the canisters were still spewing the poison.

Two minutes.

The final dragon landed and placed its canister next to the others, pausing only a second to nudge one of the open canisters. <It has begun!> The dragon took off before I could attract its attention.

My ears rang with the din of dragon conversation above. They'd wrapped themselves around the temple, and globs of acid drooled down the sides.

One more glance at Sam and Deborl. They were still fighting, still grunting and trying to kill each other. I could help, as soon as I got this poison into the temple.

I pulled out the temple key and pressed the square. A door shimmered on the white wall, and I yanked it open, ready to shove the canisters inside, but singing stopped me.

-Ana!- All the sylph flowed across the roof, burning hotter. Beyond them, a dragon hung off the roof like a ladder, glaring at me.

"Help Sam!"

-No time.- Cris tangled around me. -Push the poison inside. We'll heat the canisters. Hopefully the explosion will be enough.-

"Cris, no. Who knows what that could do to you?"

-Don't argue. This is our redemption. We need to fight for it.-

One minute. I didn't want to let the sylph be trapped in there with all that poison, but Cris was right: this was their fight, too. As quickly as I could, I began shoving twenty canisters of poison into the temple.

The doorway was all misty gray; I couldn't see anything beyond, but the sylph threw themselves inside as I pushed the last canister in with a grunt.

Over my shoulder, I caught a glimpse of Sam wrestling Deborl to the ground. The younger boy stopped struggling, but his chest heaved with breath.

Sam looked back at me. "Are you all right?"

The door slammed shut as the last of the sylph vanished into the gray, and the shriek of dragon conversation made my head spin.

My SED beeped. Beyond the wall, the sun fell below the horizon.

Deborl's outstretched hand closed around a laser pistol, and he brought it around.

"Look out!" There was no way Deborl could miss that shot.

Sam jerked away from the other boy just as darkness washed across the roof.

Soul Night was upon us.

And the temple was dark.

29

JANAN

ABOVE, DRAGONS ROARED in triumph as they coiled
muscles and spit acid onto the dull, white stone. The reek of
acid poured through the air, making my nose burn and my
lungs ache.

The temple was dark.

It was Soul Night.

We'd done it.

I ran for Sam, tracking the blue light of the laser pistol
Deborl held. All I could hear was screaming and dragons and
the incessant ringing in my ears. I was blind with darkness
and deaf with noise, and my whole body ached with burns
and fatigue and grief.

"Sam!"

Stone cracked above, and bits of rock pattered against the roof like hail, drowning out the sound of my voice. There were other voices below, too, thousands of people screaming.

Twilight bled across the world, the sky an eerie violet that deepened into night as I pushed myself toward Sam. He was nothing but an outline of blackness as I called his name. He was still standing, at least. And the blue targeting light came from below him, which meant Deborl hadn't gotten to his feet yet.

The light swung around toward me, dazzlingly bright as it darted over my eyes.

I dropped to the ground and rolled away, the lump of my backpack hindering my movements. Scattered shards of temple bit into my knees and bare hands, but I huddled low to the roof and crawled toward Sam. I'd been a fool to give away my position.

Deborl, however, either didn't realize how obvious he was, or didn't care. The blue light moved through the darkness, bright enough to keep my eyes from adjusting, not bright enough to see by.

The roof shuddered as a chunk of stone fell from above. Pebbles sprayed like shards of glass, slicing open my exposed skin where they flew by. Roaring and the thunder of dragon wings muffled my cries of pain as I moved away from the place Deborl had almost shot me.

I could see Sam; he was silhouetted against the glow of

spotlights, which shone on the market field and industrial quarter. Did he know he was so visible? I wanted to call out a warning, but the chaos of falling rock and screams would drown my voice.

I searched for the blurs and outlines of Deborl, and where his targeting light originated. He lay on the far side of the roof, just a smudge of dark against the glow of lights.

Slowly, I drew my pistol and covered the targeting light with my finger. I aimed at Deborl and took long, measured breaths to steady my hand. The clatter of rocks and voices and wing beats faded for a heartbeat.

I fired.

Deborl screamed and the world came rushing back. The shriek and roar and cracking of stone loomed overhead. Soon, the temple would come down on us.

I scrambled to my feet and ran for Sam. No time to check if the other dragon was still waiting on the edge of the roof. We'd find a way down.

Before I could cross half the roof, the world jerked and I tumbled over. Stones stabbed my palms and elbows as I rolled onto my back. Pain sliced through my shoulder blade and my spine. Chunks of rocks gouged at my skin, and fire flared in the back of my head.

Overhead, immense shapes flew from the tower and roared. Claws scraped. Stone screamed as it was torn apart.

Then light blazed, white and blinding above me.

374

I threw my hands over my eyes and rolled over, as though I could protect myself from the burn. Even huddled over, arms wrapped around myself, all I could see was white white white as tears poured from my light-seared eyes. It felt like they were bleeding, like color was fading out. My head throbbed with blinding light.

I was blind.

What if I was blind forever?

I howled against my knees, against the rocks and roof, but I couldn't hear my own voice in the tumble of rocks and the roar of dragons and the shrieking of telepathy and the screams of people and the crash of the earth shaking itself apart.

Gradually, the white dulled into gray. I sat up and squinted through my fingers.

The light still blazed, but I could see grades of pale gray.

Rocks plummeted to the roof and to the market field below, but they were smaller chunks now, shaken from dragon talons or wings. The pebbles seemed to rain down silently, the sounds of their impact covered by the din of everything else.

Darkness in the south drew my attention.

A plume of brown smoke boiled into the air, as though something had exploded there.

No, not smoke.

Ash surged upward, chased by red and gold lava. The world shook and rippled again as a massive black wave heaved itself straight toward us.

"Ana!" Sam's voice sounded dim and far away.

I pointed at the eruption on the south edge of Range. Purple Rose Cottage was obliterated by now. And Sam's graveyard. The cabin where he'd become my first friend. The forest where I'd explored as a child. The clearing where I'd watched Soul Night celebrations fifteen years ago.

All gone.

Soon, we would be, too.

Footsteps rushed toward me, and Sam draped his arms around my shoulders.

Had we stopped Janan? The temple was so bright, it seemed unlikely. And though dragons flew from Heart as fast as they could, they wouldn't outrun the eruption. There'd be another, soon. And another.

I didn't want to talk to Sam about any of that, though. I faced him. Blood poured from a wound on his head, matting down his black hair to his skin. Scrapes and bruises marred his face, but he was still the handsomest man in the world to me.

"I love you," I said.

"I love you." He kissed me softly. Grit brushed between our lips.

The temple burst apart.

Shards of brilliantly lit stone flew in all directions, hitting my back and arms and face. Agony flared across my entire body as Sam shoved me down and held himself over me, as though he could protect me from what was happening.

Sam cried out, but neither of us could move. Rock piled up around us, shining with templelight. Dust rushed up, making me cough and gag, no matter how I pulled my shirt collar over my face to filter each gasp.

The rain of stone went on forever. It was a race: what would kill us faster? The eruption fire speeding its way here, or Janan's ascension.

When the noise dulled, Sam sat up, and I followed. The explosion had been violent, but quick. Rocks lay strewn across the roof, and the city below looked as though it had been covered in fine white powder, which glowed.

And the prison—it was gone.

I glanced southward, checking on the wave of fire and ash and pyroclast. A gray-and-black cloud of debris and fire rushed upward and outward. We had minutes at best.

"Come on." I scrambled to my feet and helped Sam up. His movements were stiff and pained, and we picked our way around glowing rubble, toward the crater on the east side of the Councilhouse. We were lucky the force of the temple's explosion hadn't destroyed the Councilhouse, too.

"You're too late." Deborl's voice was scratchy and weak from the opposite end of the Councilhouse. He just wouldn't die. "There's no stopping Janan."

I ignored him and held tighter to Sam's hand as we gazed

at the bright pit below. People huddled around it, their voices muted as they wiped blood off their faces, or swept shining grit off their clothes. Some hadn't gotten up after the blast, but most had survived. They gaped at the place where the temple used to be.

"Oh, Ana." Anguish filled Sam's voice. "I'm so sorry."

At first, I saw only light.

The white stones resolved themselves into stairs. Or tiers. And skeletons. Silver chains shone in the strange illumination, glimmering as a dark figure in the center shifted and stood.

He looked small from this far above, but I remembered seeing him before: short and thick, bushy brown hair on his head and face. He'd looked *strong*, then, even dead or asleep or whatever he was.

Now, power surged through his movements as he grasped the chain linking the skeletons to one another—to him—and strode out of the temple ruins, dragging the dead behind him.

Janan had returned.

30
PROMISES

I ROCKED BACK on my heels. Sam's hands dug into my sides to keep me upright, and he said something by my ear, but I couldn't understand the words. All I could think was that we'd failed.

Janan had returned. Ascended. Both, because he was here and he was *powerful*.

We had failed.

Below, as Janan strode out of the decimated temple, the crowd split in two, leaving a wide, rubble-strewn path to the phoenix cage. They were silent, save the awed whispers and weeping. Stones continued pattering to the ground like the last moments of rain.

Silver chains clanked and clattered, and bones chattered

as Janan heaved almost a million skeletons out of the pit. He dragged all the skeletons I'd seen inside the temple before; there'd been one for everyone in Heart, everyone who reincarnated.

Janan dragged nearly a *million* skeletons by those chains. He was impossibly strong. Impossibly alive.

As the crater emptied, I found dozens of skeletons left behind: darksouls.

The world roared and trembled as the pyroclastic flow burned through the forests of Range, rolled across the valley of Midrange Lake, and thundered toward Heart.

This was it.

I wanted to close my eyes, but I watched my death coming. It would be fiery and immediate, and terrifyingly beautiful.

The black wave crashed against Heart and split around the city wall, as though the stone were a blade. The particles of rock and ash and fire surged, blocking out the moon and stars. Everything beyond Heart was dark, burned away as the eruption blast continued, but inside Heart was bright with thrown temple stones and the glare of spotlights.

Heat poured through the city, a flood of sulfuric summer that made me shake and sweat.

But we weren't dead.

I turned toward Sam, sure I wanted to say something about the way the pyroclastic flow split, unsure what exactly.

Deborl stood behind Sam, a jagged piece of stone raised

over his head. Blood and grit poured down his face and clothes, and his expression was distorted into something savage and raw.

"Sam!"

He turned just as Deborl brought down the stone and thrust it into Sam's shoulder.

Sam yelled and dropped to the ground, clutching the wound. Blood flowed down his sleeve, bright and red in the templelight all around.

Rage clouded my vision as I stepped around him and shoved Deborl away, putting all my remaining strength into it.

Deborl staggered and caught himself. His expression was wild, feral.

I gave a wordless shout and shoved him again, but Deborl was ready this time and held his ground. He lifted his hands to hit me, but before he could act, Sam surged up and threw his weight against Deborl's smaller body.

Deborl fell over the edge of the roof and tumbled down the slope of expelled temple rock. His body struck stone again and again until it landed at the bottom, motionless as it lay in odd angles. Broken, with only darksoul skeletons for company.

Janan didn't stop moving out of the crater, or even acknowledge Deborl's fall. The clack of chains and bones overwhelmed all other sounds as Janan hauled the skeletons from the temple ruins and onto the market field.

People stepped back even farther.

Dragon thunder snapped as Acid Breath's army returned to the city, now only half the original number. Their scales were covered in ash. The pyroclasts had shredded wings. Many swerved through the air, too burned or beaten to navigate properly. A few dragons dropped to the earth as they entered the city, the air relatively clear of the particles that would suffocate us. Their bodies crashed and made the ground shudder, uprooting trees or knocking over buildings where they landed.

Other dragons landed more gracefully, heaving as their talons raked the ground, while a few dove at Janan with their teeth bared and fury in their eyes.

Janan stopped in the middle of the market field and lifted his free hand.

No, it wasn't free. His fingers were wrapped around the hilt of a long knife, the blade shining gold with phoenix blood. The blade arced over his head, flashing silver and gold, and every dragon diving toward him was thrown backward.

The beasts roared and clawed at the air. Wings flapped and limbs flailed, their serpentine bodies twisting violently before they landed around the city, unmoving.

I ached for them. We hadn't been friends, but we'd been temporary allies. Acid Breath had liked my music.

Low groaning drew me back to Sam. He was kneeling

again, clutching his shoulder. Blood flowed from between his fingers.

"Let me bind it." I dug through my backpack for the bandages and antiseptic. "We'll get it cleaned out and you'll be fine."

He shook his head. "I can't feel my arm."

That seemed bad. I tried to recall if Rin had said anything about losing feeling in limbs after injuries, but nothing came to mind. All I could think about was Sam, the way he groaned and clenched his jaw against the pain. "No, you'll be fine. Just move your hand so I can wash the cut." I was a terrible liar, and my voice didn't sound as light as I intended, though I tried.

"There's no point." He sounded weak, exhausted, as though he were already dying.

He couldn't be dying, though. He hadn't lost *that* much blood.

"You need to go," he hissed. "Hide."

I shook my head. "Where would I hide? There's nowhere left. I'm staying with you."

Sam closed his eyes and nodded. "Guess you're right. What happens now?"

I had no idea. I'd assumed that if we failed, we would be dead. The possibility of living beyond the moment of ascension hadn't occurred to me. "We watch. Maybe there will be another chance. We need to be ready to take it."

"Yeah, okay." He didn't believe me, but he didn't argue.

We sat together on the roof, facing the industrial quarter and the cage. Janan finished crossing the market field, his every movement precise, careful, as though he'd forgotten what it was like to have a physical form.

"Where are the sylph, do you think?" I asked.

While Sam was distracted by the scene below, I cut his sleeve off and worked on binding his shoulder. The wound was bad. Bits of stone were stuck inside him, glowing, and I couldn't stop the bleeding long enough to get a good look at anything. It was just red. And bad. A hole in my Sam. I poured antiseptic over the gash and held a bandage over his shoulder, pressing as hard as I could.

"I don't know." Sam stared at Janan, at the cage. "They went inside the temple, and they're not here now. Maybe he . . ."

"Maybe he did the same thing to them he's been doing to newsouls." I choked on tears as I pressed another bandage against the soaked one on Sam's shoulder. I could almost hear Rin's instructions in my head: *Don't let up the pressure, no matter what; put new bandages over the old one until the bleeding stops.*

His voice was low and exhausted. "Did we send them to their deaths?"

"We didn't send them. They went because it was a way for them to contribute. It was something they could do. They

384

didn't want to be spectators in their redemption." I'd failed them, though. I hadn't stopped Janan.

Below, he was threading an end of the chain through the bars of the phoenix's cage. The racket was incredible as he dragged the silver and skeletons, and for the first time, the phoenix under the cloth moved.

"Did you see that?" Sam leaned forward; the bandages slipped on his arm. "What is he doing?"

"The phoenix moved."

"Why doesn't it fight?" Sam whispered. "It could fight and free itself."

"Maybe they drugged it or hurt it. I don't know."

"It could burn itself up and start over."

"Not here." I shifted closer to Sam. "Can you imagine being in such a vulnerable state? Between lifetimes with your enemies all around you?"

Sam looked at me, and he wasn't just a boy anymore. He was an oldsoul, one who'd spent a hundred between-lifetimes in Janan's grasp.

He'd told me once death felt like being ripped from oneself, like being caught in talons or fire or jaws for years until he was reborn. He hadn't known then that Janan was his enemy, but now he knew. He could refer back to those memories with new light. And new fear.

"The phoenix will let it happen, whatever happens next. Unless more phoenixes come to save it." How long had it taken the other phoenixes to save the one from five thousand years ago? Hours? Days? Weeks? And what *would* Janan do with the phoenix? Nothing good, that much was sure. "I want to save it," I whispered.

Sam's expression lifted. "Save the phoenix?"

I nodded. "Whatever Janan is doing next, he needs the phoenix. Deborl sent Merton and the others—his best warriors—to find a phoenix and bring it Heart. We couldn't do anything for it before because we didn't want to ruin our chance of the poison working, but the poison is gone. Whatever Janan is doing, he's not done yet, and we're not dead. We can still do everything in our power to keep him from succeeding."

Sam smiled. "Yes, we can."

Below, the chain was threaded all around the phoenix's cage, and people were grabbing hold of the silver links and dragging the skeletons into loops around the cage.

If Janan had said anything to them, somehow instructed them, I hadn't heard it. "We need to get closer."

Sam looked down the side of the building. The slope wasn't exactly sheer, but it would be difficult to climb, especially since Sam couldn't feel his arm. He had nerve damage. That was what Rin would have said. It would take months to heal, if it ever did.

I pressed a third bandage against his shoulder and taped them as tightly as I could. "We can't go straight down. We don't want them to see us." Though it seemed unlikely anyone would. They were all staring at Janan, waiting for something.

For a moment, I entertained the idea of staying up here and shooting Janan, but I'd already seen how easily he dismissed dragons. My pistol was no match. And besides, he was immortal. What could possibly hurt him now?

I glanced beyond the city wall one last time, the heavier pyroclasts settling while the ash and lighter particles hung in the air, making Heart seem encased in darkness. Inside the city, dragons rolled and gasped, fighting the ash they'd inhaled. The exploded debris from the temple still shone with templelight, eerie and beautiful against the blackness outside.

Not far from the Councilhouse, I found what I was looking for.

"Come on." I slung my backpack over my shoulder and helped Sam to his feet. Janan's people were still arranging the skeletons, so we had a little time. He was immortal. He probably wasn't in much of a rush.

Sam and I staggered across the rubble-strewn roof until we reached the northern edge.

A dragon looked up, blue eyes foggy with weakness. The ringing in my head was faint, along with Acid Breath's voice. <We have failed. The song lives on.>

Oh. When they'd dived earlier, they hadn't been attacking Janan. They'd been going after Sam's skeleton. If only Janan had known, he probably would have let them.

I held tight to Sam's arm and spoke to the dragon. "Help us get down."

<Why?>

"He has a phoenix down there. We're going to save it." Oh, such bold words.

<Why do I care about a phoenix?>

"If we save the phoenix, it will ruin whatever plans Janan has. I thought you liked revenge."

Acid Breath let out a long cloud of ash-choked breath, then lifted his head until his chin rested on the edge of the roof. He drew back his mouth, showing the fangs as long as my forearm. <Hold on.>

Sam looked at me and shook his head. "I'm not holding on to that end."

"Yes, you are. If he hurts you, I'll shoot him in the eye."

Acid Breath sighed. <I won't eat you. Or boil you.>

"There, he promised." I tried not to show my reluctance as I approached Acid Breath's face, but my heart pounded and it seemed strange that of all the things that had happened tonight, this should scare me so much. What was one short ride in lieu of stairs?

I crouched and waited for him to part his teeth a little so I could hook my arm around the fangs. "You too." I motioned for Sam to do the same as me. He used his good arm to brace himself, staring stoically at me as he did. I reached forward and helped steady him before telling Acid Breath we were ready.

The drop was sudden and swift, as though the dragon wasn't used to such weights in his mouth. Which was ridiculous. I'd seen him eat a bear midair.

His chin thudded on the ground, jarring us as we landed. Sam leapt away, staggered, and leaned on the Councilhouse for support.

<You're all tangled together now. Ugh. I should eat you both.>

Dragons just couldn't be nice.

"Thank you." I rested my hand on Acid Breath's snout. The scales were cool, coated with ash. He'd breathed in too much, probably burned his lungs, too. He was dying.

<Go away.>

I nodded and left him. It was my fault he and his army were here. My fault they were dying in this city, rather than in the north, moving all the dragons to a safer location. Safer for now, anyway. The ash would rise into the upper atmosphere. It would block sunlight and smother the world.

I hoped Orrin and his group were far away.

"Let's go." I linked my arm with Sam's good one and helped him around to the front of the Councilhouse and the half-moon steps. "Do you need to rest?"

He was pale and trembling, but he shook his head. "I'm fine. I can do this."

"I know you can." I paused halfway up the stairs and let him catch his breath. "But if you need a quick rest, I under- stand." He'd lost a lot of blood.

"Don't be ridiculous. I'm just upset that you've made me ride that dragon twice now." He flashed a weak smile, and my heart folded up with fear and hope and anxiety. He was being so brave.

"That's the last time, I promise. No more dragons."

He nodded a little and started climbing the stairs again. "I'm going to hold you to that."

I held his hand while I considered what we were doing, how unlikely it was to succeed. Did I even have a plan? It seemed like I was doing what I always did: rush in blindly with one ambitious goal.

Ruin Janan's life by saving the phoenix.

"Maybe I can annoy him to death," I muttered.

"I've never heard a plan more likely to succeed." Sam paused as we reached the top of the stairs. "Inside, I think. We can exit through one of the side doors."

"Good idea." The glass on the double doors had blown out at some point, probably during the eruption. Our boots crunched the shards, and inside, we had to stop so I could pull out the biggest pieces. I didn't want either of us to slip.

The Councilhouse was dim and silent. The air smothered our steps, and Sam's rasping breath. We paused in a wash- room to better clean Sam's shoulder and rinse the blood and grit from our faces and mouths, but after a few long drinks of water, we hurried on. Janan wasn't moving quickly, but there was no time to waste.

"I wish I knew what he planned on doing with the phoenix," I muttered as we headed through the library. Then I realized how stupid I'd been. How blind.

I'd assumed we would all die in the first eruption, and that would be it. No reincarnation. Nothing. But Sarit had been right when she said Janan needed people to rule. He wouldn't let them die.

Five thousand years ago, he hadn't become the leader by lying to his people. He'd have needed to be strong, able to protect them. He would have kept his promises.

He'd promised to become immortal, then return to do the same for them. That didn't mean they'd have equal power. It meant he ruled them for eternity.

I dropped to the nearest sofa and buried my face in my hands. "Sam," I said. "Janan is going to make you immortal."

31
VOICES

SAM COLLAPSED NEXT to me, breath heaving.

I studied him, the bloody mess of his hair, the gray pallor of his skin, and the red of injury and infection on his shoulder.

He wasn't doing well. His body was giving out, and unless we found a medic soon, I couldn't imagine he would recover. Sam was dying, slowly and painfully, and we both knew it.

"Are you sure?" His expression held a terrible mix of hope and despair. He didn't want to die. No one did. And if everyone would soon be made immortal, maybe Stef and Armande and Whit and Sarit would be reborn.

But not me.

"I think so," I whispered. "That's why he wanted a phoenix. That's why he has that knife."

"No one will do it." Sam's voice dropped. "No one will consume millions of newsouls to be immortal."

I didn't argue, but I didn't agree. They'd let Janan consume newsouls five thousand years ago. And they'd supported Deborl over the last few months. Some of them had gone out and captured a phoenix. Whit had accused me of losing my faith in people, but was it any wonder when everyone had bowed to Janan five thousand years ago? Some had changed—some knew better now, or loved newsouls and protested because of them—but for people, the memory magic meant they never had to feel the guilt of what they'd done.

"Besides," Sam said, "the temple is gone."

"Maybe he figured out another way."

"Maybe." Sam closed his eyes. "I wouldn't do it. You know I wouldn't."

"He has the skeletons out there, from your very first lifetime. You might not have a choice."

Sam heaved himself up, swaying on his feet. "Then we have to stop him."

"Do you have a plan?"

"Besides you annoying him to death?" He offered his hand to help me up. I took his hand, but didn't let him bear my weight. "The cage is hooked into electric lines. Maybe that's keeping the phoenix from fighting back, or maybe Janan needs that in order to . . . you know."

I knew. "So we head out the library door, try to blend into

the crowd, and creep through it until we find the source of the electricity."

"That sounds good." He released my hand and pulled up his hood. "We should hide our faces."

I reached up and adjusted his hood, smoothing his hair off his face. "Do you know where the electricity originates? Maybe one of those small buildings we came into from the aqueduct?"

Right before Whit died.

"No, I'm not sure. I wish . . ."

He wished Stef were here. I did, too.

"We'll find it," I whispered. "It's one of those buildings."

"I'm sorry, Ana." He touched my shoulder, not quite disguising the fact that he needed me to balance. "I'm sorry for our selfishness five thousand years ago. This isn't what life is supposed to be like. We're supposed to live, then die, and maybe there's something else after, like you said. Something good. I'm sorry that we were so afraid, and that we still are."

I hugged him. "If you hadn't, then I'd never have known you. I'd never have heard your music. You've been the most important person in my life from the first notes of Phoenix Symphony. I can't regret what let us be together." Even if our time was short. No matter what happened next. "I love you, Dossam." Tears blurred my eyes, and everything inside me ached as I pulled away. I wanted to tell him a hundred times. A million. I needed him to feel my love in his soul.

If only there were time.

As we headed to the door, I couldn't help but wonder what would happen if we stayed here. If we waited long enough, would Sam be miraculously healed when Janan finished outside? Would I be allowed to stay with him, at least until the ash had dispersed and I was sent back into exile?

We'd never know.

I pushed open the library door, but instead of slipping invisibly into the crowd, we came face-to-face with Janan.

He was only a little taller than me, but he wasn't small. He was *compact*. Thick arms crossed his chest, all bulging muscle in spite of millennia without moving, and his eyes were deep-set and piercing. The wild hair might have made him look comical if the rest of him didn't scream deadly power.

I spun and started to run, but Janan reached out and snatched my arm. His fingertips dug into my skin, even through the sleeve of my coat. I tried to pull away, but his grip only tightened, and he grabbed Sam's arm, too. The hurt one. Sam cried out as his arm wrenched out of place, but Janan's expression remained hard and angry.

He shoved us at a pair of red-clothed guards. "Bring them."

As hands closed over me, I struggled to free myself, but there were too many. They were too strong, in spite of the fact that they'd been through eruptions and explosions, too. Some were bloodied and gasping. That didn't stop them.

Sam fought back, but his arm was weak and he'd lost too

much blood. Someone punched him in the gut. He doubled over and hung limp in their grasps.

I kept struggling, hitting and kicking wherever I could. If I could get away, I could figure out how to free the phoenix. But when I looked out beyond my immediate attackers, all I could see were people. Thousands of them. I'd never make it through.

I slumped. My whole body ached, and my heart twisted with fear and grief as I let them drag me to the phoenix cage. Skeletons waited around the cage, same as they'd sat in the red chamber of the temple, though now they were partially draped over one another, to make room for all the bodies pressing around, everyone looking eager and anxious and afraid.

Silver chains shimmered in the glow of the rocks. The skulls were eyeless but watching. Almost a million of them. One for every person here, and for people who'd left with newsouls. None for those who'd died in Templedark, though; those were still piled in the crater left behind after the temple exploded.

Sam and I were slammed on the ground near the cage, just inside the circles of skeletons. Janan stepped inside with us, watching impassively as Sam groaned and clutched his shoulder, his face contorted with pain.

"Sam!" I tried to crawl toward him but someone hit me, knocking me back down. My elbows slammed on the cobblestones, then my head. My thoughts swam like liquid.

"So, the mistake still lives." Janan's voice was harsh and deep, like a canyon speaking. "You intrigue me. For millennia, I've been alone but for my Hallow, and then you arrived. You flew past me. My new Hallow explained your father's poison and how you came to be. And that you've tried to make a place for yourself in spite of everything."

I glared up at him.

"I would be a poor ruler if I didn't want my people to be happy and satisfied with their lives. I find that people who are content are less likely to cause trouble, as you have been doing."

"How can I be content when you're eating newsouls? When you're manipulating the memories of your people? And lying to them?" My words came ragged and worn, though they'd felt full of strength and hate when I opened my mouth.

Janan nodded. "Yes. I understand your anger. Which is why I'm going to make you an offer."

"You have nothing I want," I growled.

Janan stepped around me, toward the cage.

"What are you doing?" My voice didn't carry. He acted like he didn't hear me. I checked around me. The people who'd dragged Sam and me here were gone, back with the crowd beyond the skeletons. I wondered what they thought of the two of us being up here. Like we were favored. It was so we wouldn't try to escape, though.

Slowly, while everyone was distracted by Janan moving alongside the cage, I slid off my backpack. Was there anything useful inside? I tried to remember what we'd packed this morning. Medical supplies. Sticky gloves and boot covers; those were still on the roof. Flute; it would be a miracle if that wasn't broken. A small tool kit Stef had scrounged for me. The knife Sam had given me a year ago. I wanted to scoot close to him and see if he was okay, but I needed to stop Janan. Sam would understand. He'd tell me to stop Janan first.

Janan drew his knife and slipped it into the cage and the cloth-covered bundle on the floor. My heart thundered as I crept closer. Surely he wouldn't kill it yet.

The first rope snapped under the sharp blade. Then another. Was there anything I could do? I felt paralyzed, my thoughts thick and useless.

One by one, the ropes sliced apart and the heavy black cloth fell away.

It seemed a small sun appeared before me as the phoenix rose up and screamed, powerful and polyphonic. An orange glow turned white, and tears poured down my cheeks as immense wings lifted above its head, all glory and flame and black ash raining.

The phoenix was twice my size, with glittering plumage more beautiful than anything I'd ever seen. It had a hooked beak and great talons like a raptor, but I remembered the story from the temple books: the phoenixes hadn't killed

Janan and his warriors, because they didn't want to end their cycle of rebirth.

Everyone gasped, and the crowd went perfectly silent as the phoenix gazed around at its captors.

I'd expected its eyes to be made of light, like every other piece of it, but when the large round eyes landed on me, they were black like moonless night. Like night if the stars had all gone out. They were deep and ancient and filled with sorrow.

Quiet rushed over the world. Even the blackness of ash outside the city seemed muted. Janan stepped onto a raised platform to address everyone.

"Five millennia ago, I searched for the key to immortality. When I was imprisoned for my knowledge, you came to free me, but I had another plan, one that would ensure we could all live eternally. Now I have returned to fulfill that promise." Janan raised his voice. "Though I tried to protect you, I could not stop what you call Templedark or the slaughter that came that night. We've lost so many of our own. Nevertheless, we must begin to rebuild. As I've said, I want my people to be content."

Janan turned his gaze on Sam, who pushed himself back into a sitting position. His shoulder was bleeding again, and his arm hung limp at his side. His skin was pale and shone with sweat as he edged closer to me, though his movements were slow and clumsy. He couldn't do this much longer.

"Some," Janan went on, "will never be content, knowing

what they have lost. While I can do nothing for those fallen during Templedark, to show you I am not truly without heart, I will add one to our ranks."

Sam looked at me. I looked at Janan. A low murmur rippled through the crowd.

"You'd make me immortal?" I asked. "Like everyone else?"

Janan nodded. "You and Dossam care for each other. You've fought hard to be part of this community." He swept his arms over the crowd. "You were exiled, but that doesn't have to be true any longer. You can live forever with your friends. With Dossam."

My heart stumbled on itself. Life with Sam. With music.

"Ana." Sam's hoarse whisper drew me closer to him. Our eyes met, and he didn't have to say what he was thinking. He'd already told me a thousand times.

He would choose me.

No matter the price, no matter the consequences. Sam would choose me.

My heart broke.

"You understand why I can't, right?" I touched his face. My eyes ached with fresh tears. The salt stung cuts on my face.

He nodded. "I understand."

I brushed my lips against his, then climbed to my feet to face Janan. Here was a chance to make the others see.

If there were any who'd been too afraid to speak up.

If there were any who'd wanted to make a choice, but hadn't known how.

If there were any who wouldn't stand for the slaughter of a phoenix and newsouls.

"What is the price of immortality?" My voice sounded wisp-thin, only a thread of a song, but I urged strength into it.

Janan spoke easily. "One life never lived. One tiny spark that will never know." He motioned at the phoenix, which gazed over the assembly with unreadable eyes. "And this."

Couldn't everyone see how wrong this was? Whit and Orrin had insisted there were good people we were leaving behind. I *wanted* that to be true. I *wanted* them to stand up for what was right and prove all my fears wrong.

But no one moved.

What about the people we'd freed from prison? When I glanced over the crowd, I spotted familiar faces, but when our eyes met, they looked away.

"Five thousand years ago, you told everyone the phoenixes had imprisoned you because of the knowledge you gained, but that isn't true. They imprisoned you because you captured a phoenix and tortured it."

Everyone was silent. Staring.

"The phoenixes wouldn't kill you for what you'd done, but they did give you eternity in a tower. Instead of repenting, you began exchanging souls. You reincarnated people because you couldn't bear to be without them, and then you made them forget."

Janan cocked his head and remained silent.

The whole city was silent, save ragged breathing and groans of dragons dying and the muted roar of the pyroclastic flow surging past.

No one was listening.

"It's true." Sam forced himself to sit a little straighter. "You stole our memories."

Whispers sizzled through the crowd.

"You made them forget because you knew the guilt of trading a newsoul every lifetime would crush them," I said. "You didn't want them to know what you'd done."

"You didn't just trade their lives for ours," Sam said. "You took newsouls, and you *ate* them. You consumed their souls for power. Our reincarnation was bought with that stolen life."

"No. No." The voices came from the crowd. Some of the people I'd freed from prison moved about the others, muttering and pointing.

"What I did before was wasteful," Janan said. "Now I know a better way. One soul for infinite life. That's all it will take now. No more death and rebirth. No more reincarnation. Just life." Janan motioned to the phoenix. "And I have this."

"I would die for other people," I said, "and other people

have died for me. We do it because of love. But I won't accept an unwilling sacrifice. Not the phoenix, and not a soul that's never lived."

Janan nodded. "Very well. I was afraid you might feel that way, but I'd hoped otherwise. We will continue without you."

The crowd hushed. Everyone watched me; I could feel their stares. Only, I had no idea what to do next. I'd hoped to inspire them, make them see the truth, but no one was moving.

No one was willing to speak up.

"Wait," someone called. Someone from the prison? "You made us forget?"

"What was that about newsouls?" another asked, and voices poured from the crowd, talking to one another, shouting questions at Janan.

"They're just newsouls. They don't know what they're missing."

"We thought newsouls would replace us, but we've been replacing them this whole time."

"We've had more than our share of lifetimes, and the cost . . ."

"I'm afraid to die."

"The girl is right. We can't do this."

The questions and demands for more information intensified. I couldn't believe it. They cared? Not everyone, but some were asking questions and pressing through the ring of skeletons, and Janan looked stunned, like how could they not accept the trade?

He didn't understand the value of one life. He underestimated the impact one soul could have.

My friends had been right after all. There were good people here.

At my feet, Sam grasped my ankle. "Help me up."

I bent and wrapped my arm around him, taking as much of his weight as I could bear while he found his feet. He swayed, but steadied himself and added his voice to those standing up to Janan.

"I won't be part of this!" someone shouted.

Hope flowered inside me as people closed in on the cage, on Janan standing there with his knife. The phoenix watched people turn on their leader.

"Very well," said Janan. "If you will not all accept my gift, I will give it to no one."

"No!" Toward the back, someone threw a punch. A fight broke out, and screams again rang through the night. Blue targeting lights flared and people yelled, calling to Janan for help, but he just stood on the dais and watched chaos erupt through the industrial quarter. What was left of the city would destroy itself unless someone stopped it.

Stopped Janan for good.

But what could stop something like Janan? He was human,

but immortal now. He had nothing to fear.

I'd once thought dragons had nothing to fear, but they were terrified of Sam and what he held. If the phoenix song was life and death, if it could destroy something as formidable as dragons, maybe it could affect Janan as well.

As the crowd pressed closer, louder, and Janan's smile grew wider, I bent for my backpack and removed my knife and flute case.

"What are you doing?" Sam gripped my shoulder for balance.

"There's a phoenix. I'm going to make it use its song. Unless you think you can do it on command?"

"I don't know." His eyes grew wide. "I don't know how."

"It's okay," I said. "I understand." He was broken. Dying. All his hope and confidence stripped away. I held his hand as he staggered with me to the cage while Janan was distracted by the fighting.

The phoenix was quiet now, watching everything, though I couldn't guess its thoughts. I left Sam leaning against the bars while I searched for a latch. But if there were a way to open the cage, it was near Janan.

"Hey, phoenix."

The black eyes turned on me.

"I want to free you."

Its head tilted.

"But I need you to use the phoenix song. The one dragons

are afraid of. Sam knows it, but he doesn't know it. And his arm is hurt too badly to play my flute. I need your help."

"You just go right up to anything and talk to it, don't you?" Sam closed his eyes and smiled. "I love that about you."

"Everything else has talked back so far." I turned to the phoenix again. "I need your help. Please."

The phoenix shook its head.

No?

Because it wouldn't take a life and risk its own cycle of rebirth?

Then what was I supposed to do? How was I supposed to stop Janan? How was I supposed to ensure newsouls had a life?

I'd already failed the sylph.

Hadn't I?

On the dais, Janan lifted his knife into the air. A man went flying backward, like the dragons had earlier. Janan was just adding to the chaos.

If he'd consumed the sylph when they entered the temple, were they already gone? Or slowly digesting as the newsouls had?

Fine. I'd try it myself. I lifted my flute and started to play.

The flute whispered a song, high and thin with my nervousness. But Sam looked up. The phoenix softened. And Janan spun, looking for the source of silver sound and defiance.

I began with four notes, hesitant but hopeful as the flute's voice swelled into a familiar waltz. I played waves on a lakeshore and wind through trees. Lightning strikes, thunder, and pattering rain.

It seemed impossible one flute could do all that, but I wasn't alone. Sam hummed with me, heat and anger and honey sweetness as I played the music of my heart. His heart.

He was doing it, the magic. *We* were doing it.

When I looked at him, he was smiling.

More voices joined. Men and women close by caught the note Sam hummed, and sang with him. They formed a wall around Sam and me, the cage. And when Janan raised his knife to flick them away, nothing happened.

Another rush of voices raised up, strange and unearthly and coming from somewhere I couldn't see, but they sang wild harmony and countermelody.

Even the stomp of boots and the clash of weapons joined our song, weaving into the music with the thunderous bass of surging pyroclasts.

I poured my soul into this, the threads of voices weaving into sound that seemed to transcend music. This was something altogether new, strange and lovely and magical.

Music thickened over the night as though this was the only thing in the world, the only thing that mattered. Janan dropped to all fours and shuddered as smoke peeled from his body, black and undulating.

Sylph.

The fighting stopped as more people began to notice what was happening, began to add their voices to the song. Lightning snapped through and Janan screamed as blackness overwhelmed him. All my sylph freed themselves and left Janan lying on the dais, unmoving. Scarcely breathing.

As the voices rose higher and sylph added their own melodies to the waltz, I lowered my flute and approached Janan.

My knife, a slim rosewood handle and tiny steel blade, found its way into my hand. I climbed the dais and crouched next to Janan, looking up only a moment to find most of Heart watching to see what I would do. A few people held back others, but most—most just sang and watched, because somehow this was my choice.

Oldsouls or newsouls. Beginnings or never-endings.

Sylph flowed around me, Cris next to me, and waiting by the phoenix was Sam. He looked tired, barely alive, but when I closed my eyes, I remembered the way he'd held me after I hadn't killed Deborl. He'd said he was glad I hadn't.

I looked back at Janan. Could I show compassion for a man who'd caused millennia of pain for newsouls, who'd captured a phoenix twice now, ready to sacrifice it for his selfish desire to live forever?

Who was I to decide who lived and died? That was a decision Janan had been making for others for thousands of years. I wanted to be nothing like him. I wanted to value life, all life, regardless of how despicable some of it could be.

And who knew—maybe there was something else after death. Just because it was unknown didn't make it bad. It could be good.

I sheathed my own knife and took Janan's bloodstained knife from his hand.

Light and power flooded into me, dizzying and far too much for one soul to hold. I fell back, and the last thing I heard was the phoenix singing four notes.

32
LIGHT

THE SKY WAS deep violet when I opened my eyes.

My skin tingled and my heart thrummed too fast. Maybe this was what it felt like to be struck by lightning.

Janan was gone, as were most of the citizens of Heart, though the skeletons were still there, their silver chains dull and tarnished. The expelled temple rocks were murky white now, no life left in them. The sylph were gone, too.

"Sam!" I jerked up and scrambled to my feet, stumbling down off the dais before I realized Sam wasn't standing by the phoenix cage anymore. He was slumped on the ground, breathing shallowly. Someone had placed my flute in his arms, but it slipped from his grasp as I dropped to my knees before him. "Sam."

He made opening his eyes look like agony. "Ana. I waited for you." His voice was a pale breath, a memory.

"Didn't anyone help you?" I checked the bandages on his shoulder; they were new, but damp with sweat and blood.

"There's nothing to help. I'm sorry." His good arm jerked upward, but it fell and he sighed. I took his hand and pressed his palm on my face, now slick with tears. "That was it, wasn't it?" he asked. "The phoenix song?"

"I think so." It had felt like magic, and it had stripped Janan of his immortality. Sam had been humming. So had others. The sylph. And the phoenix.

Had I used the song? Or had Sam?

Did it matter?

The dragons had been afraid the phoenix song would destroy them. The song hadn't destroyed Janan; sparing him had still been my decision, in the end. But we'd made him mortal again. If no one else killed him first, he'd one day die of old age.

Sam's fingers curled against my cheek. "You have it in you now. The light. I see it. Beautiful."

"I don't know what you mean." But I did know, didn't I? My heart raced, my thoughts were sharp and clear, and *something* had changed inside me.

I looked around, but the only one left was the phoenix. The cage door hung open and the phoenix itself perched nearby, wings tucked against its sides.

"Ana," it said, voice high and low and everything in between.

Now it spoke back?

"The sylph have gone to absorb the fires beneath the caldera, to settle it and keep it from erupting further."

"No." Cris had told me that wasn't possible. It was too much. "That will kill them."

"Yes," said the phoenix. "And they will be reborn, per our agreement. They will have one life, the life they would have had if they hadn't followed Janan that day."

"What about everyone else?" What about Sam? I could still feel his pulse fluttering weakly under his skin, but for how much longer? What happened when he died? I'd already lost everyone else.

"That," the phoenix said, "is your decision. Dossam is right. The fire of infinity has passed from Janan to you. You took it when you took his blade. You may keep it, or you may give it away, though your body might not survive a second transfer of the light."

Meaning I could die. Still— "I don't want it, not if I have to be alone."

The phoenix bowed its head. "Then I think you know what to do with it. But know that it will work only once. As the sylph are receiving their second chance, that is what you will give to the others."

Then Stef and Whit and Sarit and Armande might be

alive again. And Sam. Would I, too?

I bit my lip before I asked. The answer might sway my decision, and there was only one decision I could make.

"Thank you."

The phoenix surged up, trailing sparks and ash as morning paled the sky and stars grew dim. The pyroclastic flow was gone. The sky was clear. Dawn was still and quiet. My sylph were saving the world, redemption at last.

Only the quiet gasps of my weeping and the rattle of Sam's final breaths cracked the air.

I had to work quickly.

I put my flute back into its case, kissed Sam's lips, and approached the nearest section of chain.

"Ana?" Sam rasped. "What are you doing?"

"I'm choosing you."

"Wait, think about this."

"I am." I forced a smile as I knelt. "And I'm choosing life. I'm choosing *you*." Before either of us could say anything more, I closed my hands around the chains that linked everyone together, and released the light. It burst out of me until I was a star exploding.

And I could see everything.

33
BEGINNINGS

IT MUST HAVE been years and years later when Sam awoke
to existence once more, because everything had changed.

What was left of the white city bore veins of obsidian,
scars on stone that no longer healed itself. Midrange Lake
had become a lake once more, forests had grown back, and
animals had returned. After the eruption, Range filled itself
with new life.

By the time Sam returned, everyone seemed to understand
that this was their final reincarnation. This was it. Only one
life. Cherish it.

But Sam already knew that. When he dreamt, it was of
the last moments of his previous life, and Ana talking with
the phoenix. Then Ana glancing back at him, choosing

him, and giving up the light.

The ache of missing her carried through death, through his first quindec, and though he searched for her, the world was filled with newsouls now. Orrin, Lidea, and Geral had long ago returned from their quest to protect their newsouls, and soon there were schools for the new and old. Soul Tellers still had jobs, finding the oldsouls born and cataloging newsouls. Sam spent months poring over the results, looking for Ana, but her soul had never been recorded into the database. If she'd been reincarnated, no document could tell him.

Maybe she would return. Maybe she would not. She hadn't known when she let go of the light. He'd seen the question in her eyes, and seen her decide not to ask.

He wished she had.

On a sunny morning, Sam and his friends sat around a table by Armande's pastry stall, sipping coffee and listening to a flutist play somewhere across the crowd. The music was familiar; lots of people played "Ana Incarnate" since Phoenix Night.

So many strange faces crowded the field. The din of conversation surrounded the table, all laughter and haggling and babies wailing. It was market day, which brought traders and buyers from the new settlements around Range. And students, he hoped. Music teachers still had to eat. The sign he'd made, advertising openings for students, had already received several curious looks from both children and adults. He tried to ignore the questions people asked one another when they thought he couldn't hear: Was he the Dossam who'd written "Ana Incarnate"?

"How's the new piano working for you, Sam?" Cris asked, searching his empty coffee cup for one more drop.

"Spectacular. When Orrin is reborn, I'll compose something for him. I still can't believe that with everything going on during his return to Heart, he managed to convince people to help collect supplies for the piano." Sam shook his head. His friends were amazing.

"I want a sonata." Sarit leaned her head against Cris's shoulder. "And a symphony. Yes, I think that will do."

Across the table, Stef laughed, his voice deep and full. "You don't want much, do you?"

"Only what I deserve." Sarit grinned and took a bite of her sticky bun.

Sam closed his eyes and enjoyed his friends' presence and the sweet cacophony of Heart, but the flutist playing "Ana Incarnate" somewhere toward Phoenix Memorial caught his attention. A deep ache welled up in his chest as he saw her again: Ana, giving up the light; Ana, choosing him; Ana, giving up her life to ensure that others survived.

The grief was infinite.

Something about the vibrato caught him, and a section of triplets. Familiar . . .

"Are you okay, Sam?" Stef raised his eyebrows.

"I think so." They all knew how he felt about the waltz, both a blessing and a curse. Most days, he wished no one would ever play it again. But this flutist. The way they played. Sam shivered. "I have to see something."

He pushed himself away from the table and navigated the crowd of tents and people, catching a glimpse of himself in a mirror he passed: white-blond hair, fair skin already red from sunshine. The stranger in the mirror every lifetime never got less unsettling.

He passed advertisements for newsoul-focused communities, others for oldsoul-only communities. Not everyone was satisfied with their second chance.

Where the temple once stood, now there was a memorial, an obsidian phoenix wreathed in roses of every color. The flutist played somewhere on the steps leading up to it.

He pushed between tents and stalls until finally he saw a girl on the stairs, lost in the music of "Ana Incarnate." Heavy black hair tumbled over her shoulders, and her limbs were all angles, like someone who hadn't fully grown into her body. She would be tall, and for someone who looked barely a quindec, she played remarkably well.

He wasn't the only music teacher in Range, but still. The way she moved with the music. The way she connected with it.

As he pushed through the crowd, the girl's attention snapped up, and she looked at him. Her cheeks tightened as she played toward the coda, as though she were trying not to smile.

He couldn't breathe. Couldn't hope. Couldn't stop remembering the light flooding from Ana into the silver chain.

Sam climbed the stairs two at a time as the black-haired girl played four long notes and lowered her flute. When she bent to place it in her case, obsidian-black wings stretched behind her: the phoenix statue.

He wanted to believe. Wanted more than anything.

He stopped only a step away from her while people milled around, ignoring them. Stef called his name in the distance, but he didn't turn.

"Is it really you?" He'd never wished for anything so much.

The girl looked up at him. Her eyes were so blue they put the sky to shame. She could have been anyone, but she'd drawn him with her music. Even if he couldn't trust his eyes, he could trust his ears and heart. She wasn't *just* anyone.

With a strangled cry, he caught her in his arms. "I've been too afraid to hope," he breathed. She was hugging him back, and they were both trembling. "I've missed you so much."

She pulled away to turn her palms up, revealing pale scars. Chain links. When shadows passed over her skin, the scars glowed.

Ana leaned close and whispered, "I've been reborn."

418

ACKNOWLEDGMENTS

UNENDING THANKS TO:

Lauren MacLeod, my agent. I can't imagine doing this publishing thing without you. From midnight crazy emails to editorial advice to contract negotiations: you handle it all, and more. Thank you for always believing in me.

Sarah Shumway, my editor. I've always thought the best kind of editor is one who can see through a messy draft to the heart of the story and help the author tell the tale they intended. You are that kind of editor, and I couldn't be more grateful. Thank you for always pushing me to look deeper and work harder.

The entire team at Katherine Tegen Books, including:

Alana Whitman, Aubry Parks-Fried, Lauren Flower, Margot Wood, Megan Sugrue, Stephanie Stein, and King Snarkles, an epic team of epic people (and stuffed hedgehog) who make epic things happen for epic books. Love you ladies (and hedgie)!

Amy Ryan and Joel Tippie, art director and designer, who gave the Incarnate trilogy a series of amazing covers and gorgeous insides. You guys are magic.

Brenna Franzitta and Valerie Shea, production editor and copy editor, who not only catch missing commas but all sorts of stuff that would completely embarrass me if it ever saw paper. Thanks for making me look smarter than I really am!

Casey McIntyre, my publicist and occasional superhero. I'd throw a parade in your honor, but I don't think I could organize it without your help.

Lauren Dubin, production manager, who doesn't get nearly enough credit for all she does.

Laurel Symonds, editorial assistant extraordinaire, who Gets Stuff Done. You are amazing.

And, of course, Katherine Tegen herself, publisher of so many amazing books. Thank you for giving the Incarnate trilogy a home. I can't imagine a better place for Ana and Sam.

Friends who doubled as critique partners for this manuscript:

Adam Heine, who read a super-early (and bad) draft of *Infinite* and still wanted to be my friend. Thanks, man. (As for whether I've actually taken a ride on a dragon, well, I can't say. In public.)

Christine Nguyen, the sweetest smooshface who ever lived. You brighten every day. Thank you for always being so enthusiastic and loving. You are to me what Sarit is to Ana.

C. J. Redwine, my Brain Twin. Not only are you hilarious and talented and one of the strongest people I've ever met, you're also one of the best friends I could have asked for.

Corinne Duyvis, who also read an extremely early version of this manuscript. You're a trooper! (But seriously, no petting wild bears, okay?)

Gabrielle Harvey, who does her best to keep me from looking like a musical dunce (all mistakes are my own!), and who also helped create Dossam's Greatest Hits. One day, we will persuade someone to make Phoenix Symphony real for us. One day!

Jill Roberts, my mom, who always believed in my dreams— sometimes more than I did. Thanks for never doubting me.

Jillian Boehme, an amazing reader and an even more amazing friend. I can't imagine what my life would be like without you. Thank you for always being there when I need you. (Sorry I typoed your name in *Asunder*. I love youuu!)

Joy George Hensley, for being such a steadfast friend. Your support and enthusiasm keep me going. And maybe we should make *Pride & Prejudice* & Cupcakes Day an annual thing. Or biannual. Or weekly.

Kathleen Peacock, one of the most humble and fiercely

loyal people in the whole world. I'm eternally grateful that we are friends.

Myra McEntire, who is one of the strongest, most determined people I know. You are an inspiration.

Sarah Schaffner, my sister, who really should have been mentioned in previous acknowledgments as well. Thank you for your "give me more Ana and Sam" threats. I mean, encouragement. You're the best sister in the world.

A few people whose friendship and encouragement has meant the world to me:

Amanda Downum, Bria Quinlan, Brodi Ashton, Celia Marsh, Cynthia Hand, Elizabeth Bear, Francesca Forrest, Gwen Hayes, Hannah Barnaby, Jaime Lee Moyer, Jeri Smith-Ready, Kat Allen, Kevin Kibelstis, Kristen-Paige Madonia, Lisa Iriarte, Mandy Buehrlen, Nina Nakayama, Phoebe North, Rae Carson, Robin McKinley, Stacey Lee, Valerie Cole, Wendy Beer, and many, many more. I've been blessed with so many amazing people in my life that I couldn't possibly fit everyone in here. If I (shamefully) neglected to mention you, here's a blank space for you to write your name:

The Apocalypsies, for continued support and camaraderie.

The Pub(lishing) Crawl girls, for being such an awesome force for good in my life.

Team Incarnate, with a special high five for Julie, who keeps this thing running.

My book bloggers (you know who you are) who continue to post and tweet about the series and recommend it to friends. Love you guys. Never change.

Countless booksellers, teachers, and librarians who get books into the hands of people who will love them. You are incredible. Thank you for all that you do.

God, who I will never be able to thank enough for this wonderful life and all the incredible people who surround me.

And as always, you, the reader, for picking up this book. I've been so fortunate as to receive heartwarming notes from some of you, and to even meet a few of you in person. You make this whole experience real. Thank you for caring. Thank you for reading. Thank you for being you.

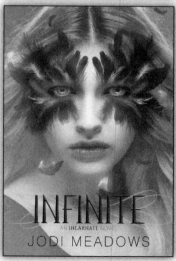
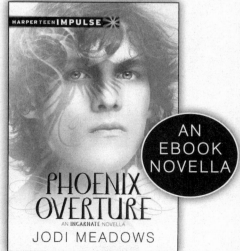